P9-CLR-959

What people are saying about …

Glamorous Illusions

"A fascinating mix of travel and intrigue, heartache and romance, *Glamorous Illusions* sweeps you away on the Grand Tour, exploring London and Paris through the eyes of a young woman who longs to find her place in the world. The title captures the story perfectly, as Cora delves beneath all that glitters to discover what is real and true, while not just one man but two vie for her affections … ooh, la la! A grand start to a new series from a seasoned author who writes from the heart."

Liz Curtis Higgs, *New York Times* best-
selling author of *Mine Is the Night*

"Who am I and where do I fit in this world? These are just two of the important questions addressed in this poignant story that takes the reader from an impoverished farm in Montana onto an opulent cruise across the Atlantic to stately England and finally to the city of love, Paris. With fresh characters, a touching story, and plenty of adventure and romance, you'll get swept away in this lavish world of the young and wealthy."

MaryLu Tyndall, author of *Surrender
the Dawn* and *Veil of Pearls*

"From a bankrupt farm in 1913 Montana to the glitter and glamour of a European Grand Tour, *Glamorous Illusions* is the trip—and the read—of a lifetime. Absolutely one of my favorites ever, this book is a stunning adventure from first page to last. A truly masterful storyteller, Lisa Bergren has penned a magical journey of the heart and soul that will leave you breathless and longing for more."

Julie Lessman, award-winning author
of The Daughters of Boston series
and Winds of Change series

"A Cinderella story lingers in the pages of *Glamorous Illusions*. Open the book and be swept into a story of heartache, strength, and romance. Add in the sweeping beginnings to a Grand Tour of Europe, and I found all the ingredients for a story I couldn't put down."

Cara C. Putman, author *Stars in the Night*
and *A Wedding Transpires on Mackinac Island*

GLAMOROUS
ILLUSIONS

GLAMOROUS ILLUSIONS

THE GRAND TOUR SERIES

LISA T. BERGREN

David C Cook®
transforming lives together

GLAMOROUS ILLUSIONS
Published by David C Cook
4050 Lee Vance View
Colorado Springs, CO 80918 U.S.A.

David C Cook Distribution Canada
55 Woodslee Avenue, Paris, Ontario, Canada N3L 3E5

David C Cook U.K., Kingsway Communications
Eastbourne, East Sussex BN23 6NT, England

The graphic circle C logo is a registered trademark of David C Cook.

All rights reserved. Except for brief excerpts for review purposes,
no part of this book may be reproduced or used in any form
without written permission from the publisher.

The website addresses recommended throughout this book are offered as a
resource to you. These websites are not intended in any way to be or imply an
endorsement on the part of David C Cook, nor do we vouch for their content.

This story is a work of fiction. All characters and events are the product of the author's
imagination. Any resemblance to any person, living or dead, is coincidental.

LCCN 2012935339
ISBN 978-1-4347-6430-0
eISBN 978-1-4347-0533-4

© 2012 Lisa T. Bergren

The Team: Don Pape, Traci DePree, Amy Konyndyk, Caitlyn Carlson, Karen Athen
Cover Design: JWH Design, James Hall
Cover Photographer: Steve Gardner, Pixelworks Studios

Printed in the United States of America
First Edition 2012

1 2 3 4 5 6 7 8 9 10

032912

God is not disillusioned with us. He never
had any illusions to begin with.
—*Luis Palau*

PART I:
THE CALL

CHAPTER 1

Montana, 1913

~Cora~

As the locomotive reached the train station, I strained so hard to see my folks that my eyes hurt. I looked left and right, but the town was as sleepy as always. It wasn't as if I had to search for them among throngs—I saw no one but old Clifford Miller across the street, climbing into his wagon with some effort, and Susan Johnson entering her hardware store.

Likely just late, I decided, making my way forward between the seats before we had fully stopped, then climbing down the steep steps to the wooden platform.

"Miss?" asked a man's voice behind me.

I turned in surprise, holding my hand up to my old hat as I felt a pin slip, and then—embarrassed that I'd forgotten to even look for it—took my valise from the conductor's hand. "Thank you."

The railroad man looked beyond me to the vacant platform and street. "Someone comin' for you, miss?"

I nodded eagerly. "Yes. My parents. They must've been delayed. They'll be along shortly." A long whistle sounded. Not that there was anyone around to rush aboard. Protocol, I supposed. That whistle, usually heard from three miles distant, was a part of all my childhood years. A warm sense of home filtered through me, making me smile.

The man lifted his brows and nodded back with a curious smile as the train began to chug into motion. "Good day, then."

"Good day," I returned, watching as he stepped aboard the steps and disappeared inside the train.

The train station—little more than a water tower, a platform, and a tiny hut of a shelter—was in the center of Main Street, which was all of two blocks long. I shaded my eyes and looked to the massive mountains behind the station, which were a pale blue in the afternoon sun. Dunnigan had once been a gold-rush town, established to supply the miners who had streamed into the mountains, seeking their fortune. But it had seen its heyday come and go. Now the buildings were in need of paint, and half the storefronts were abandoned. These days, it existed solely to supply the local farmers who stubbornly eked out an existence on the prairie in the shadows of the Rocky Mountains' peaks, farming and ranching.

But oh, did it feel good to see those mountains again. I closed my eyes and lifted my face to feel the cool breeze coming off them, down to us on the eastern plains. The feel of it, the scent of pine and sage and dust…all were of home. I craned my neck again, eagerly looking down the road in the direction Mama and Papa should be coming from. But no one was on the road—and I could see a good mile before it disappeared over a hill.

Mr. Miller, with his balding head, giant, flapping ears, and sagging jowls, pulled up alongside the platform. "Well, if it isn't Cora Diehl," he said with a smile. "Welcome home, girl."

"Thank you, Mr. Miller. I don't suppose you've seen my folks today, have you?" A stab of anxiety shot through me. What if something was wrong?

"No, miss. Drove right by your place on the way in. Didn't see hide nor hair of 'em. But I can take you out." He nodded toward the foothills, in the direction of home.

"Oh, that's all right," I said. I could walk the three miles faster than Clifford Miller's old mare could haul us.

"Nonsense, girl. I'll take you. And if we meet your folks on the road, then that's less time on the road for them."

"Oh, Mr. Miller. I don't wish to burden your mare…"

"Come, come," he said, waving me forward. "If old Star can haul hay, she can haul a bit of a girl like you. Unless that valise is full of bricks." Even though his tone was gruff, his watery eyes twinkled.

I smiled. I was hardly *a bit of a girl*. I was a woman grown, but I supposed my old neighbor would always see me as the five-year-old who would come to call, uninvited, and trail him around his homestead. "As long as you're certain it's no imposition."

"Imposition? *Pshaw.* Just being neighborly. Did they not teach you that in teacher college?" He reached over across the seat to take my hand as I clambered up.

I met his teasing grin. "No, we didn't cover that particular subject."

"Hmph," he said, flicking the reins.

We moved out, down the road. Mr. Jennings, the saddler, came outside to sweep his front stoop and waved as we went by. "Welcome home, Cora."

"Thanks, Mr. Jennings! See you soon!"

"Hope so! You stop by and tell me all about that teacher college, all right?"

"I will!"

I didn't know what was keeping my folks, but it didn't really matter—I felt welcomed already. The welcome sight of sleepy Main Street; the warm, dry wind as it swept dust across the road; the cheery red barns and tidy fence posts... After the busy bustle and noise of the city, the quiet and normalcy of the long summer stretching before me felt peaceful, like a blanket settling in around my shoulders, urging me into a porch swing.

"So I take it that Normal School over there in Dillon still suits you," Mr. Miller said.

"It's wonderful," I said. "I've learned a great deal. Two more years, and I can teach anywhere in the state."

"Should come home. Settle down with Lorrie Cramer."

I lifted my brows. "Isn't Lorrie Cramer seeing Louisa Anderson?" I said politely. Not that I really cared. Lorrie Cramer was a nice boy. Quiet. Hardworking. But all he ever thought about—all he ever *wanted* to think about—was farming. In the last year, I'd decided I loved learning. It fed me. Expanded me. Shaped me. I'd be eager to return to school, come fall. And I knew I needed a man who longed for the same.

"Ach. He doesn't care about Louisa. He's always had an eye for you." Mr. Miller gave me a sidelong glance, and I smiled. While I couldn't help but find Lorrie's attention flattering, I didn't want him to set his cap for me. Because he and I would never be more than friends. We just weren't well matched.

Mr. Miller and I chattered on about his rheumatism, the strange, dry winter followed by the dry spring, the shortage of spring lambs, calves, and foals. "Wind started in January," he said, "and hasn't let up yet."

In all my years on the farm, I could only remember one year when my papa was happy with how much rain we'd had—when it came, how it came, how long it lasted. Every other year, it was the common refrain of every farmer I knew—*if only the weather...* But even in Dillon, we'd noted the uncommonly warm winter, the lack of snow at Christmas. Papa would likely be fretting too.

I squinted my eyes, trying to see the house now that we were over the hill and about a half mile distant. The wind was gathering in strength as we neared the mountains, sending waves of dust across our path. All along, I was certain we'd meet up with my folks, and with each bend in the road, I grew more anxious.

My heartbeat accelerated. Something was wrong. Or was it simply my imagination running wild?

I thought back to the last time I'd heard from my mother—a letter two weeks ago, with the ticket enclosed. Perhaps they never got my reply confirming I'd be on this train, on this day? That was likely it. Everything was fine. Just a misunderstanding.

But the words inside my mind didn't match the fear gathering in my chest, making me fight for breath.

They'd know I would be on that train. They'd expect me. Today. An hour ago.

As we neared the farm, I could see that the wagon was pulled up to the house—Sugarbeet ready for a run to town. So what had kept them?

Mr. Miller gave me a sidelong glance. He had fallen conspicuously silent. At last, we turned onto our farm's long lane, and I could bear the slow pace no longer. "Please. Stop the wagon, Mr. Miller. I need to get out."

"Just a bit farther, Cora. I'll deliver you to your stoop."

"No," I said, shaking my head. "Please."

When he only frowned, I half stood and jumped to the ground, even as he abruptly pulled back on Star's reins. I was out and running before he came to a full stop, tearing down the lane as if a mad dog were after me. I lifted my skirts and ran across our yard and into the house. "Mama?" I called, opening the door. "Papa?" The house was quiet.

I turned and saw that Mr. Miller was only halfway up the lane. I ran across the yard to the barn, hesitating at the door. I peered into the dark recesses. "Papa?"

That was when I glimpsed her. My mother. Weeping over my father, who was sprawled over the straw-strewn floor of the barn, his neck and head in her lap. He looked semiconscious, deathly pale.

"C-Cora?" Mama asked, looking up at me, her face red and blotchy. "Oh, Cora. I didn't know what to do," she sobbed. She reached out to me, and her expression was so full of raw need and fear, I brought a hand to my chest as I sank to my knees beside Papa.

He was breathing. But his eyes were wide and vacant, and his hand was so cold—

"Cora!" Mama said. "Please, baby. Take Sugarbeet and run for the doctor."

CHAPTER 2

~Cora~

In a stupor, I ran to unhitch Sugarbeet, then hurried her back into the barn to throw my old saddle over her back. I glanced at Papa again and, with shaking hands, reached under Sugarbeet's belly for the strap, then cinched it tight. I mounted and trotted past my dazed neighbor, who was frowning up at me in confusion. "Going for the doctor!" I shouted. "Papa's in trouble. Will you stay with them?"

Mouth agape, Mr. Miller nodded once, and I was off.

I made it to town in a quarter of the time it had taken Mr. Miller to travel the same road home, and Doc Jameson followed behind me on the way back, coming at a good clip in his smart buggy. By the time he reached us, Mama and I'd managed to get Papa on top of a blanket. And once Doc Jameson gave us a nod of approval, together we moved him into the house.

We were fortunate that Papa was a slight man, nothing but lean muscle and bone. I'd met his height before I was thirteen and outgrew him by a couple of inches by the time I'd turned fourteen. "You grow as fast as the weeds in my fields," he'd teased me. But he also encouraged me to stand straight. "Never stoop, Cora. Nothing finer than a woman as lovely and straight as you, with her head held high. My own Lady Liberty," he called me. "My elegant girl."

Please don't let him die, Lord. Please. Please, please, please, I prayed, as I'd been praying ever since I left the barn to fetch the doctor.

We set Papa on the sagging bed—the same bed he and Mama had bought when they arrived here nineteen years ago. Our house wasn't much, and it felt smaller than I remembered. But it was as tidy as ever, and I found the sameness of it comforting.

Mama sat beside Papa, holding his hand, as Doc Jameson continued his examination. Mr. Miller went to the front window, gazing out with a sober expression on his face, worrying a handkerchief in his hands. And I stood in the corner, watching the doctor's expressions as he listened to my father's heartbeat through his stethoscope and then timed his pulse by pinching his wrist and keeping track on a pocket watch. Papa seemed to be sleeping now, his face relaxing and seeming even more lopsided than it had been when I first arrived.

Doc Jameson looked up at Mama and then over at me. His brows lowered. "Best take a seat, Cora. You look as white as a new snow. Don't want you keeling over in a faint."

I obediently sank beside Mama on the bed. *Tell us,* I urged him silently as he seemed to gather his thoughts. *Out with it.*

"Alan's had a stroke," Doc said with a grimace. "Now, I can give him some medicine, but mostly we simply have to wait it out to see how much he'll recover. Some folks make a full recovery, go on to live out a long, full life. Others are partially incapacitated. And still others suffer another stroke that takes them."

I frowned. I couldn't imagine my papa, so strong, so virile, now so incapacitated. I looked from his slack face to his wet pants, then away, embarrassed for him.

Being stuck in bed or a chair would kill him, even if another stroke *didn't* come hunting him. He loved to work hard, day in, day out. With the animals. In the fields. Numbly, I stared at the kitchen table, where we'd shared so many good meals, laughing and talking. I could picture him there, at the head, his eyes crinkled up as he smiled, a big gap between his teeth. The way he pounded the table when he laughed…

Doc Jameson rose, went to the sink, lifted the water pump lever once, and then let the meager trickle partially fill a cup. Then he poured some powder from an envelope into it, swished it around, and moved back to Papa's bedside. "Help me get him up, Alma," he said to Mama.

She did as he asked, but she'd said nothing since I'd returned. Only stared with wide, frightened eyes, her thin fingers to her lips, and moved like a wooden puppet, pushing through one task and then the next.

They managed to pour the mixture down Papa's throat, raising him and thumping on his chest when he choked, coughed, let it dribble down his chin and neck. I wondered how much of the medicine reached his gut. But Doc Jameson seemed unperturbed. Maybe he had figured that a certain amount would be lost and had accommodated for that in what he'd measured. Or maybe giving him medicine at all was a stage act, designed to give me and Mama a measure of peace. *Please, Lord. Please, please, please—*

"Cora," Doc said, gesturing me toward the kitchen. I'd known the man all my life, just as I did nearly everyone else in town.

Doc had been in this house the day I was born, had delivered me into the world. He wrapped his arm around my shoulders as we walked to the window, and his touch felt like a comforting uncle's. Mr. Miller had left, mumbling something about "informing the pastor—back tomorrow." Even now, his wagon was turning left out of the lane, making the journey back to town behind the old horse that was more than ready to be put out to pasture. But bless Mr. Miller's soul, he was trying to help. Trying to do something for us.

"Cora, I'm glad you're home," Doc said in a whisper, glancing past me, back to my mother. "This has been quite a shock for Alma."

I nodded.

"You need to be strong for her, Cora. She'll need you now more than ever."

I glanced up at him. "But Papa…"

The hope died in me as Doc slowly shook his head, his eyes full of pain and sorrow. "I can only do so much for him, Cora," he whispered, glancing over my shoulder toward Mama.

I wanted to sink to the wooden floor and weep. I had trouble breathing.

"But he's only forty-eight," I gasped out. Plenty of men died young, but not men as strong and virile as my papa.

Doc simply stared back at me with his gray eyes, waiting me out, his lips clamped in a sad line, his eyebrows peaked in the center.

"How long?" I managed.

"A day. Maybe two," he whispered back.

"Why not tell her?" I asked, finding breath in my fury. Grasping for strength.

"Because she needs to hope. Every family needs hope. And every family needs someone prepared to cope if the worst happens. I'm sorry, Cora," he said, dropping his arm from my shoulders and turning to face me. "But you have to be that one. I hate to burden you so. But you're a woman grown now—"

"Yes," I admitted, suddenly wishing I was eight again. "Yes. Fine. I understand. So we are to simply...wait?"

He took a deep breath and straightened. "I'll return in the morning. If he survives the night...who knows?" He offered a tentative smile.

I took a breath. "So we need only get him through the night."

He shook his head slowly, caution in his eyes. "It's often a mercy if the Lord chooses to take them sooner than later."

"How can you say that?" I said, my voice rising, sounding foreign, strangled. I turned toward him. "Get out. Get out!"

He stared at me as if I'd gone mad. "Now, Cora," he said, glancing toward Mama with concern, waving his hands in an effort to settle me.

I opened the door. "My father is going to make it through the night," I said. "Come tomorrow and see for yourself."

He licked his lips and then reached for his hat, tucking it atop his silver hair. He gave me a long, compassionate look. "I'm sorry, Cora."

I inhaled a stuttering breath, trying to calm myself. "Thank you kindly for coming to see to my papa, Doctor."

He turned and walked out. I quietly shut the door behind him, resting my head against it. I felt the wave of strength leave me as soon as he was gone, leaving me feeling weak-kneed and empty. *Please, Lord. Please, please, please...*

"Cora," Mama said softly. "What did he tell you?"

I turned toward her, holding the cool metal knob of the front door behind me as if it would hold me upright. "We need to pray especially hard for Papa tonight, Mama. If we can get him through the night…" My voice cracked, and I brought my hand around my belly, the other to my mouth. Then I swallowed back the lump in my throat and stood straight. I forced a small smile to my face. "When we see the sun, he'll be through the worst of it."

She knew I was lying. At least in part. That I was protecting her. But she didn't seem to have the strength to do anything but cling to hope. Just as Doc Jameson had predicted.

CHAPTER 3

~Cora~

I paced the floor all through the night. Mama fell asleep after midnight, curled up beside Papa, who was cleaned up and in his pajamas. Over and over she started awake, half rose, and placed a shaking finger beneath his nose, making sure he was still breathing. When I couldn't bear to watch the scene unfold any longer, I quietly pulled the drapes around their bed, sealing off their room from the rest of the house.

I begged God. For Papa's life. For a few more days. For a chance to say good-bye. I chafed at the memory of Papa grasping the last dime from his coin purse and handing it to me for the train ride to school. It'd taken everything they had to send me to the Normal School in Dillon. They'd gone without, scraped by…

Was it my fault, this? I glanced toward the threadbare curtain as doubt and fear assailed me. *Am I to blame for his stroke, Lord? Make me suffer, then. Take it out on me! Not him, Lord, not him.*

In the early morning hours, I stood in front of the east-facing window, taking heart as a faint golden glow appeared on the horizon.

I again padded over to my parents' room and edged the curtain aside, watching until I saw the shallow rise and fall of my father's chest. *He's alive. He made it through the night!* Then I returned to the window, shivering in the morning cool but warming with hope as the sunrise spread a deep pink across the land.

It was then I noted the scrawny, withered stalks of the winter wheat, stunted and struggling in the dry, lumpy furrows. It should have been harvested weeks ago. Not that it mattered. I'd seen good crops, and I'd seen bad. This was one of the worst.

Concentrate on Papa, Cora, I told myself, my eyes returning to the sunrise. *We can cope with the crops later.* But could we? I knew my parents had borrowed against the farm to send me to school. What if this crop failed? And how would Papa bring it in? *I'll bring it in. If I have to handpick every measly grain head myself. I will not let them down.*

"Cora!" Mama cried.

I turned and stared at the curtain, my chest filling with dread again. I glanced to the sun, which was just peeking over the horizon, too bright now to stare at directly. *Please, Lord…*

"Cora!"

"Coming, Mama," I managed. I forced myself to walk across the small space between us and edged through the gap in the curtain…

And found my papa sitting up and smiling. It was a lopsided smile, one side of his face desperately sagging, but truly, it was the prettiest sight I'd ever seen.

"Papa!" I cried, rushing to him. He laughed softly and wrapped an arm around my shoulders.

"Cora, honey," he said, his words slurred.

Mama wiped tears from her face. "It's a miracle," she said, shaking her head. "A miracle."

We sat there together for a long while, crying. *Thank You, Lord. Thank You, thank You, thank You...*

Shortly thereafter, the women of First Lutheran began to arrive. Mr. Miller had succeeded in spreading the word of our situation around the church. I went outside to greet them, wanting Papa to rest, knowing they'd be full of questions and nervous conversation. When Mrs. Ramstad heard he'd made it through the night, she got all teary and fanned her face, even in the chill of morning. "Thank You, Lord," she said. "My, my." She handed me a basket of fresh-baked rolls. Mrs. Humphrey brought an egg casserole, patting my hand and telling me to eat "lots of it, honey, because goodness knows, you're thin as a rail." Mrs. Kessler brought bread, hugging me so tightly to her ample bosom, I thought I'd suffocate. Mrs. Reinbarger brought a roast and potatoes, seasoned and "ready for the oven by three."

All promised that their men were coming by to see to our farm as soon as chores were done on their own, and they made me promise to give their love to my mama, who wouldn't leave Papa's side for even a moment, and to send for them if I needed a thing. I was saying good-bye to Mrs. Reinbarger when Lorrie rode up the lane, astride a horse, next to Doc Jameson's buggy.

Lorrie politely waited for the doctor to tie up his reins and approach the porch before he came up. Doc's eyes met mine. "He made it?" he whispered.

I grinned. "He's sitting up!" I crowed, wanting him to feel guilty for his gloomy warnings the night before.

His gray eyes widened, and he shook his head in wonder. "I always knew your father was one of the toughest men this side of the Rockies," he said. "May I?" He gestured toward the door.

"Please," I said, waving him in. I turned back to Lorrie, who'd paused halfway up the stairs, hat in hand. He was wiry and strong, about my height, with an unruly shock of Swedish-blond hair.

"Cora, welcome home," he said. "Not quite what you expected." He lifted his hat toward the house. "Good news, though," he finished awkwardly.

"The best," I said, unable to do anything but smile. "Evidence that God can see us through the darkest of nights."

"Uh, yes." He glanced nervously over his shoulder, toward the barn. "Can I see to your chores? I imagine your cow is in need of a milking."

I frowned, ashamed that I was just now hearing her bellowing from the barn. "Oh! Yes, yes. Please. That would be so helpful. And give the horses some fresh water and hay?"

"Done." He turned and walked down the few steps as I pivoted to head inside.

"Thank you, Lorrie," I said over my shoulder.

"Not at all," he mumbled, and rushed off across the yard. I stared after him. He really was a good man, a good neighbor. And even if I couldn't return his feelings—if he indeed had an interest in me—I was thankful he'd come to help.

The days passed, and Papa rapidly regained his strength, confounding Doc Jameson and frustrating Mama's efforts to keep him at rest. He'd insisted, since that first day, on getting himself to the outhouse, using only a borrowed cane and dragging his left foot along. After a week, he turned Lorrie back before he was even off his horse, insisting we could see to the animals and farm on our own. It tore Mama and me up inside to see him stubbornly carrying on even as his body fought him. Helpless, we could do nothing but pray for the best, for God to finish His healing work in him.

Papa leaned hard on me, and I had willingly picked up the milking, the mucking of stalls, the feeding. Now, sweat poured down my face and back as I pumped water into an irrigation ditch, desperately trying to save at least one portion of Papa's winter wheat from drying up in the relentless wind.

I wondered how this would end. If Papa would ever be well enough to manage the farm on his own. I paused, panting, and straightened, feeling every aching muscle in my back as I shielded my eyes to see what he was up to. He was in the far corner of the field, hoeing, hacking away at weeds that stole precious nutrients and moisture from the soil—from those stalks of wheat that hadn't been sliced down by the wind and dry soil.

I bent and studied a stray stalk near the water pump, a seed that had been cast too far to stand a chance in the nearest furrow but still stubbornly soldiered on, struggling to live, though the elements had cut away all of its leaves. I fingered the perilously thin head. Those in the field were faring little better. How many bushels would we salvage if we managed to even get a harvest?

I'd seen Papa staring out at the skies with worried eyes each afternoon. Hoping clouds encircling the mountain peaks would edge our way. His concern over the weather wasn't anything new, really. But there was a new weariness behind the eyes, a downturn around his mouth, beyond the effects of the stroke. Did he not have the money set aside to seed another crop? Should we not be plowing, getting ready for the spring wheat in the other fields, as late as it was to plant it?

The rusty old water pump seemed to mock me. Every lift and press was a chore, the resulting squeal like laughter. It came to me then. What was niggling at me, down low in my heart. I was fretting about my future. Wondering how Mama and Papa would do without me when it came time for me to return to school. Wondering how we'd be able to afford it at all if the crops failed…

Selfish, Cora Diehl. You're being selfish. The Lord has given you the day. This day. With your papa alive—alive! And not only alive—up out of his bed. Moving and working. All that you prayed for. I shook my head, ashamed of myself. *Forgive me, Lord. I am thankful. I am.*

I bent and grabbed hold of the pump handle, trying to find gratitude in my heart for the miserly spurts of water that emerged from its mouth, filling the trough that slowly flowed outward. It was hopeless, really. Could I water more than forty yards this way? I'd been pumping for a full hour, and the stream had yet to meet the end of the irrigation ditch and begin to spread—that hungry first channel sapping away every drop. So I went inside to get a bucket, deciding that delivering the needed liquid to the farther rows by hand would at least give them a chance at survival. I knew it made Papa feel better. Doing all I could.

I settled into a rhythm in the task, praying in time with each pull and push, then walking the sloshing bucket to the next section. *Make a way, Lord. Make a way for this water to sustain this field. And Lord? You know my heart. Learning, Lord. Teaching. I want to teach so badly… Please. Make a way. Make a way for us all. Make a way for this miserable wheat. Coax it back to life. Amen.*

CHAPTER 4

~Cora~

We watered. We weeded. We prayed. But in the end, we knew there wouldn't be anything to harvest. Papa retreated inward, replying to Mama and me in monosyllabic words, blaming himself, even if every other farmer on the eastern slope had suffered the same outcome.

And our fear grew. We had not plowed the north forty. Each morning, he made no move to hook up Sugarbeet to the plow, nor did he head to town for the sacks of seed I knew we needed. He took to walking the east forty for hours, treading the paths where the winter wheat had so utterly failed. Mama baked bread, taking loaves and the extra milk to sell to the mercantile every morning, returning with meager supplies. I fed the horse and chickens and pigs, mucked the stalls, milked, and helped Mama with the garden. But we were each waiting, really, in mute helplessness, unable to do more.

One morning, Mama stood beside me at the east window, and we watched Papa. Dragging his left foot along, bending to pick up a handful of dirt, and then crumbling the clod, watching the dust fly away.

"It's like he's visiting a grave," I muttered. "We have to get the north forty planted, or the bank will be coming to throw us out of the house." I was guessing, but by the look on Mama's face, I knew I was right.

"We can't, Cora."

"Why not?"

She turned to me, so pretty, even in middle age. So strong. "There's no money for the seed. My bread and the extra milk are bringing in enough to buy the necessities, but no extra. Thank God we have a garden and animals to keep us fed."

I paced away from her, thinking. Then it came to me, the solution. "I have to go to town."

"For what?" she asked, her eyes narrowing in suspicion.

I ignored her question and just went to my part of the house, through the drawn curtain, and sat on my bed. Next to my bed was a nightstand with a deep drawer. After a moment's hesitation, I reached in and pulled out the elegant box, running my fingers over the lid. JASPER'S, the logo read in a fine script. NEW YORK, NEW YORK.

I flipped open the lid and wondered anew over the triple-strand pearl choker with the rhinestone clasp. Out of all the fine birthday gifts I'd received over the years from a nameless benefactor, this one that had arrived on my sixteenth birthday was undoubtedly the finest. Papa had teased me about a secret admirer. But I'd caught the worried glance he and Mama shared, the one they shared every year. I knew they knew something about it, but they wouldn't tell me, no matter how much I pestered them. And I pestered them plenty that year. They simply gestured toward the crumpled packaging. "No return address, Cora. How are we to know who would send you such a thing?"

It was extravagant. And beautiful. I'd tried it on so many times, lifting my hair, fantasizing about my hair in elaborate curls and a gown to match the necklace. Wondering and wondering about who had sent it to me and never coming to any suitable answers. Most of Mama and Papa's relatives were dead or distant. And none of them were well-to-do.

It was a treasure. My treasure. But really, where on earth would I wear such a thing? Once I had my teaching credential, I'd likely be out in the country. Even if I managed to find a position in one of Montana's cities, there would be no ball or society function fancy enough where I could wear a necklace such as this.

"Cora?" Mama asked, hesitating outside my curtain.

"Please, Mama," I said. "I can't talk right now." She'd only try to talk me out of it. But I was inexplicably sad to let it go. I shook the necklace in frustration. It felt foolish to be so attached to a thing. But it'd been such a sweet surprise, such a fun mystery… I'd spent nights dreaming that there was some wealthy, distant relative, and we would be his beneficiaries when he passed on, bestowed with a fine house, fine clothes, fine carriage…

I took a long, deep breath. I was no longer a mindless adolescent, dreaming of escape. I was an adult. Life was good, but harsh and demanding, too. I snapped the hinged box shut and rose. Quickly, I wrapped it in a handkerchief and tucked it under my arm, flinging aside my curtain. Mama was back at the east window, watching Papa. "I'll be back soon," I said.

She didn't turn. She didn't respond at all. Even though I assumed she knew exactly what I was about to do.

———◦◇◦———

The bell on the mercantile door tinkled as I walked in, and Mr. Donnelly looked over his spectacles at me from across the counter. "Well, if it isn't the other lovely Diehl. To what pleasure do I owe having both of you come to call in one day?"

I grinned and pretended ignorance. "Papa's been in already too?"

Mr. Donnelly chuckled. "Now Alan's a handsome man, but..." He lifted a brow, and then the merriment left his face. "How is he today, Cora?"

"Stubborn as an ox." I glanced around, making sure we were alone in the store. "But he seems to be stuck in a corral he can't escape."

"Oh?"

"We need to get our spring wheat in the ground. I'm guessing we can't do that because Papa hasn't been able to pay his bill to you."

The man's eyes held a weary mix of regret and guilt and frustration. "You know it wouldn't be right to discuss that with you, Cora," he said.

"I understand. Then I wondered if I might pay down his bill with this." I pulled the box from under my arm and unwrapped it on the sleek, shiny wooden counter.

He whistled lowly. "Jasper's, huh?" He pulled it closer and flipped open the lid. He cocked his head and then turned so the necklace sparkled in the light from the front windows. "My, my," he mumbled, lifting the pearls to his teeth to test if they were real. "My, my." He turned back to me. "Where did this beauty come from?"

I shrugged my shoulders. "Jasper's, New York, just as it says on the box. I know nothing more than that. It showed up on my six-teenth birthday, with no return address. I never found out more."

"Well, it's a treasure, to be sure. If we lived in Butte or Billings, I'd gladly take it off your hands but—"

"Please, Mr. Donnelly," I pleaded, desperate now. "It's our only hope. If we don't get this crop in the ground, if there's not another harvest, we'll lose the farm. I won't be able to get back to school and finish my credential, to say nothing of Mama and Papa's struggle. Please."

He was staring at the necklace, thinking. I knew I'd pushed him into an uncomfortable corner. But I had no choice.

"Please," I whispered.

He turned miserable eyes up to me. "Cora, honey, there's not a farmer on this side of the mountains who will turn in a cash crop this year. It's just been too dry. They'll all be busting their backs, trying to break even. But your folks…"

He couldn't say more, but I understood what he meant. They were so behind with the new mortgage on the farm, they didn't have a prayer of breaking even. It was the farmer's cycle—go into debt all year, pay it off come fall harvest, begin again. But Papa was in deeper. Because of me and my schooling. Which explained my father's morose behavior.

"Take it, then," I begged. "Apply its value to his debt."

"I can't." He lifted the box. "You think I could sell this here? Or even the next county over?" He cocked his head again. "Not likely."

My eyes went over this meager jewelry case, filled with lockets of fake gold and silver, along with a few hair clips and broaches. "Then hold it for me. Use it as collateral against my own credit line. If we can't pay you, come harvest, you can sell it for whatever you can get, the next time you go to Billings."

He raised his eyebrows. "It's worth far more than the seed you're after, Cora. Far more." He lifted the box in my direction, offering it to me.

I paused. "Then sell it, keep twenty percent, and give me the remainder after you take out your costs," I said. "Or…or lend me the money for the train and I'll head there tomorrow and come back with the cash to pay you."

He stared at me in surprise.

My face burned with embarrassment. So forward! So demanding! What had come over me?

Desperation. Desperation to save us all.

"No," he said resignedly. "If I take it as collateral, you at least have the chance to get it back if this cursed dry streak eases." He flipped the lid closed and wearily pulled out a ledger. I held my breath. But then he began to write my name at the top. He was going to do it. Coming through for the Diehls yet again.

"Oh, thank you, Mr. Donnelly," I breathed, sinking into relief.

"Don't thank me, Cora," he said grimly, looking at me again as if he wanted to say more and then shaking his head. "Don't thank me."

CHAPTER 5

-Cora-

We never discussed the particulars of how I'd obtained the best-quality seed—Mr. Donnelly insisted I take it if I wanted "the crop to have half a chance."

Papa greeted me at the barn. He ran his hand over the sacks in the back of the wagon and then gave me a sidelong glance. "You really are a woman grown, Cora. Thank you."

"It's because of me that we're in this mess. If you hadn't sent me off to Normal School—"

"No," he said, laying a gentle hand—his good hand—on my forearm. "That was not a mistake. That was a stake in your future. We'll get you back there, Cora, come fall."

"God has my future," I said, and Papa met my eye and smiled in approval.

We immediately set to work that afternoon. Papa and I even plowed into the night, working with a lantern. Within a week, the north forty was plowed, the seed scattered.

We paused at the corner as we finished. I was filthy and exhausted. But it was done. "Let the prayers begin," Papa said, casting a searching glance to the dry, cloudless skies.

I studied his face. One side still sagged. I couldn't bear the hope I saw in his eyes, despite the grim *Farmer's Almanac* predictions, despite the talk at the Grange Hall. Because it made me fearful for him. He was so infernally optimistic. He never held back, never tried to protect a portion of his heart.

He saw me staring at him, read the question in my eyes. "Love believes all things, hopes for all things, Cora. God loves us. Sees us. He'll see us through."

"Yes," I said numbly.

But I knew, deep down, that I was protecting a portion of my heart, even if he refused to do so.

———◇◇◇———

We were blessed with a decent rain three days later, and we knew every farmer across the valley was cheering as we were. It took only a week for us to find the tiny bright-green sprouts beginning to unfurl beneath the dry soil, looking stubbornly healthy, hopeful, despite their harsh environment. Papa took to circling the north forty twice a day, dragging his bad foot along, but he stood straighter, with barely a stoop to his shoulders. Whatever became of the farm and of us, it heartened me, as it did Mama, to see him doing so well.

I'd finished my chores and helped Mama prepare noon dinner, but Papa had not returned to the house to wash up and eat. "Go see what he's up to," Mama said.

I checked the north forty first. Not seeing him there, I moved toward the barn. He was probably working on some equipment, or soaping his saddle. "Papa!" I called. "You passing up dinner?"

There was no answer. A shiver of apprehension ran down my back. I forced myself to slide open the barn door and peer into the relative darkness.

He wasn't in the central area of the barn. "Papa?"

Sugarbeet was nervously prancing back and forth. I swallowed hard and peeked around the wall.

Papa was sitting, leaning against the stall wall, his hand to his chest. He was pale and sweating profusely, his eyes wide.

Oh, no! No, no, no...

"It's okay, Papa," I said, kneeling beside him and placing my hand over his.

But the look on his face made my heart break.

The doctor emerged from Mama and Papa's room, slowly closing the curtain behind him. He looked with sad eyes at me and Mama sitting at the kitchen table, our tea long cold. Slowly, he pulled out a chair and sat down with us. "He's resting now. But it's bad. He needs more care than you can give him. Even more than I can give him in town."

"Where? Where does he need to go?" I asked dully. As if we had the means to take him anywhere!

"Seattle. Or better yet, Minneapolis. After he's stable enough to travel."

I eyed my mother, a flicker of hope in my heart. Her parents lived in Minnesota. I returned my gaze to the doctor. "Would he survive the trip?" I asked in a ragged whisper.

He nodded. "I think so. Again, if he makes it through the night…"

The room grew quiet.

"What about the farm?" Mama said distantly.

The doctor shifted uncomfortably. "His farming days are over, Alma. He needs to leave here for good, so those fields out there don't torment him."

I tried to swallow, but my mouth was dry. I stared at the surface of my cold tea like a circus conjurer trying to catch a glimpse of the future. "When's the soonest we could get him on a train?" I said.

"If he makes gains half as fast as he did last time—within a few days, a week."

"Would you travel with him and Mama? Or should we hire a nurse?"

He nodded, hesitated, then, "It'll be expensive. I don't suppose you have any savings…"

He knew the answer already. We'd already paid for his services in bread, eggs, and our lone fat piglet. I put my head in my hands.

"We have no savings," my mother said lowly. "I could stay with my folks in the Twin Cities. Would the hospital take him? Out of charity?"

"Possibly. Maybe Swedish Hospital. I'll telephone them and see."

"Thank you, Doctor," she said.

"I'll stay here," I said, looking at Mama, "look after the farm."

They both cast doubtful eyes toward me. But there was resignation in them too. If the crop was doomed to fail anyway, why not leave it to a woman to try and save it?

————◦◇◦————

I settled into a routine in the days as we prepared to send them off. Papa made strides, but his thinking wasn't clear and his speech was garbled, leaving me wanting to focus only on the next step of every day.

Rise with the sun. Wash my face. Take off my nightgown. Pull on my stockings and brown work dress. Lace up my boots. Mumble good morning to Mama. Dump Papa's bedpan. Stumble to the barn as the dawn slowly lit the sky. I tried to appreciate the nuances of color, the hope of a new day, but try as I might, the summer and my future beyond it spread out in a dismal gray. I wasn't ever going to return to the Normal School. It was as likely as me reaching the moon now. And the death of that dream left me moving like a train on its track, rolling across one foot of ground after another, making headway but feeling nothing.

The sound of the buggy on the gravel road almost didn't raise me from my milking stool. I couldn't cope with another nosy lady from church, nor find another task for one of the men to make them feel useful. I just wanted to be left alone. My cheek rested against the warm hide of the cow, my hands on her teats, squeezing her dry with a rhythmic *swish swish swish* into the clean, dented bucket. I paused once, twice, and resumed each time, thinking *I don't care I don't care I don't care*, but then I paused again as I heard the buggy pull up before the door of our old farmhouse.

I could tell from the clean, well-oiled sound of the wheels, the spirited step of the horse that drew the buggy, that a stranger had come to our small farm. A stranger of means. Not even the doc's buggy made such a quiet approach, little more than gravel dividing and a gentle clop of a horse's hoof. I spoke lowly to the cow, stroking her girth, promising I'd be back, then went to the barn door to peer out toward the house.

Mama was on the porch, wiping her hands on her apron as two men disembarked from the finest buggy I'd ever seen, its black lacquer coated with road dust. Approaching my mother, one took off his hat as he rounded the back, revealing thick, wavy gray hair that matched his silver beard and mustache. He was a man of perhaps sixty-five years, but his movements were those of a younger man, still vital, strong. His shoulders were straight, even rigid, as he paused at the bottom of the stairs.

My mother sagged to the side, wrapping an arm around the post as if for strength, and covered her mouth.

I stepped forward, frowning in concern.

Mama caught sight of me then. Dropped her hand from her mouth to clench the fabric at her breast, straightened. The stranger, hat in hand, followed her gaze toward me, then turned to say something to Mama, too quietly for me to hear.

Mama protested, but the man shook his head and looked back at me. They were arguing about something. Over me?

The other man, younger and clutching a doctor's kit in hand, shifted from one foot to the other, clearly uneasy. The older man said something, Mama nodded, and the other one climbed the porch steps and went inside.

I forced myself to begin walking across the dry, dusty expanse between barn and house, the incessant wind driving clouds of dust, waist-high, across my path. I placed one foot in front of the other, half drawn in curiosity, half afraid of what I would learn. Where had this other doctor come from? Who had called him?

The older man's eyes were a light blue, I saw when I reached the house. And although his face was heavily lined, what I noticed most were the laugh lines around his eyes. I glanced at Mama, wondering why she was so pale, why she wasn't speaking, but then I saw that she was trying. Her mouth opened and closed, but no words came out.

"You are Cora," said the gentleman.

"I am," I said warily.

"I am Wallace Kensington," he said, his hand against the fine lapel of his jacket.

I blinked twice, swallowed hard.

There was only one Wallace Kensington in the whole wide state of Montana. Copper king. Ruthless senator. Owner of banks and newspapers and much more.

"Pleased to make your acquaintance," I said with a slight nod.

"Mr. Kensington has brought his physician to see to Papa," Mama mumbled. "Would you like to take a seat?" she said to him. She gestured up toward the porch swing.

"You are most kind," Mr. Kensington said with a polite nod. Was it my imagination, or did his eyes linger overly long upon my mother?

Why? Why would Wallace Kensington, of all people, know about my papa? Bring a physician?

Mr. Kensington gestured for me to follow my mother up to the porch, and he went to retrieve a rocker from the corner and bring it near, every movement distinguished, refined. I sat down, still trying to figure out what had brought him here, while Mama went after some tea. Had they discovered copper beneath our soil, here in the foothills? Was he after our water rights, meager though they might be? Did Papa owe his bank, as well as Mr. Donnelly at the mercantile? Whatever it might be, surely there was someone else of less consequence in his company who could've come to call…

Mama emerged through the swinging porch door, chipped china cups rattling on a tray. She looked gray, as if she were about to faint, and I jumped up to take the tray from her and nod toward the swing. She almost fell into it, avoiding looking at our guest.

But he was staring intently at me anyway. A prickle of warning ran down my neck. "Tea, Mr. Kensington?" I asked, feigning calm.

"Please. One sugar."

I poured and placed one sugar cube on the saucer with a spoon and handed it to him.

"Thank you," he said, searching my face, not the tea in his hands.

I handed Mama a cup, then sat down next to her. Mr. Kensington was sitting back in his chair, rocking slightly. Mama was sitting as straight as a poker, gripping the handle of her teacup so tightly that her knuckles were turning white.

"Alma, shall I tell her…or would you prefer to do so?" His tone was surprisingly gentle but was undergirded with a level of authority. Still, my mind was racing. "Alma"? How had this wealthy man come to be on a first-name basis with my mother?

"I will," Mama said. She set her cup down on the floor beside her and then turned to take my hands in hers.

I noticed her fingers were terribly cold, which was odd on such a fiercely warm day. I glanced from her to our visitor and back to her, seeing the tears in her brown eyes. "Mama," I whispered. "What is it? You're scaring me."

"There's no good way to put this, Cora. Papa…he never wanted you to know…" She glanced toward the window. Could he hear us? From inside?

I squeezed her hand. "Know *what*, Mama?"

She turned back to face me, sniffed, and blinked several times. The tears were gone. "Cora, I've not been truthful with you, all these years. When your papa and I married…" She took a deep breath. "I was pregnant." Embarrassment sent flames of red up her cheeks. She stared into my eyes, hers begging for my forgiveness, begging for me to understand. But I still didn't. Pregnant? It was frowned upon, socially horrifying, wrong in God's eyes, but at least they had married—

"Cora," she said in a rush now. "You are not Papa's child. Not by blood."

She squeezed my hands hard then, as if fearing I'd reject her. *Not Papa's child…*

As if in a dream, I turned from her to Mr. Kensington and stared into his eyes. Blue, a light blue, like mine. My breath caught. The angle of his nose, the fullness of his lips…like mine. He nodded slowly, carefully, as if I were a skittish colt about to run back to the barn.

I wrenched my hands from Mama's, clenching them into fists. "How?" And then coloring at the thought, I rushed on, "When?" Again I chastised myself for my stupidity. I knew exactly when they had been together. And how.

It was my turn to stare at the floor.

Mr. Kensington cleared his throat and leaned forward. "Does it matter that I loved your mother?"

"No," I said, shaking my head, tears sliding down my face. "No," I repeated, staring him in the eye. "Because you obviously did not care enough to *marry* her. To properly assume your role as my *father*. Thankfully, I have a father now. A decent, upstanding, loving man. Everything that you apparently are not." In my fury, I'd unconsciously risen.

"That he is," Mr. Kensington said, unperturbed.

I stopped short. "You know him," I whispered. I glanced at Mama, but her eyes had glazed over, as if lost in those days some twenty years before.

"I did. He was a teller in my bank in Butte."

"And I was a servant in Wallace's home," Mama said.

I sank back to the swing. I'd known Mama and Papa had met in Butte. Courted there, they said. Moved here when Mama found out she was expecting me. To start a new life, far from the noise and crowds of the city, and to take over the farm from my aging grandparents.

"Your mother has always been a fine-looking woman," Mr. Kensington said. "And a kinder girl I'd never met. Words cannot express how sorry I was to see her go."

Well, I should say! You were baking your cake and eating it too...

"My wife and I..." He paused. "We were having some problems. She was busy with the children, her social endeavors, and I—"

Wife? Children? "P-pardon me," I sputtered. "I...I have siblings?" Vague memories of newspaper reports of the Kensington children and their exploits drifted through my mind, along with a hog's-pail mess of other thoughts.

"Three. Vivian is twenty-two. Felix, twenty-one. Lillian, eighteen."

An older brother, by a year. Sisters, on either side. Half siblings. I shook my head, now feeling faint. I'd always wanted a sister, a brother. Begged Mama as if she could deliver one like a Christmas orange—

"And do they…do they know of me?"

"They were told but two days ago."

I didn't know why it irked me, that they knew of me before I did of them, but it did. It grated. The humiliation if this got out… I shook my head.

"Wallace was kind enough to pay our expenses, and then some," Mama said, her hands in her lap, her eyes on the window, far away.

"I suppose when one is wealthy, one can make any sort of *trouble* go away," I muttered.

Mr. Kensington's lips thinned, and his brow furrowed. "I never wanted you to go away. But don't you see? In Butte, you would have been ostracized, seen as little more than my illegitimate child. Here, you could reach maturity, be protected from the gossips and the foul-minded."

Mama was nodding, agreeing with him. "Wallace introduced me to Papa—"

"You hadn't met before?" The story was getting stranger with every turn.

She shook her head. "But we were fast friends. And in time, we grew to love each other. You know this is true."

I stared at her, covering my mouth with my hand, unable to keep it closed. Anger boiled just under my skin. Had I seen it? Or had it all been a farce? An elaborate stage play with Wallace Kensington as director?

"Why did Papa go along with it?"

"He's a good man, as fine as your mother," Mr. Kensington said. "He found banking wasn't to his liking. Came to me, confessing his desire to be done with city life and return here, to help his parents on their ailing farm."

"And so you paid him. Paid him to take my mother and me off your hands. Take us with him. Make us go away." My mind fought to take it all in.

He stared back at me and paused. "We came to an agreement. Beneficial to all."

Mama nodded in affirmation.

It was a nightmare. If only I'd wake…

I'd thought I couldn't bend any further beneath the weight of struggle and grief. I was wrong. *Papa is not my papa at all…* The pain of it seemed unbearable.

Mr. Kensington swirled his spoon in his cup for a moment, then set it on his saucer. "I grew concerned when I learned of Alan's stroke. That was when I knew I had to come. But when news reached me he'd had another—"

I stood up abruptly, my hands in fists. "You had us followed? Hired someone to send you reports?" Who had telephoned him? Doc Jameson? Mr. Donnelly?

The necklace… My breath left me in a *whoosh.*

It'd been from him. As were all the other gifts. The fountain pen, the leather-bound books. There was no other logical explanation.

"My dear girl," he said, frowning, "you are my blood. My kin. And while I have never been a part of your life, you have been a part of mine since the day you were born." His face mellowed. "Please accept my sorrow over the pain you have suffered. Clearly, I should have come sooner."

Come sooner. My eyes met his. "What exactly do you want, Mr. Kensington?"

He laughed under his breath, never dropping his gaze. "Direct, isn't she?" he asked my mother.

"She's never been one to hold back her thoughts," Mama said.

"No, I don't suppose she would be." He set down his cup and rose, matching my stubborn gaze. "Cora, I am here to help both you and your, uh, parents. I've brought a doctor to town—the finest in Butte—to escort them to Minneapolis and see to Alan's care. I shall cover any and all expenses."

I cast an alarmed glance at Mama, but she wouldn't look at me.

Mr. Kensington studied me. "You, Cora, have your own prospects. The family is about to take a couple of weeks on the lake at our new summer home, before the children are off on their Grand Tour. And I believe, given what has transpired, you've long been destined to accompany them."

CHAPTER 6

~Cora~

Mama's mouth dropped open. I gasped. Leave the farm? Go with *him*? Mama lifted nervous eyes in my direction. They held an odd mixture of horror and...hope.

In contrast, Mr. Kensington's eyes were steady, watching me as if he were learning all about me, learning how to anticipate my next words. I felt dissected, analyzed.

I didn't even know where to begin. My knees were shaking, so I abruptly sat down again, as did Mr. Kensington. "So..." I said, "you think you can bring me home with you? That your children will simply accept me as a long-lost sibling and we'll be one big, content family?"

"I do not. You shall be introduced as my daughter, but none of it will come easily."

"And...your wife?" I asked. Mama fidgeted with her hands and looked away.

"My wife passed away a year ago."

49

Aha. "Did she ever know about me? Did you ever dare to tell her?"

"I did," he returned steadily. "She knew as soon as we found out that Alma was pregnant. And she knew I was bound and determined to do right by you."

This surprised me. He'd been honest with them. With them all, in time. And here I was, the last on his list. "I can't simply leave here. The farm—"

"The farm is dying," he said. "There won't be a property in the valley that brings in a profitable crop this autumn. There is no way a woman can keep it running. And there's no way Alan will be back—" He broke off abruptly, then cast an apologetic look at Mama.

"You've sold me short, Mr. Kensington."

He considered me for a moment, a small smile at the corners of his mouth. "Forgive me," he said, one eyebrow raised. "You are clearly most capable. But you're also bright. Admit it, girl. It'd be a waste. You might make it through this summer, but what becomes of you next year? More work, backbreaking work. For what? If there's one thing I've learned through the years, it's this—put in the hard work, but only if there's a chance of a fine profit. If not, look for another opportunity."

He set aside his teacup and leaned on his elbows, steepling his fingers together. "You have two years of Normal School under your belt. Top of your class. Come fall, you should go back, finish what you started. I can make a way for you to do that. And more."

How had he—

"You came home for the summer," he went on, "anticipating helping out your folks, then returning to school, correct?"

"That was my plan, yes. But plans change."

"Yes, they do," he said meaningfully. He paused, picked a piece of lint from his trousers, then looked back to me. "I'm giving you an opportunity to seize the finest 'change of plans' any girl on the eastern slope has ever been offered. Leave this behind. Accept your place with my family, and I will take care of you and yours."

We stared at each other for a long moment. I hated him then. For making me face it. Forcing me to turn away from what my papa, my *real* father, had loved all my growing-up years—this place. To turn away from making his dream work and…do what? Embrace Wallace Kensington's?

"No," I said.

And yet…I couldn't help myself. Had he really said his children were going on the Grand Tour? Did he mean of Europe? And he would actually fund my return to Normal School?

I hated myself then too. For the way my heart leaped inside my chest, pounded with excitement, pleasure, for the first time really, since I'd arrived home.

I glanced at Mama, who continued to stare out toward the fields, eyes wide and vacant. "I can't leave Mama. Not now. Not with Papa—"

"You are not *leaving* her. You are merely parting for a time. It will be good for you both. And your papa—Alan would want what is best for you."

I waited for Mama to move, join in the conversation, but she was mute. I knew she wanted to get Papa to the hospital and to see her parents. They were very old—I hadn't seen them in fifteen years. They had begged us to come to Minnesota for years. But the train tickets were too expensive. Until now.

I didn't like it. Wallace Kensington couldn't come in here, make us all do as he saw fit. Who was he to us? Other than a shadow of our past? He didn't belong here. We would make it on our own. Find a way to get my folks to Minnesota, find a way to get me back to school...

"I think, Mr. Kensington, that you have overstepped your bounds." I rose to my feet. "Mama and I can look after ourselves, thank you. I appreciate that you went to such lengths to honor a promise made long ago. But I do not feel a need for any father in my life, other than the one inside this house. And I prefer to make my way with Mama at my side. We are a family. We need not intrude upon yours at this late date."

His eyes registered surprise. He sat back, took a slow sip of tea, and gave me another small smile as he set it down on the saucer. "My dear Cora, I'm afraid there is no choice in the matter for you. I must insist you return with me. You shall see what it is to be a part of my family—as well as the one you share with Alma and Alan. It is the wise choice."

"How dare you—"

"How dare I offer you more than you could've ever dreamed?"

"How dare you waltz in here and presume—"

"Presume to prescribe a future with hope and promise?"

I shut my mouth abruptly, glaring at him. Then, "Are you quite finished?"

"Are you?" he asked.

"I am a free woman, Mr. Kensington. Grown. I can do as I wish. I may be blood kin to you, but I am not your employee." My eyes cut to Mama, but hers remained on the barn.

"Regardless, you shall do as I say."

I let out a sputtering, exasperated laugh. "And if I do not?"

He traced the edge of his chipped china saucer. "That would be ill advised." He said it with such confidence that it finally hit me. He could make it impossible for us here. Buy the bank and call our note, if he didn't own it already. I'd read enough of the man in the papers. There were rumors of him paying off the law. Judges. He was ruthless. Stopping at nothing to get what he wanted.

"I do not wish to deal with you harshly in order for you to accept my gift, Cora. But you shall accept it. One way or another."

Mama finally broke out of her daze and leaned forward. She tried to touch my hand, but I pulled away. "Cora, maybe this *is* best." She sighed and glanced back toward the window. "Papa's not improving… Who knows how long we'll need to remain in Minnesota. You'd be free of this place, free to pursue your own dreams. See some of the world. Finish your education. And your papa can get the care he needs." She turned back to me. "Perhaps this is God's doing, a way out for us. Not a trap, but rather a bridge to what He has for us next."

She was agreeing with Wallace Kensington? Or simply giving in to him? How could she? I stared at her, my heart heavy. What would Papa say if he could be a part of this?

I searched her eyes, and in them I saw grief and weariness, but also a trace of hope. For me. But for herself and Papa, too. Ever since Papa's last stroke five days ago, I'd seen none of that. And it pushed back at my rage and indignation, forcing me to reconsider.

I rose and paced a moment, thinking it through. All my life I'd envied those who didn't have to work all day to get more than a little meat and potatoes to the table. Envied those who could attend any class they wished, purchase any book they wanted, board steamships and travel. And now it was here. An option. A whole new world of options.

And Papa... I glanced toward his bedroom window. His best chance would be in Mr. Kensington's doctor's hands, getting him to a hospital. Perhaps with good care, he'd find renewed health again. But what then? I shook my head.

"If Papa survives the trip and regains his health," I said lowly, "the loss of this place will break his heart."

"Now it is you who are selling Alan short," Mr. Kensington said. "He is a man who understands himself and his limitations. I have other investments about Dunnigan. And I am prepared to expand them. I'll purchase this property for three times what it is worth. Enough to pay off the debts, as well as give your folks a little nest egg to begin again, wherever they wish."

I stared at him and then looked again to Mama. Her eyes were pleading now, begging me to accept. As well as rife with regret and remorse.

Why would he offer three times the value? To make it impossible for Mama to say no? My eyes narrowed in his direction. There was something more—

"Come now, Cora." He interrupted my thought. "Use that keen mind of yours. There is really only gain in this deal for you and Alma and Alan."

I shook my head, wondering over his audacity. I wanted to scream at him. I wanted to kick him off our porch. I wanted to run.

But there was little choice, much as I hated it. He'd offered us everything we needed and more. To turn away was to be a stubborn fool. And Alan Diehl had not raised a fool.

"I...I need some time to think about it," I said.

"Of course. Although as I understand it, every day Alan is not in a city hospital—"

"I understand," I bit out.

He gave me a hard look, mouth open. Clearly, he was unused to interruptions.

"I'll give you the night," Mr. Kensington said, rising and reaching for his hat as his doctor came through our front door, closing it quietly behind him. "I'll return in the morning for your answer."

He turned to my mother. "Alma, you and Alan will travel in one of my private train cars to Minneapolis. We'll do everything we can to make you both as comfortable as possible."

"I haven't agreed to *go*."

He ignored me and looked only to my mother. "There will be enough in your account to more than see to your needs, as well as the proceeds from the farm's sale. Is there anything else you need done before you go?"

"Our—our things," she said dimly, looking toward the house.

I thought about what it contained. A dirty, threadbare imitation Oriental rug? A settee, sagging in the middle? The chipped china? The small clock on the wall that hadn't kept good time for years? Was any of it worth keeping?

"I'll have some people come out tomorrow to collect anything you'd like to store," he said. "It will be waiting for you, or you can send for it when you have need of it."

I had to admit it. He said it with utmost respect; when surely he must have understood that we had very little of worth.

"All will be in order, so you can take the three o'clock east, and we can take the three-ten west. *If*, of course, Cora finds herself amenable to our plans." He gave me a curt nod.

Our plans? This was purely a Kensington plan, from start to finish.

You can keep your money and your promises, Mr. Kensington—we need nothing but the Lord, the land, and each other. We'll find a way. Somehow. Someway...

But my fierce words remained unspoken, as gagged as my mother's protests seemed to be.

———◇◆◇———

I was trembling, unable to face Mama, as Mr. Kensington and his doctor drove away.

She joined me at the sink, watching through the kitchen window as his black buggy grew tiny in the distance, a small cloud of dust rising behind his wheels.

"How could you?" I asked softly, not wanting Papa to overhear. "Give yourself to that man?"

She paused. "You just met him. Wallace Kensington does not give up when he wants something. And for a while," she said, her voice growing so quiet I almost couldn't hear her, "he wanted me."

I considered that for a minute. I knew Mama had grown up poor, her father a lumberman, her mother a cook. But she'd had a taste for adventure and had traveled west, eager to find work. I'd always known she had worked for a wealthy family. I'd daydreamed about being there too, peeking in on their well-to-do life. Never knowing I was one of them by blood.

I dug my fingernail into the pad of my thumb, trying to wake from this mad dream. Yet found I was still in the middle of it.

"Did he—did he…force himself upon you, Mama?" I couldn't imagine my mother, altar guild chairwoman at church, Sunday school administrator, Grange Hall coordinator, ever willingly taking part in extramarital relations. I couldn't believe I was even asking her this now.

"No," she said softly. "God help me, I went willingly. We were different people then. Both of us weak and in need." She turned to me and touched my shoulder. I was two inches taller than her, wider in the shoulder. But at the moment, I felt too small to face her. Too scared. I reached for a teacup, placing it in the sink to wash.

"Cora," she said.

I pursed my lips and glanced at her from the side.

"Forgive me, Cora," she said. "It's not how any child should start out life. But it was your start. Wallace made it as easy as he could on you. Your papa, too. I should have told you earlier. I should have." She sighed, and a tear traced her cheek. "I'm sorry."

"Oh, Mama," I said, looking back to the window, the valley road still and empty except for Mr. Kensington's buggy, tiny in the distance. I twirled the rag inside the teacup that was already clean.

"Your papa, he wanted you to think of him as your father, through and through. He didn't see any need to—"

"No need? To break the news that the most powerful man in the state was my father by blood?"

"Well, I'm not certain he's the *most* powerful."

I lowered my voice for fear Papa would hear me. "Did Papa think I'd never find out?"

She sighed and turned back to the sink. "He hoped not." Her voice cracked. "We both hoped Wallace would forget. That he'd see it was easier if he just left you, us, to live our lives. Only the yearly birthday presents made us think he had not."

She looked to me, deep care in her eyes. "Your papa loves you, Cora. You must believe it. And I think Wallace truly believes this is the best thing for you." She paused and turned toward me, taking my hands. "While it will be undoubtedly difficult, Cora, I believe it's an answer to our prayers. Don't you see? How else can we get your papa the care he needs?"

I bit back one angry retort after another. The Lord was answering my prayers by destroying my life, taking me from the people I loved? By striking down my papa so this pretender could come and claim me?

But then I remembered. My prayer for Him to make a way for us. It wasn't the way I'd imagined, but I couldn't deny that a way had been made. I sighed and closed my eyes. "I know Papa loves me, Mama. And I love him all the more for loving me as his own."

She stared out the window. "I'd made a mess of things. Made awful, sinful choices. And God redeemed it all. Redeemed me and my life. I've been happy here, with you and your papa. Despite the struggle and disappointments, our love has made it all worthwhile. Our parting will only be for a while. For you to see what's possible on your own, unhindered by your responsibilities to us and this farm. Your future won't be as you imagined it, but there are good things ahead for you too, child. I know it."

I clung to the hope and promise in her words as I fretted over what was ahead, thinking about meeting half siblings for the first time, strangers.

Would they welcome me? Begrudgingly let me in? Hate me? I was just glad Mrs. Kensington was dead and gone before I, her husband's illegitimate daughter, came to join the clan. Maybe in her absence, the children wouldn't feel quite so threatened...

The cup cracked in my hand, a jagged edge splitting it in two. My mother and I stared at it for a long moment.

"One less thing to pack," she said, offering a resigned smile before turning away.

CHAPTER 7

-Wallace-

The doctors decided it was best if Alan didn't know what had transpired until he was well enough to tolerate it. The poor man would probably not understand for weeks that his daughter had been spirited off.

Wallace paced and pulled the watch from his small vest pocket, checking the time again, trying to hide his agitation. Five minutes until the conductor called for them to board. He'd never missed a train yet, and today would not be his first. He was eager to get back to where he belonged, in Butte, see to his business before they met the family at the lake. He'd spent too long away as it was.

At last Cora emerged from the private car, wiping the tears from her cheeks, blowing her nose in a handkerchief. *So she's bidden Alan farewell.* Alma followed her out. They were ten steps away, on the other side of the platform, holding hands and weeping. Shortly, Alma would accompany her husband to Minneapolis. The woman still looked good to him, two decades after he'd sent her away. Still trim, and with that warm smile that lit up her brown eyes. *Another man's wife now*, he reminded myself. He tried to train his eyes on their daughter instead. She was plainly flustered and upset, and he'd heaped a new grief upon her, wrenching her away like this. But there was no way around it. The time was now. He felt it in his bones. And when he felt something in his bones, nothing could keep him from acting.

He'd thought about coming for her before. To at least propose the option of meeting her siblings so they could get to know one another. But once the tour plans were settled, he'd scanned the maps and the train schedules, tinkering with the idea of seeing to his other investments on the eastern slope—and coming to call. Alan's failing health had galvanized him. Cora was better off with the Kensingtons now, a new era upon her. She'd take the tour, find healing in the distraction, then finish her education. Under his tutelage, she'd come into her own. Into her destiny as a Kensington.

And if his surveyors had been right in their analysis of this region, he'd gain more than just his daughter…

He stole a glance in her direction, saw that a couple of ranch hands on the far side of the platform did the same. She was beautiful, with hair the color of ripened wheat, fair and shining in the sun, and glacial blue eyes so eerily like his own. He'd always imagined her having Alma's dark hair and eyes. But instead, they were his exact shade of blue. Felix had inherited them too. If any of his other children doubted Cora's paternity, that alone would put the matter to rest.

Wallace would see that she discarded her drab brown dress and bought some proper gowns and traveling suits in Butte. If he brought her to the lodge in what she wore now, everyone would immediately look down on her. Not that they wouldn't anyway. Winning the family over would be like pulling copper from the big hill without a shovel. But just as he'd brought the state its first proper smelter, he'd find a way to help Cora find her place with the family.

She was kin. His child. What was he to do? Sit back, allow her to struggle, when his other three had every single thing they ever dreamed of? He swore under his breath, laughing at the memory of her spirited responses the day before. Maybe she'd even teach her half siblings a thing or two.

He checked his watch again and cleared his throat. Alma glanced his way, reached up to touch Cora's cheek, and gave her a brave smile. Cora embraced her mother once more and then bustled past him, never meeting his eye as she boarded the train. Alma stepped toward him. "Watch over her, Wallace, won't you?"

He nodded gravely. "I will. What she has ahead of her will be the most difficult and wondrous experience of her entire life."

Alma's brown eyes studied his. Her mouth was drawn. Alan and Alma's train began to move; Wallace heard the whistle blow for his, the conductor crying, "All 'board!" But he stayed with Alma. "She'll be safe, Wallace?" she asked, starting to walk alongside the slowly chugging train.

"She will be well protected. Trust me." He took her hand and helped her step onto the stairwell platform. She stood there for a moment, gazing at him, and then over at his train car, their daughter framed in the window. Then Alma turned and climbed the steps in a way that took him back twenty years to when she climbed into the coach that took her away, when her belly was just beginning to swell with child. *When I knew I loved her, but had to give her to another man.* For the sake of his marriage. His other children. For Cora's sake too.

Hat in hand, he watched until their train grew small in the distance.

————◦◇◦————

The conductor let out a low blow of the whistle as their train began to move in the direction of Butte. Wallace took hold of the handle and climbed up and in. Cora had found their seats, right by the window in the first-class car.

Wallace sat down across from her, his hands folded over the end of his cane, between his knees. The cane was more for show than need, but Wallace thought it lent a rather distinguished air. Cora's eyes followed her mother's train, the caboose now sliding out of view.

He'd done it. *Collected my lost girl.* He shook off the guilt that tried to settle over his shoulders, seeing the pain in her eyes, around her mouth. She'd be reunited with Alan and Alma soon enough. It was time she learned about and embraced her Kensington side and all that meant for her.

They didn't speak. He figured it'd be best if she addressed him first. He'd said enough. She undoubtedly needed time to unravel all she'd discovered. He closed his eyes as the hours went on, lulled by the swaying motion of the car and the rhythmic sound of wheels crossing one segment of track and then another and another. He dozed, feeling every one of his sixty-odd years as the pressure of the last days edged away.

————◦◇◦————

He woke to a servant setting a table between his seat and Cora's, then jumped when he saw her empty seat. His heart skipped a beat, and he looked quickly around the car, putting aside the silly thought that she'd leapt from the train. *She's merely gone to the ladies' lounge to freshen up before luncheon.*

The servant slid an impeccably white linen tablecloth across the small table, then, drawing from a cart, set it with sterling silver and crystal goblets. Even a small vase with a rose. The train line was clearly trying to better its image. Usually one got no such service except on one of the bigger lines. Dimly, he remembered his late wife telling him something of the sort—that the line had plans to upgrade its first-class cars. That'd been a year ago or so, not long before she died.

The servant unfolded a napkin and set it across his lap.

Cora arrived then, and the servant moved to pull out her chair. Wallace rose, but Cora did not look at him until seated, her own napkin across her lap. She took a drink of water from the goblet and declined the wine from the decanter when Wallace raised it in silent offering. "Your other children…" she began, eyes on the goblet as if she could see her siblings' faces in it. She raised her eyes to meet his. "They will loathe me."

He considered her words. "The wind will be against you for a time. But stick with it, and you will win them over."

She raised an eyebrow. "So you believe that I can enter their circle—a girl raised on a dirt-poor farm miles from the nearest city— and we will be one big, happy family?"

"Perhaps not happy. But it shall be tolerable, in time. I hope you shall invest yourself in the opportunity, regardless of how your siblings treat you. To see England, France…Austria, Italy. To complete your education, enter the social circles that are your birthright…Is it not every young woman's dream?"

She took another long drink of water and sat back as the servant brought them china plates laden with fried chicken, steaming mashed potatoes and gravy, and "*haricots verts*," the man said.

Uppity name for little green beans, Wallace thought.

He never suffered such foolishness lightly. His staff knew to never refer to a foreign word if there was a perfectly good one in English. *Consommé* was *broth*, in his house. One needn't put on airs just because one was wealthy. But with Cora being so fragile, so tender, he elected to hold his tongue for now. He didn't wish to upset her with anything further, no matter how small.

He hoped that bringing lowborn, sensible Cora into the mix might break his heirs out of some of their less admirable traits. He loathed the lack of a work ethic in Felix, Vivian's overdeveloped sense of pride, and Lillian's spoiled entitlement. Perhaps in the arrival of a new sibling, there'd be a sense of competition that would sharpen them all in some ways and mute the less desirable aspects.

"Most young women I know dream of little more than marriage and children," she said, so softly that he barely heard her. The question had lingered so long he had almost forgotten asking it. She chewed her bite of chicken as if she lacked the strength to swallow.

"Do you leave behind a young man?" he asked, studying her. Perhaps he'd received less than complete reports.

She shook her head, eyes on her plate. "I've never been courted."

He took a bite, considering how to respond. "That shall not be the case for long, my dear. You are a fine young woman, inside and out."

She met his gaze then, finally swallowing. A blush rose at her jawline—from what? His endearment? Or because he had given her a compliment? Soon afterward, she sent away her plate, apparently too upset to eat any more while Wallace finished every bite. It surprised him, knowing how little she'd had growing up. And now she pushed away a free meal? Well he remembered the days when he was lucky to get a full meal on his plate.

—◇—

~Cora~

There was so much I wanted to ask him. About my mother. About their relationship. About his other family, his children. About what it was like when he first got to Montana, in the territorial days. About his stint as a US senator. But it all swirled around my head so fast that I couldn't grab hold of one strand long enough to pull it from the ball.

Thoughts of Mama and Papa made me feel even more dizzy. Would I ever see Papa again? That thought weighed upon me more than any other. He'd looked so frail, his eyes sunken into his head, that it still sent a chill down my spine. Yet Mama had insisted this was God's provision.

God's provision? I scoffed at the thought. How could this pompous man across from me be sent by God?

"You're undoubtedly curious about the tour," he said as the train neared Butte's station later that evening.

I blinked twice, thinking I'd like to know more about it, yes, but there were a hundred other things—

"We'll stay here in Butte for a bit. Tomorrow morning, you shall be seen by the family physician. Then your maid, Anna, will see to your wardrobe."

I glanced down at my plain brown dress. I supposed I did appear as one of his lesser servants. But a physician? "I'm not ill."

"Yes, well, the bear—the guide for your Grand Tour—insists that all who are to come have a thorough examination." He waved me off, as if that was all he could say about such an indelicate subject. "Tonight, I must see to business. We shall dine together tomorrow evening, giving us time to become…acquainted. Then we shall board another train and head north. We'll take a week upon the lake before the tour party departs."

"So soon?" I managed to say.

"I believe it will be exactly right. Long enough for you young people to get to know one another, but not long enough for things to"—he paused, seeming uncomfortable—"come to a boiling point."

I eyed him quickly. "Distraction is key," he said. "And you all shall have constant distraction on the Grand Tour—your minds occupied by the travel itself, by art, culture, language—so you do not dwindle into lesser conversations."

Lesser conversations. Such as my parentage. The thought of it made me blush furiously. Why, oh why, had my mother never told me? Given me the opportunity to prepare for this day?

Our train was pulling into the station now. Mr. Kensington— my *father*, I reminded myself, though I highly doubted I would ever be able to call him *Father*—was still speaking of our itinerary. "… trains to New York and then embark on a steamship for the week's crossing. And there," he said, pausing, blue eyes twinkling, "the adventure truly begins, does it not?"

I paused. "Somehow, I believe it already has, Mr. Kensington."

He raised his head and regarded me for a long moment then. "Indeed, it has."

───◇───

It was ingenious, really. Sneaking me into town while the family was away. Mr. Kensington was greeted left and right, but apparently by mere acquaintances, no one important enough to introduce me to, regardless of their lingering glances. Or was it the other way around? That I wasn't important enough to introduce? I burned with curiosity—how did he intend to explain my presence to the world?

He seemed to be in a hurry. To get to his office? Or to squire me away?

I tried not to gawk as we climbed into a finely polished red Great Smith touring car, driven by a man in uniform and smart cap. "Davis, I'd like to introduce you to my daughter," Mr. Kensington said. I was stunned by his boldness and turned to look at him. "Miss Cora Kensington," he continued. "She has been away for some time but is finally home with us. Cora, this is Davis, our driver."

The tall, thin man took off his hat and gave me a little bow. Still spinning over Wallace's words, I belatedly nodded. *Kensington?* Was that how it was to be handled? I'd be plainly introduced as Wallace's daughter? With the family name? I supposed I thought he might explain me away as a niece or a second cousin. Not be so...

forthright. But then he *was* Wallace Kensington. Would anyone do more than blink and nod? At least to our faces?

We pulled up to the grandest home I'd ever seen, upon the widest boulevard I'd ever seen. There were fine homes in Dillon, for sure, but none as large as this one. I glanced around to the hills above us, amazed again that there were no trees or grass for miles around Butte, although it was plain that many had tried to coax them to life. It was haunting, really—the dry, smelter-burned landscape and the massive, perfect houses lining the streets. As though someone had set a fancy town in the middle of a rocky, dusty desert.

The "hill," as they called it, rose above the heart of the city, riddled with mines and ramshackle houses and a steady stream of people traversing her roads, even at this late hour. But here, on Granite Street, were several blocks of houses as only my father and his companions could have dreamed it. Thirty years ago, this city had been full of tents and log cabins. Now there were two- and three- and even four-story homes of brick and finely milled lumber and tiles upon the roofs, glinting in the moonlight with flecks of copper.

Davis drove us up to and then under the front portico. A butler, two maids, and a footman came out of the house. "Most of the servants are accompanying the children," Mr. Kensington said, as if embarrassed by this slim accounting of servants.

In quick succession they were introduced, bobbing in deference as they met the long-lost Kensington daughter. Their faces giving away nothing, as if this were an everyday occurrence. My eyes narrowed. Perhaps I wasn't the first or last... If my father had been a philanderer once, what would have kept him from other dalliances?

I shoved the ugly thought from my head—half drawn to the idea of not being the only black sheep in the family, half repulsed—and followed a maid to a corner bedroom upstairs. My father had introduced her as Anna, gruffly telling her to make appointments with the dressmaker and milliner as well as prepare to leave Butte in two days—she would attend me at the lake, as well as in Europe. Anna accepted it all with hardly more than a blink and a bob of a curtsy. She was about my height, as dark in hair and eye as I was light. She eyed my dress and said, "Mr. Kensington has asked that your supper be brought to you in your room. After your long journey, you must be weary and need your quiet time."

I nodded, but exhaustion was the last thing I felt. Every nerve in my body, every portion of my brain, seemed taut, attuned to all that was new about me. I felt more awake than I had in weeks. As Anna shut the door, I walked around the room that was as big as our kitchen, sitting room, and one bedroom combined back home. I admired finely framed oil paintings, the textured paper on the walls, the elaborate carved ceiling molding atop fourteen-foot walls. The furniture was intricately carved, the rich red sheen boasting of cherry and mahogany. In front of a full-length mirror, I reached up to take the pins from my hair, tired of the sensation of pulling, tightness, when everything else in my life seemed to be tugging at me. I yanked ten out, placing the wires on a table and running my fingers through my hair, watching as it fell in waves across my shoulders.

When I moved over to the leaded-glass window, I paused and looked out to the back of the property. I glimpsed Davis unloading our luggage with the help of another manservant, in what I assumed was a carriage house. But my eyes were drawn to the huge, old oak, the lone live tree I'd yet seen in this town.

I was taking in the sparse leaves, noting how sickly they appeared, as if the giant was suffering, struggling to hold on against the ravages of time and smelter smoke, when I saw the dark-haired young man sitting beneath it. He leaned against the big trunk, eyes closed as if dreaming he were in the midst of a forest. He had fine features—a strong jaw, well-defined eyes and cheeks, wide shoulders. One hand rested on his thigh, and in the other hand, pressed against his chest, was a leather-bound book.

I finally remembered myself and lurched backward, praying he hadn't opened his eyes, hadn't seen me staring.

Who was he? A brother? Were they not all at the lake, taking their leisure? A servant? He was too finely dressed for that. My heart was hammering in my chest. But why? Did I not have the right to look out my window? Was I not a Kensington? At least in name? *Cora Kensington*, I repeated in my head, trying to get used to the sound of it. *Cora Kensington. Hello, I am Miss Cora Kensington.*

I felt a pang of sorrow. All my life, I'd been Papa's girl, Cora Diehl. Was I so easily purchased?

Still, I edged around the corner to steal another peek, chanting my new name as if it was the key to enter through a forbidden door.

But the young man was gone.

CHAPTER 8

-William-

She'd appeared as an angel in the window before him. Fair hair falling in golden waves across the shoulders of her dark gown. Wide, light eyes, somber in their steadiness. Lips pursed like a deep pink bow.

And then she was gone.

He waited for a moment, hoping she'd return, then looked away, knowing his uncle would be infuriated if he found him gazing toward their employer's home like a leering toad. If there was one thing Will had learned after helping to escort three groups of the States' well-to-do children about Europe, it was that the young women were off limits and the young men were only friends as long as he was in their father's employ. It went best if he kept to his assigned role—as escort, guide, teacher, protector. Assistant to his uncle. *Bear*-in-training. He and his uncle were hired to illuminate their clients' worlds, expand their minds, engage their imaginations. Nothing more.

"It's enough," his uncle always said, "is it not? They are the privileged class, and we are privileged to serve them in such a grand endeavor as the tour."

Will wrenched away from the tree and strode toward the porch swing. But curiosity was getting the best of him. This was the first he'd seen of their group of young clients—other than his old schoolmate Felix Kensington. He hoped she would emerge down below, seeking more fresh air than her bedroom window allowed. Join them for supper. So he could get to know this Cora whom the servants whispered about incessantly. What was going on?

But neither of the Kensingtons joined them upon the porch, or for supper, nor in the map room, where they reviewed their plans for the journey—for the dozenth time—nor for breakfast the following day.

Will began to wonder if he had imagined that he'd seen Cora Kensington at all. He puzzled over the fact that she was not with her sisters, her brother, or the Morgans, the other family taking the tour. That she had tarried here, behind them all. From the study, as morning light poured through a wide bay window, his uncle and he looked up to see a maid go to the front door, greet a doctor, and then lead him up the wide, carpeted staircase.

They shared a concerned glance. Examinations were supposed to have been completed last month. Was she ill? That would be a poor way to begin. The Grand Tour was a lavish but taxing journey. Constantly on the move, constantly taking entertainment, viewing museums, meeting others, attending dances and dinners. They'd dealt with people becoming ill while touring; they did not wish to *begin* with anyone ill in their party.

Only a maid's whispering to another, later in the day, relieved him of his concern. Miss Kensington was apparently off to a dressmaker and shopping for the day. If she wasn't too ill to attend a fitting, then she was likely not ill at all. *Cora*, he said in his mind. *Like coral.* Would she find a dress in that color? It'd be a fine choice for her. Much better than the brown that made her look so pale.

"Will," his uncle barked. "Pay attention. We are in Paris. Tell me of the principal delights of the World's Fair of 1883."

Will's eyes narrowed. The old man was trying to trip him. "The *Exposition Universelle* of 1889 was a sight to behold."

His uncle let a small smile tug at the corners of his mouth.

"The Eiffel Tower was built as an entrance to the fair," Will said, "of puddled iron lattice, principally designed by Gustave Eiffel. In 1889 alone there were over two million visitors to the Tower."

"Good," said his uncle. "Go on."

"Buffalo Bill hosted one of the most popular attractions, bringing in Annie Oakley for his 'Wild West Show.' There was an African village with over four hundred native occupants, which also proved popular."

"And who came to see such a marvel on the Champ de Mars?" his uncle asked, quietly reminding him of another fact he wanted worked in.

"Many, but the Prince of Wales, Paul Gauguin, Vincent van Gogh, Henry James, and Thomas Edison were among them."

"Very good," his uncle said with begrudging admiration. Will had learned more than his uncle gave him credit for. It helped, too, that Will was mesmerized by the Tower. He couldn't wait to see it again.

Uncle Stuart walked to the maps pinned to the wall, with notes tacked to it at appropriate junctures, outlining their excursions, their lessons, their entertainment. "Now tell me of the Kensington and Morgan family connections on which we shall rely."

Will knew it was imperative that he remember these relationships, given that it would be his uncle or him who would introduce the young people to long-lost relatives, friends, and business associates of their fathers'. Will was puzzling over Count Montague and his connection to Mr. Kensington when the Kensingtons appeared in the map room doorway.

"Come now," his uncle chided. "Count *Montague*," he said, as if just repeating his name would jog Will's memory. Inwardly, Will winced, knowing the tone made him appear as a chastised child before the Kensingtons. He couldn't bear to look their way.

"He is a cousin via a great-uncle by marriage," Mr. Kensington filled in for Will. Will smiled his thanks, barely glancing in Cora's direction.

"Not that he'll know that," Mr. Kensington went on. "He'll only be interested in housing my children in exchange for trying to purchase ten shares of the Montana Copper Mine," he said with a grin, clapping Will's shoulder. "Gentlemen, I'd like you to meet my daughter Miss Cora Kensington. Miss Cora, this is Sir Stuart McCabe, your bear, and his nephew, William McCabe."

Stuart gave her a stately bow and then took her hand and kissed it. Will did the same afterward, ignoring the unseemly blush climbing her neck and cheeks. It was almost as if she'd never been formally introduced to a man before, so uncomfortable was she. Will backed away quickly, admiring how beautiful she was in her gown. He'd seen similar fashions on women in the papers out of Paris—such a fashion statement would be exclaimed over by their hosts. And her eyes were the same striking glacial blue as her father's, ringed in long light-brown lashes, tinged with blonde. With her hair done up and the color high in her cheeks, she'd have no shortage of dance partners as they made their way through the various balls of the tour. Her embarrassed glance told him he'd been staring too long. Will offered her a smile, then forced himself to look away.

"Is this our route?" she asked, moving between them to the maps on the wall.

Will's uncle nodded at him, giving him permission. "Indeed," Will said, stepping to her side. He reached up to point at the map. "We shall take a train to New York, and a steamship directly to England. Shortly thereafter, we shall cross the Channel to France. Your father told us that you all have spent more than enough time in England."

She paused, glancing downward, not at all the response he'd expected. Had something bad happened to her there? He pressed on. "We shall sail up the Seine to Paris. It's a grand way to come upon the city for the first time. After some time in the city and a visit to Versailles, we'll then journey south, to Provence."

Her eyes were already scanning ahead of where he gestured. "We end in Italy?"

"Indeed," he said, frowning over the wonderment in her tone. Had her father told her nothing of what lay ahead? It was best if the group began with a certain amount of preparation, knowledge. "After Austria, we shall spend a great deal of time in Italia, from the top of the boot to the bottom of the heel, as my uncle likes to say. Torino, Verona, Venezia, Firenze, Siena, Roma, and beyond."

"It's the cradle of the Renaissance, the heart of our trip," his uncle said, leaning in front of Will to smile at the heiress.

"And the best place to spend concentrated time," Will said wistfully. It made him long for Italia, speaking of the place. There, of any place in the world—and he'd seen much of it in the family business—he felt a call to return, as often as possible. But it would be months before they reached her borders.

"It's very far from here," she said, so softly Will barely made out her words.

"Indeed," he said, trying to soothe her anxiety with an encouraging smile. "But that is part of its draw. It's like nothing you've known before."

She gave him the tiniest of smiles in return. "You make it sound magical."

"Indeed," his uncle said. "Clearly our favorite," he added, giving Will a look, telling him to fall silent. "Though we strive not to prejudice you before your arrival. This journey is about discovery, Miss Kensington. Of yourself, of others, of the world."

Her smile grew a little larger. As if she were thinking, *You have no idea*. It made Will curious, but he held his tongue. His uncle saw it too. He glimpsed the question in the older man's eyes, but both remained silent. In time, they'd know more of Miss Kensington and her siblings, as well as the Morgans. As guides, it was part of their journey of discovery too. Nothing brought people together, nor allowed such intimacies, as swiftly as traveling in a group.

But when, over supper, it was clear that Miss Kensington had not known that another family would be joining their party, nor that her father would not be with them the entire way, Will was fairly burning with curiosity.

Cora's knife clattered to her fine china plate and stared at her father. "You…you are not coming with us?"

Mr. Kensington slowly wiped his mouth and then gave them all a merry smile, meant to cover the embarrassment of the moment. "Why no, Cora. Surely you know that the Grand Tour is for young people alone. It is part of your coming of age. That is difficult to accomplish if your *parents* are hovering nearby. But please don't fret… Sir Stuart and his nephew, as your guides, will see to your safety. Along with a troop of servants. You'll find yourself more than adequately cared for." He looked as though he wanted to reach across the massive table and pat her arm. But even if he could have, her stiff demeanor and the distant look in her eyes revealed that she didn't want anything of the kind. What had transpired between them? Did she not wish to go? Was that why she was belatedly joining the others? Why she seemed to know nothing of their plans?

She sat straight, and Will admired the slight shadow beneath her clavicle, the long stretch of her graceful neck—then he cursed himself for noticing. He glanced at his uncle at the end of the table, but he was industriously chewing on a piece of bread, staring at his soup as if trying to ascertain its ingredients. But Will knew he was chewing over Cora's words as much as the bread.

"Mr. Kensington," she mumbled, glancing down at the table. "I fear I am most dreadfully weary. May I be excused?"

Mr. Kensington? *How odd that his daughter would call him that.*

"Certainly," he said, rising. Will and his uncle did the same.

"Good evening, gentlemen," she said with a courtly nod.

"Good evening, Miss Kensington," they said in unison. Only her father called her by her given name.

When he was sure she was safely upstairs, Uncle said, "Mr. Kensington, if the girl is sickly, perhaps—"

Mr. Kensington let out a snort. "The girl's as healthy as a horse. Had the doctor check her out this morning. She's merely suffered a great deal of change in the last weeks, which has left her...at odds." He cleared his throat and glanced down at his plate.

From there, he proceeded to tell them the full story—that Cora was the product of an illicit affair with a maid. Mr. Kensington had only recently met her, after the only father she'd ever known was stricken by ill health.

"I had no choice," he said, as if he needed to justify himself. "They were on the verge of losing the farm—and this shall not be a winning year for farmers. There would be no opportunity for her to return to Normal School. And when I heard her father was ailing..." He shrugged, took a bite, chewed, swallowed. "I went to collect her. It was best for her. And my responsibility to act."

Will sat back, dumbfounded.

Cora, wearing that drab brown dress, fretting over the only father she'd ever known, adjusting to the idea of being the illegitimate child of a copper king—

It took everything in Will not to shake his head and groan. They'd negotiated difficult family dynamics before on tour, but this situation was so laden with dynamite powder, they'd likely explode before they even left Montana.

CHAPTER 9

-*Wallace*-

A heavy silence fell on the table after Wallace Kensington finished speaking. Only he continued to dine, cutting apart his tender slice of roast. He knew he was acting as if he'd just shared the current price of copper and his projected profits, rather than the devastating truth that would challenge them all ahead, but he didn't want them to back out of the tour. He had to make them believe they could do this task, despite the poor odds. If he failed, his children and the Morgans would forever blame him—and Cora—for ruining their trip.

"So," Stuart said carefully, "Miss Kensington was not aware of her parentage until this past week?"

Wallace considered that, squinting, as if he had to count back, then nodded with a grin. "Heavy load to drop on someone, isn't it?"

The older man stared back at him. "Surely you understand what a tremendous task is before her, Mr. Kensington. She shall be meeting not only her family for the first time, but some of the world's finest citizens. And if it gets out that she is…that she is of…"

"That she is my illegitimate daughter," Wallace said sadly. He knew he was casting her into a vast net that would be nearly impossible to escape—but it was part of her journey of discovery. Part of what would prove to him that she was a Kensington by blood as well as by name. It was best for her, this path of challenge. And if there happened to be copper on the Diehl property he'd just purchased, she'd benefit further, down the road. *Better to sweat out the profits from the rock, than that meager topsoil...*

"It shall haunt her, sir," the old bear said. "And cast a pall over the entire party, I'm afraid. We may not get half the invitations we'd hoped for. Some families might turn us away outright."

"So be it," Wallace said gruffly, waving a hand of dismissal in their direction. "There are more than enough funds for you to rent a chateau or villa or mansion here and there, if the distant kin see fit to shun you. But, gentlemen, remember who I am." He placed his hands on the table and leveled a gaze in their direction. "You know as well as I that they may whisper behind closed doors, but they will be more than gracious to your face. They shall be eager to learn everything they can of me and mine. If for no other reason than opening a door for future commercial relations or potential strategic marriages." At that he held up his finger and lowered his brow. "You are to see to it that the girls get their fill of flirtation but no proposals, understood?"

"Understood, sir," Stuart said. "A common request from fathers stateside."

Wallace shook his head. He'd heard all about the European dandies with their fancy titles and rambling mansions, desperate for cash. More than one of his friends had shipped off a daughter to find love as well as title. But not him. He wanted his daughters to return. All of them.

He let out a dismissive sound. "They'll be curious about this latest batch of nouveaux riche from America. How they are dressed. How they conduct themselves. Fodder for their circles of gossip."

Will and Stuart straightened, taken aback. But Wallace cocked his head and raised his fork. "Oh, don't look so surprised, gentlemen. I know how they are. Some will open their doors to the children. I'm confident of it."

The guide took a deep breath and let it out slowly, pinching the bridge of his nose as if he had a sudden headache. "You might be surprised how provincial the Europeans may be," Stuart said at last. He paused a moment, then, "But sir, would it not be easiest if we simply introduced Miss Cora as a second cousin? None would bat an eye at—"

"No," Wallace growled, hitting the table, then remembering to keep his voice down. "Absolutely not. I spent twenty years ignoring that child," he said, pointing upward, "and I'll do nothing but right by her now. Her birth certificate testifies that she is a Kensington. It is time that the world knew I am father to *four* children, each of whom I recognize as my own. It may be more *comfortable* for us to call her something else"—he paused, shaking his head—"but we shall not. We shall not. We will face the truth and get beyond it."

The men were silent for a moment. Then the bear said, "But you will not be with us, Mr. Kensington. We will be the ones who bear the brunt of this coming storm."

Wallace let out a dismissive snort. "All of these young people are far too absorbed in themselves to care one whit about Cora."

The bear paused. "In our experience, sir, the younger generations of privileged families tend to spend an exorbitant amount of time considering social standing and such."

Wallace stared at him. The guide dared to contradict him? His first impulse was to excuse them from his employ. But deep down, he knew the bear was absolutely correct.

Both Morgan and he had concocted this plan to send them on the tour because they saw their children for what they were. In need of culture and refinement, yes. Spoiled. Used to things going their way. Each given to their own weakness. But good at the core, each and every one of them. Facing Cora would help transform them into the adults he knew they could be—or plunge them headlong into their deepest weaknesses.

It would be what it would be. "I understand that this is both the chance and challenge of a lifetime. That I've added a...*nuance* to the group that could not have been anticipated. But it must be faced head-on. And for your trouble, I will double your fee."

The old bear stared back into Wallace's eyes, calculating, considering. It didn't take him long. He held out a hand to shake with Wallace. "We shall see it through," Stuart said.

But Wallace had already known he had him.

Everyone could be bought. Everyone.

~*Cora*~

My father never knew I'd heard every word that he'd said to the guide and his nephew, laying bare my humiliating personal history, negotiating my inclusion in the group as if I were simply a difficult sack of goods to sell. His words had echoed over the finely polished wood floors, up the stairs, to the landing where I hovered, alternately entranced and horrified.

I sat down when he said that my name was Kensington on my birth certificate. I wondered over that. Was it true? I'd never seen the document with my own eyes, had always taken Mama's word that she kept it safe in her box of papers. I put my head in my hands when he said he intended for me to be introduced everywhere as a Kensington. What did that mean for me? That I'd face ridicule, mocking, through the whole journey? The guides clearly felt I was a liability.

Spotting a maid coming up the stairs, I rose and scurried to my room, not wishing anyone to know that I'd been eavesdropping. And then I spent hours pacing my bedroom floor, wondering if I should have declined his invitation to come on this trip, even if it meant finding our own way to make it on the farm and care for Papa. Here in Butte, knowing a little more of him, I felt fairly certain he had traded upon our insecurities and fears to get what he wanted.

But could I do it? Face the world as the illegitimate child of Wallace Kensington? Without him by my side, protecting me, driving back those who challenged the notion—even as our guide and his nephew had just done in the dining room? What was I to do if someone dared to remark on it? Grin and bear it? I shook my head and rested my hand atop it.

Lord, please help me. Give me courage. Hope.

How I envied my sisters and brother. They'd never known anything but this house, this name, this existence. As much as I loved my parents...how could they have loved me, as well as lied to me, all those years? My siblings had never had such doubts.

They always knew they were Kensingtons. I shook my head, hating Mr. Kensington, hating my mother's weakness, hating Mama and Papa's lies—even if they meant to protect me. I felt as if I'd fallen into a narrow hole and could not move, let alone begin to claw my way out.

It didn't help that the June evening was uncommonly hot. This time of night, most of Montana cooled down, allowing sleep. But after tossing and turning for hours, I knew I'd never find my rest. My mind was in as many knots as my sheets.

I had to get out. Out of this house. For a walk, to clear my head. To pray.

I threw on my old brown dress and my tired, worn boots, wanting the comfortable, the known, weary of drowning in a sea of new. Only when I felt the last button at my neck, the familiar rub of the rough fabric against my skin, did I begin to breathe easier. After a moment's hesitation, I dared to turn on my lamp. I listened intently, worried the light might draw a servant or my father. But no one came.

I moved to the dressing table, wound my hair into a knot on top of my head, and hastily pinned it in place, not even checking the mirror to find out how well I had done.

My mind was solely on my exit. Outside, in the air, I might catch a bit of a breeze, feel as if I could move freely, without being examined. I crept down the stairs, glad that the fine carpentry meant there were no creaking boards to betray my flight. At the bottom of the stairs, I looked one way and then the next. All the lights were out except for one by the front door. Were any servants even awake at this hour?

Feeling every hair rise along my neck, I pushed forward, not looking back until I'd unlocked the door and turned the knob. Then, with one last glance around the huge foyer and empty stair, I slipped out of the house, quietly closing the door behind me. I didn't pause, but scurried down the steps and the walk, wincing over the creaking wrought-iron gate that betrayed my escape. But I moved through it as quickly as I could and then down the walk as if it were completely common for a young woman at two in the morning.

Oh, but the freedom! For the first time, I considered where I was. In the middle of one of Montana's biggest cities. A shiver of daring rolled down my back. Even at this hour, I could hear touring cars and horses' hooves a few streets over. The red-light district, I surmised, and turned in the opposite direction. I wasn't such a bumpkin that I would allow myself to get caught in that sort of place. I made my way toward homes progressively much smaller and modest in scale than the Kensington mansion.

More like my own house, the only home I'd ever known. Now owned by Wallace Kensington. It made me feel dirty, as if Mama and I had betrayed my father by selling it. How long might I have lasted, trying to run the farm on my own? Mr. Kensington had been right that we were lucky to make it through the winter every year. Would we have been forced to sell before Christmas anyway?

I shook my head. It felt better to hold on to the anger. The resentment against the man listed on my birth certificate. At least my anger was mine. Something that Wallace Kensington could not take from me until I was ready to let it go.

The neighborhood felt welcoming, even in the darkness. Less frightening than the mansions, because these houses seemed like homes where I might see Mama, feel her welcome me in a hug. *Mama, Mama*, I thought, my heart twisting in a braid of anger and sorrow. She'd been weak, weary, primed for Wallace to strike when he'd shown up at the farm. And this invitation—an escape route from the farm, hope for Mama and Papa, a way out for me—had shaken us back to life, partially. Out of our own sense of paralysis.

I'll give that to you, Mr. Kensington, I said silently, begrudgingly.

I climbed and climbed the steep street, liking the feel of the incline and the way my heart beat from the exertion rather than the constant fear I'd battled in the last days. At home, I'd spent hours hoeing the garden, hours milking, hours repairing shingles on the roof, hours chopping wood. Did the wealthy ever feel their hearts pound for anything but excitement?

I reached the end of the street and looked left and right. The neighborhood gave way to a poorer district to my left, but there were finer houses to my right. Above me, I could hear shouts and machinery—sounds of the mines, working around the clock. It was odd to be in a place that was not quiet come dark; it felt vaguely unsettling, off. I couldn't imagine spending the night working deep inside a mine, then sleeping the day away. It seemed unhealthy, not ever having time beneath the sun. Not that anything in Butte felt healthy. The smelters' smoke spewed into the air night and day, mixing with wood smoke from cooking stoves and becoming a cloying cloud that settled around the city, choking every living thing. Even now I didn't feel I could take a deep breath, the odor acrid, vaguely metallic.

I longed for the wide, open plains, the swaying grasses and ripening grain of summer. The wind off the fields, smelling of nothing but earth. Roads with a few horse-drawn wagons rather than the noisy motor carriages and horse traffic clogging the streets…

So lost was I in thoughts of my home, I didn't see them approaching me until it was too late to avoid them. Three men, one who'd clearly been drinking too much, staggering left and right, his companions laughing at him. I cut across the street, as if heading home, but one of the men moved to intercept me.

Fear made my every pore tingle. What was I doing? Out at such an hour? Even at the Normal School, we were not allowed out unchaperoned past sunset. It wasn't proper. Moreover, it could be dangerous. I paused, wringing my hands in front of me, then dropped them, recognizing that the pose appeared weak.

"Hey there, miss," the man said, pulling his hat from his head and giving me a broad smile I could see even in the dark. "Aren't you out a little late?"

"I am. But I'll be home in just a moment."

"May I see you to your door?" he asked without pause. He'd detected my lie. I heard the other two shuffling behind me.

"No need. I am well aware of the way."

"Still," he said, falling into step beside me, laughing over his shoulder. "Wouldn't feel right, leaving a *lady* on her own in the wee hours of the morning."

I hesitated over his emphatic use of *lady*. As if it were a joke. Exactly who did he think I was?

"Just got paid today," he said with another smile in his voice. I didn't dare look his way and kept walking. "Me and the boys, we're in the mood to celebrate. Come out with us. We'll treat you right."

"No, thank you," I said with every ounce of authority I could muster.

He looked at his companions, and the drunk one cackled with laughter. But then all three were looking beyond me.

I glanced over my shoulder and inwardly groaned, feeling like a small child caught stealing candy from the mercantile's jars.

William McCabe.

"Is everything all right, Miss Kensington?" he asked, stepping up beside me.

I didn't know if it was the invocation of the family name, or his presence, or both, that set the threesome back a step, then two.

"Everything is fine, Mr. McCabe," I said. "These gentlemen were just heading home."

The first man had his hat off now and was partially bowing as he backed away. "Beggin' your pardon, miss. We had no idea. We..." He looked at his friends, and then they turned tail and ran, rounding the corner and disappearing into the dark.

I folded my arms and faced him. "Do you always have such an ill effect on strangers, Mr. McCabe?"

He let a slow smile spread across his face. "Only when one of my charges decides to take her morning constitutional at *two* in the morning."

"Is that what I am? Your charge?"

"In a manner of speaking, yes." I liked how his brown hair curled at the nape of his neck and around his ears. His quiet, confident manner. But I didn't like that I was noticing such things now, when we were alone, in the dark.

I am his charge. I let the thought incense me. Just the latest of many humiliations.

"I am twenty years old, Mr. McCabe, not a toddler in need of a nanny," I said.

I turned on my heel and began walking back to the house. He easily fell into step beside me. "No, you are clearly no toddler. But lovely young women are in need of an escort, especially at this time of night."

My face burned with embarrassment over his praise—and my stupidity. I had no business going out alone. I knew that now. If he hadn't arrived, might those men have tried something untoward?

I was suddenly trembling, my knees shaking.

"Take my arm, Miss Kensington."

I edged away from him. "Don't call me that."

"What else am I to call you?" he asked. "Please. You've suffered a fright. Take my arm, and I'll get you home straightaway."

"No! Leave me be!" With that I took hold of my skirts and ran, feeling idiotic—truly like a toddler—but unable to stop myself. I could hear him behind me, keeping pace, could feel my hair pulling loose from my pins, but I couldn't stop. Not until I was on our block.

"Miss *Kensington*," he said, over my shoulder, as I dashed across the boulevard, urging me again to slow. "*Miss Kensington!*"

At last I slowed to a walk, pacing over the dead grass to the old oak where I'd first seen him, my hand on my head as I gasped for breath. Warm light streamed through a window above us, but no one seemed alarmed. There was no one peering out the windows, looking for us. I glanced at him in surprise.

He leaned down, hands on his knees, panting and staring at me.

"You...told no one?" I asked.

He shook his head and straightened, mouth still open as he fought to regain his breath. "You are a decent runner," he said wryly. "Does your Normal School field a racing team?"

I ignored him. "Why did you not sound an alarm?" I asked.

His eyes searched mine. "You seemed...not yourself. I understood you were up to nothing nefarious—only needed some fresh air. Such at it is in this copper town. I merely sought to keep you in sight in case you needed aid."

I sighed and turned, taking a few steps away, disgusted with myself. "Lucky for me."

He remained silent.

I looked over my shoulder at him. "Thank you, Mr. McCabe."

He nodded once, staring into my eyes.

"You will say nothing of this to Mr. Kensington?"

"Only if you promise not to venture out on your own again, without escort."

I turned to face him. "Even in the light of day?" What sort of promise was this?

"Even in the light of day." He paused, licked his lips, and then met my gaze again. "Miss Kensington—"

I bristled at the name. I was a Diehl. Always would be. "Cora," I said, closing my eyes. "Please, call me Cora."

"Only if you will call me Will." He paused for a breath. "It must be difficult to learn something so foundational about yourself..."

I turned away, feeling the heat of a blush begin to climb my neck, not wanting him to see, though I doubted he could in the relative darkness.

"Regardless of the shock of such news," he said gently, "you must take great care. As a Kensington, there are those who would consider you a means to their own ends. Not all would turn tail and run as those three back there did. And we shall be traveling to many places in which you might become…lost."

As a Kensington. I considered his words. He spoke of danger—such as kidnapping. But there would be other risks ahead, risks that might seem more benign. Men who would entertain courting me just because of my name. Not because of my mind, or my perspective, or even my visage—but because of a potential connection to Wallace Kensington. I let out a humorless laugh.

"Something amuses you?" he asked.

"No. I don't know why I'm laughing. There is truly very little I find amusing in any part of my life right now."

He cocked his head in an endearingly caring manner, a curl of brown hair flopping over his temple and right eye. "For what it's worth, you have a friend in me, Cora. The journey ahead—I'm praying that with each day you will find clarity and greater understanding of your identity. Not only as a Kensington. But as the woman you were created to be."

I lifted my chin and considered him. I liked the way he spoke, and his quiet confidence, which reminded me a little of my papa. "Considering what is ahead, I could stand to have at least one friend, Will."

He smiled gently and reached out his hand to shake mine, as if we were striking a deal.

"Thank you, Will," I said. The shock of his warm skin against my cold hand made me immediately drop his, aware that we were both without gloves. But he reached out and held onto my other hand, not in a threatening manner, but in a way that told me he was waiting for me to meet his gaze. I looked up at him, my heart fluttering. He was a big man, quite a bit taller than I, with wide shoulders.

"You shall not go out again unescorted, Cora?" he asked softly.

"I shall not," I said. "You have my word."

"Good."

I waited for him to release me. Why was he staring at me so intently? I shifted, uncomfortable. I hoped he wouldn't try to—

"Then off with you, friend," he said, turning away, making me think I had imagined a hint of romance between us. "It will not do if a servant finds us both sneaking out in the middle of the night. You shall get me dismissed."

"Never," I said softly, turning to do as he bade. I'd tell Mr. Kensington the whole wretched story before I would see Will and his uncle lose this opportunity to be our guides. I…needed him.

I glanced back at him as I climbed the front porch stairs, but he didn't look my way. He stared up, up into the leaves again. I wondered what he was thinking about. I wondered who William McCabe was, exactly. And if he had always wanted to be a Grand Tour guide, or if he had simply found himself thrust into this madness as I had.

CHAPTER 10

~William~

Cora was largely silent on the train trip north, seeming to ignore their conversation about the tour itinerary, yet her eyes alternately widened or narrowed as Will spoke of the sights they would see. They traveled in a fine private rail car with the name *KENSINGTON* emblazoned on its side—one of three, he'd been told—which would in time be transferred from the train in Kalispell to the one that would take their party east.

Mr. Kensington caught Will looking Cora's way a couple of times. He held his gaze to let Will know he'd seen and then went on with their discussion. Will could feel his uncle's scowl too. But he couldn't help himself. He longed to talk to her, even for a moment, to ask her how she felt about meeting her siblings. He could see the small furrow between her delicate brows, the way she anxiously rubbed her gloved hands.

What would it be like to meet sisters and a brother for the first time as an adult? He himself had never had a brother or sister, so

Will had never really known what a true sibling relationship was like. He'd only had glimpses of it on the three tours they'd made alongside the States' most spoiled children. Mostly, when those trips were done, he departed eager to be alone. To bear no intrusions upon his quietude until he wished to seek others out—that was what he craved most.

Later in the morning, Cora went to rest in the sleeping section of Kensington's private car, and her father took to reviewing a pile of papers at his desk in the far corner. Will's uncle unfurled a newspaper, gesturing toward another, wanting Will to read. He liked Will current on recent news, ready to dialogue with their clients. Will scanned a few headlines, but when his uncle became absorbed in an article, he opted to stare out the window instead.

The train stopped only to take on water and coal, and with only two passenger cars connected to Kensington's private ones, Will realized they might rumble right on through the next Montana town as they had the last.

Luncheon was served right at noon, but Cora did not join them. Mr. Kensington asked the waiter to take a tray to her. Will doubted she'd eat any of it. His own stomach was in knots. *How must she be feeling right now?* Afternoon cocktails were poured precisely at one—tawny scotch in crystal glasses that Will sipped reluctantly as they idled at the Missoula station, ready to cover the last few hours' journey to Somers. From there, they'd travel by touring cars to the Kensingtons' new lake home.

Cora emerged at last, just as they pulled out of Missoula, the train slowly gaining speed. She stumbled as the car hit a bad stretch of track, and Will reached out to steady her. "All right, there?"

"Fine, fine," she said, straightening her crumpled jacket back into place. It was another fine ensemble, in a light teal that complemented her sparkling eyes. She obviously wished to look her finest before meeting the rest of the clan. But she turned down her father's offer of wine "or something stronger."

Will liked that she had the fortitude to say no. Both to her father and to drink, especially given what she was about to encounter. Though a part of him wished she might take even a little to settle her nerves. His mind went back to the night before, to how lost in thought she had been when she walked, then ran. What sort of lady ran? He hid a smile at the memory. It only brought home the fact again that Cora Kensington was not the typical young lady they were accustomed to escorting. It wouldn't be long until the rest of the family discovered it too.

Will slammed back the rest of his scotch in one gulp, hiding his distaste from Mr. Kensington in order to not offend. He wasn't given to drink, but there were occasions in which it helped to take the edge off. And if he were to fit into the social situations that were sure to come, he had to be able to drink his share of champagne and wine and keep his wits about him, even if their clients did not. *Most especially if their clients did not.* Two summers before, his uncle had drunk him under the table to bring that lesson home. Will had been so inebriated he couldn't stand the next day. But it gave him the understanding Uncle wanted him to have—how much he could imbibe, and how much he could not.

They were greeted in Somers, a tiny logging town on a lake, by two men in touring cars, who loaded their trunks and set off in short order—Mr. Kensington and Cora in the first car, the bear and Will in the second, eating their dust. They closed the windows tight, which made the car stifling hot. Sweat rolled down their temples and cheeks. Will didn't know why they didn't give it up and just let the windows down. Dust still circulated inside the cab of the motor carriage, despite their best efforts. But, according to Uncle, sweat was preferable to soil, every time.

They jostled over a bump in the road that sent them sailing upward, hitting their heads on the canvas roof. It was the umpteenth such bump they'd encountered.

"Sorry about that," said the driver. "Not much longer."

Both Will's neck and tailbone were grumbling their complaints. Regardless of the fine cars, the locals had not yet built roads to properly accommodate them. As if to underscore that fact, they passed one farmer after another atop wagons, with horses or oxen plodding along, pulling them.

Will stared out his window. The vast Flathead Lake glittered to their right, with mountains on either side of her, like two lines of guards. "Biggest freshwater lake west of the Mississippi," said Uncle, dabbing a handkerchief across his face.

They turned at last and headed south into another valley that ran parallel to the one they'd just exited, divided by a smaller mountain range, undulating in ample, matronly curves covered in green. They entered the trees then, tracing the edge of a river on a newly hewn gravel road. In half an hour they pulled to a stop, and Will wiped his face of sweat and dust before the driver came around to open his door. They climbed out, and Will ran his hand through his hair, then reluctantly placed his hat atop his head.

Mr. Kensington was helping Cora out. Will caught a glimpse of her slender ankle and calf as her dress slid back.

"Keep your eyes to the ground, Nephew," Uncle said, giving him a nudge to the center of his back.

Will looked after him, but his uncle was already on the move. Uncle Stuart ambled toward their employer with a hitched gait that told Will the old bear's rheumatism was acting up—sitting for a long time was always difficult for him. Will hurried to join them.

It was early evening, but they could hear shouts and laughter, water splashing. In the still heat of the evening, covered in the grime of the road, it sounded beyond inviting. Will wanted to hurry onward, but Cora was slowing. Mr. Kensington stopped and turned, whispering something to her. Will and Uncle Stuart tarried, keeping a discreet distance. The servants, with a cartful of luggage, did the same behind them.

Mr. Kensington stared at her kindly and tucked his head, waiting, concerned.

She glanced his way, softly said something to her father. Will could see the confusion in her eyes—the desire to trust him, the obvious doubt just beneath it.

Mr. Kensington waited a moment and then lifted his chin, obviously ready to brook no further argument. He turned and offered his arm.

And, after a moment's hesitation, she took it.

They moved forward, over the bridge. They could all see them then, in the distance—a group of six young people Cora's and Will's age, splashing and running, the water droplets glittering in the golden late sun. There was a delicious chill off the lake, as well as the loamy, earthy scent of the shore.

One caught sight of them and hollered, waving. Mr. Kensington smiled and lifted an arm in return.

Will watched as the group gave up on their play, heading toward servants who waited with towels on the shore, like nursemaids ready to wrap up damp toddlers. Will stifled the urge to shake his head. Such were the follies of the rich.

Mr. Kensington, Cora, Will, and Uncle Stuart took a newly laid stone path, which was already filling in with deep green grass and moss between the crevices. The sweet smell of just-milled lumber permeated the air. The buildings—five of them within sight now—were clearly influenced by their cousins in the Adirondacks. Fine, strong bones, lush curves in the roofs, intricate, stacked stone, copper flashing and gutters—clearly, no expense had been spared. How many craftsmen had Kensington imported to complete it?

A man tackled Will from behind. Will didn't even have time to react. As the damp of his attacker's swim clothes soaked his and they rolled in the grass, he knew who it had to be. Will laughed and turned, seeking a good wrestling hold, missing his opportunity. His opponent wrapped an arm around Will's shoulder and neck in a secure hold from behind.

"Felix," Will said with another laugh as if he were giving up, staring up into the sky. He could hear his friend panting behind him. "It's good to see you, too."

But when Felix eased his hold, Will turned and managed to gain the advantage, pinning him to the ground. "Is this to be our entire tour?" Will asked, tightening his grip.

"Only if you and your uncle bore me to drink," Felix said, panting and laughing beneath the weight of him. Grinning, Will rose and offered a hand up.

Felix grasped it, embraced Will briefly with a clap on the back, and then took a step back. "What's it been? Two years? Three?"

"Two," Will said, as if it didn't really bother him that Felix couldn't remember when he'd left university. When Felix could carry on and Will couldn't, even after he'd sold everything he had and still came up short of tuition.

So here they were. Once fraternity brothers. Now client and employee.

Felix's grin put Will at ease, just as it had all those years ago. His blue eyes—so much like Cora's and their father's—shifted from Will to Mr. Kensington to the young woman beside him. "Heard you brought another hen to the nest," he said. "This ought to be interesting."

Will turned, and his uncle joined him. They watched as Felix approached his father, respectfully shook his hand. Then he turned toward Cora. Will held his breath as they were introduced. She looked pale, full of trepidation. Then Felix was saying something, and Mr. Kensington threw back his head and laughed, patting him on the shoulder. Felix gestured down to his dripping swimming clothes and then back at Cora. Cora smiled then, and Will couldn't help grinning with her.

Trust Felix to make it easy. Will didn't know why he'd worried that Felix would treat Cora in a disrespectful manner. Felix genuinely loved people, even if he didn't think of them unless they were under his nose. His sisters, on the other hand, and the Morgans…

One at a time, Will, he told himself. *One down, two to go.*

CHAPTER 11

~Cora~

My half sisters, Vivian and Lillian, did not reappear until supper, nor did any of the Morgans. When they saw us coming across the bridge, they'd scurried indoors, apparently wishing to make themselves presentable before our introductions—which clearly hadn't bothered Felix. I supposed I ought to be grateful for the respite, the opportunity to freshen myself, but the anticipation was excruciating. I began a letter to my mother but, when I could come up with nothing but angry, bitter words, abandoned it. Then I tried to pray, asking for the right things to say when I met my sisters, but received only silence. Dimly, I understood that God was not likely to answer the pleas of a petulant, frustrated woman, but I wasn't ready to let it go. *Oh, Mama, how could you... How could you?*

Giving up on any sense of peaceful solitude, I moved outdoors and down the path that led to the lake. Mr. Kensington spotted me before I could duck away, and he waved me over to meet his business partner, Mr. Morgan, a sprite of a man, all of five foot two and a hundred pounds.

"How do you do?" I repeated after him, giving his small hand a single shake and nodding slightly as my maid, Anna, had trained me to do.

"Please, my dear, join us for some lemonade," Mr. Morgan said, gesturing toward a rocking chair next to my father on the small stone patio. The pleasantries soon over, the men moved back into conversation about the Montana Copper Mine, debating the skill of one manager over another. I tried to sit still, delicately sipping lemonade and staring at the lake, but my nervousness made me feel as if the lemons had become whole, the sour rind choking me. So I ended up merely holding the sweating crystal goblet and tried not to fidget.

Will and his uncle ambled by, strolling beside the lake, but they didn't come near. Perhaps they wanted to steer far away from the explosion that was bound to occur. I watched as Will bent and took hold of a flat rock, then skipped it across the still surface of the lake. Mr. Kensington and Mr. Morgan went on endlessly speaking of what was happening at the mine, the smelter, mostly ignoring me. For that I was relieved. I didn't have it in me to make conversation. Not when I was about to meet more of my family.

Family. I thought of my parents, in Minneapolis. Wondered how Papa was faring. I wished I was with them, with my grandparents, anyplace but here, regardless of how lovely it might be. The lush, verdant lawn and sparkling lake were a stark contrast to our hardscrabble farm, so riddled with brown, so lacking in life. Here, everything was green, from the grass beside the lake, to the small bend in the shoreline where lily pads grew, to the giant pines reflected in the water.

To our right, the river flowed, just past the footbridge we'd crossed. To our left was the widening lake, which, according to Anna, stretched for miles to the south, around a slow bend.

I fought the urge to rise and walk, to trace the water's edge and round the corner to see the rest of it, rather than sit here awaiting my fate like a fat hen facing a starving farmer's wife. Happily, these families had more than they'd ever need to eat—perhaps they'd forget about me. I smiled to myself and took my first full breath in what seemed hours.

"And who is this stunning creature?" said a tall, thin young man about Felix's age. I looked up, but with the sun behind him, he was little more than a silhouette.

A girl giggled at his side and hit him playfully on the arm. "You know very well who it is, brother."

Mr. Kensington and Mr. Morgan rose. My father reached to help me up, but I ignored him, wanting to touch him as little as possible. I straightened my linen coat, knowing I'd become frightfully rumpled again, sitting there.

"Mr. Hugh Morgan and Miss Nell Morgan," Mr. Kensington said, "allow me to introduce my daughter Miss Cora Kensington."

I nodded. "How do you do?"

"We are well," Hugh said, looking me over with more intensity than seemed proper. "And you?"

"I'm well, thank you," I said, lying through my teeth. I'd been better the day I took to my bed with measles.

He was tall and slender, with foppish, wavy brown hair that swept rakishly close to one of his dark-brown eyes. Like Will's did, but more contrived. Unnatural.

His younger sister, Nell, was as round as he was slender, reaching my shoulder and sporting ringlets of brown curls around her red-apple cheeks. Dark lashes lined her sparkling eyes, and she grinned in delight at me. "Miss Kensington, I do believe you are the most interesting thing to happen to our traveling party yet."

"Nell," Mr. Morgan chastened with a low growl.

"Yes. I would imagine," I said.

Hugh continued to look me over with calculating eyes. I felt like I was an insect under a magnifying glass, and he was trying to scorch me with the sun's rays. I ignored him, looking instead to the man who had to be his brother. He was rapidly striding our way.

Hugh turned and saw him too, as the patriarchs moved off toward a table where a steward poured from crystal decanters. Mr. Kensington mumbled an explanation over his shoulder about leaving us young people to get acquainted. Even though his presence continually agitated me, the thought of him leaving me alone with these strangers made me feel terrible. Undefended.

The eldest Morgan's approach did little to alleviate the sensation. He strode right up to me, arms folded, and looked me up and down. "So, the claim jumper has made it into the fold," he jeered. "A tidy arrangement for you, miss."

I frowned. *Claim jumper? Surely I misheard him.* "I beg your pardon," I said, reaching out a gloved hand. "My name is—"

"Cora Kensington," he ground out. "If you think you can shimmy into our lives and claim a part of Vivian's inheritance, you have another thought coming."

"First of all, my name is Cora Diehl," I said. "And I assure you, I have no idea of what you speak."

His eyes narrowed. "We're not simpletons, Miss *Diehl*. You wormed your way into our summer plans," he said. "Everyone knows what you'll be after next."

Nell nervously giggled and put a hand on his arm. "Andrew, really," she tried. He shook it off.

"See here, Andrew," Hugh said from his other side, "the girl just arrived. Could you not be a tad more gracious?"

"To an interloper?" Andrew asked, looking me over in derision as he straightened. "The *maid's* daughter?" The way he said *maid* had me itching to grab something breakable and throw it at him. "She'll cast a pall over our entire group. We may as well change our plans and remain here in seclusion for all the invitations we'll get!"

A collective gasp sounded over my left shoulder, and with cheeks aflame, I turned to see Felix, looking chagrined, with a young woman on either arm. My sisters. *Half sisters*, I reminded myself. Could our meeting be more humiliating?

"Remain here in Montana?" said the older one, so perfectly poised and dressed she reminded me of a model from *Harper's Bazaar*. Straight shoulders curved down into a tiny waist and out again at her hips. She moved past me and took Andrew's arm. "What silly notion has taken you over now, Drew?"

"Forgive me, darling. Seeing her here..." His tone deepened as he looked at her, total adoration in his eyes. So the eldest Morgan was courting the eldest Kensington. Now things were making sense. Inwardly, I sighed. The families were far more melded than I had hoped. I'd thought perhaps the Morgans would at least accept my presence with less strain, that they might be a door by which I could enter their circle. *No such luck.*

She turned toward me and offered me a limp hand and a steady gaze from her hazel eyes. "Cora," she said firmly, "I am Vivian, your elder sister. Trust me, Andrew has his charms. He tends to be bit passionate. He'll warm to you in time. As we all will." Her words were kind, but her eyes were cold.

I swallowed hard and took her stiff hand in mine, awkwardly giving it a little shake. She was as forthright and firm as our father, doing what was expected, but I got the feeling she couldn't stomach my presence any more than her beau did.

"And I'm Lillian," said the other girl, far more friendly in her tone. She had blonde curls to match Nell Morgan's brown ringlets, but she was slender, with green eyes less muddy than her older sister's. *Our* older sister's. "Friends call me Lil."

Did that include me? I didn't dare to be too presumptuous. "I'm most glad to make your acquaintance, Lillian."

A shadow passed through the younger girl's eyes. Had I made the wrong decision, not wishing to assume she was inviting me to call her by her nickname? Felix laughed and clapped his hands. "Well, now that that awkward moment is over, shall we give our new friend and sister a bit of air? She looks like she might faint dead away."

With a mixture of mutterings—some dismissive, some empathetic—the group separated and walked across the wide lawn to the main lodge, where a servant was ringing a dainty bell, calling us in to dinner. Hugh waited till most of the others moved ahead, giving me an intimate, predatory smile that sent a shiver down my back before he turned to follow our siblings.

Only Felix remained behind. He took my hand and tucked it into the crook of his arm as we climbed the hill. "Be careful with that one," he whispered, nodding toward Hugh's back. "He fancies himself a ladies' man."

"Yes, quite." But as I figured it, I had something to fear in each of them. Even Felix. Surely he couldn't be as at ease with my presence as he pretended now… "Felix, you know I didn't seek out your father—"

"Our father," he said, his blue eyes moving to the older man, who raised his crystal glass in our direction as we entered the dining room. Mr. Kensington probably thought our introductions had gone just fine. Could he not have stayed with me for just a few more minutes to ensure they did?

"Father told us exactly what happened," Felix said.

"I didn't even know he existed a few days ago," I said. My only chance with these people was for them to know *he* came to *me*—demanded…no, *forced* me to come, really. "I didn't seek him out. I didn't ask for anything."

"I know."

I paused then and decided there was little to lose in asking. "Then why must the others look upon me with such distaste?"

Felix hesitated and brought us to a stop. "Our social standing, and the political battles Father has weathered—have made us somewhat wary and clannish. It is difficult for many to join in, and here you are, blood kin…expected to be one of us. Give us some time, Cora. You'll come to see the good in each of them, just as we shall with you."

I gave him a grateful smile. "I hope so. Or this summer shall feel like a decade."

—◇◇◇—

Supper was served on an overwhelming array of china and sterling silver, beginning with a clear consommé—*broth*, as Mr. Kensington corrected—that I feared would end up dripping all the way down the front of my new linen; more little green beans; sautéed mushrooms; and *beef en croûte*—tender cuts of the finest meat I'd ever eaten, wrapped in a perfectly browned pastry. Mr. Kensington belittled it, apologizing to Mr. Morgan for the plain broth, the ill-developed green beans, the mushrooms, and tough beef. I couldn't see the need for apologizing. Never had I had such sumptuous food. It was no wonder that little round Nell ate and ate—I'd do the same if my stomach wasn't in knots.

Father had seated me at his right hand, which drew more than a few looks from the Kensington and Morgan children. The conversation was cheery, but there was an underlying tension around the table. After we were seated, not one of the Kensington or Morgan children looked my way. Even Felix. My stomach clenched in anxiety. Was this to be my entire summer? Oh, how I longed to be with Mama and Papa. *Help me, Lord. Help me find my way.*

As dinner progressed, the conversation moved from the lighthearted topic of the rising temperature of the lake to the more serious topic of the rising power of the men who labored in the mines, threatening to form unions.

"It's only a matter of time until they try to strike," Andrew said, his eyes shifting to his father, then to Mr. Kensington. I could see that he itched to be in the office with the elder men, rather than on some "frivolous tour," as he referred to it. Anna had told me he recently graduated with an MBA from Harvard, and clearly he thought he knew enough to take the helm of the Montana Copper Mine, if not of the company itself.

"A strike would be foolhardy," Mr. Kensington said, leaning back in his chair. "But it wouldn't be the first effort we've weathered."

"All a matter of waiting them out, isn't it, Wallace?" Mr. Morgan said with a conspiratorial smile. He cut a big bite of chicken and looked over at his children. "We can outlast them without even feeling it. Every time. Most of them are lucky to have two weeks' pay set aside. And for every one that would strike, there are ten men who'd like their job."

The younger Kensingtons and Morgans nodded. Felix and Andrew clinked their crystal goblets together in an unspoken toast. I swallowed hard, past a ball of anger threatening to choke me. *Keep quiet, Cora. This is none of your affair—*

"So you believe the laborer has no rights at all?" I blurted out.

All eyes turned toward me...except for Will's. Had he winced?

Andrew looked at his father and Mr. Kensington and then said with barely concealed anger, "You are new to our company, Miss Cora. So perhaps you are not yet aware that Montana Copper pays their laborers a dollar more per week than any of our competitors. I'd say that's caring for the worker's rights where it counts most."

I stared back at him. "You are right," I said in a measured tone. "This is very new to me. How many men does Montana Copper employ?"

Andrew sat back and smiled a little, as if thinking me addle-minded. Will stared down at his half-eaten meal. Dread bubbled in my belly, but I could do nothing but press on.

"Seven hundred," Mr. Kensington said. "We employ about seven hundred."

"Seven hundred," I repeated, thinking. "Suppose half of them have a wife, children. Montana Copper would be responsible for"—I shrugged, figuring—"two to three thousand people, in total? Or thereabouts?"

Mr. Kensington's eyebrows lowered. All eating and drinking ceased. "Thereabouts. But I wouldn't say—"

"How much is their weekly pay in total? Working the average shift?"

"See here, Cora," Felix said. "Must we spoil dinner with such mundane conversation?"

"Twenty dollars," Mr. Kensington said, staring hard at me. Giving me latitude. I had to admire him a little for it. Especially when I was clearly bent on making a point at his expense.

"Twenty dollars for the week, eighty for the month."

"So the country girl can do her figures," Vivian said.

I ignored her, warming to my topic. "What's the cost to rent one of those row houses?"

"Twenty a month," Mr. Morgan said, narrowing his brown eyes.

"Hmm," I said. "I've *lived* the economics you just described. It leaves little extra. If someone in his family takes ill…it can wipe them out. Their landlords might boot them out of the house, and then where do they go?" I lifted the sterling fork in my hand. "This piece of silver alone would feed a family of five for a month, maybe two. Does that not seem a tad"—I paused to gaze around the table—"unfair?"

Vivian dabbed at her mouth, took a sip of water from a crystal glass, and peered at me as if considering my words, but not truly doing so. I could see the loathing in her eyes.

Before she could speak, Mr. Kensington said, "Would you have us pass along all our profits to the laborers?"

"I am well aware that you have worked very hard for what you enjoy today. I do not begrudge it of you. Truly. But why such sharp disparity? Surely you have *all* of this as well as ample funds in savings and investments." I shook my head, trying to think about what I wanted to say most, before the opportunity slipped away. "And what of your children?" I gestured to the others at the table. "The only thing that divides us from that laborer who toils far beneath the surface of the earth in our fathers' mines is the blood that runs through our veins."

"Or *half* our blood," Vivian said with a sniff.

"*Vivian*," Mr. Kensington warned.

I didn't flinch. "Half my blood, then," I said with a prim nod back at Vivian. "But if I cut open my wrist alongside yours, would it not appear as the very same red? Despite your effort to be a blue-blood, *sister*, you are as red-blooded as I."

I dared to look around at them all, staring them down. A small smile tugged at the corners of Will's mouth, but the others looked alternately aghast or furious.

"Are you quite finished?" Andrew asked, a muscle twitching in his neck.

"Not quite," I returned softly. "A little more than a week ago, my parents and I were struggling to bring in enough on our farm to feed ourselves more than once a day. We had meat, but only on Sundays. Bills came due, often before we were ready to meet them. Somehow, God always provided, but it was hard. And life, for you..."

"We are in no need of your moral compass," Andrew said. He waved at me dismissively, and Hugh and Vivian murmured their agreement.

"Aren't you?" It was out before I could catch myself.

Felix laughed in surprise, and Mr. Morgan joined in. The younger girls stared at us all with wide eyes.

"Perhaps we are," Mr. Kensington said with an indulgent smile.

"You have no right to judge us," Vivian said, her eyes narrowing. "You don't know the pressures there are, living as the upper class. We don't struggle to survive, I'll grant you that. But we face other challenges, equal challenges." She glanced over to Andrew as if for support.

"You're right," I said. "I haven't walked in your shoes." I stared at my hands in my lap, thinking, then raised them up. "But these hands," I said, "are blistered from hauling water and hoeing gardens and roping animals, not from needlework or tennis. I'd wager I understand the men in the employ of Montana Copper far better than you will."

Vivian's mouth was hanging open as she stared at our father, who was nodding gravely, but then she abruptly shut it. She turned back to me, rage in her eyes. "So then tell us, *sister*. How might you circumvent a strike?"

"Move forward boldly. Generously. Assure them there's no need to unionize—make them believe Montana Copper is the best employer a man could ask for. You already pay them a dollar more per week than your competitors, which is truly commendable, but adding yet another dollar would do wonders for those families. Or better yet, some profit sharing. If the mine makes such and such, they earn an extra amount. Consider a doctor to care for their needs. Years down in the mines leaves many of them struggling with consumption." I'd seen it for myself, in Dillon—those too ill to work the mines any longer. "Others with failing eyesight. And the mines are so dangerous… If an explosion occurred, and the company could pledge to take care of the men's families, it'd mean a great deal. Loyalty. For life."

I looked to Mr. Kensington, suddenly nervous, checking his expression to see if I'd gone too far. But he only looked back at me with something akin to pride in his eyes.

"That would be an exorbitant expense," Andrew said.

"I beg to differ. Such care would be winning for you in multiple ways. You'd attract the best workers possible. Not only would your men be in better health, they would be in better spirits. And men in good spirits and health are more efficient in their work. You may indeed galvanize them to produce even more, which means good profits for you, in turn." I shrugged. "It could quite possibly negate the added expense."

I picked up my napkin and rubbed my mouth, trying to occupy my hands. The rest of the table was still, each looking down at their plates as if waiting for the wrath of their fathers to unfold. But Mr. Kensington wasn't angry. In fact, he was smiling. "I do believe the girl is right." He shook his head, then looked over at his partner and thumped Mr. Morgan on the shoulder. "What do you say, Morgan?"

"Well, it's something to consider," he said noncommittally.

"More than consider. I'll tell you what, Cora. At our next board meeting, I will bring up every one of your suggestions. And I shall put my shoulder behind them."

I stared at him in surprise and managed a single nod. "Thank you."

"Well," Hugh said with a clap of his hands, "now that we have resolved the fate of our workers, who is up for an evening canoe ride?"

"Oh, me!" said Lillian, clapping her hands, probably relieved both by the change of topic and the prospect of escaping the heat.

"And me!" said Nell.

The others all eagerly nodded, and Mr. Kensington waved them off, excusing them from the table. None looked at me as they departed. Right after, Will, his uncle, and Mr. Morgan did the same.

I stared at my food, which all looked far from appetizing. What had I done? Had I ruined any opportunity I might ever have with my siblings? The Morgans? I'd always had a difficult time remaining silent when I sensed an injustice and—

"Cora," Mr. Kensington said softly. I dragged my eyes to his. But he was rising, standing beside his chair. "If you are finished with your supper, I'd like you to come with me."

I did as he asked, following him out the swinging screen door to the porch, knowing he'd likely wish to call me into account in private. I'd so overstepped my bounds…Mama and Papa would be horrified.

"Please," he said, gesturing to one of two rockers.

I gratefully sank into it, trying to catch my breath and slow my rapidly beating heart.

We rocked together in silence for a while, each of us looking out through the trees to the still lake, which reflected the last vestiges of the late-setting sun. "It will be all right in time, Cora," he said.

I shook my head, hating that I was fighting sudden tears, refusing to cry but unable to speak, knowing my voice would crack. I folded my arms across my chest. "No, it won't," I dared, swallowing hard. I shook my head. "This won't work. I must be away from here, from them. I'll leave in the morning. You can give us back the farm. I can return, finish bringing in the harvest for Papa—"

All tenderness left his voice. "No, Cora. You will not. That chapter is over."

I frowned. "Even you must see that this plan cannot succeed. Or do you simply wish to torture me for a time, then send me off as you did my mother?"

To his credit, he didn't return my fire. He simply rocked and waited till I calmed down. "Kensingtons beat the odds," he said, "every time. You will succeed—far more than you can imagine."

"How can you promise that? You...you won't even be with us! This is my choice, not yours." I rocked a few more times and then rose. "Pardon me. I think it best if I—"

"No," he said. "The choice has been made. Your course has been set. The world is beginning to know you as my daughter."

I laughed softly. "Montana, maybe. I doubt the *world* has taken notice."

He touched my arm. "You would be surprised."

I glanced over my shoulder at the others, now changed out of their evening finery and loading into canoes, then back to him. "I don't understand. Why not squire me away at Normal School, where I can finish my teaching degree in peace? Why foist me upon them?" *And them upon me?*

"Because you will be good for one another," he said. "Tonight is but one example." He raised his hands, heading off my argument. "You will get your credential. After you complete the tour. Trust me. It will be worth it in the end." He raised a finger of warning. "Not easy. But worth it."

I sighed and leaned against the rail, looking out.

"How do you know?"

"Gut feeling." He joined me at the rail and gave me a wry grin through gray whiskers, cocking his head. "Made a good deal of my money off my gut feelings. They told me there wasn't enough copper in the big hill to be worth the effort. But I knew I simply had to find a different way. That's what you'll need to do with your siblings, and the Morgans, too."

I considered that. "Why not come with us, if it's so important for you to see us all together?"

He gave me another smile. "I'd only impinge upon your progress."

"Mr. Kensington," I said, "there is so much I don't know. I'll embarrass you, as well as my sisters and brother. Being raised on a farm—"

"What was I before I was a copper baron?" he interrupted. "A banker. Before that, a miner. Before that, a trader. And a guide. A packer. We all start somewhere." He patted my arm. "Anna will help you," he said. "Her mother schooled your brother and sisters on manners and the way of gentility. Anna can do the same with you."

I pushed away a fleeting thought of Anna being yet another of his unclaimed children. It was an ugly thought. If he'd claimed me outright, surely he would have claimed any others.

"I'd wager that young William there shall be a solid companion for you." He nodded to our right.

I followed his gaze to the giant cedars. Will was watching us but pretended not to.

"Look to him, Cora. He's a good man, a trustworthy sort."

He left me then, clearly never considering that I might wish to do anything other than what he suggested. All I wanted was to get out of my confining clothes and let down my hair and bury my head beneath a pillow, shut out the world. Was that too much to ask?

Apparently, yes, I thought resentfully, striding toward Will as if he himself had created all the pressures that pulled and pushed at me from every side. He had moved to the beach, with his back to me now, skipping rocks as twilight faded. Across the narrow lake, we could hear two loons calling, the sound haunting, echoing across the water. Beyond them, there was laughter. The Kensingtons and Morgans.

Were they laughing at me? I forced myself to block them from my mind, to concentrate on the lake, the water. What were they to me? People I met today, that was all. We shared blood. The One who mattered to me still found me worthy, still loved me, whether I knew when to curtsy properly or not. I drew in a deep breath, letting the motion soothe me.

Will tossed a flat slate-gray stone out, and it sailed, turning before resting briefly on the water, jumping and jumping in progressively smaller skips.

"Twelve," I said. "Quite a feat."

"Not much of a feat," he said with a gently appraising look. "More of practice paying off." He stepped forward along the beach, looking for his next perfect stone. How I wished I could take off my slippers and wade into the cool, welcoming waters! I remained where I was, seriously contemplating sitting, unlacing my shoes—which were pinching my toes—and wading into the water until it covered my head. Screaming underwater, where no one could hear me. Until it was out of me, all out of me.

"Cora."

I looked up at him, quickly, wondering how long he'd been trying to gain my attention. "Yes?"

"It…it will be all right, in time."

"Yes, well," I said, "let us hope so."

"Soon you'll be getting along swimmingly with these people."

I laughed at the irony of his word choice. He paused, looked me in the eye. Finally, when I could bear his gaze no more, I shrugged.

"Watch this rock," he said.

He sent the next one in a long, wide arc across the water. It made nine jumps. He leaned closer to me, pointing. A shiver ran down my back at his proximity. But I reminded myself that he was only being kind. Friendly. "See how the skips get progressively closer until the rock is claimed by the lake?" He straightened. "That's what it will be like for you, Cora. Getting easier and easier until you have it. Until you're exactly where you want to be."

And where exactly did he think I wanted to be? I stared out at the intermingling, fading circles cast by the impact of his last skipping stone and smiled. "Thank you, Will."

He picked up another rock and sent it flying. "Not at all."

I was in a small cottage with four bedrooms, with one for me, the other two assigned to my sisters, and the fourth housing our maids, including Anna. I tossed and turned, listening to the crickets outside my window, thinking of the water and my desire to swim until I'd had enough. Till I could rid myself of the angst that tugged at me, my homesickness that kept begging me to find my way back. I thought of my conversation with Mama just after I'd found out about her and Mr. Kensington. I'd never reassured her of my love, my forgiveness for the years she'd lied to me. Not lied—*neglected* to tell me the truth. But was I ready to forgive her? I thought not.

My sheets in knots, I lit a candle and checked my watch. It was past one in the morning. Perhaps, relieved of my itch and chilled by the lake water, I could cuddle beneath my covers and sleep until noon, leaving only part of the day to negotiate the labyrinth of difficult people that suddenly populated my life.

I threw back my quilt and went to a trunk, using the light of the nearly full moon to find my bathing costume, purchased along with the rest of my trousseau in Butte. I'd never had a bathing costume at home. When we'd gone to the swimming hole on the Thompson farm, we'd just worn old dresses. But it'd been years since I'd been swimming at all. Suddenly, I couldn't wait.

In the white-and-black suit, which covered me from neck to thigh but left the rest of me scandalously bare, I was glad for the dark of night as I ventured out. I tiptoed down the hallway and slowly opened the screen door, desperately hoping I wouldn't wake anyone. At least here, there were no drunken miners. We were the only people for many miles.

Gently, I closed the door and crept down the front steps, then over the lawn, wincing as rocks and pine needles bit at the tender soles of my feet. When my toes met the icy water, I paused, already cooled by the air coming off the surface. The moon's reflection danced on the inky water, barely moving atop ripples that called to me. I stepped in, taking care to not splash, moving slowly, methodically until I was thigh deep. Shivering in the icy water, gooseflesh covering me from toe to scalp, I considered turning back but could not fathom returning to the cottage without doing what I'd wanted all evening.

Chest deep in water that threatened to set my teeth to chattering, I reached up and let out my braid, letting my hair fall around my shoulders and float upon the water. I could feel the gentle pull of the river to my right, tugging at my legs, and wondered how it would feel to swim against the current farther down, where it increased in velocity. If I floated on my back, how long would it take to carry me to the bridge? I smiled and ducked under the water then, taking several long strokes with my arms and kicking, liking the feel of freedom. The bathing costume was far easier to swim in than a dress. I could see how they'd come into fashion.

My lungs bursting for lack of air, I slowly rose to the surface, barely disturbing the water as I blinked and peered toward the shore. A few gaslights lit the pathways near the main lodge, but no one walked upon them. It seemed all but me were asleep. For the moment, I was perfectly, blessedly alone. I turned over on my back, floating, looking up at the moon and the few stars bright enough to see, stretching out my arms and feeling my body turning, the river calling.

For several minutes, I forced myself not to look, not to see how far I'd drifted, considering it a good exercise in relinquishing control. *God, God,* I prayed *I am so far away from everything and everyone I love. Why? Why have You brought me here?*

I waited for a vision, a word. Something. But all I could see was the endless dark sky. No voice filled my ears, only the progressively louder sound of the water about me. I rose, and with some surprise realized I'd drifted a good fifty feet. I was not far from the mouth of the river. It was fortunate I hadn't waited another minute to look around.

The rocks here were slippery with moss. I slid and winced, feeling the hard edged points and crags of every stone beneath my feet. My exit was far less smooth than my entry, and I was thankful, once again, for the privacy of the moment.

That was when I smelled it. Cigarette smoke. Eyes narrowed, I searched the heavy shadows of the big cedars until I found the source—the orange, burning ember, the cloud of smoke casually released.

I stood straighter even as my face burned, not wanting him to see me cower. Knowing I'd discovered him, he pushed off from the trunk of the tree and moved to intercept me. Hugh Morgan. "It's late for a swim," he said lowly, sucking on his cigarette.

"After the heat of the day, dust from the road, it was exactly what I needed," I said lightly, passing by him.

"Had I known, I would've joined you," he said, falling into step with me. Even in the dark, I could feel the heat of his gaze on my bare arms, which only made me shiver all the more. "I almost did, bathing costume or no."

I shot him a horrified look. Just what was he saying? "It hardly would have been proper. I would have left immediately." I doubled my pace.

"Cora."

Reluctantly, I paused and turned. I could just make out the handsome, angular lines of his face in the warm light of the gas lamp. He forced a smile. "I am offering you friendship, Cora. Seems to me you could use as many friends as you can find in this group."

I straightened my bathing costume, wishing it wouldn't cling as it did. Much as I hated it, he was right.

"Thank you for your offer of friendship, Hugh," I managed to say. "But what do we have in common that would bind us as friends?"

He took a long pull on his cigarette, considering me. He blew it out to the side and said, "A reluctance to embrace all that the family name offers? Or maybe something as simple as a penchant for evening dips?" A catlike smile spread across his face as he tapped his cigarette on a low fence, letting the ashes fall.

"I prefer to bathe alone." I forced myself to stare back at him.

"Pity, that," he said, laughing under his breath. "Even in the light of day?"

"Oh, I wouldn't mind joining everyone tomorrow for a dip after the noon meal."

"Good, good," he said, nodding.

I didn't want to think of Hugh Morgan as an enemy. After all, he was right—I needed all the friends I could get. But I couldn't deny the way my hands clenched at my side, as if I was preparing to fight. What was it about him that felt subtly predatory? Dangerous?

Slowly, I unclenched my hands, pretending I was relaxed, in charge. "Perhaps now I can sleep. Good night, Hugh."

He smiled and winked, taking another long draw on his cigarette. "Good night, sweet Cora," he said, every syllable full of innuendo. "Or shall I call you Ophelia?"

I knew he referenced the Ophelia of *Hamlet*, famously floating upon the waters. "Cora suits me well," I said, forcing a smile and turning, feeling his eyes still on me.

Still, as I donned my nightgown and slipped under the covers again, I sighed in relief. I was finally ready to fall into a deep slumber. But just as I was edging off into unconsciousness, my eyes popped open.

Ophelia had mourned her father, like I did in a way. My *real* father—Alan—who had loved me and raised me, yet lied to me about who I was… If he'd had the strength, would Papa have had the right words for me, when Mama did not? Would he have known what I should say, do now? Here?

Never had I felt farther from them. I stared out the window, glimpsing stars among the ghostly silhouettes of trees, and thought of Ophelia, convinced no one loved her, drowned and floating upon the water.

CHAPTER 12

~Cora~

Will's first lesson on the history of England took up most of the day. The others filed out afterward, intent on a canoe race to the island. Not one had spoken to me since last night. Even Felix.

Will shoved his big map book and his notes into a satchel as I gathered my things and hurried toward the door, my head a swirling tornado of thoughts—wondering about my papa, my inability to keep my mouth shut, how the rest of the summer would go...

"Cora," Will said as I passed him.

I paused and dared to look up at him. He truly was boyishly handsome, but it was his eyes, so warm with compassion, that moved me most. He smelled of fresh pine and warm leather, with a little dose of sharp ink, which stained several of his fingertips.

"How about we take our own canoe ride?"

"Oh," I breathed, "Please. There's no need—you..." I stopped and brought fingers to my aching temple. "I've created a breach. I'll find a bridge, in time."

"Undoubtedly." He gave me a small smile. "Allow me to assist you in building it. Let's go out on the lake."

I shook my head and squinted at him. "How is that not like inviting oneself to a party?"

"It's not a party. It's a lake. And there are still several empty canoes available on shore, I'd wager."

I sighed. "How about a horseback ride instead? Up into the mountains? Far from here?" Hope rising with each progressive question.

His smile broadened. "It shall be much cooler on the lake. Come," he said, already moving toward the door. "We needn't be near the others. We can take our own route."

———◇◆◇———

Will steadied the canoe as I lifted my skirts and made my way forward. Out on the lake already, Nell was with her brother Hugh, Andrew with Vivian, and Felix with his sister Lillian. So far, Felix and Lil were in the lead.

"Hold tight," Will said, shoving off. I watched over my shoulder as he perched on the edge and then carefully climbed aboard, barely tipping the canoe. We glided forward, behind the others, but that was all right too. I liked being able to see them all—while staying out of their line of vision.

"Been in a canoe before?" he asked lowly.

"Never," I said over my shoulder. "Perhaps you can tell by my stroke."

"You'll do better if you hold your left hand on the top and your right hand low, toward the blade." I studied his example and then repositioned my hands, as he continued, "When you paddle, dig in. Think of the water as soil, and you're pushing back as much as you can. I'll steer. You can trade sides as you need or leave it all to me."

I looked ahead and saw that Hugh and Nell were racing Felix and Lillian to the tiny island. Andrew and Vivian casually followed behind. None of the other women were resting; I'd do my part. And I found that as I did, it felt good to move, to push my muscles. I was used to hard work on the farm; the last few days had demanded little more from me than lifting a teacup or lacing up a corset. No—Anna saw even to the corset and clipping up my wretched stockings. Exerting myself now felt like a relief rather than a burden.

"Would you like to see a beaver den?"

I nodded, and he turned our canoe south, into gentle waves moving toward us. I silently admired his prowess and wondered if he was looking at me or at the lake as we paddled. I sat straighter, aware of him in a new way. And not an entirely good way. *He's our guide, nothing more*, I told myself. *You need a friend, Cora. Don't ruin the one friendship you may make this summer.*

The sun was still climbing, making the water a more true blue versus the morning steel and evening's still green. It was the first time I let my guard down, really drank in the beauty of where I was, appreciating it rather than missing Dunnigan or wishing I was in Minnesota with my folks.

Perhaps it was the physical break from the others that allowed me such a moment. I paddled hard with Will, inhaling the scent of rotting grass and rich mud on the banks of the lake. We rounded the bend, and above us, to our right, was a lone, heavily treed mountain.

And to our left were many others like it, lush and green—above them, magnificent purple snow-covered peaks, high above the tree line. The lake below reflected their silhouettes on either edge as the water stilled with the onset of evening.

I inhaled deeply and closed my eyes, listening to our paddles dip and pull, pause, dip and pull. Then opened my eyes to again take in the grandeur.

"Your father chose his property well, did he not?" Will asked, his voice behind me somehow just right with the view, warm and woodsy.

"Indeed," I said, stiffening at his use of *father*. "But had it been me, I would have situated the cottages and lodge here, where we could see the whole length of the lake and these mountains." I shook my head. "Why would he not place them here? Around the bend with the view?"

"Perhaps he wanted each guest to experience what you just did," Will said quietly. "That moment of awe as it opens up before you."

"Perhaps," I said. But I didn't know. It seemed out of character for my father, in some ways. From what I'd seen, he was never understated, always forthright. Would not such a bold man wish to place his summer home in the boldest location possible? But then, what did I really know of Mr. Kensington? We'd only met six days ago.

"Here we are," Will said. I glanced back at him and saw that he pointed at the shoreline. "A groundskeeper told me they've been denning here for decades."

"It appears so!" I said, admiring the massive pile of sticks that made up the lodge. The beavers had dammed a small inlet to the lake, creating a large pond on the other side of a slight hill. As I glanced to the shore, I could see that trees had been felled twenty feet from the edge. "Industrious, aren't they?"

"Indeed."

We pulled up close to the den, peering into its depths. It looked as if the structure went down a good six or seven feet. "That's amazing," I said in awe. "How do they know how to build such things?"

"God plants the knowledge in them." He smiled. He really had a quite friendly face, I thought, and with that brown hair that curled at the nape of his neck...

"So it's inborn, eh?" I asked, steering my mind toward more appropriate thoughts. "It really is something, isn't it? That God designs every little facet of creation, knowing how one element affects the next. That these beavers with their hardworking ways will create a pond where there once was forest, and that in turn changes the whole ecology."

His blue eyes—darker than mine—smiled back at me. As if he wanted me to think about my own words. Then, "You've studied ecology?"

"Ecology and biology. Next term..." I paused, briefly wondering if there would *be* a next term of Normal School. "Next term, I shall even study a bit of zoology. Perhaps I'll write my paper on beavers," I said, smiling over my shoulder at him.

We resumed paddling. "Beavers have the most curious eyelids," Will said, gently paddling to keep the current from shifting us away from the den. "They're translucent, allowing them to see underwater."

"Fascinating," I said. "I wish I could do that." We shared a small laugh, and as it faded, I thought it might have been my first real laugh since leaving home. "Did you learn such facts at the university?"

"Ah, no. I wanted to study architecture at university. I had to…take a sabbatical for a couple of years. My uncle wanted me to apprentice as a tour bear anyway. He thinks a man learns far more from the tour than anything they can teach in a college, and it's the family business and all. But I hope to return and complete my degree in a year or two."

"I see." I could hear the burn and hesitation in his voice and gathered he'd run out of money. Now here he was, with Felix, who would complete his education come fall, and Will had had no choice but to drop out. *So I am not the only one who feels less-than in their company. The only one who feels forced into being here.*

Gratitude surged through me at the realization. It made me feel closer to him than any of my kin.

"There's one," Will whispered excitedly. I scanned the surface of the water and then saw the small nose and broad cheeks of a beaver, his teeth clenched across a tender sapling still sporting its first green leaves of summer. His broad tail spread behind him, and a triangular ripple widened beyond him in his wake. He reached the den, lumbered up it slowly, and deposited the young tree, nosing it into just the right position.

"Beavers are notoriously slow on land, but excellent swimmers. If alarmed, he'll slap the water before diving, a sound that will carry a good distance under water, alerting any other beavers in the area that there's danger about." As Will finished speaking, the beaver turned and sidled back into the water, disappearing beneath.

He nodded toward him. "And that coat allows him to be in the water in the coldest of months."

"So he doesn't feel as cold as we do," I said.

"Indeed not. Nor did he fear us much, did he?" He cast a wry grin in my direction, and I shook my head. "Shall we go to the island now?"

I stared out at my siblings and the Morgans, realizing this had been his intention all along,—to ease me into their company again. "If we must," I said with a sigh.

Will chuckled lowly behind me. "We must. In time the ripples will be fewer and fewer—"

"Yes, yes," I said, digging my paddle into the water as if I really wished to reach them. "They'll get closer together. But how long will that take?"

"You force them to think, Cora. They have to respect that, even if they disagree with you. That respect will make things easier, in time."

We paddled in silence for a while, gradually drawing closer to the group, but they were still a good quarter mile distant. "You'll come to enjoy the tour," he said quietly. "Travel expands us in ways we never know are possible before our feet touch foreign soil. I'm glad you will experience it."

I frowned a little. I needed *expansion*? I already felt as if my heart and mind had been wrenched open.

But as we paddled, my irritation faded. He was the lone person who could understand a measure of my angst. As well as the opportunity at hand. "I…I'm afraid that I'll spend so much time negotiating my *struggles*," I said, nodding toward the three canoes ahead, "that I won't have time to truly embrace those opportunities."

He laughed lowly, and I let the warm sound settle around me like a gentle hug. It rang of friendship and camaraderie and understanding, and in that moment, he again made me feel not quite so alone. "Cora, I ask you to trust me in this. Regardless of whether or not the Kensingtons and Morgans accept and include you, I will ensure that your trip is nothing but enlightening, an experience of a lifetime. You shall come home transformed."

I looked over my shoulder at him. "That is quite the audacious promise."

He gave me a mischievous smile that lit up his brown eyes in a way I found utterly charming. "Indeed."

"I must confess I hadn't thought of you as the audacious sort, Master William."

"Then, Miss Cora, you have not yet begun to know me at all."

I smiled and turned around. *Perhaps not. Perhaps all before me is not preordained. I can make this what I want of it.* I looked up to the mountains. *Let me see what You want me to learn along the journey too, Lord,* I prayed. *Please, please, make it not one long trial from beginning to end. Just a measure of civility from them is all I—*

"Ahoy!" called Felix, when we were but ten feet away. "The tutor and the new student decided to join the rest of the class, eh?"

"After a brief detour, yes," Will said. "Felix, are you perspiring?"

"A bit, yes," Felix said, wiping his forehead with a handkerchief. "It's terribly hot this afternoon, don't you think?"

"Let me assist you," Will said, ramming his paddle against the surface of the water. A perfect arc jumped across the remaining gap between us. Lillian shrieked as most of it hit Felix, with a small amount splattering over her.

"Why, you!" Felix cried, a grin splitting his handsome face. He immediately took aim at Will, but instead sent a spray of water that squarely landed on my torso.

I opened my mouth in shock at the cold surprise.

"Oh, Cora!" Felix cried, his eyebrows lifting in apology.

But before I could think of it, I laughed and immediately took aim. Most of my water sprayed at Lillian, and across their canoe onto Andrew and Vivian.

It was my turn to be aghast. "Oh! I'm so sorry! I only meant to—"

But Hugh and Nell jumped into the fray, splashing back at me, and behind them, Andrew and Vivian. We screamed and shouted, and for a good three minutes, we were nothing but a group of splashing geese in the middle of the lake, honking in outrage and laughter. When we finally paused, I was out of breath and utterly soaked, my hair falling from its bun, around my shoulders, my skirts clinging to my legs.

Never had I looked worse.

But never had I felt such relief.

In spite of all the posturing and digs, in spite of the tension, for a few precious minutes, we were nothing but barely grown children, connected, laughing.

And in those moments, I caught a glimpse of what it might be to be one with them. A family.

PART II:
CROSSINGS

CHAPTER 13

~Cora~

Our parting with Mr. Kensington, at the harbor in New York, was awkward. I was torn between my desire to keep him with me for one more moment, as a buffer between me and my reluctant siblings, and my desire to finally be free of him. He was the constant reminder of my deepest hurt, the secrets he and my parents had conspired to keep.

I stood a few steps away as he tenderly hugged and kissed the foreheads of Vivian and Lil. The girls teared up. He moved on to Felix, shaking his hand and holding it as he shared a stern word of warning. He patted his son on the shoulder, then leaned closer to say something else, as Felix threw back his head and laughed. Then my siblings turned and joined the Morgans—the youngest girls squealing and jumping up and down in their excitement, pointing up at the vast ship that loomed above us—and Mr. Kensington turned toward me.

I felt faint. From the steps I was about to take? Or from the prospect of leaving him? I knew not. He opened his arms, offering a hug, but I gave him a sad, rueful smile. I did not belong in those arms. He was no more my father than any other man I might've met a few weeks prior.

But I had to offer him something, so I held out my hand, dragging my eyes upward to meet his, hoping it'd be enough.

He gave me a soft smile, his blue eyes tilting upward too—and yet laden with a barely concealed layer of grief—and then took my hand in both of his. His fingers were thick, like sausages, and his palms warm and dry. "Cora, sweet Cora," he said, holding on to me as if I might pull away. "Have a good journey. Know that you are not as alone as you feel. Alan and Alma did right by you, girl. They gave you what you need to make it, come what may. I've only given you the means to go."

I was grateful to him, honoring my parents that way. "I thank you for the opportunity, Mr. Kensington."

At my words, he lifted his chin slightly. Still, he held my hand, and I resisted the urge to yank it away. "This is but the first step for us, Cora. Once you're home and return to school, I wish to come and call upon you occasionally. I wish to know you, Cora, and you, me. Someday, perhaps we'll be at ease in each other's presence."

"Perhaps," I said stiffly.

"Perhaps," he said, nodding and giving me a real smile then. He lifted my hand and quickly brushed his mustached lips over my knuckles. "Take close care, daughter. I will pray for you every step of the way."

Pray. My father prayed? The thought startled me.

"Oh, and this arrived for you this morning. A telegram from your mother." He smiled as he reached into his coat pocket to extract it. His eyes twinkled, as if he already knew it contained good news.

"Thank you," I managed, taking it from him. And then there was nothing more to say. So I turned, picked up my valise, and followed the merrily waving Morgans and Kensingtons aboard the long, steep gangway up to the enormous ship.

At the rail, I paused, looking down to the dock and the city beyond it, my last glimpse of America for some time. I tore open the telegram.

Papa faring better –STOP–Under best care here –STOP–Bon voyage dearest –STOP–We love you–STOP

"Bon voyage, Mama," I whispered. "Take care of him." Then I tucked the telegram inside the vest of my traveling suit, directly next to my heart.

———◦◇◦———

It took me days to stop fretting that we were on the sister ship to the *Titanic*, which had so tragically gone down the year before. Like the rest of the country, we'd devoured every detail about the horrible accident. But Will and his uncle, as well as my father, rushed to explain that the *Olympic* was as trustworthy as she was beautiful—and White Star had worked diligently to add more lifeboats and adopt emergency procedures that would keep the tragedy from being repeated. We'd gone through several drills, each passenger moving to their assigned lifeboats, which lined the decks. I'd seen crewmen testing each rope and pulley that would allow the boats to descend to the water, hundreds of feet below.

"No one wants to avoid another tragedy more than White Star," Will had said, at my side.

LISA T. BERGREN

But it remained in my mind nonetheless. The first few nights, I'd awakened in the middle of the four-poster bed in my luxurious first-class stateroom, crying out, thinking of children drowning in the corridors of the third-class decks below. It didn't help that Felix delighted in bringing up stories of the *Titanic*, trying to scare the younger girls, Lillian and Nell, who shrieked in horror and hit him on his arms with their fans. According to him, waiting relatives of those who went down with the ship awoke at 2:20 in the morning, after dreaming of their loved ones drowning. The exact time the big ship sank.

I'd thought it to be nothing more than a ghost story until Will shrugged and reluctantly nodded. "There were reports of that happening, yes," he said.

There was murmuring all around the table, wondering at such a mysterious event. It made me think of arriving home in Dunnigan and *knowing* something was wrong.

"Is it true that you can smell an iceberg?" Andrew asked Will as we sat around a table in the Grand Dining Saloon, nearly identical to the one that had been on the *Titanic*. We had a private alcove which held one massive table where we could take all our meals together.

"Pish," Vivian said dismissively.

Will lifted an eyebrow toward his uncle.

"I believe it's possible," our elder guide said, sitting back and stroking his gray beard. "The icebergs break off of great glaciers. The minerals inside give off a distinctive odor as the iceberg melts. When we get to the mountains, we'll visit an ice cave. You shall know then of what I speak."

"There was a lady aboard who said the evening smelled strange," Felix pressed. He lifted his nose in the air and frowned a little. "Do any of you smell something odd now?"

"Oh yes, I do too." Andrew frowned.

"As do I," Hugh said, feigning as if to rise in alarm and flag down an officer.

Nell and Lillian grew pale as they looked to their elder brothers. Then Vivian said, "Are you three quite through with your game? If you don't stop, both of these girls will end up in my stateroom bed tonight, and there is not enough room for all of us!"

The young men laughed, and the girls immediately relaxed. Lil slapped Felix on the arm, and Nell threw her napkin at Andrew.

"Perhaps you gents should ease up on the *Titanic* talk," Will agreed. "Or we might all find our sleep disrupted by nightmares."

"Don't tell me you fear going down with the ship, Will," Felix said, eyeing the girls again to see if they'd heard.

"You're just working them up," Will chided. "You know as well as I that we aren't going to sink."

"These waters would make our lake in Montana seem like a warm bath." Felix shivered.

"Master *Felix*," the bear intoned.

Felix gave him a guilty smile. "All right, all right," he said, raising his hands in surrender.

Our meals were served à la carte by circulating waiters who offered eleven courses from giant silver platters. Such meals unfurled over a languid two to three hours. I stayed largely quiet during those dinners, electing to watch and listen, learn what I could of each person, and engage at just the right moment. After our rough start, I was hoping we were making incremental progress. But they still all treated me as someone they had to tolerate more than welcome.

After dinner, the women usually retired to the lounge to play cards and do needlework while the men went to the smoking room. I had no idea what they did in there; I only knew that getting within fifty feet of the doorway set me to sneezing and coughing. Each night, instead of joining the ladies, I made my excuses, returning to my stateroom to read.

After my terrifying dreams of the previous nights, I was exhausted and eager to escape the confines of protocol. To strip off my long gloves and clinging corset and icy blue evening gown and attempt a good night's sleep. I'd decided that being a woman of society meant that you dedicated half your life to dressing for the next event. Never in my life had I changed clothes so often, nor owned so many, and after the novelty had worn off, I longed for the simplicity of the farm, where a girl could wear a dress she could breathe in, move in. Where I could do as I pleased. But as we finished our raspberry sorbet—a delicate, icy treat I'd never had before—I learned there was to be a dance in the first-class lounge.

The younger girls were all atwitter about the opportunity, hoping certain gentlemen they'd seen would be in attendance. I scraped out the last of the melted raspberry liquid from the bottom of a crystal glass so fine I worried I'd break it, and I closed my eyes, remembering picking raspberries off enormous, thorny bushes with Mama last summer. Of baking Papa a pie, with the perfect crust…

"May I take your plate, miss?" asked a steward.

I opened my eyes to discover that most of my companions now stared at me.

Even Hugh stared at me with curiosity in his eyes. For once, there was no trace of lust. "Your face, Cora," he said in a gruff whisper. "A fond memory?"

I felt the burn of a blush and studied the napkin on my lap. "A good memory, yes."

He gave me a small smile and then, when I offered nothing further, looked to his sister, Nell. "There shall be no dancing with any gents aboard ship unless you grant me the first."

"And me the second," Andrew said, with nothing but brotherly care in his green eyes.

I smiled, looking at Nell, who loved her doting brothers. It had been the first thing I'd discovered about the Morgans that I could sincerely appreciate. They genuinely loved one another. And I adored how the older brothers watched after Nell when her own father rarely seemed to take notice of her. It made me long for brothers of my own, or for my papa. Would I ever feel connected to Felix in that way?

"Whoa," Hugh said, shifting his eyes from Nell to me again. "What happened to the fond memory?" I was surprised at his kindness—and his awareness.

I lifted my gloved hands to my cheeks. Was I so easy to read? I had to find a way to hide my emotions a bit more if I was to negotiate day-to-day life with these people. I forced a smile to my face and pictured Papa in my mind, strong in his saddle, reaching down to lift me up to sit behind him.

"There now, that's better," he said. Hugh rose and pulled out my chair. "Save me a dance, Miss Cora."

"I'll only stay for a little while," I hedged. "I'm dreadfully tired."

"And I'll be terribly disappointed if you slip away before I show you my prowess on the dance floor."

Nell looped her arm through Hugh's and glanced back at me, pride alight in her brown eyes. "He is quite good. He wins the annual ball award every year."

"Well, at least the last few years," he said.

"I'll do my best to linger," I said, pretending to be won over. Anna had tried to teach me the basic steps of a waltz and others, but I had yet to try them out with a man. I hoped I could escape before the Morgans and Kensingtons finished their first dances and looked around for me.

I was making my way to a chair on the edge of the parquet floor in the sprawling, grand room, which was modeled after Versailles, when Will took my hand. "May I have the first dance, Cora?"

"I, uh…I am rather new to dancing," I said.

He gave me an encouraging smile that lifted the corners of his eyes, and I nodded my assent. He reached for my dance card to sign his name next to the first of eighteen songs.

"I am rather experienced at tutoring," he said. He let the leather-covered card fall back to my side, hanging on a cord over my elbow. "In all subjects," he added with a nod.

"All right." We immediately turned toward the floor to join the other waiting couples. Anna had told me there would be frequent dances in the months to come. Almost nightly, when we reached Europe. The sooner I learned how to navigate them, the better.

"You look lovely tonight, Cora," Will said in a whisper, looking down at me. "One would never guess you hadn't been haunting grand saloons like this all your life."

"All a part of my elaborate mirage," I said, waving my fingers in an arc like a magician performing a trick.

He chuckled, and I smiled. He offered his left hand, and I slipped my right into it, then settled my left on his shoulder as he put his other hand on the small of my back. It was quite different to be in his arms, rather than Lorrie's, the only other man I'd ever danced with. For one, Will was much taller. Broader. Substantial. Lorrie had been strong, but slight, and only about my height.

I studied the musicians in the corner, watching as they tapped a beat and began the song, wondering how many counts it would take to finish the dance. How many counts there would be before I could make my excuses and depart.

But Will pulled me along, uttering directives that only I could hear. After a couple of minutes, I stopped counting and began to feel the rhythm of the music within. I paid attention to the nonverbal cues he gave. His fingers pressing, arms tightening, the subtle turn of his body. I tried to match each stride, to stay on my toes, to float, as Anna had taught me. But I'd never understood what she meant when she said that it could simply *flow*, be as natural as drifting with a river current, until I danced with a man who knew how to dance.

I looked up at him as the song ended and smiled. He smiled back at me. "You're a natural, Cora," he whispered, lifting up my right hand, allowing me to ease away from him, then turn under his arm and end in a demure curtsy as he bowed.

"And you're a fine tutor," I said.

My smile faded as I saw a shadow cross his face. He seemed to force a casual smile as I followed his gaze toward Hugh, who approached us, ready for the next dance.

I accepted Hugh's hand and looked for Will over his shoulder when we turned, but he slipped between two couples and disappeared in the crowd at the edge of the floor.

"Do you know the Castle Walk?" Hugh looked at me with honest interest, not in judgment. And his eyes held no trace of the inappropriate advances that had shadowed our earliest encounters. Had I misjudged him?

"A bit. Dancing is rather new to my life," I confessed.

"Happily, it's not new to me. Just follow my lead."

Hugh was almost as tall as Will—over six feet—but thinner at the shoulder and waist. And as soon as we began to move, I knew why he won the dance contests. He was built for it. Powerful, but lithe. If I'd begun to feel the current of the dance with Will, I knew what it was to float on clouds, following Hugh's lead.

I grinned when I completed the half turn and dip, without his cue, and saw the measure of suspicion and surprise in his eyes.

"Few get that on first try," he said. "You've been practicing with more than Anna."

"I haven't. This is my first time on a formal dance floor ever."

"Well, then," he said, turning me backward for eight steps. "You are a quick study."

"In more ways than one," I said.

He smiled at me. "I'm understanding that more and more."

Embarrassed at his praise, and irritated that I lapped it up like a stray kitten coming across a bowl of milk—from Hugh Morgan, of all people—I lost track of the music and stepped down on his toe.

Caught, our knees cracked together, and we both winced. If he hadn't responded immediately, we might have ended up falling. But he quickly took command, easing me back into the dance. "Let me amend that..." he teased with a gentle smile.

"I'll get it in time."

"Of that, I have no doubt, Cora," he said in my ear. Did his hand at my back caress me slightly as he spoke those words? Or was it merely me, becoming more aware of him touching me? I shifted, uncomfortably clear that he was now pressing a new advantage. I'd cracked open the gates...

And yet, as Lillian danced past us in the arms of a handsome young man, then Nell, giggling in Andrew's arms at something he'd said, I remembered the water fight in Montana, when I'd glimpsed what having siblings would feel like, and felt a measure of it again. Not begrudging half siblings suffering my presence, but whole siblings who wanted me there. *What is it, Lord? What do You want me to take from this summer?*

I would've missed this, I thought, as Hugh led me about the dance floor, had we had the resources to fight Wallace Kensington. I would've missed knowing how to dance more than a square dance in the Grange Hall. Knowing about things like fine gowns and gloves and etiquette and food like I'd never dreamed of and ships with dining rooms that sprawled as big as eight houses.

I liked knowing about these things. Learning. Growing into something more, something far grander than I'd ever imagined. And then I felt a stab of guilt, thinking about Mama and Papa. Had they not raised me to be everything fine? Regardless of what I looked like on the outside and ate, were they not the ones who taught me to be loyal and strong and forgiving and honest and hopeful? Had they not shown me that true worth came from my life in Christ, from who

He'd made me to be? Yet here I was, becoming quickly as shallow as Lillian, as superficial as Vivian, allowing Hugh's hand to drift ever so slightly downward…

The stab of guilt shot straight to my heart.

Oh, Lord, I sighed even as I danced, *forgive me. In many ways, I am as self-centered and shallow as they are.* The song ended, and I smiled empty thanks up at Hugh. I saw other young women send lingering glances his way and knew he would dance as long as the musicians played.

"Don't go far, Cora," he said, kissing my gloved hand as the last note ended. "I'd like another dance."

"Perhaps another evening," I said. "I do think I'll retire now."

He looked me in the eye, then dipped his head. "Very well. I'll regretfully allow you to escape," he said with a nod. Then he turned away and approached the prettiest girl on the far edge of the floor. So, he'd been scouting his next dance partner even as we danced, even as he made me feel like I was the only girl he had eyes for. I laughed at myself, wondering at my foolishness. I didn't even care to flirt with Hugh! But I'd been drawn in like a silly twit. I'd have to keep my mind stalwart when he came around. There was something subtle about him—something like the tiny tropical vines I'd read about, those that grew inches in a day, gently winding, entwining around objects, until they were engulfed. *Lord, I'm going to need Your help*, I added to the prayer I'd uttered before.

I left the dance floor and moved to the deck door, suddenly eager for some fresh air. Here in the Grand Saloon, it was suddenly warm, thick, *close*. My dress felt sticky, more clingy than ever. A steward opened the door for me. "Care for an escort, miss?"

"No, thank you. I'll be fine." That was something else I'd discovered about my new first-class life. People believed a woman incapable of making it minute by minute without assistance. As if she had to be watched every second. Was that part of what drove Andrew and Hugh to watch over Nell, without their mother in attendance? A shiver ran down my back. I rather liked my independence. I didn't need Felix or any other man considering what step I should take next.

I moved to the deck rail and inhaled a long, deep breath of the cold night air. It instantly steadied me. I glimpsed stars and moved to a portion of the deck free of lifeboats, where there was nothing but sea and sky before me. The lights of the ship reflected in the waves far below. I continued walking toward the bow, loving the feel of the wind on my face and the sound of the water as we cut through it. I grabbed a blanket from a deck chair abandoned by someone who'd paid the steep dollar rental for the day, knowing that while the air felt good to me now, in minutes I'd be chilled.

An officer walked by me, giving me a slight bow with his hand on the brim of his hat, as if he intended to take it off but didn't. "Good evening, miss."

"Good evening."

I kept going, skirting the wide deck in front of the bridge, until I was at the very front of the ship. No one else ventured here this night, perhaps electing for the more sheltered walkways, protected from the elements. But I welcomed the fierce wind whipping at my gown, plastering it across my legs, between them. I pulled the blanket closer around my shoulders like a shawl, glad I had it when I was finally at the front of the ship. Here I could feel the rise and fall of the giant *Olympic* as she crested each massive wave. I sensed no weakness within her and wondered again at her sister failing her passengers just a year before. She felt strong enough to slice through ten icebergs.

I was glad I'd yet to suffer seasickness, but here, feeling the rumbling, submerged power of the ocean, my stomach flipped. Dark skies, littered with a canopy of stars between banks of clouds, met the sea ahead, building on the front end of a storm that the captain had warned us of at dinner. I reached out to grab the cold metal railing with each hand, my feet splayed for better stability, and watched as the dark waves rolled near and we conquered each one. Climbing, cresting, cascading down the far side.

It came to me then.

With God's help, I could conquer the seas ahead. Whatever storms I encountered on the path before me. I was not alone. My God traveled with me. What I'd learned from Mama and Papa was with me still. *God makes me strong*, I thought, *capable*.

Yes, the storm was daunting, but I had only to take each wave as it came.

CHAPTER 14

-William-

From the concerned look on his face, it seemed Uncle Stuart had been shaking his shoulder for some time when Will finally came to and sat up, reaching for the bedpost to steady himself. Somehow he had been able to sleep even as a storm railed against the *Olympic*.

He and his uncle had been through rough seas before. But this storm was clearly different.

"They'll need us," said the elder man. "Get dressed. I'm heading up."

Will nodded and watched as the portly older man made his way to the second-class cabin door. It slammed behind him.

How would Nell and Lillian fare in the face of this storm? After all the talk of the *Titanic*? And Cora? A girl of the plains?

He'd watched her leave the dance floor after dancing with Hugh, exiting to the deck. Trailed her to the bow, where she stood at the very front, like the masthead of a pirate ship, her hair unraveled and flying behind her, along with her skirts. He thought about approaching her, escorting her in, but he sensed she needed the moment alone.

So he'd kept to himself, leaning against a wall in the shadows, keeping watch over her but not interrupting. Observing as officers and deckhands passed, each eyeing the lady at the bow in curiosity and appreciation. Rubbing his hands as the evening's chill seeped into his bones. But still she stood there, as if she had become one with the ship. He didn't leave, her father's entreaties to watch over her ringing in his ears, until she turned from the rail.

He'd slipped down the deck and between two lifeboats, waiting until she passed within ten feet of him, looking magnificently windblown, alive, and chilled, and then disappeared inside like an apparition, a mermaid who'd sprouted legs, claiming an ancient human heritage.

If this keeps up, we might all wish we were mermaids and mermen tonight, he thought, trying to pull on his trousers and landing painfully against a post as the ship lurched from one side to the other, out of rhythm with its previous cadence. A rogue wave? Outside his door, he heard men shout and women scream—one nearby. *The cabin across from me?* The big ship slowly returned to its previous climb and sway.

Quickly, he finished buttoning his trousers and went to the door, his shirt hanging out, his feet bare. He reached for the door, timing his movement with the next wave, moving forward as he held out an arm to either side of the hall walls when the following wave rolled through. He looked upward, thinking of his clients and his uncle, but he couldn't ignore what he'd heard. He knocked on the cabin door across from his.

An older man, balding and gray, swung the door open with the next wave. He lurched back with it.

"Whoa," Will said, reaching out to steady him. "You all right, sir?"

"We're...we're hurt. One of the beds wasn't bolted down right. It fell over. My wife..."

Will peered in. The electric lights flickered. But he saw her leaning forward in her nightgown, with her head in her hands. Long gray waves of hair flowed on either side of her face. Her head was bleeding. And the man held his belly, as if he, too, was in pain. "Let's get you two to the doctor," Will said.

He moved in. "I'm Will McCabe," he said to the man.

"Oscar Welch," said the husband, giving his hand a tentative shake. "Think we're going down?"

"Twice for the White Star Line? No chance." Will forced as much confidence into his voice as possible as he made his way, step by step, the waves rolling under them, to the woman. "Can you stand, ma'am?"

She looked up at him with a puzzled expression, as if she sensed his presence but couldn't hear what he'd said. "What?"

"Can you stand, ma'am?"

Her eyes rolled back in her head, and she collapsed. Will caught her and lifted her easily into his arms, then looked back at Mr. Welch. "Sir, can you follow me? Hold my shoulder, if you can. I'll lead you through."

"I'm with you, son." Mr. Welch reached up and touched Will's shoulder. Will bit his lip, looking down at the woman. Was she breathing? He managed to open the door, then held it against the wall with his hip as he considered where to go. The doctors and their offices were on the fourth deck, below them. But with that big wave, others might have fallen, been hurt. Will closed his eyes and forced himself to concentrate. If the first-class passengers were ailing or suffering, the doctors would attend to them first.

"We're going up," he said to Mr. Welch.

"But the doctors—"

"The doctors will be on the top deck." He eyed the old man over his shoulder. "With the first-class passengers."

Mr. Welch paused a second and then nodded. "Go, son. I'm right behind you."

Will and his uncle were almost directly beneath the staterooms that housed their clients. He assumed, as they painstakingly climbed the steep metal-and-wood stairs, that this had been by design. Wallace Kensington's design. Did the man not think of every detail? And would he fire him when he found out that Will had gone to the aid of this elderly couple rather than his own children?

At that moment, Will didn't care. He did what his mother and father had raised him to do—help anyone in need. He'd look after Cora and her siblings—as well as the Morgans—as soon as he reached the doctor.

Their progress up the stairs was perilously slow. Will looked in alarm to the woman in his arms, so terribly unresponsive, and then back at Mr. Welch, halfway up the stairs behind him. "Sir," he said. "I need to get your wife to the doctor. We're going…" He paused as another rogue wave washed by, and now that they were out in the stairwell, they could hear its accompanying roar. It sounded like the ship was brushing past a submerged sea monster. "We're going too slow."

"Go. Go, son. I'll be behind you," said the old man. Will had no idea how dire Mr. Welch's injuries were. All he could think was, *I need to take care of this woman first.* If she wasn't already dead in his arms.

The lights died for a moment. As he held his breath, waiting, hoping, Will prayed, *Please, Lord. Let her live. Don't let her die here, now. Let us all live through this night.* Memories of Felix's stories of the *Titanic* cascaded through his mind. He found himself inhaling through his nose, trying to detect the scent of minerals in the air.

The lights flickered back to life. Will took an awkward, gasping breath, then stumbled upward, not knowing if the lights were soon to go off forever. He reached the top, fumbled with the latch, and then burst through as the lights flickered again.

The Kensingtons and Morgans lined the hallway, seated on the floor of either wall as they'd been instructed to do. His uncle was handing out life vests, and the young men were securing their sisters. All eyes moved to him as Will's eyes locked with Cora's. She was all right. Pale, plainly frightened. Without a life vest yet, but all right. He sighed in relief, surprised that he'd been worried about her.

"The doctor—we need the doctor," Will said, nodding to the woman in his arms.

"I think I saw him head down there," Andrew said, gesturing along the hall. He stood and braced himself for the next wave. "I'll go with you," he said, moving toward him.

Cora watched him, as did Will. It was the first he'd seen Andrew move on behalf of anyone but himself or Vivian, and Will felt a surge of gratitude. "Get a life vest on, Cora," Will grunted, already stepping away from her. Andrew moved to the front, offering apologies to the passengers he had to step over as he opened doors, and gradually they made their way to the Grand Saloon.

It was already full of bleeding and groaning passengers. Two ship doctors—in crisp white coats—moved among them, examining each of perhaps thirty patients. "Doctor," Will called. Were any of the patients in as dire straits as the woman he carried? He doubted it. "I need a doctor over here!"

The nearest turned toward him, and then slowly, lurchingly, made his way over to them. Andrew put a strong hand on Will's shoulder to steady him, his other hand on the wall. And Will was grateful for it. As light as the old woman was, his arms grew weary, his steps less sure.

"Put her down here," said the doctor, pointing.

Will carefully lowered her to the carpet. When she was settled, he turned to Andrew. "Stay with her. I have to fetch her husband."

Andrew gave him a swift nod, and Will was off, feeling strengthened that he'd gotten at least one of his clients to help. He moved through the doorway and down the hall, trying to catch the rhythm of the waves as he had the rhythm of the dance the night before. But it kept changing.

He reached the Kensington-Morgan hallway, and all eyes again turned to him. They all had life vests on now, at least. Even Cora. He was glad to see that the maids and valets had made it up to join their masters and mistresses too. "You are all right?" he asked.

They all nodded, eyes wide, but none appeared the least bit all right.

"Any word from the captain?" Hugh barked.

"None that I've heard. Stay tight. They'll call us to the lifeboats if needed. I'll be right back." He glimpsed Cora beginning to rise, but he motioned her to stay seated as he turned and moved through the door.

He headed down the steep stairs, frowning when he saw the old man crumpled at the bottom. He rushed to him. "Sir! Sir! Are you all right?"

The old man only groaned.

Will glanced up as more light flooded the stairwell from above. Cora was there, her hair loose and flowing around her ivory life vest. She was in her nightgown and appeared as an angel to him. *An angel in a nightgown and life vest,* he thought, laughing at himself.

"Bring him!" Cora called. "I'll hold the doors. We'll get him to the doctor too."

He nodded, his vision clearing, then bent and lifted the old man as easily as he had the woman. *Neither of them can weigh more than a hundred and twenty pounds,* he thought. He leaned against the railing, catching the cycle of the wave, timing it in his head, then pushed upward and past Cora. The ship rolled, and Cora cried out, but all Will could do was fall against the far wall and wait for the wave to pass. When it did, he looked over his shoulder, panting. "Cora? Are you well?"

She nodded, eyes wide with fear. "Are we going down?" she whispered.

He shook his head. "No. It's a fierce storm. But she's built to encounter such storms." He gave her a wry smile. "And there are no icebergs within miles, I'd wager."

She smiled back at him gratefully, then moved past him, reaching out an arm on either side to steady herself as more waves rolled past. As she walked, she reached down to touch a whimpering child's head, a frightened woman's shoulder. Dispensing hope, courage, even when her own was in short supply.

When they made it into the Grand Saloon, Will saw Andrew cradling the old woman's head, blood seeping onto his trousers, as the doctor carefully bandaged her. The measure of care and selflessness made him pause. *Perhaps I've misjudged him.* Before this night, he'd doubted the man would turn to aid anyone for fear someone would leave dirt on his hands. He sensed Cora pause beside him, perhaps wondering over the same thing. Or simply waiting for him to move forward.

His eyes moved to the doctor as he gently laid the old man beside his wife.

"Another?" the doctor said, as if discouraged that Will would burden him so.

"Sorry. Husband and wife," Will said. "Their bed tipped in the storm."

"A bunk?" The doctor's eyes narrowed as he bent to examine the man.

Will rose and put a hand on his head, looking over the group of injured and crying passengers. Their numbers had grown in his brief absence. But that was when he felt it. The distinct easing of the pitch of the waves. He timed it, really paid attention through two more, then glanced back at Cora. "Feel that?"

Her eyes were wide, so blue—so terrifically blue against the white of her gown and cream-colored life vest. She nodded. "Oh, Will," she said in relief. "Is it passing?"

"I think so," he said, reaching out to wrap an arm around her slender shoulders. He meant to hold her only a moment, aware of the odd intimacy of touching her. It didn't matter that her shoulders might be bare in an evening gown on the dance floor. She was in her nightgown.

It was then he felt Andrew's narrowed eyes upon him. The man's eyes flitted from Cora to him and back again.

Will abruptly released her. "Let's get you back to your family." She hesitated, and it was only then that he realized what he'd said. *Family.*

Andrew shifted, clearly uncomfortable. "I'll stay with them," Andrew said, pointing toward the older couple. "Do what I can to aid the doctors. You might see if there are any others in need of assistance."

Will nodded and then took Cora's hand firmly in his, leading her down the hall. They had to pause periodically for the waves, but it was remarkably easier going than it had been just fifteen minutes past. When they reached the Kensingtons and Morgans, Felix and Hugh and their servants stood, while the women remained seated.

Felix looked pointedly down at Will and Cora's intertwined hands. Will abruptly released Cora even as a knowing expression entered his former classmate's eyes. His smirk rankled Will.

"Everyone all right?" Will asked.

"We're all right," said Felix. "What of those two you brought through here?"

"I'm not certain," Will said, shaking his head. He took a deep breath and rubbed a hand through his hair. The waves outside had eased more, yet. "Excuse me," Will called to an officer who was rushing past. "Are we through the worst of it?"

"Yes, sir. Still heavy seas ahead. But nothing like what we've just been through. It's safe to return to your cabins," the officer said, looking down the line of passengers huddled in their life vests. "We'll reach calm waters in an hour or two. Perhaps you all should attempt to get some sleep in the meantime. You can sleep in your vests if it eases your minds."

They nodded, and he left, but they all stayed where they were. Will knew it'd be a while before they felt safe enough to do as he suggested. He hooked a thumb over his shoulder and leaned toward his uncle. "Since all is well here, I'd like to go back to the saloon and see if I might be of assistance. Andrew's back there with the elderly couple."

"Your place is here," Uncle Stuart hissed. His eyes brooked no argument. He was angry that Will hadn't been with their clients the whole time. With him. His eyes held fear, and Will knew he'd been worried for his nephew's safety.

"I'll go," Felix said, putting a hand on Will's shoulder.

Will, struck by his friend's kindness, nodded once, and Felix began picking his way down the hall, which grew more crowded by the minute. Cora was reaching out to Nell, stroking her plump arm. Will liked that she cared for the youngest of the Morgans, but he wished she would look his way. Even once. He wanted to see her face, know that she was calm, no longer frightened. He frowned when he remembered the feel of her strong but slender fingers in his hand, the feel of her shoulder beneath her thin gown, as if it had been seared into his memory. *Entirely improper, that*, he chastised himself.

"William," said a feminine voice. He turned, hoping it was Cora. But it was Lillian, admiration large in her green eyes. She reached out and touched his forearm. "I just wanted to say," she said, dropping her gaze and then slowly looking up at him, "that I thought it most heroic of you. Helping that couple as you did."

"Yes, well," he said, looking past her to Cora, who had been watching them. She glanced away. "I did as anyone else might."

"Might," Lillian said meaningfully.

"Oh, leave him be, Lil," Vivian said, reaching up to pull her sister back down to the floor. She leaned closer, until she was nose to nose with her sister and said, just loudly enough for Will to hear, "What'd I tell you? No fraternization with the guide. It's entirely improper."

Will turned away and took a few steps to an empty spot along the hall, then slid wearily to the floor. He closed his eyes and leaned his head back, letting it rock back and forth with the waves. Vivian espoused only what he himself did—no fraternization between client and guide. Yet why did her words burn?

He knew why. Behind his shut lids, he could see only Cora, the angel at the top of the stairs, and earlier, outside, in her ice-blue gown, at the fore of the ship.

Cora.

It can never happen, he thought, squeezing his eyelids hard, as if he could press the memory into such a slim slice that he would forget.

But he couldn't.

CHAPTER 15

~Cora~

After the storm, I immersed myself in life aboard ship, wishing to concentrate on anything but the dangers present. Something had shifted with the storm; the girls and Vivian seemed to more readily accept my presence rather than look over their shoulders at me as an intruder. We took to the saltwater pool during the women's hours, watched the young men play squash from the gallery, played shuffleboard ourselves, and took tea at Café Parisien, decorated to look like an authentic café in Paris. "You'll see for yourself in but a week," Will said, when I asked him if the eatery was really like those in France. The thought of seeing Paris thrilled me.

And it terrified me too. What was a simple girl from a farm in Montana to do among the highborn society of England and France and Italy? It was finally sinking in that I was going. That we were almost there. Almost ready to formally begin our Grand Tour.

Will and his uncle took turns giving short lectures each day about British history and the imperial impact on world politics. We would not be long in London; after only a few days, we'd be on our way via train to port, then a ship to Paris, sailing up the Seine.

"Do you think we might meet the king?" Lillian said, clapping her hands.

"I doubt it," the bear said drily. "We *might* catch a glimpse of him at some point. But you will be introduced to your distant relatives, who no doubt will introduce you to their friends. If we're most fortunate, we'll be ushered into parties where even the king and queen consort might attend. That is how the tour works best; we meet people with whom we are associated in some form, and therefore we can secure proper lodging as well as introduction to the region's most scintillating society."

"I thought the tour was to expand our education, our understanding of the world," I said. There was little, I thought, that could bore me more than hours of tea and idle conversation with people I didn't know, whether they be kin or not.

"Indeed. Getting to know the people of these lands will offer us a far richer and deeper education than if we simply traveled the tired tourist routes." Will's uncle smiled at me benignly. "Trust me."

I sighed and turned away. The old bear surely remembered the obstacles they were likely to face with me along. People were expecting the legitimate children of Hubert Morgan and Wallace Kensington.

It wouldn't take long for the whispers to start once they found there were now three and a half Kensingtons where once there were only three.

I felt the seas beneath my feet, the gentle roll and rock, long after I'd disembarked and made the journey to London via train. It took six hired touring vehicles to transport us and our belongings from the train station to the estate on the outskirts of the city where we were to lodge. The traffic lessened as we continued west along the Thames, where the homes and estates grew larger. One lane after another led to magnificent manors and huge Tudor mansions. I gaped at the monstrous homes, wondering how many people such mansions could hold. My companions, Lillian and Nell, peppered our driver with questions about who lived in each and what sort of lavish parties they hosted.

But when our driver turned down a lane that was more of a boulevard, with manicured, mature trees down the center and perfectly laid gravel on either side, we all fell silent. Before us sprawled a palace of light-yellow stone, with crenellated walls and towers on either end and flags waving in the wind. So formidable was its effect that we half expected guards to patrol the towers, watching for enemy assault. Servants stood outside, as if awaiting our arrival.

As soon as we stopped, a man in uniform stepped forward to open our car doors. Another came around and assisted me out. "Welcome to Syon House, miss," said the butler.

"Thank you," I said, staring up at the palace wall high above us.

"Don't gape, Cora," Vivian whispered, firmly taking my arm. "It is unseemly."

"Oh, right," I said, feeling every bit of the shame her tone cast upon me. She'd lectured Lillian about that enough.

I fell into step beside her as we followed Andrew and Will up the steps and into the Great Hall. The sprawling room was like a sketch from the history books come alive. Decorated in the Greco-Roman style and made almost entirely of stone and plaster, the Great Hall was a good fifteen degrees cooler inside than out. Magnificent marble statues occupied alcove after alcove. My eyes traced the beautiful blue-and-white marble beneath my feet, and the fine, fluted columns that rose to the domed ceiling. Never had I been in such a fine structure. And someone called this their *home*?

When two servants had brought us all a glass of champagne, a butler at the door said, "Ladies and gentlemen, permit me to intro duce your hosts, the Duke and Duchess of Northumberland."

In walked a rather homely couple in their late thirties, dressed in the finest clothing. The duchess's hand rested gently atop the duke's open and raised hand. She wore a cream-colored suit dress and a long string of pearls, her hair perfectly coiffed. He wore a distinctive summer suit, brown with cream pinstripes, and perfectly shined shoes. One by one we were introduced.

The duchess's eyes roamed over Vivian, Lillian, and me. "I misunderstood, Master McCabe," she said. "I believed you were bringing six guests. Did Mr. Kensington or Mr. Morgan adopt another child en route?" She laughed at her own joke. My sisters and Nell twittered nervously along with her. Felix edged slightly away from me. I only stared at our bear, hoping he would find a way to smooth this over without immediately addressing the truth of my paternity.

"It appears that way, does it not?" he said easily. "Mr. Kensington hadn't yet convinced Cora to come when we sent our letter to you. She was rather embroiled in her life in the States and hesitant to join the others for the tour. I hope it's no imposition."

"Not at all." The duchess turned cool eyes on me. I imagined her running through a version of the family tree, checking out pedigrees, and discovering where my branch ran awry of the others. I fought to keep a smile on my face, my feet still.

She turned to speak to a maid over her shoulder and then gestured to all of us. "I'm certain you all are weary from the road, as well as famished. The servants will show you to your rooms, and you can freshen up."

"Tonight, there is to be a grand party in the conservatory, as well as fireworks," said the duke, "a tribute for my wife's birthday." He glanced benignly at his wife. "You are all invited, of course."

Nell and Lillian immediately murmured their birthday wishes, which seemed to make the duchess bristle. I'd already seen that the British seemed somewhat cool in their demeanor. Removed. Or did the duchess just not care for the idea of the party at all? The reminder of her advancing years?

"Yes, well," she said, turning toward the bear. "You may meet our butler, Jensen, here in two hours. He will take you on a tour of the palace, as well as introduce you to the grounds. Then, you can take the others about at your leisure. I imagine you'd find that agreeable?"

The older guide nodded. "Very much so. Beyond kind, my lady."

"Not at all. The house and her artwork hold a fine piece of British history. It is our good pleasure to share it with you, a fitting beginning to your tour. Tonight at seven, please join the party outside. Once you make your way to us, we shall make proper introductions."

"Thank you, your Graces," the bear said, giving them a genteel bow.

They both nodded, gave him an affected smile, and then left us.

Vivian let out a pent-up breath, looking relieved that we'd dodged the bullet. Her eyes flicked over me and on to Andrew, who took her hand with a smile and kissed it. "See there? All is well," he murmured.

"Yes, well," she said, her eyes passing over me again. "For the moment anyway."

I found my luggage in the arms of a tall manservant—Jensen, I assumed—who peered down at me through tiny spectacles. Anna, my maid, was beside him, holding my smallest trunk.

"May we see you to your room, Miss Kensington?" said Jensen, lifting a haughty brow.

I glanced around. I wasn't the only Kensington here. So why single me out? But then I saw Vivian's flared nostrils and narrowed eyes. Apparently my pause had been a misstep of some kind. I turned back to Jensen. As demurely as I could, I said, "I'd be most appreciative."

"Right this way," he said, gliding up the staircase off the western corridor. Other servants met with the rest of our party and followed behind us.

On the ground floor, in the center of the foyer where the curving staircase lifted to the second story, there was a massive golden vase atop a marble pedestal.

The servant glanced back and saw me gawking at it. "A gift from the king of France to the third duke. The duke, as Britain's ambassador extraordinary, attended his coronation in 1825."

"I see," I said. "It's quite beautiful."

"Quite," Jensen said.

I wondered what it would be like to attend a coronation. What it would be like to be an ambassador. To bear such a title as duke, let alone ambassador extraordinary.

We walked down a long hall, the manservant's heels clicking on the marble floor. I looked back, but here, no one else followed us. Perhaps it was why I had been picked first—I was the last-minute addition. My sense of pride faded as we passed eight or nine rooms, doors open as if to display each immaculate, elaborately decorated apartment, until we apparently reached the one selected for me. My escort bent and slipped a key into the lock and opened the door, then waited for me to go in first.

My mouth dropped open as I went immediately to the window. The man set down my bag and then came to the window too. "The duchess thought a woman so reluctant to leave the wilds of America might enjoy a view of the wood from her window."

"Indeed," I said, admiring the sprawling gardens before me. To the right, I glimpsed a huge glass conservatory, lines of servants coming and going from it, getting ready for the party.

More servants arrived with the rest of my trunks. Jensen excused himself, but Anna stayed to help me unpack a few of my gowns. "May I press the one you wish to wear this evening?"

I started, still not used to servants looking after my every whim. "Please." I moved over to the trunk, looking for the blue dress that gathered at the shoulder and came together at the waist, making me feel like a Grecian princess. And with no sleeves, it would be cooler this summer evening, when I was liable to be sweating through one introduction after another. "This one," I said, pulling it free and handing it to the maid.

"Ahh, that's a beauty, miss," said Anna. "I'll have it back to you in the lick of a ladybug's tongue. Then we'll do up your hair."

I smiled. "Sounds quick indeed. Maybe I can do my own hair If—"

"Don't even consider it, miss," she said with the bob of a curtsy. "It's best if I see to it."

I laughed under my breath. She had just offended me and offered me nothing but service at the same time.

"Do you need some help in locatin' your slippers and undergarments, miss?" Anna said.

"No, thank you. I'll just take a sponge bath and perhaps lie down until you get back."

"Of course. Take your rest. I'll see to your gown. You be needin' anything else, miss? A spot of tea? A bit of biscuit?"

"When you return," I said, "that'd be wonderful. Say, are you happy to be back in England?"

She looked to the window and smiled, more broadly than I'd ever seen. "More than you know. But we'll only be here for a few days, so I aim to not get too attached."

"Will you see family while you're here?"

Her smile faded. "Not much of my family left in England proper. But I would like to see if I might find my aunt. That is, if I could have an evening off, miss." Her eyes went to the floor as if she'd asked for too much.

"Oh," I said, "please. Take a whole day. Just let me know when you wish to go."

"Thank you, miss," she said with another quick bob, holding up my wrinkled ice-blue gown. "I'll be back shortly." She left then, quietly closing the tall door behind her. I felt like an interloper, looking around the room. Who was I to be giving anyone a day off? Who was I to be here, in this incredible mansion of a house, in this beautiful room? My eyes roved over every wall. It was decorated in whites and blues, but it had a warmer feel than the Great Hall, given that there was more painted woodwork and paintings and rugs atop the marble floor.

I returned to the window and peered out through the wavy plate-glass windows at the trees but thirty feet away. I figured out the mechanism to release the window and, with a creaking push, opened the massive panel, taking a deep breath of the fresh air that smelled of gardenias and lavender. I glanced down and saw that my movement had caught the attention of two gentlemen, one with dark hair and the shadow of an evening beard, the other fairer. Both smiled and nodded in my direction, then respectfully looked away, continuing their walk.

I left the window open but stepped back, out of sight, in case it was deemed improper for me to be seen in my bedroom. The gentlemen and ladies below were already in fine clothing worthy of a soiree. Hurriedly, I went back to my door, opened it, listening for any other voices—was I the only one in this wing?—and then, hearing nothing, gently closed it. I moved to the sink and, after undressing, quickly washed myself. I glanced in the mirror and unpinned my hair, brushed it out, then brought it back up in a knot. After the second try, I sighed and silently agreed with Anna—she was better at fixing it than I.

I opened my bag and fished out a tin of powder. In a few minutes I looked refreshed and more ready to be in the company of the ladies below.

A gentle knock sounded at my door. I pulled out a dressing gown and quickly slipped into it, wrapping it tight around my body as I peered around the corner of the door. It was my maid.

Anna bustled inward and lifted up the dress, perfectly pressed, toward me. "Need assistance, miss, putting on your gown?"

"That'd be grand, Anna. It's all a bit uh, *much*, to handle on my own." I took the gown from her hands and laid it on the bed. "Thank you for pressing it, Anna."

"Not at all, miss." She ducked back out the door, took a tray from another servant, and brought it to a small table beside my bed. On it was a tiny china pot, steam lifting from the spout, a cup and saucer, and a small plate of "biscuits"—dense butter cookies.

I smiled. "Thank you, Anna."

"My pleasure, Miss Cora. Ring the bell when you're ready for me to attend you." She pointed at three small brass levers by the door, labeled *Maid*, *Butler*, and *Kitchen*.

"I shall," I managed to say.

The maid slipped out, and I poured myself a cup of tea with trembling hands while I kept glancing at the levers. Back home, Anna and I might've been friends. Here we were clearly mistress and servant. Oddly, I felt more like a pampered princess than dismayed by the injustice of that. *Oh, Mama and Papa, what is happening to me?* How I wished they were here. Sharing in this adventure with me, giving me advice. But then I thought better of it. Even if Papa had not been ailing, I sensed that they would have encouraged me to take this journey. *You have to find your way, Cora,* Mama had said in the train car as I kissed Papa goodbye. *You know the way.*

I do?

Yes, she'd said, staring into my eyes, as if willing me to understand what she meant. *You are a fine woman, Cora. And you're about to find out what it means to be a Kensington. Once you discover what that means—and what it doesn't—you'll know. You'll know.*

I puzzled over her words, wishing I could go back to that train car and force her to explain what she meant. It'd be easier if I didn't feel so terribly alone. Just when I'd thought I was making headway with the Morgans and Kensingtons, Vivian treated me with disdain, as she had downstairs, and it all fell apart.

I sat down heavily and took a bite of my cookie, closing my eyes as the delicious chunks melted over my tongue. I sipped from my cup of strong black tea, then lay down on the bed, staring up at the ornate plaster ceiling. *Even the ceiling is beautiful.* I turned my head and looked about the room again. *I think I could become rather accustomed to such beauty.*

The thought of it startled me. I sat up abruptly. *So soon, Cora,* I chastised myself. *So soon we become used to the finest things…* I shook my head, remembering how I took Mr. Kensington to task over his sterling and what he paid his workers. I massaged my right temple, feeling the beginning of a headache forming there. My father had promised nothing more than this tour and the completion of my education at the Normal School after. That was it. Staying in places like this would soon feel like a distant memory. No. I had to appreciate it but not adopt it as my own. It wasn't mine to hold.

I couldn't let it mold me, leaving me wanting more. I had to take from the tour what I wished, not allow it take me and change me. I had to be strong. True to what I knew was right, good. *Maybe that was what Mama had been talking about…* My fingers rubbed across the smooth, luxurious fabric of my bedding. Never had I felt such finery. I clenched it in my hand and let out a groan. Even the blankets seduced me!

I rose and stepped into my corset, then reluctantly pulled the lever to ring Anna. I stepped behind the dressing screen, and a minute later, she tapped on the door and peeked in. "Miss Kensington?"

"Yes," I said, flinching over the name. "I'm here."

She came around and with fast and sure hands, took the ribbons and pulled them tight, lacing them up my back. With each turn, I felt less able to breathe. Back home, we'd taken to girdles we could slip on and off ourselves. Here, it took more "structure," as Anna liked to call it, in order for the gowns to hang correctly. I spread out my feet, bracing, as she finished her work and quickly tied it at the top.

"There now," she said, turning to reach for the blue gown that so perfectly matched my eyes. She gathered it up in her hands and then carefully settled it over my head, pulling it down over my body. The luscious silk brushed over my skin and the skirts settled around my ankles.

"Ach, miss, you're a vision. Every duke, earl, and valet will be staring after ya. At least they shall be once I see to your hair." She led me to a chair before a mirror and quickly brushed it out and wound it into a sleek chignon. Afterward, she pinned a rhinestone-and-feather headband firmly in place.

"Isn't it a little…much?" I asked doubtfully, staring at my reflection in the small oval mirror. I felt like a curious bird with the feather atop my head.

"No, miss. You are perfect," she purred, clasping her hands in delight as she stared over my shoulder at the reflection in the glass.

"Thanks to you," I said.

I rose and smoothed my bodice.

"I only made more of what God Himself began," Anna said, nodding again in appreciation. "You'll surely upstage the duchess in whatever we put you in, so mind your choices. Keep to the center of the crowd." She leaned in and brushed away a speck from one of my shoulders, then looked into my eyes. "Politely answer every question but do not seek others out. Allow them to come to you. Blend in as much as possible. You understand?"

"I do," I said, grateful for her coaching.

"You'll be fine," she said, giving me a bright smile. She patted me on the shoulders and then slipped out the door.

I hesitated, not quite ready to follow. In the corner, I glimpsed my reflection again and did a double take. Slowly, I approached, studying my image in the long oval mirror. Classic. Simple but elegant from head to toe. I looked like I belonged here. In this palace. With these people.

From the outside, I looked like I was one of them.

But on the inside, I knew I was nothing more than an interloper.

CHAPTER 16

~William~

Jensen led them toward the gardens, remarking on different portraits of famous statesmen. For the life of him, Will couldn't remember his third duke from his sixth duke of Northumberland. He only knew his host. It rankled—how much was really vital to remember? Surely if he couldn't remember it, the Kensingtons and Morgans wouldn't. Was it not much more important to center on those things that they might apply later on, in their lives in America? But still, if he forgot a detail, he'd hear it from Uncle for hours tonight.

He'd changed into his formal coat and waistcoat, more appropriate for the evening's festivities, and now he was suffering. He ran a finger under his tight collar and bow tie, hoping to catch a deep breath in the heat of evening.

Guests were starting to arrive en masse.

"I heard Antonio is here," Uncle had said earlier. "Keep an eye out for him."

"I will," Will agreed. He looked forward to seeing the man again. On the last tour, Antonio had become like an older brother to Will. And if it hadn't been for him in Napoli, Will would've been robbed and left for dead by a gang of six young men.

Antonio rounded the corner, laughing with a young earl as if they'd already shared a drink and a game of cards. Will grinned and shook his head as the older man spotted him and hurried over, arms wide, so Italian in his greeting. If the Brits thought Americans were uninhibited, they had to be continually shocked and appalled by the Italians.

"Will!" Antonio cried, thumping him on the back and lifting him off the ground. He pronounced his name like *wheel*, and it deepened Will's gladness to hear it. "Oh, my friend, how I have missed you!" He drew back, gripping Will's shoulders and smiling broadly. He was several inches shorter than Will, but sturdy and strong, like a boxer.

"It is good to see you, too, Antonio." He turned and greeted the nobleman at Antonio's side, a young man of about seventeen, sandy haired and slim. On two previous tours, the earl had mentioned joining their party when he came of age. "Has Antonio convinced you to visit Italy yet, Lord Carlisle?"

"Very nearly, yes," said the young earl. "When will your party reach her this time?"

"Six weeks from now we'll reach Venezia," Will said. "Two weeks later, Firenze. A week later, Roma and Napoli. It's an interesting mix."

"I've heard," said the young man, raising an eyebrow. "Though I confess fraternizing with American girls is the most intriguing aspect of the offer."

"It's a common draw," Will said, covering his irritation over Carlisle's comment as his uncle neared.

"You should bring them out to the lakes," said the earl. "A turn in the district would be enlightening. For us all."

"Truly?" Will asked, pinning him down. He'd seen his uncle do this a hundred times.

"Truly. Next week?"

"It'd be a delight," Will said regretfully. "But we're to take the train to Dover and catch a ship in three days' time. And until then, we plan to spend all our time here in London."

"But they cannot miss the lakes," the earl said, his brow furrowing.

"Unfortunately we simply cannot manage it this time around. Perhaps the next group we bring?"

"Yes, yes. Certainly. Consider it done."

"You honor us with your invitation, my lord. May I send word when the time comes?"

"Good enough," said Lord Carlisle, shaking his hand. "Mother will be alternately aghast and entranced with the prospect of having a group of Americans in. It shall be the most intriguing thing to happen to our manor all year."

"At least you'll have time to prepare her."

The young man moved off, and Antonio and his uncle smiled at Will. Antonio clapped him on his shoulder and looked proudly at Will's uncle. "He has learned much, has he not, Stuart?"

"A great deal," agreed his uncle.

Will smiled. He glanced up and saw, descending the stairs, the ladies of the Morgan and Kensington families. For a moment, he didn't see Cora, but then he knew it was her behind them, pausing at the top as the sun set. Her form was a silhouette as she descended, sunlight streaming around her. As she drew closer, he saw that her gown was the same color as her big, beautiful eyes.

Beside him, Antonio sucked in his breath. "She is a vision, that one. Do you know her name?"

Will tensed. "Indeed I do. She is one of our *clients*. Cora Kensington."

Antonio shot him a quick look of confusion. "Cora? I do not remember such a name from the list—"

"She was a late addition," Will said, brushing past him, moving forward to greet the group. He shook hands with the men and bowed toward the ladies. When he got to Cora, Antonio was again beside him, waiting for an introduction.

"Miss Cora Kensington," Will said, "this is Antonio Lombardi, a fellow guide, specializing in Italia. He shall attend us on the tour."

Antonio offered his hand and then bent to kiss hers. "You are ravishing, Miss Kensington. I shall have to stand beside you every moment to protect you from the young men of my country."

Will suppressed the urge to sigh as he watched Cora smile and blush. Antonio was as charming as he was handsome, even if he was twenty years their senior.

She gently pulled her hand from Antonio's, and Will saw his chance. "May I introduce you to some of the others, Cora?" he asked, offering his arm.

Cora gave him an appreciative look that warmed him, and he cast a sly, triumphant look at Antonio as they turned, arm in arm. He had no business competing for Cora's attentions; he knew that.

He only wanted her to succeed, flourish on the tour. Make the most of it. Nothing more. *Nothing more*, he repeated in his mind firmly.

But he could not deny that it felt good to be drawing the eye of everyone they passed. He wore the finest clothing he owned, even if it was two sizes too small, and Cora…well, she looked incredibly beautiful. "A most handsome couple," an older woman murmured as they passed. Will remained silent; had Cora heard?

The rest of the Morgans and Kensingtons were already mingling, having discovered relations they'd met in America, apparently, who in turn were introducing them around. Uncle Stuart looked back over his shoulder, concern shrouding his eyes, and then his brows lifted when he saw Cora with Will.

"What is it?" Cora asked quietly.

He glanced at her in surprise. "What do you mean?"

"You stiffened when your eyes met your uncle's. What is it?"

"Uh, nothing," he said. He saw a group of five young men turn from their conversation and gaze in Cora's direction, clearly talking about her, eyes alight in anticipation of finding a way to be introduced. But how long would it be before word got out that she was Wallace Kensington's illegitimate daughter? Knowing well how these people worked, it wouldn't be long. There was a certain prejudice against Americans to begin with—especially the nouveaux riches like the Morgans and Kensingtons—but anyone with scandalous parentage? The bluebloods could be merciless, regardless of their own dalliances.

"How much of our tour will be spent in evenings like this?" she murmured.

"Mmm, they'll be frequent. Every few nights, at least." She was silent, and he cocked his head, waiting for her to meet his gaze again. "You don't enjoy parties?"

"It takes a great deal of effort. I'm interested in the landscape, the history, the monuments, the art… The people are obstacles I have to negotiate, I'm afraid." She looked around the courtyard. "There were hardly this many people in my entire town back in Montana."

"Ahh, but the people are part of the tour," he said as they entered the massive glass conservatory. "Perhaps you can think of the whole tour as a canvas, and the people merely one element within it." He held open the door for her, and she swept by, smelling of verbena and lemon. Or was it the plants around them? Inside the conservatory, the temperature rose by a good ten degrees, and tropical plants lined each edge. Exotic birds sang and flew above like some sort of elaborate stage set for a play about to unfold. "Understanding the people of each country we visit—truly getting a sense of who they are—is part of the experience," he said.

They came across a group of young people Will had met the previous year in France. Quickly, Cora was introduced around and was soon surrounded by admirers. They wanted to know what life was like in the wilds of Montana and if gold was still available for the taking. She seemed to be holding her own, so Will allowed two sisters to spirit him off to introduce him to their mother. They were bent on taking their own Grand Tour in the coming year and wanted him to be their bear.

Warmed by their praise and joined by the girls' father and brother, Will spoke with them for a good long while, outlining the basics of the tour and pulling away to discuss finances with their father. It was exhilarating, thinking of guiding on his own, without the shadow of his uncle following his every move. He could make more money and possibly return to school earlier than planned.

The first notes of the orchestra wafted through the air past the open windows of the conservatory. As one, the group began to shift to the doors, and after promising to dance with each of the sisters, Will guiltily looked around for his charges. In the last hour, he'd not glimpsed one of the Morgans or Kensingtons. In particular, Cora. Where had she gone off to?

He moved to the buffet table, hurriedly heaping some tender roast chicken, a creamy soufflé, and some carrots onto his plate before turning to look again. There, in the far corner, was Vivian, speaking with the duchess and some of her friends. He moved toward her, thinking that if he found one Kensington, he was liable to find the others. He shoveled several bites into his mouth. It was always hard to find time to eat at such parties when one was constantly chatting or dancing, but his stomach was screaming for sustenance. It was no wonder that so many ended up tipsy from the champagne when it was brought to them on endless passing trays and quickly swallowed.

Outside, a second massive pyramid of crystal glasses had been set up, and a servant on a ladder was beginning to pour, sending the golden liquid cascading down in a champagne waterfall. The crowd sighed in admiration, clapping at his success. Will noted that they were already much more cheery than when they'd first arrived. Such was the effect of alcohol, before everything headed downhill.

He took another bite of the chicken and took a step toward Andrew and Vivian, still looking around for the others.

That was when he heard her. Vivian, speaking to the duchess's friend.

"I confess I have no idea what my father was thinking. We didn't even know of her a month ago. And now she's to be on tour with us? What will people think?"

"Miss Kensington!" Will said, covering his bark with a belated, pretend cough. "Forgive me, but may I steal my client away for a moment?"

"Certainly," said the duchess's friend, looking a tad pale, her eyes wide with excitement. It was early, and yet Vivian already had found the biggest gossip around.

Will took Vivian's arm and ushered her away, working very hard not to grip too hard, nor walk too fast, even though he wanted to storm her out and give her a good thrashing. When they were ten paces off, they turned, and he glanced back. Andrew was frowning in their direction, clearly wondering what was going on, but Will ignored him. "*What* are you doing, Vivian?"

She pulled her arm from his hand and sniffed. "Protecting our good name."

"Protecting? You just—"

"I just made a preemptive strike," she said, crossing her arms. "The duchess knows already, Will. She *knows*. It took her but an hour to find out the truth."

"Who—"

"What does it matter? All we can do now is to make sure that everyone knows we didn't invite Cora in. It's either gather against her or fall with her."

Will's mouth dropped open. "How can you say such a thing?"

"It's the truth of it. If we wish to fraternize with these people, we need to deal with it as my father wished—head-on—and deal with the repercussions. We shall be accepted or we shall not. Now if you'll excuse me…"

Will clenched his fists at his side. "It's not you who will bear the repercussions, Vivian. It will be Cora. Through no fault of her own."

Vivian paused, and a flash of doubt ran through her eyes.

"You've ruined her," he growled. "Before we've even begun."

Vivian lifted her chin. "I didn't ruin her, Will. My father ruined her mother. He might want to make her into a woman of society, give her the opportunity, but she will never be more than a Molly Brown to these people, or to me. If we do not make it clear that we are different, that she's been thrust upon us like an unwelcome gift, we'll be treated the same. We'll all be ruined."

"Isn't that what it means to be a family?" Will asked. "To stand together?"

"She is not family to me," Vivian said. "She is a stray dog my father brought home."

With that, she walked off, and Will turned away, setting his plate on the nearest table, no longer hungry.

———◇◇◇———

It emerged exactly as he feared.

When he reached the dance floor, outside on a massive stone patio beside the conservatory that was ringed with strands of electric lights, many couples were already dancing, including Cora with one of the gentlemen who had been eyeing her when they arrived. Will watched as the duchess and her friend joined the group at the far edge. They laughed as they bent to speak into each other's ears.

His uncle and Antonio joined him, and with one look, both sobered and surveyed the crowd. "What is it, Will?" Stuart asked.

"They know," he said simply.

Antonio's eyes moved to Cora. Apparently, he'd been informed of the truth already too. "It did not take long."

"No," Will said bitterly. Not when her self-serving half sister came right out with it. But had Vivian been right? Had the duchess already uncovered the truth? They'd been foolish, thinking they could keep it quiet.

The dance ended, and another song began. Another gentleman stepped up and bowed toward Cora. She accepted his offer, and they set off on a fox-trot. But his eyes didn't stay on her. They traced the crowd on the far side, suddenly aware that everyone seemed to be murmuring about them—and judging by their expressions, not in an admirable way.

It made Will wince as he watched people bend toward one another, whispering, laughing, and glancing in Cora's direction. By the time the dance was done, no one from the far side stepped forward to offer to dance with her in a third.

Will was moving before he realized what he was doing. He only knew he couldn't leave her there, alone, with no idea of what was about to happen to her. He stepped toward her as her partner thanked her for the dance.

Will smiled down at her and cocked his head. "Fancy a dance with a bear-in-training?" he said.

"A dancing bear," she returned with a grin. "I thought they were only in circuses."

"This might constitute a circus of another sort," he said, taking her into his arms. He was glad when the musicians began another waltz. Immediately he led her forward, then back, swaying in time with the music. She was enjoying herself, and he hated to be the one to break into her brief joy. But if he didn't tell her, she'd soon discover it herself.

"Cora, as this dance ends, I was wondering if you'd do me the honor of a walk."

She looked up at him with curiosity in her big blue eyes, measuring him, trying to decipher the reason for his request.

"Only a walk, nothing more," he assured her.

"I...I see."

Was there a glimpse of disappointment in her tone? Or had he imagined it? He lifted her hand, and she turned under it, then smoothly returned to his arms.

"So why the invitation to stroll?" she asked.

"A friendly intervention," he said softly. "I'll explain more on our walk."

Her eyes studied his, and then she finally glanced over his shoulder at the crowd around the perimeter of the floor. It only took a minute before her eyes abruptly returned to his, alarm alive in them. "They know," she whispered. She flubbed a step, but Will pressed his hand to her lower back, helping her back into the beat.

"They do," he said. He kept his expression neutral, as if they were merely continuing their conversation. "I guarantee you that you are not the only person here with questionable parentage."

"But I am the only one they're talking about."

"Smile. Keep that head high, Cora."

"I...I can't."

"You can."

They reached the end of the dance, but there was none of the pleasure in it that he'd enjoyed aboard the *Olympic*. Cora was distracted, clearly counting the moments until she could flee. But he held her arm in his. "Walk as if you're in no hurry," he whispered. "Return their glances with confidence, as if to say you know they know, but you don't care."

"I cannot," she said, staring at the handkerchief peeking from his breast pocket.

"You can," he said. "Begin with me. Look up at me. Return my smile. You can do it, Cora. Take a deep breath." He smiled at her, willing her to join him in the charade. So much of society was a charade, keeping up appearances. Regardless of what one felt within. He hated that part. But it was part of the game. And he was determined to see Cora through it.

Her gaze finally met his, and then she forced a smile. "You've come to my rescue again," she murmured.

They turned and began walking. "You may feel dreadfully alone, Cora," he whispered. "But you never are."

CHAPTER 17

~Cora~

"Thank you, Will," I managed. But the crowd seemed to close in on me, one solid swaying mass. One individual indecipherable from the next. "You've brought me far enough. I can make it on my own from here." I hated myself for it, but I abandoned him then; I dropped his arm, turned, and walked away, shoulders straight, head high. Ignoring him as he whispered my name like a groan, as if he felt a measure of my pain. Walking through the crowd as if I had someplace to go. But inside, I knew I was fleeing before I broke down in front of them, in front of Will.

I made my way through the palace, nodding to servants, determined to hold back my tears. Hurrying now that I was safely away from the crowds, half blinded by my welling eyes, I turned down one wrong hallway and had to go back. I slowed when I heard the bear's raised voice from a parlor.

I crept closer to the doorway. I could not see who else was inside, only robin's-egg blue walls and decorative white molding inside.

"Nevertheless, I see no recourse," said the duchess. "Kindly resume your journey in the morning. I will say you were eager to continue on with your travels."

I took a step back. She was tossing us out?

Horrified, I moved back to the main hall, found my corridor and hurried toward my room. But my eyes narrowed when I saw Anna and Jensen outside. They straightened as I neared, as if they had been waiting. I slowed but forced myself forward, each step feeling as though I were plowing through mud. Hurriedly, I wiped my face of tears, hoping my fragile state wouldn't be too obvious.

The maid blushed as she bobbed a quick curtsy. "Beggin' your pardon, miss. But we're to see you to another room for the night."

My frown deepened as my head swirled in confusion. "All...all right," I stammered. The tall, elegant butler ducked inside, grabbed hold of my biggest trunk, and waited for us in the hall. Anna did the same, opting for a smaller trunk. "Jensen will return for the rest of your things, miss," Anna said. "This way."

We walked to the end of the hall and through a large, decorative door that led to a set of stairs we took down. Behind this door was another hall, the walls a simple white, the doors plain. Servants' quarters. Cold washed through me. I alternately hated myself for my wounded pride—wouldn't I have once been honored to be even in this hall of the palace?—and burned with fury at the affront.

The maid didn't look at me as she set the trunk down. Numbly, I sat on the corner of the bed. It was a simple cot with clean bedding. A pillow. A blanket. There was a small window, and through it I glimpsed the very top of the conservatory. The conservatory where people were laughing and drinking and talking right now...probably about me. About the Kensingtons and the nouveaux riches and the audacity of them, thinking they could bring just anyone into these social circles…

The servants disappeared and reappeared a few minutes later with more of my clothing. "Is there anything you be needin', miss?" Anna asked. "I could help you find a nightdress and change—"

"No, no," I said, as kindly as I could. This wasn't her fault. *Whose fault? My mother's? My father's?* "I'll be all right, Anna. Thank you."

She paused at the door. "It's a cruel thing they've done, miss. Don't let it get to you…" She wrung her hands, her face earnest. "Just don't allow them to get to you, Miss Cora. Get a good night's sleep. We'll show them what you're made of."

With that, she disappeared, closing the door behind her. I wanted to give in to the grief that was heavy in my chest. But now my eyes were dry, as if the sadness were set aside in a locked trunk. Present but unreachable. *Shock,* I assessed distantly. Like I felt after Papa's stroke. Stunned. Unable to speak or even react.

Papa, Papa, I thought, my heart breaking at the sound of his name in my mind. *If only you hadn't taken ill. We'd be home, working together.*

He would've been cordial to Wallace Kensington. Soberly respectful. But there was no way he would've let him steal me away. Not that Wallace had really stolen me. I'd come of my own free will. But had I? No. I'd come out of love for Papa.

Lord, why? Why bring me all this way? For what? For this? For this? I studied the white plaster of the ceiling as if in it I could see my God. I wanted to shake my fist at Him in frustration. Why put me through this? Why not just leave me on the farm if He wanted me to suffer? I turned and lay down on the bed, my fingertips rubbing over the rough linens, so different from the lush accommodations upstairs but more like what I'd known at home. There, their touch would comfort me.

But now they only made me feel unclean, unworthy.

Less-than.

A quick rapping at my door awakened me.

I blinked several times, the memories of last night coming back to me. I didn't know when I fell asleep, or how long I'd slept—only that my headache had faded, leaving me with a thick, groggy sensation. I sat up and looked down at myself. I'd slept in my evening gown. I reached up and pulled the headpiece—now crumpled—off my head, knowing I was making my hair all the more a mess.

The knocking resumed. "Miss Kensington?" said a woman's voice.

"Coming," I muttered, forcing myself to my bare feet. At some point in the night, I must've kicked off my slippers, but I didn't remember doing so.

I opened the door and found Anna, with Will right behind her. His mouth fell open at my disheveled state. Abruptly, he closed his lips. "Cora, I had no idea you had been moved. I—I'm so sorry."

"It's all right. I obviously slept well enough." I seemed to be over the humiliation.

"But in your evening gown, miss!" said Anna, bustling in. "I'll see to her, Master Will. Go and tell the bear we'll join the family on the patio shortly."

He nodded and departed, anger and sorrow fighting for space in his eyes.

I turned to stare at my five trunks crammed into the room, but I had no idea where to find proper clothes, no matter what I'd said to Anna last night. What was on the agenda today? The British Museum, if I remembered right. Would that be before or after we moved into a hotel? I sank to the edge of the cot, feeling overwhelmed, lost.

"Hmm," said Anna, going directly to the smallest trunk. "I think I put your green suit in here. Don't you think that would be appropriate today?" There was barely room enough for her to move between the trunks and the bed.

I thought about the beautiful grass-green jacket that fell so elegantly down my torso, and the matching straight skirt and parasol. "Certainly," I said.

"Well, then, up with you, so we can get you ready for the day," she said, her tone firm, as if to wake me from my odd, foggy reverie.

I obediently stood and reached behind by back to undo my gown, suddenly anxious to be out of it, out of anything that reminded me of the night before. But I could not reach the hook and eye, nor more than a few of the buttons.

Anna sighed and came over to me, brushing aside my hands and unbuttoning it for me. She held it as I slipped out of the sleeves, and then she pulled it up over my head as if I were a child. Then she moved to a small stand and poured water from a pitcher into a bowl. There were no en suite bathrooms, nor was there running water in this portion of the old palace. "Get to it, then. See to your bath." She looked up at me, but I felt like she was looking down her nose at me. "Quit feeling sorry for yourself, miss. You must deal with your lot. This is not the end of the world." She gripped my shoulders and waited until I looked her in the eye.

I was standing there in my corset, in a servant's room, with a servant of my own behind me. Nothing made sense... Nothing had made sense in a long time.

"You might feel alone, miss, even forsaken. But you're not. The bear is livid, by the way. I've not seen him so angry in a good long while. And if not him, look to your Lord. He's seen it all. What you've been through and what's ahead. Trust in Him, girl. He'll see you through this."

Trust Him? Hadn't I trusted Him through the last weeks, through all the change? And for what? How much more humiliation was I to suffer?

I turned to the basin and dipped a cloth in, hurriedly wiping my face, my neck, and my body. Then I pulled out the remaining pins from my hair and brushed it out, thinking, growing angrier by the minute. "*God* watched the father I loved, laid out on a barn floor. *God* watched as Mr. Kensington came to collect me as if I were a prize horse he'd bought, the 'long-lost daughter.' *God* watched my siblings treat me with outright disdain. And last night, *God* saw me brought low. *This* is how the Lord cares for His people?" I turned to face her, invigorated by my fury.

Anna raised an eyebrow at me, her lips a grim line. She looked back up at me and lifted the hem of the green skirt so I could step in. Once it was on, she gently but firmly turned me around to button up the back, then urged me toward a stool. Her eyes met mine in the reflection of the mirror above the basin. "*God*," she said, her tone gently reproving, "brought Mr. Kensington to you, and with him, a world of potential. As I see it, each of our lives is a journey, Miss Cora. A path that takes us over the mountain or down through a dark valley. But He never abandons us. Never. *That* is how He cares for us—walking with us every step of the way."

I stared at her image in the mirror, thinking over her words. She seemed to catch herself, regret in her eyes. "Beggin' your pardon, miss," she said, with a tiny curtsy.

"No," I said, with a wave of my hand. "Please." I rubbed my face, feeling a tinge of shame. "I'm not myself today." *Not myself.* I hadn't felt myself for weeks. Not since I left home…

She took the brush from the counter and gave my hair a few more strokes, then expertly wound it up in a sweeping style. "Put some blush on those cheeks. You will not go down to that patio and face them with anything but confidence. Your mother may have been little more than a maid like me, but your father is a man of great influence. And your God? Well, He is enough, Miss Cora. Enough." She laid a light hand on my shoulder. "Shall I wait for you outside the door and see you down to the patio?"

"Thank you, Anna," I muttered. "I'll get myself there in a moment."

She gave a quick bob, turned, and left, quietly closing the door behind her as if she were suddenly a subservient sort of person, rather than the outspoken, brash woman she had just shown herself to be. I closed my eyes and held my head in my hands, thinking about her words.

She was right, of course. Much as I disliked admitting it.

I straightened to powder my face, then unscrewed the lid of a beet-juice jar and hurriedly rubbed some color onto my cheeks. I studied my reflection in the mirror.

Here, I wasn't the daughter of Alan and Alma Diehl, simple folk but upstanding citizens, the friends of every one of their neighbors. Here I was despised, open to the world's ridicule, the illegitimate child of a copper king who was one of the wealthiest men of the world.

I had been claimed, not left to subsist on a dirt-poor farm in Montana. It was not a fair deal, but it was a deal. There was still much to gain from walking this road. It wasn't easy, but at least there was a road forward, upward, outward.

And my papa, my mama…they'd want me to take it. To put one foot in front of the other. To see where it led.

CHAPTER 18

~William~

He'd never been so proud of one of his clients as he was of Cora that morning. She'd emerged from her room and joined them for breakfast on the patio as if she belonged nowhere else.

It took true inner strength to conduct herself so, especially after what she'd faced the night before.

The duke and duchess had excused themselves from joining the group, citing a "previous engagement," but before they'd known the truth of Cora's parentage, there had been no plans other than to spend the day with their guests. It was fine by Will. This way, their group could speak of the subject at hand and be done with it.

Cora sat between Hugh and Andrew Morgan, facing her siblings. A servant poured her some tea and placed a scone on her plate. Hugh passed her a heaping bowl of clotted cream, his eyes lingering on her with fascination. Will shifted uncomfortably. There was no way that Hugh Morgan was the right man for Cora.

The girls ignored her. Perhaps they didn't know what to say. Uncle Stuart had had a firm word with Vivian that morning, telling her that what had happened here last night could not happen again. If it did, the Kensingtons and Morgans would part ways for the duration of the tour. They had to pull this out by the root, or it would continue to spread like a weed, growing into ever-new areas, destroying opportunity after opportunity. Vivian had been horrified at the thought of not being with the Morgans. They all knew she was looking forward to a romantic proposal somewhere along the way, despite Andrew's efforts to keep his intentions a secret.

Uncle Stuart cleared his throat. "We shall be moving to a hotel for the next few days, so after breakfast, please return to your rooms and see that the servants gather your things. While we enjoyed the duke and duchess's hospitality last night, it's been made clear that we would be better served moving to other quarters until we embark on our voyage to France."

Cora's blue eyes flashed toward Will as she finished her breakfast. She was clearly worried, even if she was covering it well. Was this just the beginning of their trials? He popped the last bit of his scone into his mouth and excused himself, following Cora as she rose to leave.

She walked only to the corner of the patio. Her long, strong-but-graceful fingers gripped the marble balustrade as if for strength.

"You should send me home," she said as soon as he neared her. She didn't look his way, only stared out.

He stood beside her, looking out onto the grand lawn, the conservatory, the gardens—more a forest—that stretched for acres. "Your father wished you to stay. It's for the best."

"Even after last night," she said, more as a statement of confirmation than a question.

"Even after last night," he confirmed.

"You...you're moving us to another location today. Resolving our immediate issue. But this will happen again."

"I doubt it. It might challenge us here and there, and when it does, we shall intercede again. We lack no resource, Cora. Your father and Mr. Morgan have given us a healthy account to fund the trip. Even if we must stay in hotels and cottages and villas that we rent, all the way."

She sighed and looked out again. "My father's asked a great deal of me."

"He has."

"I don't think I'm up to the task."

"Does it matter that I disagree?"

Her silence told him what he needed to know.

"I will destroy the Kensingtons' and Morgans' chances among respected society," she said. "Make them pariahs as well as myself."

"You *are* a Kensington," he said. "Your presence will help them discover *who* is truly worthy of respect, as well as a measure of self-respect." He paused and looked at her, reaching inside his jacket pocket. "Cora."

Slowly, she met his gaze.

"Your father—Mr. Kensington—asked me to give this to you. When the moment was right." He slid an envelope out of his pocket. Running his thumb over the smooth vellum, he offered it to her. "He foresaw this moment."

She stared at the envelope as if afraid to take it. After a moment of hesitation, she finally did so, but slowly.

Will gave her a smile of encouragement and then left her alone to read it.

—◇◇—

~Cora~

I took a deep breath and then slid my finger under the red wax, breaking the seal stamp, cracking the regal *K*. I pulled out the single sheet and unfolded it, staring out at the woods, wondering if I had the courage to read what Mr. Kensington had written. To find out what he had to say, when he apparently couldn't say it to my face. But curiosity won out.

My dear Cora,

So you've reached a juncture in which your parentage has come to light and the road now seems impossible. I assure you that any obstacle can be overcome, given time. They are momentary challenges, nothing more. I ask that you find your way forward, Daughter, not for me, but for you.

Your heritage is what it is, Cora. I urge you to make the most of it rather than let it hinder your progress. Let the challenge of the hills refine you as you climb them. The question isn't how society defines you, nor how I define you, but rather how God defines you, and in turn, how you yourself want to be defined.

When this summer is over, when you are free to go your own way, who will Cora Kensington be? Claim the name, or leave it behind. All I care is that you take what you deserve out of this life. Take the resources I've laid at your feet, and make the most of them.

I stared out to the trees again, thinking over his words, surprised by them as well as challenged. I imagined him here, stubbornly meeting my gaze, daring me to defy him. *Blue eyes so like mine...*

I pray you will understand me one day, Cora, at least in some measure. I'm a sinner, through and through. And as you've experienced, the repercussions of those sins haunt me and those I love every day. But I've made my peace with my family and my Maker. I suggest you do too.

Best,

Wallace Kensington

CHAPTER 19

~Cora~

I trailed the rest of the group the next day, still pondering my father's words as we toured the Parliament building, the Palace of Westminster. It was all well and good that Mr. Kensington could take the stand as a sinner who'd made peace with God, but he had left me to roil in the repercussions of that sin on my own.

I envied the ease my siblings had in their own skins. I missed that in myself. I'd always thought of myself as poised, secure. What had happened to that? I stood at a large window, looking out at the Thames. It was as if I had once been a riverbank, standing strong, but my confidence had eroded with repeated flooding—the battle to scrape by and bring in another harvest, my papa's illness, and finally, the Kensington wave. Wallace Kensington befuddled me. Just when I felt I had deciphered who he was and what he was about, he turned it upside down.

"Are you all right?" Felix said, standing beside me.

I jumped, having not noticed my brother was there until he'd spoken. I glanced down the hall. About a hundred yards away, the group was gathered before a portrait, and the bear was waxing on about it.

"I care very little for art," Felix whispered. "Bring on the parties and dances, the strolls among the gardens, the boat rides. Portraits of dead politicians? I'd rather stab myself repeatedly with a fork." He turned his back to the group and made a stabbing motion. I giggled, covering my mouth with my hand and ducking my head so the others wouldn't see.

"I'd rather see more mummies in the British Museum, myself," I said. I was desperate to keep him by my side, to feel like I had a friend. Few in the group had spoken a word to me since we left the duke and duchess's palace the day before. Felix gestured forward, and I stepped into pace with him.

"Sorry it's been a rough start for you, Cora," he said. "Our family's all right, once you find your footing with them."

My eyes moved toward Vivian. "I'm not sure I'll find it with all of them. Before we reached England, I'd hoped… But it seems more distant than ever."

"You will," he reassured. "In time. Keep in mind that it's almost as monumental for us as it was for you to learn of our family bonds."

I considered that. From the start, all I'd felt from Vivian was resentment. But if I were in her place, what would I be feeling? She had been so little when our father had fraternized with my mother. Yes, it was a union between two adults. But as a daughter, there had to be a part of her that wondered why she wasn't enough to keep his heart at home. Why he couldn't remain faithful to her as well as to her mother.

My eyes moved to Vivian, her hand resting in the crook of Andrew's elbow. She was pretty enough. Light-brown hair, hazel eyes, pert nose, rosebud lips. But take her out of her fine gowns, and she was far from glamorous. It was her demeanor lifted chin, shoulders back—that made her seem refined, taller than I, even though we were about the same height.

I realized I'd stopped walking, and Felix stopped with me. He followed my gaze. The group was moving on. He offered his arm, and I hesitantly took it. "You've wounded her pride," he said. "Besmirched the family name. Not that we haven't seen that happen before."

I glanced up at him in surprise. "Before?"

"Ah, yes. You can't be a child of a copper king and not hear some foul things about your father over the years. But always before it was about distant subjects—his business practices or his political ambitions."

He caught my confused look. "Greasing the palms of so-and-so and the like," he said. "Buying what he could not attain through traditional routes."

"Ahh," I said. Felix was referring to the stories of a purchased senate seat, competitors driven away from Butte, and the like. Up until a few weeks ago, they were only stories of people living far different lives in a far different place. Irrelevant to my life on the farm. Now I wished I'd studied them, knew every detail.

"We're a rather tight group, the Morgans and Kensingtons, because our fathers are so tight," he said. "Together, they built an empire. And in the shadow of their legacy, we share the same triumphs, the same threats."

I ruminated over his words. In the shadow of their legacy. Did Felix feel incapacitated, incapable of ever competing with his father's accomplishments, so therefore unmotivated to move at all? I glanced at him. He was hardly ready to delve into such personal matters as that with me. He was speaking off the cuff, without really thinking about it. Trying to draw me in, make me feel included. But something else in his words bothered me. "What do you mean by *threats*?" I asked.

The group ahead of us was poised around a Greek statue of a man, the younger girls tittering over his naked form.

Felix looked chagrined. "Forgive me. I've alarmed you."

"No. I am merely curious. Of what do you speak?"

He gave me a rather quizzical look. "Do you really believe that our group of seven needs three guides?"

I looked toward the bear, Will, and Antonio. "Well, no. But Will is apprenticing, is he not? And Antonio, is he not the expert on Italy?"

"Indeed," he said, giving me a conspiratorial grin. "But with us being abroad, neither my father nor Mr. Morgan were willing to take any chances."

I thought back to that first night in Butte, and how Will followed me, protected me. How he always seemed to be nearby. If he was always watching like that…it suddenly felt cloying rather than reassuring. Back home, I'd gone for long walks among the fields, climbing the sprawling hill in the back of our property and resting beneath a giant oak, where I could see for miles. Often, I was the only person within sight, and I'd liked that. In that place, I could breathe deeply. Rest. How long had it been since I'd experienced such a feeling? "Do *you* fear we might be harmed, Felix?"

"Me?" he said, raising dark eyebrows in surprise. "No. But with four women along, it's wise to take caution."

We rejoined the group, and when Vivian looked at us, I gently dropped my hand from Felix's arm. If she and I were to find our way, I'd need to make it as easy as possible. And for the first time, I again had hope that it just might be possible. Making a bit of an effort to stand in her shoes, in Felix's, in Lillian's, had granted me empathy, which in turn had torn down some of the wall between us. *Thank You, Lord*, I prayed silently. *Might You help them tear down some of that wall too?*

Vivian gave me such a hard look then that I almost laughed aloud. It was as if she had heard my silent prayer and was disgusted.

The bear led us to the massive doors of Westminster Hall, and we peered inside. Our guide nodded at Will.

"When it was built in 1097," Will said, "it was the largest hall in all of Europe. Originally, the roof was probably supported by pillars, but during the reign of Richard II, it was replaced with the hammer-beam form you see now, allowing the three aisles to become one massive space, with a dais at the end. Still today, it is the grandest example of medieval clear-span roof structure in Europe. In 1824—"

"In 1834," his uncle corrected.

"In 1834," Will said smoothly, with a nod of deference toward him, "a fire broke out, which destroyed both houses of Parliament, as well as most of the major buildings in the complex. Thanks to a change in the direction of the wind and heroic firefighting, Westminster Hall was spared."

"As were the cloisters, the Jewel Tower, and the Chapel of St. Mary Undercroft," the bear added.

"King William tried to get them to take Buckingham Palace—a residence he did not care for—but tradition led them to rebuild."

The bear nodded in satisfaction, and he gestured for the group to follow him. We stopped next in the Central Lobby, right beneath the great chandelier, and the older man said, "Here we are in what has been called the political center of all of Britain. From here, when the doors open, you can see the royal throne and the speaker's chair. Through this hall, every principal politician and monarch travels."

I stared up to the roof, with its venetian glass displaying emblems and heraldry. I wondered what our family crest would be. A young crow, learning to soar like an eagle? An owl, hunting at night as others slept? The heraldic crests seemed to speak of older, established families—with sedate, languid lions and medieval armory. It was little wonder that the clans with bloodlines that ran back hundreds of years felt they had greater presence than the newcomers. And a group of Americans? We were little more than a novelty to them, I was certain. Something to gossip about. And I was the center of that.

We moved down a hall and learned that the complex had over a thousand rooms. The younger girls were whispering over the queen's robing room, wishing they had a chance to slip on the ermine-collared ruby-red robe, "just for a moment," Lillian mused. It was then that I noticed we were missing a couple in our group. I turned to look for Andrew and Vivian. Had they not realized we'd moved on?

A pang of fear shot through me as I thought about Felix's words. What would happen if the eldest from each of our families was captured? What would kidnappers do to them? I turned and took several steps back, looking into one alcove after another.

It was then I spied them. Standing just to one side of a doorway in a lovely sitting room. Andrew's arm was around her waist. I could see the shoulder and back of her beautiful rust-colored gown, and I knew they were sharing a moment of intimacy. I was turning to escape, feeling foolish, when Vivian straightened and looked my way, as if sensing they were not alone. Our eyes met, and quick fury entered hers.

"Can we not slip away for but a moment without you following us?" she said.

"I...I only...never mind." I turned to hurry away, heat rushing through my face and down my neck.

Will's eyes narrowed as I neared, and Felix covered a laugh, obviously recognizing what had just gone on. I tried to concentrate on what the bear was saying, to get my mind off of what I'd done.

But all I could think about was the ever-widening gulf between Vivian and me. Why should I attempt to befriend a woman who so clearly despised me?

And yet she was the key. If I could find a way, a way to bridge the gap, the others would be far more accessible too. *Any obstacle can be overcome*, Mr. Kensington had said.

But had he been thinking of Vivian when he wrote that?

CHAPTER 20

-William-

With the group weary of history, art, politics, and religion, Will's uncle wisely prescribed an afternoon in the countryside, hiring mounts at a stable and taking the rest of the day in a beautiful park. But then, complaining of his rheumatism, Uncle Stuart had left the picnic and ride in "Will's capable hands." Will groaned when he found out, but their young clients had donned riding costumes and assembled in order. A groomsman led the way down a pebble path, while Will and Antonio brought up the rear of their group. All appeared to be in order. *Exquisite order,* Will thought, chastising himself for allowing his eyes to wander over the slim legs and curves of the young women ahead of them, particularly Cora's.

It didn't help that Antonio nudged him and gestured with his chin at what Will had already noticed. Righteous indignation ran through him, with a quick shot of shame following close behind. "Mind your manners, man," he growled, saying to Antonio what he was telling himself. Antonio's black eyes widened in surprise at his gruff answer, and then his face eased into a knowing smile.

Perhaps women were best served to always be in gowns, Will thought. Bathing suits and jodhpurs only led a man's mind to wander.

They reached the stables and entered the building where the mounts were saddled and ready. With relief, Will and Antonio set down the heavy baskets carrying a picnic the maids at the cottage had packed for them.

Will watched the stable hands help the women mount, feeling tension waft through him, especially as a man placed Cora's boot in a stirrup, his hand lingering on her calf. She was paying no attention, however, her eyes going to Vivian again and again. He knew they had had some sort of exchange the day before in the Parliament building. He didn't know what it was about—only that, ever since, Cora had stayed on the opposite side of the group from Vivian.

He gazed around. The stables advertised that they only had the finest mounts for hire, which was what drew his attention yesterday when he'd been organizing the expedition. But that meant the horses were high-spirited, and three were struggling for control—Vivian's, Cora's, and Hugh's.

He neared Vivian. "Perhaps we can ask them for a more genteel mount."

She lifted her nose in the air. "Please, William, tell me you're joking. I've been riding since I was old enough to walk."

He suppressed a sigh and turned toward Cora as her mare pranced sideways. "Cora? Would you like a different mount?"

"No. She'll settle down," Cora said, stroking the mare's neck and looking again in Vivian's direction. Was pride holding her back too?

He looked toward Hugh, but the man was already trotting off beside Felix, his back to him. Will knew he wouldn't appreciate the question.

Antonio, an expert horseman, pulled up beside him as Will mounted. "Want me to watch the young women while you attend Hugh?"

Will scowled at him. "You attend Hugh. *I'll* watch over the women."

Antonio laughed and gave him a shrug. "*Bocca al lupo.*" *Best of luck.* He rode up to Hugh and Felix, and the younger girls joined them.

"If we get separated, we'll meet at the hill beside the covered bridge," Will called after him.

Antonio laughed again and nodded toward Vivian's horse, which was taking off in fits and starts. She wheeled around in a sudden circle, frowning.

"*If?*"

Will smiled with Antonio then. "All right, *when.*" Vivian was watching Cora take her mare in a tight circle. Vivian dug her heels into her own mount's flanks, edging nearer Cora.

Even from fifty feet away, he could hear the young woman ask, "Did you ever have a proper lesson?"

Cora's eyes were steady as she looked at her half sister. "My *father* taught me. Did yours?"

"Of course not," Vivian huffed. "We had a proper riding instructor."

Will nudged his horse toward the women, knowing he needed to stop their competition, and fast.

"Let's head out," Will called.

Antonio moved toward a trail, all but Cora and Vivian behind him.

"Where are we going, Will?" Cora asked.

"To the old covered bridge."

"How far is it?"

"A couple of miles," he said. "But we'll be—"

"How do you get there?" Vivian interrupted, looking from Cora to him.

"I will show you the way." Where was Andrew? Ahead with the others?

"That's just it," Vivian said, her face flushed with excitement. "We don't wish you to lead. My *sister* is challenging me to a race."

Cora's eyes moved from Vivian to him. She didn't deny it.

"Now see here," Will said. "You are on unfamiliar mounts. It would be most unwise—"

The women turned from him as a pair of gentlemen moved in from the opposite direction.

"Pardon me, sirs," Cora called. "Can you kindly point us in the direction of the old covered bridge?"

"Certainly," one of the men returned with a touch to the brim of his hat. He paused to look Cora and Vivian over in appreciation. "It's over that ridge right there," he said, pointing up and to the left.

Will groaned as Cora caught Vivian's eye, smiled, and then kicked her horse into a full gallop. Vivian was right behind her.

"No, no!" he cried. But they ignored him, already racing up a wide, grassy hill. The gentlemen hooted and cheered them on. If he'd had time, Will would've taken pleasure in pummeling his fist into each man's face for his foolishness, but he was too busy pursuing the young women.

He pounded up the hill after them, already chagrined at the distance they had gained. His heart was in his throat as Vivian's mare jumped a log, but the woman seemed to gain confidence as her mount came down on the other side and found its pace again. Cora went wide, disappearing behind a stand of oak trees, then reappearing slightly ahead of Vivian.

They crested the ridge, out of sight again. Will lowered his head and urged his mount to go faster. He had to catch up to them, somehow rein them in. He had to. If any harm came to either of them, Mr. Kensington and his uncle would have his hide.

CHAPTER 21

~Cora~

I didn't know what had gotten into me. Only that there was no way I would allow Vivian to beat me. I'd reach the old covered bridge first if I had to jump over Vivian's mare to get there.

I knew it was foolish to push my mount so on unfamiliar roads, but I felt exhilarated in the challenge, the release of letting go all my pent-up emotions and frustrations and pouring them into the moment. And if I could beat her, arrive there first, perhaps she'd begin to treat me with a modicum of respect. Perhaps we would be able to find our footing at last and the summer wouldn't stretch before me as one long, exhausting challenge.

She was behind me, but then she cut off at a *Y* in the road. I frowned. Where was she going? Was it a shortcut? My eyes scanned the road below, and I glimpsed not only the bridge but a place where her path would likely rejoin mine. Movement caught my attention to my left, and with chagrin I saw Will closing in, determination etched into every bit of his handsome face. He'd stop me if he could.

It was his job to stop us. But for the first time on this whole journey, I knew that I was fully in charge of my own actions.

I leaned lower in the saddle, my horse's mane tickling my nose, and after a few moments, it was almost as if I could hear nothing but my own breathing, the squeaking of the leather, the heavy hoofbeats striking dirt and rock.

I glimpsed Vivian's purple coat through the trees. She would soon rejoin my road. I had to be ahead of her. Sure enough, she came alongside me, just a half pace behind.

"Cora! Vivian!" Will shouted. "Stop this! Now!"

I looked back at Vivian, wondering if she was ready to give in, give up, grant me victory. But she kept her eyes on the road, still determined to overtake me. And her determination fed my own. I squeezed my horse's flanks with my heels and held on, trying to match her pace with my movements, make it easier for my mount to carry me.

Papa had taught me to ride, and ride fast. He was no proper equestrian, but I'd show Vivian that didn't matter. That I could compete, win, regardless of where I'd been trained. I remembered the first time I could truly race Papa with the hope of beating him, and the surprise and delight on his face. His look of frustration. And then pride. *Oh, Papa,* I thought. *How I miss you.*

Vivian was surging ahead of me as I emerged from my reverie. Frowning, I renewed my efforts, but then her horse pulled up, apparently spooked by a darkly shadowed stand of trees we were passing. She whipped her mount to the other side of me, concentrating on coming up that way. She was quick; I'd grant her that. And I had to admire her spunk.

The forest began to gather on either side of the road, closing in, and I hoped it would give Vivian's mount pause. We raced into the shadows, and I welcomed the cooler air after sweating under the hot sun. But it was harder to see. Reluctantly, I pulled up slightly on the reins. Vivian quickly took the lead. We rounded a corner, her horse going wide, edging into some bramble and slowing, letting me ahead again.

I saw that the forest was clearing, and the path glowed like a trophy before me. But a huge log lay in our way as we left the trees. Vivian cast me a sly smile, obviously confident in her mare's ability to leap over it as she'd done before. I frowned. I'd jumped small creeks and stones, but never anything as large as the log. Still, nothing could make me give up. Nothing.

We were shoulder to shoulder, each concentrating on the log ahead, when our horses slowed, so neatly timed it was as if they were yoked together. I felt the forward momentum, desperately tried to hold on with my legs, but the force was too much. As the horse came to a lurching stop, I went flying over her head, grasping hold of the reins and her mane as if that would somehow correct what I knew in my gut was destined to end poorly.

I held my breath as I fell, waiting for impact, but instead landed in a pool of water, somersaulting so far that I skidded across the surface on my belly before sinking. I flailed around, trying to get my head up and gather a breath of air, gasping. It took a moment for me to realize Vivian was in the water with me, crying out, her brown hair covering her face in a soggy mat. I reached out and pulled her closer, since I was nearer the far bank, able to touch, but she whipped her arm away.

"Vivian," I gasped. "Over here. You can touch here."

She let out a sound of such exasperation and rage, I took a step back, suddenly wanting her anywhere but near me. She sounded cat-like, ready to lash out.

But she relented and swam toward me until we could stand chest deep. We looked up as Will arrived, his face sweating and ashen.

"We're all right," I said, raising a hand to him, still gasping for breath. "Wet, but fine."

"Speak for yourself," Vivian spat, pushing her hair aside. She trudged past me in the water. "Honestly, Cora. I can't believe I allowed you to suck me into such a mad race."

"Ah, of course," I said. "It's my fault."

"Of course." She tossed over her shoulder. "It certainly was not mine."

I giggled then. "Oh, no. Certainly not. I dragged you into that race. It was almost as if I had your mare tethered to mine."

She paused and looked at me. "You should have given up much sooner. Anyone could see I was the more experienced equestrian."

"No. You should have, but your pride wouldn't allow it. Not when it was I—a girl who learned how to ride on a swaybacked old nag—who was in the lead."

"That was not it at all."

"I think it was." I trudged up the bank, faltering when I felt the soggy ground give way. I slipped and fell to my knees.

Vivian looked back at me with glee in her eyes but then imme-diately slipped in the mud herself, landing back in the water with a big splash.

I moved ahead, determined now to beat her up the bank, if noth-ing else. But the edge was steep and hopelessly slippery. It seemed to be more oil than mud. My hands sunk into the muck just below the surface. I wrenched a stuck boot from where the bottom sucked at me and felt my other boot begin to sink too. I tried to step forward but stumbled, landing back in the muddy water. It splashed over and onto Vivian, who cried out.

I looked her way and laughed. Her face and purple coat were layered with grime, as were mine. She looked back at me with outrage, but then she paused. A smile split her face too as she laughed. It made me laugh harder, hearing her, and together we dissolved into giggles, our merriment so fierce we began to slip down the bank again.

"Cora," Will said, somehow now on our side of the pool, reaching for me.

Still giggling, I tried to wash off my hand in the dark water, then reached for his, grabbing hold of his wrist as he did mine. With one powerful move, he hauled me up the bank and deposited me on the long green grasses. Then he did the same with Vivian. Together, we sat and panted for breath as Will hovered over us, pacing, hands on hips, seething in anger.

"You two…," he said, finding his voice, shaking his finger at us, "could've been killed."

"But we weren't," Vivian said, shaking her head.

"You've dishonored me as a guide and ruined our afternoon plans."

"Oh, Will," I muttered, "this was hardly about you."

Vivian caught my gaze, and after a hesitation, she gave me a small smile. She looked down at herself, hands splayed, and shook her head. "My goodness. We're quite a mess."

"Quite," I said, looking down at my elegant riding suit. It would never be the same. I'd never worn anything near as fine for an afternoon ride, and I'd gone and ruined it, all on account of my pride. But I couldn't help but think that it had been worth it. Sitting there, listening to Will lecture us on the dangers of racing—of knowing people who had been paralyzed from such falls as we had just taken—I felt the first bit of camaraderie, connection, with my half sister that I'd experienced in a while. And in that connection, I felt a smidgen of hope.

That hope faded as soon as we came into view of the others. They were gathered in a group, sitting about on blankets; Hugh and Antonio were stretched out as if sleeping in the sun. When they heard us, all heads turned in our direction. Andrew stood up, plainly alarmed, and went to Vivian to hold her horse still as she dismounted. Hugh and Felix laughed outright. The younger girls covered their mouths, giggling.

"What in heaven's name," Hugh asked, still chuckling, "happened to you?"

"Cora drew me into an ill-conceived race," Vivian said, taking a damp cloth napkin from Lillian and wiping her face. "Our horses stopped, and we kept going, straight into a filthy water hole."

I suppressed a sigh, biting my lip.

"Needless to say," she said, "we must head back at once to change."

Will hovered near, a brooding guardian. He spoke at last. "It takes two to race, Vivian."

"Indeed," Andrew said, handing her a second wet napkin.

She pulled it from his hand angrily, clearly frustrated that he wasn't taking her side in the matter.

No one thought to offer me assistance. I didn't know why I cared that they seemed to not see me. Why I tried.

"So if you all will quickly finish your picnic, we'll be off," Will said. "We need to get these two into dry clothes again before they catch a chill."

I couldn't imagine how I'd catch a chill—it was a hot and humid afternoon, and while my riding clothes felt cloyingly sticky, at least they were cooler, wet.

Felix was goading Vivian to tell the story, and when she wouldn't, he turned to me.

I smiled at his glee and regaled them on how it had transpired. The girls giggled, and the boys hooted with laughter. All except for Andrew. He knew his place with Vivian and remained nothing but the attentive and concerned beau. But again, I felt the tiniest shift within the group, an inch of compassion, connection. And I drew encouragement from it.

When we returned to the cottage, I thought I'd never been wearier. Even compared to days I'd helped Papa with plowing or irrigating or seeding. Perhaps it had been the ride—and the subsequent fall—but every muscle in my back ached. So I sent my regrets via Anna that I wouldn't be attending the last dinner out and would instead remain home to rest.

I'd stepped out of the tub and slipped on a robe when I heard a tentative knock on the door. Thinking everyone would be gone by now, I glanced at the clock and then tiptoed over to the door. "Yes?"

"It's me, Cora," said a low male voice. Will.

I opened it a few inches. "I…I thought you all had left."

"We're about to go. Are you certain you do not wish to join us?" Concern weighed heavily around his eyes.

"I am." I took a deep breath. "I just need some time to myself before we resume our journey. The others will be relieved to be free of my presence too."

"You must not dodge them for the rest of the tour."

"I'm not dodging."

"Well, good then. Might you share a cup of tea with me when we return? I'd like to talk to you."

"Perhaps," I hedged. What did he want to say to me? What else was there to say?

"I'll knock softly," he said. "If you are asleep, slumber on. But if you are awake, I'd appreciate a word."

I forced a small smile to my face. "I'll come to the door if I'm awake."

"Good." He straightened and gave me a smile. Then he turned and walked away. I slowly shut the door and walked to the window, watching as several touring cars idled. One car door remained open, presumably for Will. He emerged from the cottage, climbed in, and the group departed.

No one looked my way. No one waved. Not that I'd really expected it. I'd wanted to remain behind. But when I got what I wanted, I found it…surprisingly empty.

PART III:
THE
CONTINENT

CHAPTER 22

~Cora~

I didn't know if Will knocked on my door and I slept through it, or if he never knocked at all. Only that the next morning, it was Anna's knock that made me sit upright, blinking rapidly, trying to make sense of my surroundings. I was still fully dressed, having decided that I'd hear whatever Will had to say. But I'd obviously fallen asleep.

Anna set down a tray of scones and a small teapot, then looked me over, hands on her hips. Consternation and suspicion flashed through her eyes. "So, miss. Is that what you'll be wearing, then, or would you like a fresh suit?"

I rose and ignored her judgmental look. "A fresh blouse, Anna. That'd be lovely." I pulled off my jacket and the rumpled blouse beneath and took the new one she offered, slipping it on and buttoning it up while she swiftly saw to my hair. Afterward, she wordlessly offered me a summer cape, balling up the rumpled jacket I'd worn all night. I accepted it, buttoning the huge crystal clasp at my neck.

"Did you ever get the opportunity," I asked, "to see your aunt?"

"No, miss," she said, refusing to look me in the eye. She conjured up a smile. "She was away, then..." She shook her head. "Perhaps next time through."

I'd messed up her plans, getting us tossed out of Syon. All the moving and resettling had obviously made it impossible. "I'm sorry, Anna."

"Oh! Never you mind, miss. My auntie will still be here next summer."

"You're certain?" I asked, waiting until she met my gaze.

Her face softened and she nodded. "Yes, yes. Now off with you, then. You look respectable again."

Within minutes, we were finished and out in the cars that would take us to the train station. To France.

That was something I'd never ever thought I'd be able to say.

We traveled for several hours on the train to Dover, then boarded a small sailing vessel for the crossing of the Channel.

I'd been assigned a cabin with Vivian, but I consoled myself with the news that it would only be for one night. We'd make our crossing by evening, settle into the harbor, and make our way up the Seine River tomorrow. As we drew away from England, I could see the towering white, chalky cliffs of Dover disappearing into a steel-blue sea. The weather was beautiful, if somewhat chilly, now that we were out on the water. Men dressed in crisp white pants and striped shirts trimmed sails and adjusted ropes all around us.

Holding my hat so that the wind wouldn't steal it from me, I watched them climb to dizzying heights and balance across beams to do their work high above. It was far different from the sprawling steamship that had carried us to England from America. This smaller vessel felt more visceral, as if we were a part of the sea rather than simply traveling upon it.

Will joined me and looked up to see what had caught my attention. "It takes a crew of thirty to man her."

"I can't imagine being up there, and in such waves!" I said. "They are like monkeys."

He smiled. "They've known it all their lives. Think of something that you did on the farm, before joining the Kensingtons, that they cannot imagine."

I laughed. "Mucking stalls. Milking cows. Butchering chickens."

His face broke out in a huge grin, and I thought again that he was quite handsome in a warm sort of way. His was a quiet sort of masculinity, ever present but arising in turns so suddenly that it surprised me.

"Will," I dared, "what was it that you wanted to say to me last night? Over tea?"

"Ah," he said, looking down at his feet. "I thought better of that. Forgive me for not knocking. Did you stay up waiting?"

I considered him, wondering what the secret was. "It's all right. And no, I went right to sleep."

"Good, good," he said, clearly wanting to move on.

I decided to let him be. He'd tell me when he wished. "Have you been aboard a great many ships, Will?"

"A fair number. But my favorites are those like these, sailing under nothing but the wind's power. Unfortunately, they're hard to come by. Steam is taking over the seas. Uncle likes his groups to travel this way so that we can observe the sailors work while we can."

"I suppose steam is a bit more reliable."

"Indeed. But in the Channel, they're hardly ever without wind, so it's a good bet to run a vessel like this here."

"I think I could watch them work for hours. Watch them capture the wind, harness it. It's an art, really."

"Well said. However, if you stay out here much longer, you'll continue to distract them from their work." He gestured toward a lanyard high above us where two sailors, seeing they'd been spotted spying on us, hurried to resume their work. "Come, Cora," Will said, merriment in his tone. "I'm about to give the group a lesson on wind dynamics and the history of the English Channel."

He offered me his arm, and as I took it, a shiver of excitement ran down my back. I loved the feeling of strength in his muscles beneath the smooth silk, and I couldn't resist glancing up at him again.

He smiled back at me, and I quickly looked ahead. I was in no place to take a suitor. And a romance with one of our guides was forbidden. Wasn't it? At least, that was what the younger girls spent a great deal of time chattering about, along with whispers of Will's handsome face, the strength of his shoulders, the kindness in his eyes...

I slowed, and he gave me a quizzical look. "Cora?"

"Oh, sorry," I said, picking up my pace.

By the time we reached the door, the sails were taut with wind, the waves tossing us back and forth. I clung to Will's arm, and he reached out to open the door for me.

The bow of the ship rose at that moment, and just as I stepped to move through the door, the boat tilted downward again, sending me swinging around, midstep.

Right against Will's chest.

"Whoa!" he said with a laugh, letting go of the door and putting his big hands on my shoulders. I could feel the warmth of them through my thin summer cape. "We're hitting high seas now."

"Truly," I said, embarrassed, trying to step away from him.

The ship swung upward again, and he took a lurching step toward me, catching himself with both arms to the wall beyond the door, with me between them. Worse, my hands now rested against either side of his waist.

He paused, looking down at me, but an inch away from my face, and the flash of heat I saw in his eyes made me lose my breath altogether. I stared back at him, trying to confirm what I thought I'd seen.

Passion. Hope. Desire.

But he'd already shoved off and was moving away. "Quickly now, Cora," he said politely, "or we're liable to fall overboard."

In more ways than one, I thought, slipping inside.

CHAPTER 23

-*William*-

Will groaned as he struggled to wake. Between the rough seas and thoughts of Cora, so close, so open, he'd barely slept. He rubbed his face. "Help me, Lord," he muttered. "Take away these wild imaginings of the heart."

He'd wanted to kiss her, God help him. Bend and claim those lush lips. Pull her close. Give in to the tidal force he felt within him, drawing her in. Was she attracted to him? He only knew that over the last two years, these tours had been full of insipid, superficial, mindless females. Cora Kensington was the first woman of substance, depth, that he'd met in a long, long while.

He glanced over at his uncle's empty bunk. The old man rose before the sun and usually retired with it. So, often, watching over their clients in the evening fell to Will. "It's a young man's sport," his uncle would say. But Uncle would not bless any pursuit of Cora, and Mr. Kensington—Will doubted he'd ever bless Will's courtship of his daughter, whether during or after the tour. Will had not finished his education, nor had he anything more than partial employment and a flat in his uncle's attic. Hardly enough to offer a bride.

Will rammed the palm of his hand against his forehead. "Stupid, stupid," he berated himself. How could he have let it happen? His guard had been as far down as hers had been. Yet she was still roiling in the tornado created by the Kensingtons and Morgans, trying to find her place. All she needed from him was friendship. Protection. Leadership. Encouragement. Nothing more.

"No confessions of some sort of heartsickness," he reminded himself in a growl. He'd stood outside her door their last night in England, about to knock, but could see how it would transpire. He'd wanted to confess that seeing her thrown from the saddle made his heart stop. That watching her wade into social situations far beyond her experience, with nothing but grace and poise, left him in awe. That witnessing others be less than kind to her made him long to defend her. But in the end, he couldn't see it through. It would've left them with nothing short of disaster and, quite possibly, with him on the next steamship home.

And now this. All he could see in his mind were her lips. That open invitation in her eyes, the innocent surprise and wonder that he longed to turn into understanding…

He sighed and swung his long legs over the edge of the narrow cot and glanced at the clock again. He was late. He rubbed his face, hard, as if he could rub away every thought of Cora Kensington. He needed to review his notes and gather the group for a brief lecture on French Impressionists.

Quickly, he rose and shook out a fresh shirt. There was barely enough room to move in the cramped cabin, let alone dress, but at least the seas seemed calm this morning. He bent over a small basin, added some water from a pitcher, lathered his face and, after a long look in the mirror, gave his cheeks a quick shave, leaving a bit of a beard and long sideburns. He figured that France was the country in which he could experiment some with his facial hair. Perhaps he could use it as a way of reminding himself—rub his beard whenever he got the urge to kiss Cora Kensington.

He ran his fingertips over his cheeks, checking for stubble. He was glad he had a strong chin—it wasn't as if he needed a beard to give him what God had not. But perhaps it would make him appear more mature, established. Maybe it would lend him greater authority with his clients.

He laughed at himself. At least it couldn't hurt.

Will washed and wiped his skin clean, then pulled on his shirt, trousers, tie, and jacket. The suit was a few years old and tight around the chest, but it was one of only two summer-weight suits he owned. He had to get a little more use out of it. If all went well with the tour, the promised double pay when the Kensingtons and Morgans went home come fall would not only help him come up with a semester's tuition, it might update his wardrobe. With luck, he could find a part-time job to pay for the next semester, and then take another tour to fund his final year. If Uncle would let him guide on his own, he'd be that much further ahead. He knew the old man pocketed three-quarters of what they brought in. And increasingly, lately, he'd elected to take his leisure while Will took over. Will struggled not to let it rankle him. The old man had earned it over the years. Established himself within the family business, as he expected Will to do now.

Will tried to knot his tie, but when he checked the mirror, it was off, so he untied it and tried again. And then again. Groaning, he stood with both hands on the small table and studied his image in the mirror. *This isn't about Uncle Stuart,* he said silently to his reflection. *Get hold of yourself, man. And get your mind off her.*

He took a deep breath, then slowly, steadily tied his knot perfectly. Then, with one last, stern warning look at himself, he turned and left his cabin. The passageway was narrow, and so was the stairwell, so when he reached the top, he exited with some relief. He blinked several times in the sudden bright light. When his eyes adjusted, he noticed Cora right away, her hat off, her hair streaming in waves on the wind. She was leaning against the edge, holding a rope that secured a lanyard to a cleat, eyes closed, as if feeling the rise and fall of the ship. Her face was a mask of pleasure. It reminded him of that night aboard the *Olympic* when he'd spied on her.

He heard Hugh behind him, making a lewd remark about her to another passenger. He whipped around to face them. "Keep your voices down, gentlemen," he said with a scowl, "and I ask you to keep your minds out of the gutter."

Hugh gave him a scoffing laugh. "Get off your high horse, Will." He dropped his voice. "Even a priest couldn't ignore the comeliness of such a creature." Will glanced over at another group of Frenchmen who were clearly appreciating the view too.

Knowing he was making a terrible mistake and yet unable to stop himself, Will looked her way again. She was so beautiful it almost hurt to look at her. She wasn't his to protect as a beau. Only as his client. *My client.*

Hugh's mouth dropped open. "The apprentice is falling for her," he said, slapping his newfound friend on the back in wonder. "Would you look at that!"

Will grimaced and stepped forward to grab hold of Hugh's arm. "Excuse us for a moment," he muttered toward the stranger, as he hauled the smaller man around the corner of the cabin, out of Cora's sight—and potential hearing.

"Let me go!" Hugh wrenched his arm away and straightened his jacket. "What do you think you're doing?" He edged up against Will, chest to chest.

"Maintaining order," Will said. "I know Cora's new to the family, but you will treat her with respect. I insist on it as your guide."

"First of all, she's not part of *my* family. And is your interest in her only that of guide or as something *more*?" He raised his eyebrows.

"As your guide," Will gritted out, "we are not to fraternize with our clients. Nor allow our clients to fraternize with each other. It leads to…difficulties."

"I bet," Hugh said, a smile edging out indignation. He stepped away. "What of Andrew and Vivian?"

"They were previously courting. An exception."

"I see," Hugh said. "But there's no harm in eyeing the goods if you don't touch, is there?"

"I think there is."

Hugh pounded him on the shoulder playfully, as if they were pals. "You're putting too much heart in it, man. Keep it light. Take in the flowers; just don't pluck the petals. It'll relieve some of that pressure building." He leaned forward and whispered, "That is, unless you're so inclined."

Will clenched his fists. "I'm not."

Hugh gave him a long, appraising look. "Right," he said, clearly not believing him. He pulled a pocket watch from his waist and looked from it to Will. "Isn't it time for your meeting?"

"Indeed."

"Excellent. I'll just go and fetch our Cora—"

"I'll fetch her. You go on."

Hugh nodded knowingly. "Sure you will."

"Go, Hugh."

He raised his hands. "I'm going. I'm going."

Will waited until the man moved away, toward the deck beside the main cabin where the others were already assembling. Then he ducked around the corner and stopped a few feet away from her. She was sitting now, apparently oblivious to what had gone on. Her eyes were closed, her face to the wind as if she were posing for a painting. And indeed, she was a worthy model.

"Cora," he said, wanting it to be soft, low, so he wouldn't startle her. But instead it came out strangled, with an awkward squeak.

Her eyes fluttered open, and she brought a hand to her throat. "Oh, Will. Are you all right?"

"Fine, fine," he said, swallowing hard, embarrassed. "We're gathering. Ready to join us?"

"I am," she said, turning, "though it's difficult to leave this." She glanced over her shoulder at the riverbanks lush with green grass. Will looked beyond her to the landscape at large. They'd entered the mouth of the Seine in the wee hours of the morning. He'd felt the waves diminish and smelled the shift from salt to freshwater, but he hadn't taken in the lovely surroundings. "I never expected to love the water so," Cora said. "There's something about it that reminds me of the prairies of home." She shook her head. "All those miles of swaying grass aren't so different from waves of the sea."

"Except the prairies cannot swallow you whole." He offered his arm.

"You'd be surprised," she said. "Many who've put years of toil into the ground might tell you that it swallowed them."

"An astute observation," he said. She took his arm, and they began walking. "Cora, about last night…"

She paused and looked up at him. Was that a flash of hope, interest, in her eyes? Ignoring his dry throat, he pressed on. "I apologize. It was an accident, falling against you as I did."

"Oh, I know that. Such things happen." But she waited there, as if she wanted him to say more.

He turned more fully toward her. "Still. It was… I apologize if I offended you in any way."

Her blue eyes searched his for a moment longer, then stilled, her brow lowering. "Not at all, Will. Don't fret over it any more."

His heart seemed to pause and then pounded. "Thank you," he muttered, leading her forward again.

Had he disappointed her? Did she actually want something to happen? No, he told himself. He'd confused her. Complicated matters. Crossed his own well-established line.

"What shall you teach us about today, tutor?" she asked, following behind him in the narrow passageway.

"Monet and Manet, French Impressionists."

"Ahh. Painters of idle garden parties and picnics."

"Oh, and far more. For instance, Monet painted important works in Venice and London. And he often painted his wife—with their son, in a Japanese costume, working at her tapestry, and even on the occasion of her early demise."

"In her deathbed?" Cora said, eyebrows lifting in surprise.

"Whose deathbed?" Lillian asked as they entered the small parlor.

"Camille Monet's," Will said. He moved to the front of the group, assembled in chairs in the only sitting room on the ship. "Cora asked if French Impressionists painted only garden parties," he said with a nod to her. "But Monet often painted his wife, Camille. And when she died of tuberculosis, in the midst of his grief he painted her on her deathbed. It's an intriguing work that captures the moment when the body remains but the spirit has departed."

"Will we see that here in Paris?" Vivian asked.

"Perhaps. We'll certainly see many of Monet and Manet's works in the city, but I'm not certain where that particular work now resides. We'll be taking a painting class one afternoon, doing our best at emulating the Impressionist style—"

"That ought to provide a laugh or two," Andrew said.

"Or allow some budding artists to emerge," Will said benignly. His uncle had wisely found some years ago that nothing helped young people remember particular lessons like actively engaging them—constructing one of Da Vinci's models, sketching the Eiffel Tower from beneath it, learning how to bake pastries from a French chef. On some trips, he'd even brought in a magician to teach a few tricks, and a gambler to teach the gentlemen how to play a proper game of cards. It was Will's favorite part of the tour—far better than his droning lessons.

His blood surged with excitement as he told them of the plans, and in turn, he saw their faces come alive with interest. He knew he was keeping his eyes purposefully off Cora. Glancing past or over her. He didn't dare to hover there for long, fearful that everyone, including Cora, would soon guess his interest as Hugh had. His only defense would be to make it appear that Hugh was totally wrong; then the others would come to Will's aid, passing his teasing off as Hugh's imagination run wild.

After teaching for a while, Will noticed his uncle standing beside Antonio in the back, hands on the head of his cane as he observed like a proud parent. Will wrapped up his last statements, and his uncle nodded to the window. "Think you all ought to come on deck," the old bear said. "We're just beginning to sail past the outskirts of Paris."

The group moved out the door, the women chatting excitedly, the young men jostling one another good-naturedly. Outside, they all gathered on the leeward deck, from which they could see the most buildings. Charming cottages lined by gardens, orderly farms, milking cows out to pasture... It had the same pastoral effect as Provence, where they would eventually sojourn.

Once they were assembled, his uncle began a lesson in French, reminding their clients of useful phrases and words they would likely need. As with other lessons, Uncle Stuart and Will found that clients were far more engaged in learning once they had the land in sight and knew they'd soon be encountering native speakers. Listening to them, it soon became apparent that Andrew and Felix were nearly fluent, probably having studied it in college. Hugh and Vivian's French was passable, but the younger girls and Cora had much to learn.

Will noticed that Lillian and Nell were casting surreptitious, coy glances at a couple of finely dressed gentlemen who smelled of money, from the tops of their bowler hats to the tips of their perfectly polished boots. Frowning, Will moved into the girls' line of vision, forcing them to return their attention to his uncle. He well knew that American girls were a prize for European men, who considered them deliciously naive and relished the idea of educating them…and not in the way their fathers had hoped when they sent them off on the Grand Tour.

Once word got out that these young women were copper-king heiresses, they'd be all the more alluring. Europe was rife with old titles but empty coffers. Young, rich brides were in short supply, and America was proving to be a lovely new mine shaft for such gold. Will's goal, as his uncle oft reminded him, was to make sure the young ladies' dance cards were full, that they had the opportunity to flirt and converse with men—and yet return home thoroughly single. It was part of the art of the tour—to dip in, become a part of the immediate environs and society, but then to extricate their clients before they were too entwined.

Lillian's face twisted in confusion as he blocked her from the men. Will had to stifle a smile when her eyes met his and she knew her coquettish ways had been discovered. But his smile quickly faded when he discovered that one of the gentlemen had slipped around the group and now was offering a note to Cora, with a bow.

He could feel the heat under his collar, as well as his uncle's angry, concerned gaze upon him.

Cora took the note from the handsome gentleman and nodded gracefully while the two younger girls shared a look of seething frustration.

And as the man moved off with his companion, and Cora waited for his uncle to move on with the lesson, Will acknowledged that he knew something of what the girls were feeling.

Jealousy.

CHAPTER 24

~Cora~

"I fear I must ask for the note," the old bear said, drawing near.

"For what reason?" I asked, folding my arms. I hadn't even had a chance to open it.

"To be certain that he has not compromised your character by asking anything untoward of you."

I almost laughed. But I sobered as Will and Antonio joined our circle. "I'm certain that I can keep my own character in check, thank you. If I find I am in need of counsel, I shall seek you out. Until then, kindly make way." I waited with a polite but firm smile upon my face as my mama had taught me. Eventually, the older man grumbled and glanced Will's way as if to ask for help, but Will only stared back at him, not at me, clearly unwilling to enter the fray.

"Very well," the old man said. "Do as you wish." He turned to the side and gestured me forward.

"Thank you," I said, moving past him and down the deck. Heavens, we were hardly in the Victorian age. I had a sudden urge to march with the suffragettes, be a part of change that might bring women more power, more respect.

After I'd gained a little distance, I pulled the card from its fine envelope and studied the elegant script. It was nothing but a name: *I am Pierre de Richelieu, Esquire.*

"You see, mademoiselle," said a man from over my shoulder, "we hadn't yet been introduced." He gestured toward the note card. "So I had my friend give this to you."

I smiled and turned toward him, laughing inwardly at his clever method of introduction.

"I see," I said. He was frightfully handsome, but not in the rugged manner of Will. Elegant, slim, with a face that was almost pretty. Just a couple of inches taller than I, with sandy hair and the most beautiful green eyes.

"And so you now know that my name is Pierre de Richelieu," he said, drawing a hand to his chest. He cocked his head and flashed me a smile. "But may I ask yours?"

"Certainly. It's Cora…Kensington." I felt myself blush at my hesitation over saying my last name. It still sounded so wrong in my mind, a lie on the tongue. But the man would think I didn't know my own name.

He offered his hand, and I placed my gloved one in it. He lifted it to his lips and kissed my knuckles. I could feel the heat of his lips and breath through the cloth. A shiver of delight ran up my arm and down my back. His eyes had laugh lines at the corners. And he arched a brow up as though he had all kinds of secrets he was more than ready to share. He rose and gestured to the bow of the ship. "Care to stroll the deck with me?"

"Certainly."

"I understand that you and your companions are on the Grand Tour," he said, tucking his hands behind his back while staying right beside me.

"Indeed." Apparently, it didn't take all that much to find out about the other forty passengers aboard. Who'd told him? The captain?

"Most delightful," he said. "I think you shall find France to be an intriguing country to explore."

"I hope so."

"Is this your first time on the Continent?"

"Yes."

He clasped his hands together in excitement. "Then I must show you and your friends about!"

"Oh, I think our guides have our plans in order."

His face fell as we continued to walk. "There is no time to include new plans? I thought we might take a picnic along the Seine. Your whole party is welcome, of course," he added hurriedly. A slow smile spread on his face, and he dropped his voice. "Though I confess it's you that I wish to get to know best."

"A little forward, aren't you, friend?" Will asked, placing a hand on Pierre's shoulder. We stopped strolling.

"Will, really," I said, embarrassed at his tone.

"I beg your pardon," Pierre said, bowing in deference to Will. "I have overstepped my bounds?"

"I don't know," Will said. "Have you?"

"I don't believe so," Pierre said. His green eyes slipped from Will to me and back again. "You two are not...entwined?"

"Entwined?" I asked in confusion, even as understanding dawned. He was asking if we were involved. Engaged, even. Both of us answered together, shaking our heads in surprise. Last night I'd wondered, but after this morning, Will had made it more than clear that I was nothing to him but a client.

"I am Will McCabe, her guide, as well as one of her protectors," Will said, nodding over his shoulder at Antonio.

But Pierre was clearly unperturbed. "And I am Pierre de Richelieu." He reached out a hand, and Will reluctantly shook it. "I have no objection to your playing nursemaid, Mr. McCabe," Pierre said easily. He smiled over at me. "With women in your company as beautiful as Miss Kensington, it is most wise."

Will's jaw muscles tightened. I couldn't quite tell whether Pierre was referring to Will in the role of an elderly aunt as a means of dismissing him or honoring him.

"Please, walk with us," Pierre invited. He had the air of a man who had nothing to hide. But this time he offered me his arm, and in a sudden surge of rebellion, I took it. We fell into step again, and after an awkward hesitation, I heard Will follow behind us.

"As I was saying," Pierre said, speaking over his shoulder as much to Will as to me, "it would be lovely if you—and your companions—joined me and mine for a picnic along the Seine tomorrow. Would your schedule accommodate such a venture?"

"I don't know," I said. I glanced back at Will. "Do we have time in our schedule?"

He shook his head. "No. Tomorrow is scheduled from morning until night." Was that a hint of smug satisfaction around his mouth?

"Oh," Pierre said sadly. "How about the next?"

Again, Will shook his head.

"When shall you be free?" Pierre asked, turning sideways in order to face him. But his expression was carefully inquisitive, not challenging. His hand rested on mine, atop his arm, the pressure calm but constant, as if he didn't want me to pull away.

I had to be honest with myself; I found him quite self-assured. And charming. The way he spoke, the way he held himself…

"I don't know," Will said. "We are conducting a Grand Tour and hope to make the most of every moment in France."

"As I have heard," Pierre said, again clasping his hands before him in excitement again, his face alight. "I might be of great assistance to you. I am well connected in Paris. Where would you like to go? To the top of the Eiffel Tower? The Louvre, after hours? Would you like to eat in the finest restaurant in Paris? I can get you in anywhere." He flicked out his fingers with the word *anywhere*, then drew them back, knuckles under chin, waiting on Will.

Will stopped, plainly surprised. How could a tour guide turn down such an offer? "You…you can gain us entry to the top of the Eiffel?" Will had told us that the second and third observation decks had been closed since the year before, when an Austrian tailor had died trying to jump off the tower with a homemade parachute.

"Oui. But first," he said, holding up his index finger in warning, "you must be my guests at my home. I have a lovely view that will make your visit all the more glorious."

"That would be most generous of you," Will said. One eyebrow lifted. "But our party numbers eighteen, including servants. Most find such numbers too large to accommodate."

Pierre smiled again and let out a little breathy laugh. "That shall not be a problem at my chateau. You will find your accommodations spacious. And I, in turn, would greatly enjoy the distraction of new friends to show about." His eyes shifted to me.

"Yes, well," Will said, "perhaps I can persuade my uncle to modify our plans for tomorrow evening and we can sup with you. Consider staying on for a night or two? I cannot promise that—"

"Marvelous," Pierre said, taking my hand and tucking it firmly around his arm. We immediately set off on our walk again. I glanced back at Will, who frowned at our new host's interruption.

"So, Monsieur Richelieu," I said, "tell me what it's like to grow up in such a fascinating city as Paris."

"Please, my friend. Call me Pierre."

"Thank you. And you may refer to me as Cora."

"Cora, a lovely name," he said. "And Paris…she's lovely too. Truly the finest in all of Europe," he said, genuine devotion in his eyes. "And what is it you asked? Grow up?"

"Growing up. What was your childhood like, in Paris?"

"Ah, yes. My English is decent but far from perfect. *Growing up*," he said, as if trying out the words. "I confess I did not have the most innocent of childhoods. Always into mischief."

"Oh?" I said, curious. "Give me an example."

He smiled and cocked his head, as if a little guilty about the memory. "As boys, my friends and I were convinced we must seek out the holy relics—see them for ourselves."

"Holy relics?" I said, blinking.

"Oui," he said, peering at me strangely, as if he wondered if he was using the wrong English word for something I should know about. "The crown of thorns and the drop of Christ's blood that was Sainte-Chappelle's prize until the revolution? A piece of the cross or a nail of the Passion? All in Notre Dame's treasury."

"And you were not permitted to see them?"

"No, no," he said, shaking his head. "The priests are most possessive of their treasures. They like to brag about having them but then won't share them with the world!"

"Perhaps they fear they will be damaged or stolen," I said.

He made a dismissive sound and waved his hand. "Then put them under glass, and under guard, as they do in museums. Don't make boys sneak into your church in the middle of the night to see them."

I gasped and laughed at the same time, bringing a hand to my lips. "You did not!"

He grinned, clearly proud of himself. "We did. But I cannot tell you any more of it, or the priests will unleash holy wrath upon me."

The bear had told us to expect such things ahead of us. Unlike our American churches, the great cathedrals and basilicas of Europe had long competed for stature, fame, and power through grand architecture, beautiful artwork, and housing the crypts of the famous—be they political, artistic, or religious figures. But the "relics"—bodies and body parts, as well as the cross, the nails, the crown? This was new to me.

"The most difficult to see was the crown of thorns. The old priest slept with the key under his pillow."

I knew my eyes must have been wide when I asked, "And you dared to sneak it from him?"

Pierre simply smiled and tapped his lips. "Perhaps."

"So did you see the crown, in the box? What did it look like?"

He shrugged one shoulder. "Sure, sure. It was very old, very brittle." He cast me a wise sideways glance. "But is it *the* crown of thorns? Could such a thing be preserved for thousands of years? That is somewhat suspect. But such traditions give my city a deeply mysterious layer." He smiled. "Which, I confess, I enjoy."

"I can only imagine. What is your work, if I may be so bold?"

"Ah, I am engaged in many things. My real business is in banking. But that's a rather dull way to spend every day, is it not? Money is money. People are far more entertaining." He glanced over at me. "How is it that you came to take the Grand Tour, Cora?"

I felt the back of my neck heat up, as if Will's stare were boring straight through me, wondering how I would explain it. "My father and his business partner have long planned to send their children on a tour, to both experience and understand culture, art, and history in some of the finest countries of the world. They believe it is vital for us to learn of these things to better prepare us for our future."

"Ah, they are wise men, then," he said, waiting a moment before continuing. "I have been to your country."

"You have?"

"Yes, to New York, last year. I find Americans to be lovely, open people. But rather, uh, how do you say it? Innocent. Simple." He pronounced it as *seemple*. And while some might have been offended, I thought I understood what he meant.

"We're a young country. Which leads to a certain measure of idealism, I suppose. We haven't had the time to become as jaded as the French."

Pierre's eyebrows shot up, and then he threw back his head and laughed. "Are you certain you have not yet set foot in my country?"

I laughed with him and lost myself in more of his tales, gradually recognizing that Will had left us when Antonio began watching from farther off, my guardians apparently satisfied that my attention was on Pierre and that he was up to nothing nefarious, at least at the moment. He was so different from any other man I'd met...so refined and gorgeous that I wanted to look at him all day. And he seemed equally intrigued by me.

He continued to entertain me all the way to Paris. As we neared the docks, he groaned as if lamenting that our time was at an end, and then he kissed my hand, holding it between his. "Forgive me. I've spoken far too long of myself. I wish to know more of you. Tomorrow, you must convince me that you are a woman and not the angel you appear. You shall send me word on how to reach you?"

I laughed. "I shall. And I can *assure* you that I am far from an angel."

He covered his heart. "I am not yet convinced," he said, studying me intently. "Our meeting has delighted me."

"And me as well," I said.

He deposited me beside Antonio and left. I saw that the others were gathered again, the younger girls staring in our direction, the others pretending not to look but glancing anyway.

"Be careful, Miss Cora," Antonio whispered.

I looked up at him from the corner of my eyes.

"Only one sort of man is worse than an Italian when it comes to their appetite for women."

"Oh? And what is that?"

"A Frenchman."

———◇◇◇———

After spending the night in the prestigious Ritz Hotel, the next day we went to the massive palace-turned-museum the Louvre. My siblings and the Morgans seemed to be ignoring me, as if still angry that I had even been polite to Pierre de Richelieu, making inroads before them. Apparently, I was only to follow behind and remain as silent as possible. Vivian had grumbled, "So, are we to fill our date book with just any Frenchman who comes along, smiling at our Cora?"

The way she said *our Cora*, with such disdain, still made my skin crawl hours later. She made it sound as if I were something unpleasant she'd stepped in, clinging to her boot. Every time I felt I had begun to make headway, I seemed to make some choice that again separated us. The group was intrigued to learn more about Pierre and his chateau yet irritated that our schedule had been disrupted.

The bear had assured Vivian that such disruption was not to be the case but reminded her that seizing upon invitations would greatly enhance our experience on the tour.

I sighed, thinking about it. I was tired of worrying over such things. Could we not embrace the tour and one another at face value? Take it day by day? I resolved to do so anyway. And today, before us, was the massive Louvre, housed in the remains of a palace that had stood on this spot for centuries. The sheer size of the building shocked me from the start, and when I learned that the exhibits inside covered more than five thousand years of history, I was overwhelmed all the more. There were thousands of Greek and Roman sculptures. Thousands of paintings, from medieval to modern. When the bear said that there were more than thirty thousand pieces of art in the museum, I could only gape at him, wondering how one could ever take it all in.

But what I found most arresting were the Egyptian exhibits. While I studied a twenty-foot-tall sculpture of a pharaoh, Will came up beside me and stared upward too.

"You like this exhibit," he said softly. It was more of a statement than a question.

"I thought I'd awakened in Paris this morning, but now I believe I've been transported to ancient Egypt," I said, not looking at him. Our interactions over the last couple of days had been frustrating, irritating. What was wrong with him? One minute he seemed interested, the next all business. And now...now he was just perturbed. Though I could tell he tried hard to mask it.

Conscious that Will trailed behind, I went to a case that contained a gold-encrusted sarcophagus. I wasn't sure I wanted him following me everywhere all summer. But at the moment, he and Antonio seemed to be my only companions.

"Will we be going to other museums with such treasures?"

"None as vast as the Louvre."

"That's all right by me," I said. "It's a bit overwhelming, isn't it?"

"It can be," he said with a soft smile. He was wearing a dapper lightweight wool suit. But even I could see that it was old; the jacket didn't quite stretch around the breadth of his chest.

I felt a surge of compassion for him—having to keep up appearances with the likes of the Kensingtons and Morgans, while obviously on a strict budget, couldn't be easy. "Which has been your favorite exhibit, Will?" I asked, trying to draw him out, make him forget about the past few days.

"I favor the dinosaurs at the British Museum, myself."

I nodded in quick agreement as we walked through a passageway that had once stood outside of a pharaoh's tomb. "Those were wonderful. I felt much the same there, standing at the feet of those massive creatures, as I do here. Awed." I reached out and ran my hand across the facade, wondering about the men who carved it thousands of years before. Who were they? Could they have envisioned their works being here, so far from where they'd lived? "Can you imagine transporting these monuments from Egypt to France?"

"Quite the enterprise," he said, hands tucked behind his back. His quick eyes seemed to absorb every inch of the sphinx we now studied, as if he were recording it for a sketch later on.

I shifted my eyes to the sculpture. "It's almost as if I am seeing an issue of *National Geographic* come to life."

He paused. "These artifacts, like the dinosaurs, represent mighty civilizations that once dominated, but then were washed away, buried. We'll run across bits of ancient Egypt all across Paris and elsewhere. She was plundered for her treasures. Napoleon brought some obelisks home that the Egyptians want returned."

"That's awful," I said. "Perhaps they should be."

"Perhaps. Although the Parisians are loath to give them up. They feel as if they belong here now."

"But they don't. They were stolen," I said, no longer fully appreciating the artifacts before me. Now they felt like ill-gotten loot.

"When people grow up with something, they tend to feel as if that object belongs to them, don't they?" Will paused by a group of stone monkeys, their faces and tails eroded. "Think about what was on your property in your hometown. What if there was something that had been brought there two hundred years before. Wouldn't you feel as if it belonged?"

I laughed under my breath. "There was hardly an obelisk in my yard."

"But if there had been?" he pressed.

I considered it. What if the barn hadn't been one my papa built? What if he had somehow stolen it, placed it there? Begrudgingly, I nodded. "I understand the impulse to claim it as your own," I said. "But that doesn't make it right."

"Agreed."

We strolled onward, now past cases with mummies. Never had I seen one, much less so many in one room. But the sight of my half siblings and the Morgans gazing at them made me pause.

Will paused with me, looking back and forth between us.

"Cora," he said softly, "don't let the Kensingtons and Morgans make you think you must be like them to be one of them. Don't be afraid to be who you are."

I blinked at him in confusion and irritation, my brow furrowing. "You believe I am afraid to be who I really am?"

"With them," he said, nodding toward the group ahead of us. "But also with yourself. I think you've stopped examining what has happened to you. The bounty your father has laid at your feet. Your new identity. Taking up with Pierre de Richelieu…"

"Taking up with him?" I sputtered. "We merely met. It was you who accepted his invitation."

"But it was you who drew us into that conversation at all. As if you felt you had to flirt with him like Vivian or Lillian or Nell might."

I shook my head in embarrassment. Who was he to judge me so? I hadn't been flirtatious, merely friendly. "That was not my intent," I said, gritting my teeth.

Will looked me in the eyes, then shrugged. As he edged away, moving toward his uncle, I hoped he felt the darts my gaze shot at his back.

"Haven't we seen enough?" Felix was asking the bear. "I don't know about you, but I could stand a nice nap under the sun about now."

I shook off a shiver of frustration and again fell behind the group as they agreed to leave the Louvre. Everyone asked different things of me. Andrew and Vivian wanted me to fade into the woodwork and hopefully out of their lives altogether; Hugh wanted me to return his romantic overtures; Felix had an idle interest in me, but I suspected it was truly idle; Nell and Lillian saw me as a novelty, like a doll grown tall, walking and talking; the bear saw me as a receptive student; but Will apparently saw me as something else. What? An actress, a chameleon?

I wanted to stop and get down on my knees and hold my head in my hands. Cry. Because there was some measure of truth to that; I no longer knew exactly who I was. I hadn't really known—ever since

Wallace Kensington rolled up our drive. I'd known, once. At home, when Papa was well. At school, studying.

Such memories seemed like something I'd experienced years ago, not months. Try as I might, I couldn't imagine being back there now.

Will was right. I was changing. I'd changed already. Fundamentally. It was more than my last name. Deep within, I'd turned. The question was, in what direction? What did I want out of all of this? When the summer was through, when I left this group of people, was it merely the memories and a promise of a teaching credential that I'd take with me? Or did I want to discover something more, something else about myself?

I thought so.

Help me, Lord. Help me find what You would have me discover. More of You. More of myself. More of my future.

"Cora?" Felix asked, holding the door. "Are you coming?"

I flushed, realizing I'd fallen quite a bit behind and he'd been waiting on me.

"Are you all right?" he asked.

"Fine, thank you. A cup of tea and bit of sun would do me well too," I said.

"Indeed."

We left the museum and went outside, where four motor carriages were awaiting us.

On a whim I asked, "Felix, do you ever wonder what your life might've been like had you not been born a Kensington?"

He let out a low chuckle, and his blue eyes met mine. "I try to keep my mind from anything so onerous. In fact, I try to keep my mind from anything of consequence at all."

"Oh," I said, taking his hand as he helped me into the back of the nearest car. Nell was on the other side, fanning herself, her round face bright red. He climbed into the seat beside me, and I inched toward Nell. I didn't know if it was my imagination or if she huffed as if we were intruding upon her space, when she was taking nearly half the seat.

Will slid in next to the driver, and our convoy moved out into traffic on a broad street. I thought about what he'd said, his supposition that I was trying too hard to blend in rather than be myself.

"Felix, if nothing strikes you as being of consequence," I said to him, "how do you apply yourself to your studies at university?"

Will's neck and shoulders became more rigid, and belatedly, I realized I'd asked a question that might disturb him. Felix laughed, his handsome face splitting into appealing lines of merriment. "If at all possible, I try not to apply myself there, either." He gave me an appraising look from the corner of his eyes. "The family name grants me a certain leniency. Father makes a handsome annual contribution to the school, you see. And I am a fairly adept rugby player, which earns me a little more grace. Anything else is gravy."

I stared at him, and he laughed, reaching out to touch my chin with his knuckle. I hadn't realized my mouth was hanging open, and I blushed furiously that he'd caught me. "Relax, Cora. You'll enjoy such things yourself, in time. Such is the power of the mighty Kensington name."

"Perhaps," I mumbled, looking straight ahead at the turnabout we approached, a massive Egyptian obelisk at its center.

I turned my attention to the passing traffic of buggies, wagons, handcarts, touring cars, and bicycles; then, as we turned, I looked up at the buildings, admiring one fine storefront after another. Did Pierre de Richelieu shop here?

Will had been wrong about the attention I'd given Pierre—I genuinely thought him charming—but he was right about my attempts to win over my family and their friends. I was trying to fit in too much, with a family who believed they had the right to claim what they wished, when they wished, simply because they were rich. They'd never considered anything else, of course, because they'd always been rich. Had always had things their own way.

As we drove down the lovely Avenue des Champs-Élysées—where countless couples were out strolling, all in finer clothing than I had ever seen in my life—I knew I didn't want to waste this opportunity. Mama had urged me to come, even knowing what the Kensingtons represented, good and bad. And God had allowed this to happen for a reason. The way I'd come into the world had been less than ideal, but I'd been blessed by the way I'd been raised. I was stronger than any of my siblings, as well as any of the Morgans. That I knew, deep within. I could use my strength to stand among them. To be me.

Felix nudged me. "Why are you smiling?"

"Am I?" I looked him in the eye—the same clear blue as mine—and smiled more broadly. Neither the Kensingtons nor the Morgans would ever put me in a corner again. I'd be one step ahead of them, beginning with Pierre de Richelieu.

"Ahh," he said slyly. "It's a secret."

"A secret?" Nell asked in a high-pitched voice. "Tell me!"

"Sorry," I said, feeling no true remorse as I thought about telling Pierre who I was. If he wished to cast us out, at least we'd know before we were settled into more sumptuous rooms. It mattered not to me—if he was as superficial as the duchess in England, I didn't really care to spend more time with him anyway.

Because I'd decided. To make the most of this trip—to do as Mr. Kensington had asked. To live as if I deserved it, as if I belonged here. To embrace my identity anew. To concentrate on what defined me and ignore what did not.

Come what may.

CHAPTER 25

"Cora"

By the time we returned to the hotel that afternoon, I truly wished we could do nothing but go to bed. I longed for farmers' hours—up with the sun and to bed not long after it disappeared. It seemed that in society, no one took their supper until after eight, so I was starving as well as exhausted. I honestly feared I'd inhale half my soup and then fall asleep in what remained. The day had seemed to take everything I had. My brain and my heart were full.

After a brief nap from which Anna awakened me, I hurried into an appropriate gown—a violet creation with intricate purple lace over the shoulders—and clipped on my only pair of earrings. I was eager to arrive at Pierre's and see my plan through. Then I could return to the hotel and slip beneath the cool sheets and go to sleep, a smile on my face. I merely had to tell Pierre that I was an illegitimate child of Wallace Kensington and he'd readily send me—and my companions—home for the night, just as surely as the duchess had.

LISA T. BERGREN

I was no longer going to hide who I was. I'd take on the truth of my identity with my shoulders back and my chin held high. It was up to the people around me to decide how to tolerate such information, be they kin or stranger.

At least, those were my brave thoughts while I was still at the hotel.

We drove for quite a while, and this time I traveled with Antonio, Lil, and Nell. The girls chattered on about how handsome Pierre and his friend had been, wondering what the Richelieu chateau would be like. "Perhaps it will be a lovely apartment above a little bistro."

The driver clearly overheard us and glanced back at us. His eyebrows shot up in surprise. "Pierre de Richelieu?" he said. "Surely you know of the Richelieus?"

The girls quieted at his superior tone. I doubted anyone had ever spoken so condescendingly to them. A shiver of apprehension ran down between my shoulder blades. What now? Was Pierre more than he appeared? Or less?

Antonio conversed with him for a moment in French and then looked back over his shoulder at me with a glint of warning and delight in his eye. "You remember, miss, what I told you aboard ship?"

I nodded, recalling his statement that the only sort of man more dangerous to a woman than an Italian was a Frenchman. As we slowed to turn a corner, my eyes widened, and the girls gasped. At the end of a vast lawn—a half mile deep, with its own boulevard lined by huge trees, their branches spreading over both lanes—was a gray gothic mansion, four stories tall.

The girls erupted in excited clapping and chattering. We hadn't been in as fine a place since we'd stayed with the duke and duchess that first night. This was what had alarmed Antonio. Pierre de Richelieu was not only French; he was powerful—or at least from a very powerful family. I closed my eyes, my will faltering. It was one thing to imagine taking the upper hand this time around, telling Pierre of my scandalous beginnings, watching as Vivian's self-satisfaction melted from her face…and another thing altogether to do it. Especially on such a grandiose stage. It was as though my plans had moved from a children's playhouse to the city's opera house.

We approached the grand chateau, and my heart pounded as my courage waned. The driver pulled to a stop, and Antonio helped me out, giving me a look of approval; but Pierre was already coming down the steps, eagerly welcoming us like long-lost friends. Primarily me. He took my gloved hand and kissed my knuckles, his eyes alight as he watched me.

He didn't release me; instead, he tucked my hand through his arm and led me up the stairs, speaking over his shoulder to the others.

"Pierre," I said, tugging at his arm, pausing on the last step. "M-*m'lord*."

"Oh," he moaned, "I much preferred it when you only thought of me as *Monsieur* de Richelieu," he said, looking down at me. "Better yet, simply Pierre. Can we not go back to that, dear Cora, regardless of social convention?" The way he said my name, as if he'd just called me by an endearment, brought a flush to my cheeks.

"Pierre, I fear I must speak with you immediately about something of some urgency."

"Oh?" His face clouded, and he came back down to my step. The others gathered around us, half looking ahead in gawking fascination at what we could see of the amazing foyer—decorated in Louis XIV style, with white marble, gold, and a massive chandelier—and half glancing back in curiosity and consternation at us.

This was only going to become more difficult as the evening progressed. And to wait was to allow Vivian or one of the others to share what should be only mine to share. I looked Pierre in the eye, and he covered my hand with his other, his forehead a wrinkled mask of concern. "What is it? Tell me at once, and I shall see if I can remedy it."

I let out a humorless laugh. "I think not. You have been so kind to invite us all here, to be our host. But before we take advantage of your hospitality, I think you ought to know something…" I glanced past him. Now all of the Morgans and Kensingtons were staring solely at me.

"Please," he said kindly, "tell me."

I took a deep breath and made myself look him in the eye. "Pierre, I feel it's best that you know from the start that I am the *illegitimate* daughter of Wallace Kensington."

Vivian gasped, and Andrew pulled her close. Even as my face burned, I swallowed a laugh—apparently, it was all right for her to share my birth story, but I could not do so myself. Felix turned to me, eyes wide. Hugh snorted, and the girls looked at each other in surprise. I couldn't manage to look at the bear or Will or Antonio, but instead forced my eyes back to meet Pierre's.

He was smiling wryly, more remarkably handsome than ever. His eyebrows arched up in surprise. "This is it? This is the news that burdens you so?"

"Why, yes. I…I thought…"

"Oh, my dear Miss Kensington, this is no problem here in France. In fact, you'll find such a beginning makes you all the more intriguing."

Now my eyes widened.

He smiled and patted my hand. "You left the provincial behind you when you left England's shores." He gestured around him. "This is the land of love and passion. We embrace who we are; we do not aspire to be who we are not. And tonight, we are but a group of friends who met aboard a ship. Let us celebrate as such."

He tucked my hand more firmly around his arm and led me past Will, whose eyes were wide with surprise, and Antonio, who looked on with a knowing eye. The bear put up his hands and shrugged, as if this was a surprising but utterly delightful turn of events. I struggled to find my voice again, and Pierre seemed to understand my shock, so he chattered, telling the group of his family's fourteen-generation history, how his ancestor had been a commander in Napoleon's army and had been sent as far as Morocco and Algiers before he returned home with enough plunder to establish his banking business in Paris, from then on building upon his wealth.

We entered a massive parlor with hundreds of oil paintings—four high on the fabric-covered sixteen-foot walls. A quartet in tuxedos waited behind stringed instruments the corner. After a nod from Pierre, they began to play. The furniture was refined, pristine. Servants emerged, champagne on one tray and fat poached shrimp on the other. Thirsty, I took a big swig of the bubbling liquid and wrinkled up my nose.

Pierre laughed. "You do not care for champagne? That is the finest in all of Paris."

I smiled. "Perhaps I'd like the least fine. In all honesty, I'd love a cup of tea."

He smiled with me. "Then you shall have it," he said. He snapped his fingers at a servant and bent to whisper in his ear. The servant rushed off.

Lillian and Nell drew near, eyelashes fluttering. Andrew and Vivian stood off in a corner, as if they really didn't care to be here any longer. *If he accepts me*, I thought, *they surely don't wish to accept him.* "Tell me, Lord de Richelieu," Nell said, "are any of your other family members at home? Are there others?"

I covered my smile by looking downward. Clearly, the girl was wondering if there might not be a few younger brothers around the corner…

"My friends are my family," he said, throwing his arms wide, gesturing toward all of us. "Won't you help me fill my empty halls by staying with me for the duration of your time here in Paris? I will introduce you to my other friends, and tomorrow, I am to host a masked ball. You all must be in attendance."

The girls chattered in excitement. "A masked ball!" Lillian said, clapping her hands. "Father hosted one when I came of age."

"I'm certain the young gentlemen came from far and wide to present themselves," Pierre said, nodding toward her.

Antonio had been right. Pierre was truly sweet, but he also embodied flirtation, from head to toe. I'd have to watch myself around him.

"The only question is if we can get you all costumed in time. I do not suppose you travel with costumes."

I let out a little laugh. "Uh, no." *What sort of people might travel with costumes in their trunks, other than actors or performers?*

"I thought not. But it's quite the elaborate function, you see, and many have had their costumes on order for months." He paused, chin in hand, and then raised a finger. "I have the solution." He spoke in hushed tones with a servant. The man hurried off just as the first arrived with my cup of tea.

I looked around as scents of licorice and lavender wafted up to my nose. Three more servants were stationed about the room, ready to do Pierre's bidding.

The bear was at my elbow. "If you are certain that we will be no imposition, we'd be honored to be your guests, my lord," he said. "We depart on Saturday for the countryside."

"So soon?" Pierre frowned. Then he waved a hand, his expression easing. "No matter. I shall send word to my many friends. They will be your hosts wherever you wish to go."

"You are most generous," the bear said.

I sighed in relief. Two new couples arrived, as well as a group of single men and women. Pierre moved off to speak to them, and Vivian sidled near. "Just what do you think you are doing?" she said in a strained whisper.

I gave her a sidelong glance. "Merely taking matters into my own hands for once, sister."

She stiffened. "You risked our whole experience in Paris with such a declaration." She did not look at me, only out to the others, smiling demurely toward the newcomers and our host.

"You yourself did the same thing in London. Why is it all right for you to tell of family secrets and not me?"

"You are *not* family." She said it so lowly I wondered, for a moment, if I misheard her. "You do not have the right to make such decisions."

I raised my chin and thought on that for a moment. "The truth affects me, more than any," I said.

"How selfish of you!" she said, taking a glass of champagne from a waiter. My tea was rapidly cooling in my cup. "Our futures are inextricably entwined. You would do well to remember that."

"Yes," I said. "And so would you."

She looked away, then back to me. "We shall tolerate our ties through the end of the summer, but only until then. After that, you shall go on your way, with whatever guilt money Father feels he must fill your pockets with, and we shall go ours. Agreed?"

I stared at her. Could she possibly be so cruel? And was she truly speaking for the whole group? Not that I wished to be together forever, nor had I thought of anything beyond the summer. The idea of sharing a Christmas with this cold woman and her bristly beau made me nauseous. "I can't imagine ever wishing to see you again," I said brightly.

Her eyes narrowed. "Good, then."

"Good," I repeated. I moved away, my eyes inexplicably filling with tears. She'd wounded me, just when I'd thought she'd already done all she could. I thought I was ready to handle them all, head-on, shoulders back, chin up.

But over and over again, she found new ways to twist the knife.

"Cora," Will said lowly, eyebrows lowered in concern, reaching out to me as I passed. But I shook my head and brushed by, out into the hall and down it. I turned a corner and went to the end of that, drawn by tall doors covered by curtains. I was relieved to find them unlocked, and I hurried through, quietly closing them behind me.

I was alone on a small balcony. Taking deep breaths of the cooling evening air, I desperately tried to hold back my tears. *Why do I care, Lord? Why do I care if Vivian accepts me?* I clenched the marble balustrade in my hands and leaned against it, lifting my face to the sky. I was resolving to not care, to pretend as if Vivian did not exist, to *show* her, when my mother's words came back to me. *Bitterness leads nowhere but down. Accept God's love, even if you don't understand His ways. And out of respect of that love, love others, even when you don't wish to.*

She'd said it in reference to my anger over Papa's stroke, my railing against the heavens for lowering him so, just when we had been poised at the door of such a sweet future together. In those first terrible days, I could sense God's presence, Him holding me close even when I felt so completely, achingly set adrift. Now here I was again, feeling terribly lost, but I felt none of that holy reassurance. I sighed and closed my eyes, concentrating on nothing but my breath, my heartbeat, the sound of the birds in the air, the breeze on my face.

I thought of my papa, his arms around my shoulders, holding me. I thought of my mama, taking my face in her hands and leaning forward to touch my forehead to hers. Of suppers when we spoke of nothing but the weather, or the cows, or the sprouts, or old Mrs. Chandler down the road, who needed help with the chores when her rheumatism acted up. I wished I was sitting down at the old pine table tonight, with the knots that looked like faces and food that was simple and served on one plate all at once.

But I wasn't. I wasn't.

"Help me remember who I was," I whispered to the wind. "Who I am. And show me, please show me, who I am to become."

CHAPTER 26

~William~

Uncle Stuart crowed over their good fortune and spouted praises of the French until Will fought the urge to ask him to be quiet. They were sharing a room in the hotel, but tomorrow their party would move to Chateau Richelieu, which, in Will's eyes, was a mixed blessing. On the one hand, they'd be accomplishing what Uncle Stuart wanted most—to introduce their clients to each city's society—and Will wouldn't have to share a room with the old man. But on the other, they'd be in the hands of this city's society, and there was something about Richelieu that Will didn't entirely trust—beyond the fact that he clearly had an eye for Cora.

Uncle Stuart finally stopped yammering and gave in to slow breathing, which eventually became great, faltering snores. Will sighed and turned over, pulling his pillow on top of his head. The squeaking springs made his uncle pause, as if he'd awakened him, but then slowly, the snoring resumed. Will was utterly exhausted, but his mind was racing. He thought about Cora's surprise announcement, and a part of him was proud of her for taking matters into her own hands, the other part aghast at the risk she took. But Cora's expression had been so tense as Vivian spoke to her, and when she'd fled the room as if driven from it, he worried about what the eldest Kensington had said. Cora was quiet through dinner and seemed to revive only when the costumer arrived, methodically taking notes and measurements in order to find the right outfit for each one, as well as a proper mask for the ball the following night, among previously worn and stored gowns and suits.

The thought of his charges all being in costume, in a sea of costumes, agitated Will. How was he to watch over them, protect them, in such a setting? He doubted this would be a small affair. According to Richelieu himself, it would be quite elaborate. Three hundred? Five hundred? The chateau could certainly hold that many. Uncle would have to have a firm word with the group about not taking the proffered champagne at every pass, or Antonio and Will would end up carrying each one of them upstairs as the evening wore on.

On and on his thoughts went, until he finally gave in to sleep in the wee hours. It seemed mere minutes later that his uncle was shaking his shoulder, urging him up. They were to visit Napoleon's tomb and ride through the Arc de Triomphe on horseback, as the great leader had once hoped to do himself. Then they would return and change for the journey back out to the chateau, to prepare for the evening's festivities.

Will groaned and made himself sit up, rubbing his face.

"What's wrong, my boy?" Uncle Stuart said. "Did the bed not agree with you?"

"Something like that," Will muttered.

"No doubt you were kept up late thinking of pretty Cora in Master Richelieu's arms."

Will frowned. Was the old man baiting him? "No. I had other concerns on my mind."

"No? Well, good then. You know how I feel about fraternizing with—"

"Yes, Uncle Stuart. I know."

The old bear paused, the ends of his tie in his hands. "So what is it, then? Out with it."

"It's the ball. A masked ball? How are we to keep track of the Morgans and Kensingtons? Usually, we don't encounter such things until Venezia…"

His uncle made a dismissive noise and turned to the mirror to finish tying his knot. "They'll be fine. It's precisely this sort of event that will live long in their memories." He leaned over to pick up his jacket and slipped it on. "And it's this sort of event that will garner you future tours."

Will's eyes shifted to meet his uncle's gaze. "Truly? You're ready for me to move on without you?"

"Oh, yes, yes," the old man said, waving a dismissive hand. "This constant travel is rather wearing. Too wearisome for a man of advanced years. I need to take my retirement upon some lovely porch where I can smoke my pipe, watch sunsets, and flirt with the local widows."

Will smiled, hope growing in his chest. "I appreciate the vote of confidence, Uncle Stuart."

"Not at all, not at all, my boy. You've earned it."

He looked at his pocket watch and then gave Will a meaningful look from beneath his bushy gray eyebrows. "Best be about it, then, boy. I'll go and meet the clients for breakfast. Come along shortly?"

Will nodded his head and rose, moving to the sink to run some cold water and splash some onto his face, while his uncle shut the door behind him. He stared at his reflection and grinned. *So the old man really is ready to move on...* He'd been waiting for this day forever. Uncle had hinted, intimated that he'd like to retire, but he'd never said that this would truly be his last tour.

Next year, freedom. Back to university, perhaps securing a loan for the entire year, guide another group come summer, and with luck, be able to finish the following year. Then he'd be his own man. With a degree in one hand and a map in the other.

Traffic was far worse that day on the streets than any other they'd experienced in Paris. But then they'd never arrived so close to the annual celebration of the French Bastille Day. Will frowned over his shoulder in concern for the group on horseback, as they struggled to stay in pairs, knowing they were safer riding together than they were riding single file. *At least it keeps Cora and Vivian from racing,* Will thought. It'd be impossible here anyway, in this crowd. One or both would very likely end up with a broken neck.

He rode beside his uncle. "Perhaps this is the last year to include this particular excursion," he said to the old man. "With Bastille Day around the corner."

"Perhaps," Stuart returned, his face settling into deeper lines. "Though it seems wrong to approach the Arc in any other manner other than as Napoleon wished to."

Two touring cars nearly collided in front of him, and one sounded its horn. Will's horse shied, and his uncle's mount reared. Will wrenched his reins left as one vehicle swerved by him on the right, still beeping in frustration. The girls, directly behind him, screamed. But his eyes were on Uncle Stuart. The old man's horse faltered, shifting dramatically to the left, but remarkably, his uncle clung to his seat.

When the horse was again on all four hooves, prancing about, Stuart circled and took in his group, returning his focus to his clients. "Well, that gave us quite a fright, did it not?" he asked jovially, still looking peaked. "Never fear. We'll be at the Arc in short order. Onward!" he called, raising one hand as if lifting a sword.

Will shook his head and laughed under his breath. Only he could see the slight tremble revealing his uncle's fear. He had to admire the man. He had a good forty-five years on Will and seemed able to manage days and nights that would put a far younger man in bed for days. He could still outwalk and outtalk many, and he could outdrink more. He was a force, a legend. And Will couldn't imagine that Uncle Stuart was truly ready to hang up his hat after this tour.

Day by day, Will told himself. *With what I know to be true.* Who knew if Uncle Stuart would change his mind tomorrow? Take another tour? Or twelve...

Finally they made it to the Arc and ran their reins through old brass rings on posts.

After everyone had had some water to drink, they set off on the narrow, winding stairs to the terrace atop the arch, which boasted one of the finest views of Paris's streets anywhere in the city. After two hundred and eighty-four steps, they emerged to the bright sunlight of midmorning. The younger girls traded flirtatious glances with some locals while Andrew and Vivian went off to a far corner, holding hands. Only Cora, Hugh, and Felix listened to the bear droning on about Haussmann's webbed design for the twelve avenues, Napoleon's wishes for the arch to become Paris's symbol of power, the Grand Axis that allowed one to see all the way from the arch to the Place de la Concorde. Will moved over to the edge of the terrace and looked down the wide Avenue des Champs-Élysées.

It truly was a grand design. His hands itched to sketch it, to measure it out and see it on paper as well as by sight, to learn how others had done it so he could emulate the masters. He sighed. Did he really have it in him to be an architect? It was difficult enough, seeing his way to getting through his bachelor's degree. How long would it take him to become a full-fledged architect if he was taking every summer to guide tours?

He wanted a wife, a family. His fortunes had been cast. He was to be the next great bear, leading the finest Grand Tours of Europe for America's coddled and spoiled. Why couldn't he settle into it? Uncle Stuart was retiring; he could run next year's tour as he wished. But the thought of spending every summer and perhaps more with the likes of Cora's siblings, tracing the same paths, pointing out the same nuances in each place, avoiding any true and meaningful connections because he was the bear, and they the clients—

"Are you all right?"

Will turned in surprise toward Cora. She was looking up at him with concern in her beautiful eyes. In the sunlight, he could see that her lashes gave way to blonde at the ends, matching her hair. "What? Oh, I'm fine, fine," he lied, looking away, conscious that he was staring.

"Well, good. You seemed…your expression…well, you appeared sad."

"Sad in one of the most joyous cities of the world?" he said, forcing a smile. "I think not." He gestured outward. "It's beautiful, isn't it?"

"It is."

"Tomorrow we'll go to Versailles, so you can see the grand chateau. I think picnicking on Marie Antoinette's favorite hill, and this view from the Arc, live long in the memory of those who come to France."

"Mmm. I imagine."

He turned to move toward his uncle, who was waving. Cora moved alongside him. "We'll ride bicycles—do you ride?" Will asked.

"I do."

"Good. We'll ride bicycles around the perimeter of the lake and have a picnic. As grand as Versailles's chateau is, it's far grander to be on her grounds."

"That will be welcome. I don't know how many more monuments or grand homes my mind can take in."

He laughed in surprise. "But we've just begun."

"I know," she said ruefully.

"It *is* a lot," he whispered. "I'll try to get him to slow down." He nodded toward the old bear.

She smiled back in appreciation and then moved off.

At least when he was bear, he told himself, he could modify the schedule to better suit himself and his clients. It wasn't all he wanted, but it was something.

As they were returning, Will caught a headline on a newsstand and circled back. A boy hawking papers turned to him and said, "Paper, monsieur?"

"Oui." He fished a coin out of his pocket, and the boy handed him a folded newspaper. Will eyed his clients, who had paused up ahead to wait for him, and then scanned the paper, looking for what he sought. *There.*

"*Montana Copper Strike Averted,*" he translated from the French. His eyes widened—it was about the Kensington-Morgan mine in Butte. He was deciding to read and share it with his clients later when a line caught his eye. He double-checked it and then grinned, remembering Cora at the dinner table at the lake and her suggestion. He nudged his horse's flanks and joined the others. They moved out in pairs, down the street.

"Why do you look so smug?" asked Hugh, beside him.

"Just some news from home."

Andrew looked over his shoulder at him. "What is it?"

"Your father's copper mine narrowly avoided a strike."

"That is nothing new. The men constantly threaten such an action. But they are poorly organized."

"It sounds as if they may have found their footing since you've been away," Will said. "You can read it for yourself."

Andrew glanced at him again, this time in tandem with Vivian. "And?"

"And your fathers settled it before it became an issue."

"And that is worthy of a newspaper story?" Vivian said.

"It is. Because they agreed to pay their workers an additional three dollars a week, over and above the competition, as well as some limited profit sharing if goals are met. They also agreed to hire a company doctor who will see to the men as well as their families."

Andrew straightened in his saddle as Hugh laughed under his breath. Vivian looked ahead to Cora, who was chatting with Felix, who in turn was making the younger girls giggle.

Will grinned. Yes, Cora was making headway in the family. Whether the rest of them wanted her to or not.

CHAPTER 27

~Cora~

When we returned to the Richelieu estate, we found it surrounded by trucks and horse-drawn wagons. Men moved in streams, all carrying crates of food and bottles, presumably of champagne and wine.

"How many do you suppose he invited?" I asked, staring at the hundreds of workers, some of whom came to unload our cars and see us to our quarters.

"By the looks of this, I'd say a good thousand," Will said, his tone holding no delight.

"Lucky us," Lillian said, brushing past. "We've stumbled into the grandest party in all of Paris!" She reached out to squeeze Nell's shoulder, and the two rushed up the stairs, all the more excited to don their costumes.

"At last we'll meet some eligible socialites," Hugh said, stepping next to Felix and climbing the steps right ahead of me. "Have you mastered your tango steps yet?"

"I'm ready to show a Parisian girl or two the romance of the dance," Felix tossed back.

"Good man," Hugh said. "We Americans have to hold our own."

With our host nowhere to be seen, and five glorious hours stretching out before us until we were expected to assemble again, I eagerly followed a servant up the curving staircase to the east wing, spotting the girls as they entered their adjoining rooms and slipping gratefully into my own. I went to the window, which overlooked the gardens, and paused to one side. Will was standing in the center of the garden, fingering a rose, seemingly deep in thought.

What occupied his mind so?

I grabbed hold of the blue curtains and slid them closed, encasing the room in semidarkness. My mind and heart were tired of thinking about so many others—their hopes, dreams, and frustrations. I desperately needed an afternoon with nothing to do but be idle. To sit and stare and let my mind catch up with all it had taken in. To put my thoughts in order like cans upon a shelf.

I lay down on the enormous bed and stared up at the shadows of the gilt four-poster and the inlaid ceiling high above me. I sank into luscious linens, goose down hugging every aching inch of my body. In seconds, I was asleep.

"*Mademoiselle*," said a feminine voice, a hand shaking my shoulder. "*Mademoiselle*," she said, more insistently. When I finally recognized that a French girl had no place in my dream of the Montana prairie, my eyes fluttered open. "*Il est l'heure*, mademoiselle," she said, pointing to her tiny watch. *It is time.* She moved over to the window and threw open the curtains, gesturing toward the waning light as if to say, *Hurry, the party's almost started!*

I heard the bath running, and I glimpsed Anna in my small bathroom. I smelled the lavender bath salts. The French maid handed me a huge towel, pointing to her watch again, then left.

The water stopped, and Anna emerged, smiling at me. "Nice nap then, miss?"

"Indeed." I stretched. "I think I could've slept through the night."

"Ach, that would've been a pity. You would've missed out on wearing your lovely costume." She gestured toward the bed, where a gown had appeared.

I stared with some surprise at the dress. The costumer had done nothing but take our measurements and notations as to the coloring of our eyes and hair.

But my French-blue gown covered over half the bed, its color perfectly matching my room. It had a daringly low neckline lined with lace, and the bodice drew in at the waist. *Can I breathe in that?* I wondered. The huge skirt flared out in successive waves. I laughed under my breath at its decadence and fingered the silk fabric.

To one side lay a white wig with curl upon curl in a style that reminded me of a beehive hanging low from the branches of a tree, and a grand silver mask, meant to be held by its stick. The bear had schooled us that afternoon—we were only to remove our masks in private, to those whom we wished to know our identity. No others.

I smiled. No one would know who I was. I could slip through the crowd without any of the Morgans or Kensingtons watching me. I could just be me. Anonymous again. For one night.

"My, my, miss, don't you look beautiful," Anna said, turning me toward the full-length mirror.

I studied my reflection and gasped.

She'd done my makeup to complement my Louis XIV gown—white powder, dramatic eyes, red lips, and a brown beauty mark that left me looking more like a porcelain doll than myself. But I laughed at the sight, utterly delighted. "Anna, you're a magician! Even without the mask, they'll wonder if it's me!"

She giggled with me and bent to straighten my skirts over the crinolines beneath. I frowned a little over the low-cut bodice and tried to shimmy it up, tugging at the white lace.

"Leave it, leave it be," Anna said, shooing my hands away. "You'll rip it!" She peered over my shoulder at my reflection. "It doesn't show off too much of what the good Lord gave you."

"Are you certain of that?" I said, still frowning at my cleavage.

"Trust me, miss. Compared to some of the gowns I've already seen in the halls this night, you'll look like a nun among the cloisters."

"If you say so…" I turned halfway to see as much of my back as I could in the mirror. The bodice came down in a *V* at my rear, accentuating the shape of my waist and hips. The sleeves were three-quarter length, tight along the shoulder and down my arm, then past the elbow, bursting out in another lovely layer of white lace, soft to the touch, that reached my wrist.

Anna handed me the mask.

"I'm living a fairy tale," I said numbly.

"That you are, miss. Not many get swept into a world such as this."

"No. You're right." Her words rang in my ears. *A world such as this.* I couldn't deny I was excited, thrilled to be going to a real ball. From the Grange Hall dances at home, to the more sophisticated dances aboard the *Olympic*, to the ball tonight…it seemed impossible that I was experiencing it all in such a short period of time.

I like it. I hated admitting that to myself, feeling as if I was betraying my past—all that was good and right and true of my growing-up years. I knew in part that I was giving up on the anger I'd felt toward Mr. Kensington for dragging me into this. I took a deep breath. But it was impossible to deny that this was a kind of fun I hadn't experienced since childhood.

I sent Anna off with word for Will that I'd join the ball on my own accord, so he needn't come for me. As she shut the door behind her, I clasped my hands together and twirled, again looking in the mirror. For the first time in a very long while, I felt free. On the precipice of an adventure of my own design. In a foreign land at the home of a rather charming man. I felt as if I were Marie Antoinette herself in such a gown and slippers. A fairy princess on her way to a magical ball. Never in a hundred years would I have imagined myself truly here, in a place so far from the land of my birth.

My parents would think it ridiculous, of course. The whole extravaganza would have made them shake their heads in disbelief.

I frowned at my reflection, as if I could stare down the negative voices in my head. *But my parents aren't here with me. They shall never be a part of this world.*

I straightened and let my frown fade. This was my life to live. I only needed to figure out who I wanted to be. Who Cora Kensington was—and wasn't.

And to do that, I needed a bit of time to myself. Unencumbered. Undisturbed. Indistinguishable from the rest. Tonight was my perfect opportunity.

I pocketed a handkerchief and my room key in the delicate bag that matched my gown, then went down the stairs, past a group of servants, who bobbed at the sight of me, and then down the central hall, joining others in a long queue that led to the ballroom.

I fell into step beside two other women, wanting to appear as if I were with them, but not too close. One glanced over at me, but then her companion drew her into conversation. We walked down the hall, slowing as people gathered, waiting for Pierre to greet them. People hemmed me in from all sides. Casually, I looked around. None of my traveling companions were in sight. That I could make out, anyway. I was free. For an hour? Two? The whole evening?

The crowd buzzed in fifty different conversations, all in French. Here and there, I could pick out a few words, but despite the bear's efforts to teach us aboard ship, I knew nothing but the basics. A polite smile and nod seemed to get me as far as I needed to go. I didn't really want to talk to anyone this night. I wanted to meld with the crowd and observe, feel the flow of the celebration, but from a step away. With no pressure to perform or speak. I didn't even care if I danced. I simply wanted to be in the midst of the fantastical scene.

It felt like theater to me, and the stage was stunning. Women in the grandest gowns possible; men in ruffled vests and long coats, equally as gaudy and ornate. Everyone wore tall white wigs and masks. Would Pierre know any of them? All of them? As we flowed past our host, I could see him point and name a few, delighted with the success of his party. It was part of the mystique of the evening—to wonder about each person's identity and solve each mystery. Would he know me?

If he did, the illusion of my freedom would be over far too soon. And I wasn't ready for that.

A large family was speaking to Pierre, and I saw my opportunity. I moved to the left, repeating "*excusez-moi*" over and over in a whisper, lest he hear me and recognize my voice. I waited until the guard at his side bent down to speak to a woman, her face blocking Pierre's view of me, and scurried past.

But a hand snaked out and grabbed my wrist. I gasped as I glanced over my shoulder to see who had nabbed me.

"*Nous sommes-nous déjà rencontrés, mademoiselle?*" Pierre asked. I gathered he was asking if we'd met.

"Non, monsieur," I said, making a deep curtsy. I prayed my accent did not give me away. And that he'd let me go without telling my name, as part of the evening's mystique.

"I see," he said, dropping my wrist and switching to English. "But you have an invitation to my ball?"

"Oui, monsieur."

He studied me a moment, and then a man to his left called out to him in a chiding manner, perhaps for lingering over me for so long when so many were waiting.

I hurried across the marble floor and into the grand ballroom, which was already two-thirds full, and made my way into the most crowded section, keeping my head down and listening for my American compatriots. All I heard was some German and quite a bit of English with a refined British accent, but everyone else spoke French. I raised my head and dared to look about.

A footman passed by with a tray, and I took the proffered glass of champagne, mostly because it helped me blend in. Sipping some of the liquid, I felt the bubbles explode in my mouth. I stood near a tiny table on tall legs, so that I might set the champagne down and still manage my mask. Another footman then passed with tiny, delicate croissants filled with some sort of cheese. I took a tiny hors d'oeuvre plate from his tray and then slipped two croissants onto it. They practically melted in my mouth. After him came another servant, serving more fruit, cheese, and a mountain of what I assumed was caviar.

I'd only read of caviar and was eager to try it. I put a spoonful of the black shiny eggs atop a slice of cheese and bit in. And almost immediately wished I could spit it out. I looked around, but knew there was no way for me to tactfully do so. Steeling myself, I took a swig of champagne to wash it down and then another to wash away the taste. With my tongue still shriveling in my mouth from the residue of brine, I finished off my champagne and handed the empty glass to a servant.

Despite my disappointment over the caviar, I was feeling freer and lighter by the minute, most likely the effects of my swiftly consumed champagne. The music had begun and people were assembling at the center of the ballroom's parquet floor, but it did not appear as if they were ready to dance. Others joined behind them, and still more, so I did the same, still eager to blend in. Trumpets sounded then, and a loud voice announced Lord de Richelieu, with a most impressive list of his titles. *So he's not only handsome and rich, he's from nobility, too.* I didn't know why that surprised me. Perhaps it was because he was a man who chose to travel the English Channel with others when he could obviously afford his own vessel.

Two women were announced, and Pierre walked the human aisle, his hands raised as he held the women's hands on either side of him. I felt an arrow of jealousy. Were they sisters? Cousins? Or romantic interests? I chided myself for the sting that ran through my body, as well as for thinking that I might have truly held his attention. If I were a grateful sort of girl, I'd be thankful for the invitation to his lovely estate, if nothing else. That he housed us and clothed us for his hall, rather than tossing us aside when I told him who—and what—I was. *Help me to be grateful, Lord,* I prayed. But as they passed me, another stinging shiver ran through me.

"Found you," said a voice in my ear.

Startled, I took a staggering step to the side. He caught my arm, and I knew him then. "Will?"

He gave me a curious smile and bowed, dropping his mask and my arm. "Indeed, mademoiselle. Why did you not join the others?"

"I'm sorry. I only...I was hoping for a night of...anonymity."

He studied me for a moment. "Your secret is safe with me. I shall watch over you, but from afar."

"Thank you," I managed to say. But it was the last thing I wanted—anyone watching me at all.

"Take care," he whispered, and then he left my side. I didn't watch him go, hoping none of my other companions had seen him speaking to me. Was I so easy to pick out in the crowd? Perhaps my identity was not nearly as secure as I had envisioned. Or perhaps Will was especially good at detecting what he sought out.

I took another glass of champagne. At the front, upon a dais, Pierre lifted his glass in a toast and ended it with "vive la France." *To France.*

"To France," the crowd shouted back to him, glasses high. Then they drank them all down. Eyes wide, I took a big sip but could not manage more. I handed my mostly full glass to a waiter, who looked back at me with disdain for wasting the precious liquid, but I knew if I wasn't careful, I'd soon end up tipsier than I cared to be.

"Puis-je avoir de l'eau?" I hoped I remembered that right—I was in need of water.

The waiter's nose wrinkled up further, but he nodded once. "Oui, mademoiselle." He left me then, collecting more glasses before disappearing among the crowd. I stayed where I was so he could find me again and then heard the orchestra tuning up for their first song.

The ballroom floor cleared, and Pierre and his two ladies paraded to the center. After the introduction of the song, they began the most fascinating dance I'd ever seen, with Pierre focused on one woman and then the other, as if flirting with both in turns. The crowd laughed and clapped as Pierre tried to kiss one, and she slipped away, and then the other, and she escaped him too. Two men approached, one from either end, walking in a sort of skip-hop in time with the music, until they reached the trio. Then, as the music reached a crescendo, each woman left Pierre.

He pantomimed his sorrow, and the crowd moaned in mock grief with him as the music came to an end.

Then a lone violinist rose and walked toward Pierre, playing a haunting, hopeful tune. Our host, obviously relishing his role, perked up, turning and following the violinist to the crowd, as if the musician were his pied piper, pulling him along by a string. The violinist, still playing, nodded toward a girl in blue, and Pierre nodded in turn. He took her hand, and the orchestra played perhaps twelve measures of the song as he led her about the dance floor and then returned her to her place with a regal bow of thanks. The girl curtsied deeply. The violinist continued along our side of the crowd, and the process was repeated, again, with a girl in blue. I understood then; Pierre was seeking me. As the second girl was returned to her companions, I looked behind me, hoping to edge toward the back again. But the crowd was thick, and they pressed forward, waiting to see whom he would pick next.

The music was coming closer, and my heart pounded. I turned and had to press my arm between two ladies to get them to part and make way for me. They muttered and gasped in dismay, but then our host drew their attention again. The hair on the back of my neck rose as I continued to make my way back in the crowd, knowing the violinist and Pierre were directly behind me. I had to be fairly invisible by now, hidden by the sea of people. I dared to turn and glance behind me—and saw Pierre staring right at me, a grin on his face. *"Elle essaie de s'échapper de la danse!"*

I decided he'd shouted something about me trying to escape, judging by the laughter and gasps he elicited from the crowd.

People surged around me, and helpful hands urged me forward. There was no way out. Reluctantly, I stepped forward, head down.

He took my hand and kissed it, then drew me out onto the dance floor.

As we danced a delicate waltz, his smile grew, and he raised his arm. The crowd cheered at his signal. I wondered what it meant until the music continued and others joined us on the dance floor for the rest of the song. Apparently, the lord had found his preferred dance companion.

He took a turn past me, and his eyes narrowed as he studied me. "Why so glum, Cora?" he asked. "Surely it is not the worst thing, to be chosen out of so many."

"On an evening in which I wished to be anonymous, it is."

His chin rose, and he appraised me as we continued the dance. "I see. It wears thin, does it not? The mantle of a family name, even if you are new to it?"

I smiled back at him. He, more than anyone, would understand such a weight. He'd obviously been living with it—and escaping it on occasion—all his life.

"Is it only you, Pierre? You have no kin? No brothers or sisters?"

"It is only I here. My father and mother are dead, my sister happily married in Provence. I lumber about this great house, wishing only for the right bride to help me fill it with many children."

I glanced back at him, surprised by the meaningful tone of his words. Was he testing the waters to see if I was interested? Or was it merely his most convenient line, an easy lure for women seeking their handsome prince?

But he stared back at me with a calm, steady look. He was serious. And of the right age for such a quest—probably twenty-five or so.

The dance ended, but Pierre did not drop my hand. Instead, he led me to the center of the floor, where couples lined up from one end to the other. "Now we shall dance the favorite of the peasants who gave their very lives, so that others might dance in the years to come."

Bastille Day, I thought. Like our American Independence Day, remembering those who fought for freedom…and those who died. Hugh and Felix wouldn't likely be showing off their tango skills this night—this ball was all about hearkening *back* in time. The tango was too modern.

"Follow my lead," Pierre said. "It is rather simple but elegant." He pulled me closer. "Back right, back left, right, right, right," he said, his breath warm in my ear. And then we moved, one of his hands firmly holding mine, the other at my waist. He repeated, in a whisper, the steps as we went through them, but my mind was on his hand, warm and so at ease at my back. I had the feeling he would be able to catch me if I stumbled and would make it look like it was a part of the dance. "Now forward left, forward right, left, left, left," he finished, lifting my arm and urging me under it and then around him as he waited for me to return to his other side.

We repeated the steps, but this time, he circled me. His proximity and manner sent a delicious shiver down my back. Could it be that he was truly interested in me? Of all the women at his disposal? I could feel the chill in the room, pointed toward me. *Who's the newcomer? Why her?* But warding it off was the warmth of Pierre's passionate attention, the heat in his eyes.

I was reminded of Antonio's warning about Frenchmen and their tendencies toward romance. And in school, I'd seen the handsomest boy in the county go after the most reluctant girls, ignoring all those who hovered near. I was nothing but a challenge to Pierre, something different in a sea of the same. So after the dance ended, I curtsied and said I needed some fresh air.

"I will escort you."

"No, please, monsieur. Stay with your guests. I...I shall find you later."

A stunned flash passed through his eyes, and then a hint of anger. I'd offended him. When was the last time a woman had turned down the handsome young lord? "Very well," he said crisply.

I turned to go.

"I shall be watching for my lady in blue."

I rewarded him with a smile and small curtsy. "I sincerely hope so, monsieur."

His expression softened, and I felt as if I had been dismissed with his blessing. I hurried off the dance floor, and the crowd parted, all eyeing me with curiosity. I moved directly to the far doors, which were open to the gardens, and down the steps to a place I could finally be alone again, away from any prying eyes. I breathed deeply and slowly, waiting for my hands to stop trembling.

CHAPTER 28

-William-

"Truly?" Vivian asked. "Was it not enough that she had to embarrass us all with her public proclamation to Lord de Richelieu—now she envisions herself as Cinderella at the ball? Honestly," she said, taking another glass of champagne and swigging a gulp down as she surveyed the crowd. "Now she's disappeared again!"

"Perhaps she's left behind a glass slipper," Hugh said, one eyebrow raised. He searched the crowd, his attention as piqued as Richelieu's, apparently. Will stifled a sigh. He'd much rather trail Cora about than spend time with his other clients, but he and Antonio had just traded posts. Even now, Antonio made his way out the door to follow Cora from afar to make sure she did not encounter any trouble.

The younger girls were chattering in excitement about the dance, practically standing on tiptoes as they waited for someone to come and invite them to the floor. Hugh was drifting away, ogling an elegant, slender young woman in a dusty-rose gown, while Felix was chatting up a young gentleman, probably inquiring about the next available gambling opportunity.

Will purposefully avoided the champagne, as did Uncle Stuart and Antonio, because their clients were counting on them to keep clear heads. *Like a shepherd to the sheep*, he thought morosely. For once, he wished he could let loose, swallow his own flute of champagne, and ask anyone he wanted to dance. He didn't blame Cora for her hunger to fade into the welcome folds of the crowd. He felt the same desire. To not be looked to for guidance, to not have to keep count. Every autumn, as they said farewell to their clients, it was the single best pleasure for Will—to no longer be responsible for anyone but himself.

Two young gents came near and invited the youngest girls to dance. Andrew asked Vivian to join him on the floor. That suited Will; if they were dancing, they weren't likely to get into too much difficulty. Others surrounded Uncle Stuart as word spread that this was the group of Americans Richelieu had chosen to host, and among them was the girl in blue he had specifically sought out to honor with his first dance, the one who had abruptly left him.

So much for keeping our identity a secret.

Will had stifled a laugh at the expression on the young nobleman's powdered face. It was clear their host had rarely encountered a woman like Cora. Will looked for Richelieu and found him chatting with a group, making them laugh—but his eyes kept shifting beyond them. He was looking for her. And that was not a good thing.

Will felt his uncle edge near, his eyes in the same direction. "I see it," Will said, before the bear could speak.

"It happens quickly," Stuart said.

"I know." Will knew the story well. In all of his uncle's years as a guide, only once had he had an affair get out of hand; it had ended in nuptials in Spain and a divorce in Portugal. Such matters were devastating to a tour guide's reputation, and he was determined to never allow it to happen again. Uncle Stuart left it to Will to see through, of course. He moved on, busily chatting, secure in the knowledge that Will and Antonio were on task. Will sighed, resisting the urge to rub the tension from his temples despite his ridiculous white wig.

He eased to the right and neared a man who'd been chatting with Felix's new friend a moment before, intent on finding out if he was right—that a poker game was at hand. Gambling was an acceptable enterprise among most of their clients and their fathers, but it grated on Will to see thousands of dollars lost at cards when there were far better ways to invest one's money. *Such as a poor man's education*, he thought bitterly.

Uncle Stuart took pride in teaching the young men they guided how to win at cards four out of five times—"four to save your father's money, but losing once to leave behind no enemies." On the fifth, losing hand, they were to bow out, every time. No negotiations. It was as strict a rule as no fraternization with the clients was for Will. Fortunately, the gentlemen didn't seem to mind the rule since they became experts at the game.

However, the trick was to not let the young gents become involved with games run by sharks; professional gamblers tended to frequent such events as this ball, seeking out gullible, rich young targets. And their clients, often young and green, were some of these sharks' favorite "opportunities."

Will struck up a conversation with the man near Felix and exchanged pleasantries until he offered him the bait. "Word has it there's to be game of cards later on," Will said.

The man, in his forties and relatively handsome, gave him a sly smile. "I've heard the same."

"Any chance a bloke like me could join you?"

"Certainly, certainly," he said. "If need be, we'll gather others for a second."

A second table. That wouldn't do. He had to be at the first, with Felix, to keep track of him. The heady draw of a good table—or the challenge of a bad one—had bankrupted more than one rich young man. "That's all right," he said, lifting his hands in surrender. "Best for me to keep clear of it anyway. I'm not feeling luck blowing on the wind."

"No, no," said the nobleman. "Don't back out now. Some of the finest men in the room will be at that table."

"Which table? The first or the second?"

He gave Will another smile, realizing he'd been pushed into a corner. "The first, then. I'll see that you are seated with them."

"Thank you, monsieur," Will said with a polite nod. He walked off a few paces to take a cup of punch. Uncle Stuart always gave him a stipend to enter card games when he felt it necessary; Will pocketed 10 percent of any winnings. If he lost, he had to pay Stuart back 5 percent after what his uncle deemed "acceptable losses." But he never lost. His ability with numbers would one day serve him well in business. One day. When he was finally through following around young men chasing new whims and could concentrate on his own.

There were eight at the table in the magnificent library. Will, Felix, a Brit, and five Frenchmen.

"What are the stakes?" Felix asked.

"We are at a French table, friend," said the dealer. "On the brink of Bastille Day, we speak only French. If you are not able to say what you need in French, we require you to drink a shot of whiskey." He nodded toward a small glass in front of Felix as a woman bent over him to fill it.

Felix smiled and downed the liquid. *"Même si je parle français, je peux boire?"* May I drink even if I do speak French?

The others around the table laughed. The dealer shrugged. "If your French is impeccable, then you may do as you like," he said in French.

The maid filled the Frenchmen's glasses, and the dealer raised an eyebrow and gestured to Will and the Brit, Kipling, to see if they cared for a shot.

Kipling agreed, but Will waved off the invitation.

The others drank their shots. The dealer shuffled a couple more times, passed the deck to his neighbor on the right, who cut it and then began to deal the cards. *"Cent francs minimum. Par main. Les as sont élevé, messieurs."*

It was a hundred francs per hand to play, and that was on top of the ten thousand they had to bring to the table to purchase chips. Aces were high.

"Jacks are wild?" Felix asked, studying his cards.

The dealer motioned toward his glass. *Again.* "And no, jacks are not wild," he said in French.

Felix acted surprised, then rueful. He tossed back his second shot.

Will cut his eyes to his old friend. Was he doing this on purpose? Felix was as lazy as they came, but he was never stupid. Did he want to lull them into a sense of complacency, thinking he was an easy mark? Or did he hope to drink them under the table, making them, in turn, the marks? He studied his cards and chose two, placing them facedown on the table, as did the others.

The dealer dealt them each two more cards. Will studied his hand, making a rapid decision so he could study the others' faces. The Brit and one of the Frenchmen were frowning over their hands. Another Frenchmen was moaning and groaning, clearly bluffing that he had a terrible hand—the question was, was that to make them think he had a terrific hand when he did not? The remaining two Frenchmen were quiet, polite as they waited.

The dealer nodded to the man at his right, the Brit. The young, blond man took five hundred in chips and tossed them to the center. The next two followed suit. The moaning Frenchman folded. It was Felix's turn. Will tried to look uninterested as his friend took ten chips and pushed them into the stack. *That would pay for a whole semester of tuition right there...*

A devilish thought came to him. If Felix were to lose, would it not be best if Will was the one to beat him? He could claim he was teaching his friend how to play cards well, and give Felix a bit of comeuppance at the same time. Let him know what it felt like to be the loser for once. He shoved in his own pile of ten chips, the equivalent of about a hundred dollars. As did the man to his left. The dealer paused, then stacked twenty and shoved them in.

Will kept his expression steady as he studied his cards. Could he truly win the hand with three kings? Moreover, could he really risk two hundred dollars of his uncle's money? Two hundred dollars at all?

Felix flashed him a wise, superior smile. Irritated, Will ducked his head, picked off ten more chips, and tossed them in.

The dealer laid out his cards. Full house.

Felix had three jacks.

And the man to his left had a pair of aces.

They'd all lost out to the dealer. Will nodded at the dealer, and the man hauled in the mound of chips, casually stacking them. "So, you are the Americans hailing from the wilds of Montana," said a man to his right, in French.

"You would be surprised to find out how civilized it is," Will returned in French.

"Tell us of the girl—the one Lord de Richelieu picked out of the crowd tonight."

Will clenched his teeth and pretended to be studying his cards. It would be best if Felix answered. In fact, Will was rather curious to find out what he would say.

"*C'est ma sœur,*" Felix said. *She is my sister.* He set down two cards.

"Ah, your *sister,*" said the man, with an odd inflection in his voice. Felix and Will looked across the table at him. "To your sister," he said, saluting Felix with his shot glass. The Frenchmen all drank their round. Felix and Will did too, each still watching the man across from them.

"She is most beautiful. She is not spoken for?"

"No, she is not," Will said. "And that is how her father wishes her returned to him." He offered a smile. "Pure. Not with a Frenchman in tow."

The Frenchmen roared in approval, and they all nodded and smiled, the two nearest patting Will on the back.

"You do your work, little bear," said the leader. "And keep the sheep safely in their pen. Oh, but look!" he said with mock surprise. "One has escaped to our lovely green." He rubbed the soft felt of the table between them.

"I am no lamb," Felix said.

"I hope you are not," said another. "With beautiful sisters in your company, you shall likely need to be a wolf to chase away our countrymen."

The conversation was distracting Will. He'd thrown away one of the cards he needed. Stifling a sigh, he set down two others and waited for the bidding to begin. It remained rather flat until it reached Kipling, who put in twenty chips, straight out. Felix and the moaning Frenchman—who was now leading and conspicuously quiet—saw his raise.

The Brit took the hand with four queens, but Will entered the next hand with more confidence. He was convinced the moaner was bluffing, and he'd make his bold move with this hand or the next. Three of the Frenchmen were straightforward card players, in it as idle distraction or as an excuse so they wouldn't have to dance with their wives. The real contenders were the Frenchman with the most chips, the moaner, and Felix.

Will thought he could take them all.

⸻◈⸻

It turned out he was wrong. Terribly wrong.

Will did not win. But neither did Felix. And now Will had to face his uncle, three hundred dollars poorer. He wanted to bury his head in his hands. He wanted to scream. But all he did was shake each man's hand, congratulate the winner—the moaner, surprising them all by alternately bluffing and playing it straight—and walk out beside Felix.

"Tough round, eh?" Felix said, his voice slurred. As the game progressed, he'd lapsed back into English and had downed eight more shots. Will was surprised that he could still stand. "Really thought you had a chance of *besss*-ting him." He stumbled, and Will wearily wrapped Felix's arm around his shoulders.

Will *had* come close several times. So close. He chided himself for getting sucked into the game rather than watching over Felix. He'd let pride and greed take him for a ride, and now he didn't have a horse to ride home. Uncle Stuart would be more than chagrined at the loss. Will could win it back, sure. But if he didn't have better luck at the next table, or the next, he might not end up with enough to enroll in the university again, come September.

He shook his head, wondering what had come over him. He always did better than he had tonight—always. But thoughts of Felix, and of Cora, had him all mixed up. Missing things. Unable to keep track of cards and factors of probability as he usually did. As his father had.

His father…

"What's brought you to the doldrums?" Felix slurred, reaching over his right hand and pinching Will's cheeks.

Will wrenched his head back, out of Felix's grasp. "I'm fine."

"Oh, no you're not," Felix said. "Tell me. The night's young. Let's go get a glass of champagne."

"I think not. I'll get you to your room so you can sleep off what will become one monstrous hangover."

"How come you're not drunk?"

"I like to keep a level head."

"Level heads lead to level lives," Felix said.

"I'll take a level field any day over a hill."

"You say that now. But doesn't that sound dreadfully boring, even to you?"

"I'd like a bit of boredom."

They'd reached Felix's room. Will leaned him against the door-jamb. "Where's your key, Felix?"

"I dunno."

Will sighed and began rifling through Felix's pockets, pausing occasionally to right the man when he started to slump. He slapped his cheeks. "Stay with me. Almost there."

"Almost there," Felix said, eyes dazed.

Will found the key at last, slid it into the two-hundred-year-old lock, and then half carried Felix to the vast bed. He dropped him into the center of it, went around to the other side, and, hauling on his arms, dragged him fully on. Then he unbuckled the atrocious costume boots and slid them off.

"Ahh, tha's better," Felix said, smiling, eyes closed.

"I'll be back to wake you in the morning."

"Mornin'."

Will rolled his eyes, laid the key on the table by the door, and slipped out. Other guests from the ball were returning to their rooms.

Two giggling girls passed a couple that was passionately kissing in a doorway. Will averted his eyes, his agitation rising. *Debauchery and silliness everywhere.*

I hate this life.

He corrected himself. *I hate the current direction of my life.*

What he wanted most was to return to his room and fall into a dreamless slumber. But he knew he had to go and find the others. Make sure they all got to their respective rooms…alone. Even Uncle Stuart would be assisting on that front. *Lord, give me strength*, he prayed silently. *Forgive me my envy, my pride, my greed.* He shook his head in shame and looked up, then sighed again and forced himself to continue walking. Onward and upward, Uncle Stuart always said. "Onward and upward," Will muttered.

He moved down the hall and met up with the two youngest girls, ushered by Vivian. "Ah. Off to bed, then?"

"Yes," Lillian said with a pout. "We begged for but one more dance, but Andrew and Vivian fancy themselves our parents."

"Just one more dance, Vivian," Nell whined. "That's all we ask."

"Someone has to take responsibility for you, if you shan't for yourselves," Vivian said. She gave the girls a small smile as she shook her head. "There shall be more dances. Right, William?"

"Many more. Best to get some good rest. Tomorrow is a new day—and I believe Uncle Stuart has a rather daunting schedule in store for us. Off to Versailles." He gave the girls an encouraging grin. "If you think the Richelieu chateau is beautiful, wait until you see the grand Hall of Mirrors in the Chateau of Versailles."

The girls smiled at each other in anticipation.

"Where are the others?" Will asked, turning to Vivian.

"Andrew was heading out to the gardens to smoke a pipe with Hugh. I thought Felix was with you."

"He was. He's retired now."

She gave Will a knowing look and nodded once. "I see." Then she turned and walked away.

Frustration rolled through him. She was going to make him ask? "And Cora?" he asked, as lightly as he could.

"I don't know where she's run off to," she said, raising one eyebrow as she glanced back over her shoulder. "I haven't seen her for hours." She was turning the younger girls, steering them by their shoulders down the hall again.

"Good night, Will," Nell said.

"Good night, all," he said. *Four down, three to go.* With any luck at all, he'd come across Uncle Stuart and Antonio bringing the rest, and this night would be over.

CHAPTER 29

~Cora~

I'd alternated between braving the dance floor and walking the gardens for hours, bending to examine what seemed like every single blossom and bloom within it, as if I were a budding botanist. I was waiting for the music to wane now, praying that Pierre would become distracted, enamored with some other young woman at his feet. But he found me.

"There you are," he said, prying his wig from his head and tossing it to the bushes behind me.

It made me laugh as I turned to see it hanging there. "Your gardeners will wonder just what sort of moss is growing among your vines."

He smiled easily. "I cannot help it. I could not stand it for another minute."

I hesitated, suddenly wanting nothing more than to do the same. He clearly saw it on my face. "Please. Be free of yours as well."

I quickly unpinned it and then pulled it from my hair.

"Ahh. Better, no?"

"Better, yes."

"Here," he said reaching into my hair and pulling the rest of the pins from it, running his fingers along my scalp, adeptly prying my chignon free and loosing it in waves. I stared at him in open wonder. For a man I'd so recently met, the action was entirely too…forward. But I couldn't deny that it felt wonderful, both to be touched and to have my hair loose, not to mention bucking the ever-growing list of social conventions I was tired of following. I moved my neck, stretching out muscles suddenly weary from the load I hadn't realized I'd been carrying—the wig probably weighed three pounds. "Allow me," he said, slipping behind me, gently rubbing my neck and shoulders.

I edged away. "Monsieur. Please." My tone begged him to stop.

He waved me off with a teasing laugh. "You Americans! So provincial!" His face was kind. He turned and took two champagne flutes from a waiting servant. "Come. Walk with me." He offered his arm.

"I've been walking all evening. My feet are begging me to retire."

"Then sit with me a moment," he said easily, gesturing toward a bench.

I sat down, thinking we would rest for a time, together. But then he was down on his knees, grabbing hold of my ankle.

"Pierre!" I cried.

He looked up at me and laughed. "I am merely helping you get rid of the slippers!"

I laughed in shock. "I'm perfectly capable of taking off my own slippers."

"I'm certain you are," he said, taking a seat beside me. "But does it not delight you, that I'm willing to serve you in any way?"

"There is a line," I said.

"Fine." He crossed his arms. "Then slip them off yourself."

I pried them from my sore feet and closed my eyes in relief as my toes settled into nests of green moist grass.

"Ahh, better?"

"Much."

"Now we can walk. We shall play a game in the maze."

My eyes narrowed. "What sort of game?" For hours I'd seen couples disappear among the trimmed hedges—nine feet tall with uniform walls—and return later. Sometimes an hour later.

"It is harmless," he protested, rising and offering his hand.

I hesitated. I'd spent my whole life being the good girl, making the cautious choice, following the sensible road. Couldn't this evening be about spontaneity as well as anonymity? "What does one do in the maze?"

"One strolls and finds their way to the end." He lifted a brow. "Or one races to the end and receives a prize."

"It would not be fair," I said. "You know that maze, and it's dark."

He smiled. "The men of King Louis's time would blindfold themselves and try to fetch a maiden from the maze."

I laughed. "So you suggest I take to the maze and you come after me, blindfolded? What do I win if I reach the end without getting caught?"

He tapped his lip and considered me. "What is it that you wish to receive?"

I stared at him and smiled. What did I want? "A ride in a boat at Versailles, with no conversation at all for a full hour. Utter silence."

He smiled. "Easily done. I shall do nothing but row and stare at you in awe." He reached up and caressed my cheek, but I smiled and edged away.

He caught my wrist. "And if I catch you before you leave the maze? What do I receive?"

I felt daring, impetuous. "I don't know. What is it that you want, monsieur?"

He smiled again. "A kiss. A *willing* kiss."

My heart hammered in my chest. For the first time, I admitted to myself that I wouldn't mind getting caught by this man, kissed by him. A pang of guilt shot through me as I thought of Will. But that confused me. I had no feelings for Will, did I? He was my guide and guardian, nothing more. And regardless of what Antonio said, I did not feel in danger. Not with Pierre.

"All right," I said quickly, before I could change my mind. I lifted my hand to shake his in the manner of men.

He laughed then and slowly pulled a silk handkerchief from his pocket. His confidence unnerved me.

"I get a thirty-second lead," I said.

"No. That was not a part of our agreement."

"Pierre!"

He raised one eyebrow, holding his handkerchief in both hands. "I suggest you go, for as soon as I have this tied, I shall be coming to find you, seeking that kiss."

He seemed to brook no argument, so I turned and fled into the mouth of the maze. I heard him laughing behind me, and I wondered just how difficult it would be to find my way. It was past ten and there was a little twilight left, but the shadows were deep among the tall hedges. My chest was tight with excitement and fear, and it felt good to run, even if I could barely breathe in the tight bodice of the gown.

At the end of the first channel, I turned the corner. Halfway down the next channel, there was an exit to a third row, or I could continue on to the end. I heard Pierre whistling, a mere hedge wall between us, and it sent my heart into a triple-time beat. On tiptoes, and lifting my skirt so it wouldn't *swish*, I hurried to the end of the row and took the second exit. I hoped he'd think I'd taken the first, like a scared rabbit rather than a thinking competitor.

He did, because in a moment, I heard him on the other side of the hedge again. I glanced one way and then the other, trying to figure out which way would be safest, while considering where I was in the maze and keeping track of what I'd seen already. I hoped to form a mental map.

"Little American flower? Where are you?" Pierre called.

That set me to running again, wanting to put a good distance between us. I headed right, because I knew the exit was to the far right—I just had to find my way to it. But when I turned the corner, I came to a dead end. I whirled and opened my eyes wide, trying to see in the gathering darkness. He hadn't appeared there yet. Quickly, I backtracked, and then held my breath as Pierre walked by the exit, arms outstretched before him. He paused and turned his head toward me, as if he had heard me. I was deadly still, holding my breath. He turned then and headed on. It was then that it occurred to me. He knew the way, even blindfolded. So I was better served following him to the end and then running past him at the last minute, claiming victory.

I eased around the corner, watching until he made another turn, then hurrying toward that exit point. Again and again, we repeated the process, with him leading me to the proper escape and me rushing to follow. The trick was not to lose him entirely… I scurried on tiptoes to the next turn and cringed as two men came from the other direction, laughing with delight when they saw me. *"Mais qu'est ce donc? Une belle fille, perdue dans le labyrinthe? Pourrions-nous vous aider?"*

I could not interpret what they were saying. From their tone, they were flirting. I looked the other way for Pierre. I saw him in a shaft of light from a gas lamp, just on the other side of the hedge. He'd paused, head in profile, listening.

"Non, non, s'il vous plaît," I whispered, having no choice but to head the other way.

They laughed again, and I heard them talking to Pierre as he neared them, obviously having turned around. I could barely see the three of them in the dark, but I knew they wouldn't hesitate to aid their host in finding what he sought. I turned the corner and ran down the long aisle, knowing I must be getting very close to the exit. But it was so dark that I didn't realize until I reached the end that there was no exit here.

A figure, little more than a shadow among others, appeared at the far end. My heart pounded again. I was alternately terrified and delighted, a delicious mix. He moved toward me, confident now that I was trapped, that he had won.

"Come to me, sweetheart," he cooed. "There is nothing to fear in losing this game."

I edged closer to him, wanting to be away from the wall, where he expected to trap me. I tried to control my breathing, catch my breath enough so I'd be able to hold it when he passed. I studied his footsteps, how he held his hands out. I took a couple more steps toward him, then crouched, my shoulder pressing into the hedge at my right. But my skirts were enormous. Slowly, I gathered them in, cringing as the crinoline beneath made a sound. He was almost upon me.

He was smiling, and I knew he anticipated victory at any moment. "Where are you, Miss Cora? I can hardly wait to collect my prize."

I ducked, and his hand only missed my head by an inch. He moved past, and slowly, slowly I raised my head and looked over my shoulder. He was fading into the dark shadows, so I pulled my body out of the hedge and then winced as it pulled back. I tugged, and the delicate silk, caught on a twig within, tore at a seam, bringing the whole cap of the shoulder down in a hopeless flap.

But my attention was back on my pursuer rather than the gown. He'd heard the rustling in the hedge, the tear of the fabric. He had turned and was racing toward me. "Why, you little minx!" he said in delight.

I let out a squeal of laughter, rose, and ran. Now it was so dark that I might as well have been blindfolded myself. I stretched one hand out to touch the hedge on my right, keeping my left before me so I wouldn't collide with an end wall.

I knew I was making far too much noise and that Pierre would easily follow. My only chance was to make it to the end before he did. But I was hopelessly lost, mixed up on where I was in the maze. For all I knew, I was right back at the beginning.

My right sleeve caught in the hedge, and I let out a little yelp when it wouldn't release me. I tugged and winced when I felt the branch both tear the lace and cut my wrist. Ignoring the pain, I paused, trying to settle down and listen for a moment, detect where Pierre might be. Was he in front of me? Behind?

I looked up and noticed a glow on the horizon; we were likely to see the full moon rise at any moment. Maybe if I waited just a few more moments, I would be able to see again and make my way out.

But I heard his whistle and had no choice but to press on. I couldn't tell if he was in my same channel or in the next, but he was close. I turned the corner and reached out as I moved forward. And touched a chest.

He laughed then, a delightful, rumbling sound, and I quickly dropped my hand.

"Oh," I said in a breath. Half of me was relieved that it was over; half was panicked.

"Come. I take you not to the guillotine, but to someplace special in the maze." I could see that he was pulling the handkerchief from his eyes and tucking it into his pocket. The fat full moon had risen behind me. I glanced back.

"It is lovely, isn't it?" he said.

I nodded. "Indeed." But when I turned back to him, he was gazing intently at me. I could feel the heat of my blush as I looked down, unable to stare back into his eyes, knowing what was to come.

He offered his hand and I took it with my left. My right wrist stung, and I knew that it was cut, maybe even bleeding, but my attention was solely on the feel of his cool, strong fingers around mine. We turned a corner and then another, and then ducked beneath a low-hanging arbor, full of rose vines. The night air was thick with their sweet scent as we made our way to the center, which held a small gazebo. Vines crawled up each of the six pillars, winding together in a living roof, higher than the tunnel that had led us to it. Here we could see the moon, now fully round, leaving the forest below in silhouette. I stared at it, suddenly nervous, knowing that Pierre would wish to claim his prize.

"Cora," he whispered, stepping closer to me. His hand moved to my lower back, pulling me toward him. He slowly caressed my face and then paused, his eyebrows lowering in concern over my torn dress.

"Oh," I said, pulling the cap of my sleeve up in embarrassment. "That won't do."

He laughed lowly. "And so the maze became a dragon, intent on eating you up."

"It tried, but I fought it off," I said with a smile.

His hand was feather-light as he held my chin between his thumb and forefinger. "Shall you fight me off too?" he breathed, hovering near my lips.

"You may claim your prize," I whispered in return, liking the heat between us, the shiver of daring that raced down my back. Every bit of me felt alive, more alive than I'd felt in months.

He didn't wait a moment longer. He leaned in and covered my lips with his, soft at first, then searching, pulling me closer until I was pressed against his hard chest.

When he released me, I stood there, almost paralyzed. I'd been kissed before. But that was a boy's kiss, perfunctory, proper. What Pierre bestowed upon me was a kiss like none I'd ever experienced. A kiss of passion, promising so much more. I lifted a hand to my cheek and stared at him.

"What is it?" he asked, giving me a curious smile. But then his smile faded. "What happened to your hand, Cora?" He reached out and took my right hand in his, bending to examine the blood that ran from my wrist into my palm. But all I could think about was him, and how I wished he would kiss me again.

A shiver of disgust ran through me. Was I as wanton as my mother had been with my father? Was this sort of passion, taking place in unseen passageways, the sort of thing that led them to...?

I wrenched my hand from his grasp. "Which way to the exit?"

He frowned and then turned and pointed. "Right there, at the end of this arbor. Then to the left..."

I lifted the hem of my skirt and raced down the far steps and through the other arbor.

"Cora. Cora!"

I ignored him, wanting to be out, away, alone.

"Cora, wait!"

I knew I should hold on, wait for him, be polite, even if I saw him only as my host, but I didn't, I couldn't, not anymore. He was right behind me. I didn't want to talk about it tonight. I was liable to start crying, and that would be beyond horrifying. I turned to the left and raced out of the maze—and ran directly into Will and Antonio.

"Whoa," Will said, helping me stand upright, steadying me. "We were just looking..." He was taking in my hair, my ripped sleeve and bloody hand, my bare toes sticking out from beneath the hem of my dress. And then he was looking up in consternation at Pierre, just exiting the maze, chasing me.

"Why you...," Will said in a furious sneer, pulling back his fist.

"No, Will!" I cried.

But it was too late.

He rammed his fist into Pierre's face and sent him sprawling.

CHAPTER 30

~William~

"Pierre!" Cora screamed, running to him.

But he was already scrambling to his feet, rising to meet Will's charge.

Two men from the maze had exited and were running to his aid. Antonio was behind Will, waiting for Richelieu to get up.

"No!" Cora said, coming between Will and Richelieu. She put a hand to his chest and the other to Richelieu's. "Will, there's been a misunderstanding," she said, panting. "You owe Lord de Richelieu an apology."

Seeing the insistent look in her eyes, Will could feel the color drain from his face. He'd thought that Cora had been fleeing from Richelieu, but perhaps she'd been running from the other men in the maze. He glared at the two of them, now on either side of their host. Richelieu rubbed his cheek and warily studied Will. A crowd was forming around them, including Hugh and Andrew.

"Cora," Will said carefully. "Tell me what happened. Your dress—"

"Nothing!" she said, clearly horrified. "We were playing a game of hide-and-seek in the maze, and my dress got caught in the bushes."

A look of shock ran through Richelieu's face. *"Vous pensiez que je…" You thought I…* He straightened, and his eyes hardened. Muscles in his jaw twitched. "Monsieur, I pride myself on respecting a woman's honor as well as her wishes. I am French, but I am a gentleman."

Will swallowed hard. He took a deep breath. "Of course you are. I am very sorry, my lord. I only sought to come to Cora's aid. I made a hasty assumption. Please, forgive me." He touched his chest and bowed his head. He wished the man would take a swing at him, make things even.

But Richelieu only gave him a solitary nod. "You are Miss Cora's protector, and for that I am grateful. You acted out of care for her, and because I, too, care for her, I shall overlook your attack."

"Thank you, my lord," Will said, still wishing he'd just hit him. It'd be easier to deal with than owing their host an additional debt. Uncle Stuart would lecture him for hours. Never had he gotten himself into such a mess before.

"It is very late. Perhaps it's best if we all said good night," Richelieu said.

"Thank you, Pierre," Cora said, reaching up as if to touch his cheek, then pulling away. "I am so sorry it ended as it did."

"As am I. I shall see you tomorrow?"

"We plan to go to Versailles," Cora said, apologetic.

"Ah, that's right." He hesitated. Cora did too, and Will moved on, feeling as if he was intruding. He looked at Antonio and, with one glance, knew the man would wait to escort Cora. Will led the others to the chateau, enduring ribbing from Andrew and Hugh all the way.

"I'm only disappointed it didn't come to full fisticuffs," Andrew said. "A good fight would be a welcome relief."

Will rolled his eyes. That would have been utter disaster. They were lucky, as it was, that Richelieu hadn't been so offended that he showed them out the door despite the hour. But it didn't bode well that he was so drawn to Cora that he *didn't* toss them out either.

"I've been wondering if she has a bit more of her mother in her than we'd been led to believe," Hugh said with a wink.

Will turned, grabbing hold of Hugh's ruffled jacket in both hands and ramming him into a portico column. "Don't ever speak of her in such a manner. She is a lady, regardless of her parentage."

Hugh stared back at him, eyes wide with shock.

Andrew took hold of Will's arm and wrenched him backward. "Enough, Will."

Hugh brushed his arms and narrowed his eyes at Will. "So, I was right in assuming the tutor wishes he had more of sweet Cora than the tour rules allow."

Will surged toward him again, but Andrew held him back. "Stop it," Will seethed, trying to pull his arms free of Andrew's hold.

But Hugh stepped toward him, his eyes widening with understanding. "It's true. You're jealous."

"I am not. I was merely seeking to come to her aid. As I would for Lillian. Or Nell. Or you, for that matter." He shook off Andrew's hold and then led them onward, into the chateau and toward the staircase that led to their rooms. Both men were silent for once, which told Will they didn't believe him. It didn't matter; all he wanted was to fall into bed and into such a deep slumber that, for some hours, he wouldn't remember the awful way the evening had ended. In the morning, he could cope.

But tonight, it seemed impossible.

Will awakened stiff and sore. He forced himself to his bath and into clothes, so he'd be ready for anyone who came to his door. He hoped to fit in a brief walk before breakfast, needing time under the trees, a chance to pray, in order to be fortified for the battles ahead. And there would be battles. Uncle Stuart, for one, once he found out about the altercation last night. Managing the clients, when they were less than respectful. Cora… Who knew how that would be resolved? And facing Richelieu? He cringed and rubbed his face. *Strength, Lord. Give me strength.*

He was glad he'd gotten that time in before Uncle Stuart found him on a bench beneath the trees. The portly man came toward him, hands behind his back, chin down, as if deep in thought. He sat beside Will, and they both stared at the sprawling gardens and the chateau beyond it.

"So you've heard," Will said.

"I have."

"I'm sorry, Uncle Stuart. Truly. It was an honest mistake."

"A grievous error. But understandable." He sighed. "I have greater concerns."

Will hesitated. What could be heavier on the older man's mind? "Such as?"

"Your feelings for Miss Cora."

"I have no more feelings for Miss Cora than I have for any of our clients," Will said. The words, though he wanted to believe them, felt false. He frowned.

"No?"

His frown deepened, and he met his uncle's gaze. "No," he insisted.

His uncle continued to stare at him, searching his eyes, until he acquiesced. "All right, then," he said, rising. "Time to go and face our host."

Will sighed and followed behind him by a few steps, feeling every bit the small child as he had been when he had first come to live with his uncle.

But when they reached the blue breakfast room that held eight round tables to accommodate guests for small functions, their host did not arrive. Only other guests, looking rather worse for wear after a night short of sleep. Richelieu sent his regrets via a servant, and after Uncle Stuart gave Will a meaningful look, no one chatted but the youngest girls, who were blissfully unaware of anything that had gone on the night before, besides the marvelous ball.

Will picked at his food, chewing a croissant until it was paste in his mouth, wishing they were scheduled to leave for Provence today, rather than in a few days. At least they wouldn't have to be back here at the Richelieu chateau until nightfall. With any luck, they wouldn't see their host until tomorrow, and perhaps the day's respite would have soothed his ruffled feathers.

Perhaps.

—◦◇◦—

They stopped in an open-air market in a village outside of Versailles, picking up bread, cheese, chocolate, strawberries, and wine, reputedly Marie Antoinette's picnic items of choice, according to Uncle Stuart. The groceries were loaded into backpacks, and they all took rented bicycles from a rack. Lillian shared a tandem bike with Will, since she said she wasn't very adept at riding. Will was already weary. By day's end, he'd be exhausted. That was fine by him. The more spent he was by nightfall, the more likely he would be to fall into a dreamless sleep.

Dreams were unwelcome. They frequently consisted of his mother and father, his mother welcoming him with open arms, over and over, his father patting his back... Seeing his parents made waking painful, their dream time together always cut short.

"Look out, Will!" Cora cried, riding past, the first she'd spoken to him since last night.

He opened his eyes wide and swerved, narrowly missing a tree.

"Should I be steering?" Lillian asked nervously from behind him when they were once again on a steady course.

"No, no. Sorry. I was just distracted for a moment. It won't happen again." The silly girl barely pedaled, and he had to work very hard to keep them upright. Now she thought she should steer? Frustration bloomed in his chest. Everything was falling apart around him, which he knew was an overreaction, which in turn made him all the more agitated. What was wrong with him?

Pull yourself together, Will, he told himself. Calm and collected, that was how Uncle Stuart liked him to be. Such demeanor reassured their clients. *Calm and collected, calm and collected, calm and collected...*

He focused on the dirt path before them, the long line of tall green trees on either side, the green pasture beyond a wooden fence, where horses busily grazed on long grasses. The group stopped near a small hamlet, where they reclined on the grass as Uncle Stuart lectured them on how Marie Antoinette had it built to remind her of her native Austria and often escaped there to "play" at farm life. "Immaculate livestock, bathed daily, were about, and the queen liked to feed them. She even milked the dairy cow," he said. "It was a welcome respite for the queen from the constant positioning that took place up at the chateau. She only invited her most trusted friends here."

They moved back to their bicycles to head toward the Grand Trianon, a smaller palace on one end of the Grand Lac, the man-made lake that spread out from the chateau, but Cora hesitated, staring at the timber-and-plaster buildings with thatched roofs. "Cora?" Will asked. Lillian looked from him to Cora and back again, plainly curious.

Cora jumped, startled out of her reverie, and turned to him.

"Ready?" he added.

She nodded hurriedly and passed by them. Fifteen minutes later they arrived at the Grand Trianon and walked through the massive pink columns to the patio that edged the lake. Shaped in the form of a cross, the Grand Lac was deep enough for boats and took a good hour to ride around on bikes. Riding—either in a carriage, in a coach, or by bicycle—was truly the best means to explore it.

Uncle Stuart lectured for a bit about it, and they headed off again, toward the next arm of the lake, riding along a path that traced the waterway. They parked their bikes and walked down a broad hill. At the far end, in the distance, was the massive staircase lined by sculptures, and the sprawling chateau, a monument of white. It reminded Will of a king sitting on a green throne.

"My goodness, isn't it beautiful?" Nell said.

"Can you imagine picnicking here every afternoon?" Lillian added, looping her arm through her friend's.

"It's lovely," Vivian said, waiting as Andrew spread out the blanket for them. "No wonder the queen loved it."

Women always seemed entranced by Marie Antoinette. And the young men liked the vivid drama of the French revolution, the royals driven out, necks placed upon bloody guillotines.

Felix lay down on Vivian and Andrew's blanket. "Ahh, that's perfect, Drew, thanks," he said, closing his eyes and lacing his fingers over his chest. "I'll just take a quick nap. You know, recover from our arduous ride, and then hand it over to you two for a go."

"Felix Kensington!" Vivian chided.

But Andrew merely smiled and grabbed hold of the side of the blanket with two hands, then quickly lifted it, neatly sending Felix tumbling away. The group laughed as Felix pantomimed his outrage.

Hugh spread a blanket out and gestured for Cora to join him. Will could see her hesitation, but there was little that he could do about it—after last night, the worst thing he could do was to invite her to sit with him instead. He needed to steer clear of her, pretend he hardly thought about her. At least until tensions cooled. Then—perhaps then—they could resume their friendship.

He ignored the cocky look of triumph Hugh tossed his way as Cora sat down on the corner of the blanket.

The ladies had brought out their parasols, and they'd just gotten settled, distributing the picnic items, when a large boat appeared in the center of the lake, covered with a fabric roof to keep out the sun. "What is that?" Nell asked, pointing.

"I've seen canoes and rowboats, a few small sailing boats," Uncle Stuart said, "but never a boat of those proportions on this lake."

Will chewed on a chunk of bread, thinking back to his studies on Versailles. "Didn't Louis XVI once cavort about the lake in something similar, Uncle?" he asked.

Uncle Stuart nodded, thinking. "I do believe you're right, Will. Along with yachts sent to him from distant kings and gondolas from the doge of Venice."

Six sets of oars were rowing in tandem, three on either side of the big boat, and it soon drew near. The girls giggled with excitement when a call went up inside and the rowing stopped, but the boat continued to drift toward them. At last it bumped up against the shore, and immediately, a gangplank was lowered.

"Oh my," Nell said, hand at her throat.

"What is it?" Lillian asked.

Out walked Pierre de Richelieu, dressed in a fine summer suit, complete with jacket, vest, and ascot. His hair was pulled back in a ponytail, making him appear as a prince of another period. He grinned at their surprised expressions and walked straight to Cora.

When he got closer, they all could see the purple bruise on his cheek, the slight swelling. But he was looking only at Cora.

"Miss Cora," he said, getting down on one knee. "Last night did not end as we wished, but today, I'm determined to give you your prize." He gestured back at the boat. "Please, come with me, and you shall do nothing but drift and dream for an hour."

Uncle Stuart finally seemed to awaken from his surprised stupor. "You are most kind, my lord. But I'm afraid we have to get on toward the chateau directly after our picnic—"

"All I ask for is an hour with Cora," Richelieu said, meeting Uncle Stuart's gaze and cutting a glance to Will. "We shall meet you at the chateau."

"But we have her bike," Will tried.

"That is no great difficulty. I'll send a servant to fetch it, and we'll bring it with us. There's plenty of room for it." He tucked his head and stared at the bear, waiting the briefest of moments for the approval he knew would come. Uncle Stuart nodded his assent, and Richelieu reached out a hand to Cora. "Come away with me for a bit, Cora."

Glancing back at Will, she hesitated and then placed her hand in Richelieu's. They walked to the boat, hand in hand, and he helped her up the gangplank and into the boat. A servant ran up the hill for the bike, then disappeared inside the boat, the gangplank following after him. Six sets of oars set into motion again.

"Well, for heaven's sake, cease your fretting," Vivian said, turning from the sight. "We'll see her in an hour. They're not sailing off into the sunset! I, for one, am glad that Lord de Richelieu has seen fit to look beyond last night's...misunderstanding."

"As am I," Andrew said, pouring Vivian more wine.

"I think it's the most romantic thing I've ever, ever seen," Nell said dreamily, chin in hands.

Hugh and Felix groaned.

"We have a problem," Uncle muttered to Will, sitting down heavily beside him.

"I know," Will said.

A pirate had just kidnapped one of their clients. And there wasn't a blessed thing they could do about it.

CHAPTER 31

~Cora~

It was the most extraordinary boat I'd ever been on. Like something in the storybooks about the Egyptians or Venetians, with slaves down below, propelling us forward. I doubted Pierre would be anything but a benevolent employer, but with the heat of the day, I worried over our oarsmen.

"Are they all right?" I asked, peering down through a small space, where I could glimpse men pulling hard on their oars.

"They're fine. And earning quite handsome pay. Now you must take your wished-for hour of silence and make it all worth *your* while." He put his finger to his lips and smiled at me, then led me to the end of the boat, where there was a pile of pillows awaiting me.

I stared up at him. Once again, I felt the yawning distance between me and Montana, wondering just what sort of dreamscape I'd found myself in. I might as well have been Alice in her wonderland, so foreign was it.

He laughed and brushed a hand under my chin. "Honestly, Cora. Take it as the gift it is. I ask nothing in return." He gestured toward the pillows, and I settled into them, realizing that they hid a lounge chair underneath. Pierre settled into another, several feet away, risking no sense of impropriety as a servant poured us tea and then set individual trays of tea sandwiches near each of us. We both faced forward, watching the chateau slowly edge nearer, as if we drifted on a cloud.

"How did you manage all of this?" I asked. "In just a morning's time?"

He put a finger to his lips, shushing me again, then tossed a small sandwich in his mouth and pulled a book and pencil from his pocket. The lone remaining servant on deck stood in the rear of the boat, steering it.

I'd asked for an hour of silence, in which nothing was required of me. An hour in which I could just be.

And he was giving it to me.

A part of me wished he'd simply come up by himself in a rowboat, but I supposed when one was raised in a chateau, with elaborate parties like we'd experienced last night, nothing so basic would do in a place like Versailles. His world was full of grand gestures.

I looked over at him, again opening my mouth to speak, but he shook his head, his handsome eyes crinkling at the corners with glee.

I gave in then, smiling with him.

After eating all of the tiny cucumber sandwiches, and several with tuna—or maybe they were sardines—a few brightly colored macaroons filled with raspberry cream, and two chocolates, I drained the last of my tea, leaned my head back, and listened to the rhythmic sound of the oars. It was soothing, the low rumble of a leader's call down below, the creak of them leaning forward, the *kerslup* as they dipped, the creak as they pulled backward, the drips as they raised and waited for the next languid pull.

I stared at the chateau but then closed my eyes, not wanting any more information in my head. No more pictures of things I wanted to memorize. No more effort in imagining Marie Antoinette and Louis here. I just wanted to *be* for a moment. With no one asking anything of me, no role to play, no hard feelings to soothe, no sorrow about yesterday, no fear about tomorrow. Just me. Being.

My breathing slowed, and I relaxed, my hands settled on the rough silk of the pillows, the lounge chair fitting me perfectly. For a moment I resisted, not wanting to waste my precious hour of escape on sleep, and then realizing that there really was no more perfect escape.

I remembered the song of the birds in the trees, echoing across the lake. And remembered meadowlarks at home, singing so sweetly…

"Miss. Miss," a man said, shaking my shoulder.

I awakened with a start and sat up. Pierre was gone. The servant smiled at me. Obviously, he spoke no more English than "miss," and he gestured to the chateau rising high above us, and Antonio waiting for me alongside the group's bicycles.

I'd been dreaming of Mr. Kensington's note. Of his words. *The question isn't how society defines you, nor how I define you, but rather how God defines you, and in turn, how you yourself want to be defined.*

It made me think of my mother's words too. *You're about to find out what it means to be a Kensington… And what it doesn't.*

I was a Kensington, but I was also a Diehl. Claiming both the name of my childhood as well as the name on my birth certificate was somehow key…

"Lord de Richelieu," the footman said, lifting a stiff card in my direction, offering it to me.

"Oh, thank you," I said, rising. I opened the card and sucked in my breath. Inside was a perfectly splendid and simple sketch of me sleeping on the lounge. *"L'ange au repos,"* was written beneath it. I wondered if my guess at the translation—angel in repose—was correct.

"Où est Seigneur de Richelieu?" I asked, following the servant to the side of the boat and a new, wider plank to exit. *Where is Lord de Richelieu?*

He raised a brow and shrugged his shoulders. I suspected he knew where Pierre had gone but had been instructed not to tell. I smiled and accepted his hand as I made my way down and over to Antonio.

Pierre had kept his promise, giving me an hour without asking for anything in return—not even waiting to accept my thanks. It had been a fine gift. An outrageous gift, but a fine one. The question lingered in my mind: how did it define me, to be courted by Pierre de Richelieu? And did I like that definition?

"You realize, of course, that this is merely part of Lord de Richelieu's ploy to win you with grand gestures," Antonio said as I came near.

"I take it you do not approve." We fell into step beside each other, climbing the massive staircase, and I accepted his offered arm, still feeling rather sleepy.

He shrugged. "Lord de Richelieu is like a beautiful gem on the beach. How can you pass him by?" He cocked his head. "But is he merely a beautiful bauble, or a jewel of worth? That remains to be seen."

I smiled, inwardly hoping that Pierre might be a jewel. "Agreed. But that takes time to decipher, does it not?"

"Alas, the tour affords little time for such examinations. We are soon on to Provence. And perhaps that is just as well."

Was he warning me? Trying to dissuade me from allowing Pierre's pursuit? His expression was difficult to read. "The others are already inside?"

"Yes. They were eager to see the grand chateau."

"Mm, yes."

"You are not eager?"

"I have already seen more grand homes than my mother has seen in her whole life," I said. "And they are lovely…" I turned to him. "Why is it, Antonio, that we cannot continue to hold such places in the same esteem as we did with the first?"

"It is true. We lose our sense of awe," he said, studying me with his dark eyes. "We become accustomed, and then only bigger and better impress us."

"Indeed. I'm thankful I haven't lost all of it. I think I'll continue to appreciate the unique. But I look upon this"—I waved forward—"and think it's all a bit much, isn't it? What is the purpose? To impress your neighbors? Your friends? Why not house a city of orphans, feed the poor instead? Would that not be all the more impressive?" I shoved aside an arrow of guilt as I remembered I'd just stepped off a lavish boat worthy of dreams.

He smiled and nodded. "Agreed. But you must put it into context, Miss Cora. The men who built them. Their desire to control, conquer. It mattered not if they occupied but two rooms in this grand house." He gestured toward it. "What it told the people of France was that they might be poor and starving, but their lot was to struggle, while the ruling class's lot was to live in splendor. It worked for a time, until the poor and starving had had enough and rebelled."

"Good for them for rebelling, I say."

He laughed and stared at me quizzically. "What has come over you, Miss Cora?"

I stared back at him, pondering his question. "Me," I said at last. "I've overcome myself. I am who I am. And I think…I think I'm about to claim what's mine."

—◇◇◇—

~William~

Will's eyes narrowed as he watched Cora arrive on Antonio's arm. They were in the Hall of Mirrors, and every single reflective surface seemed to showcase the pleasing blush high on her cheeks, the bright sparkle in her eyes. The gilt chandeliers above made her golden hair shine. But she seemed intent on listening to the bear as he lectured, and slowly edged her way near.

"What happened to her?" Will whispered to Antonio as the man came to stand beside him.

Antonio shrugged and lifted his brows. "I know not. She came off the boat as you see her."

So he'd recognized it too. Something that had shifted, changed for Cora.

Will searched over his shoulder for a glimpse of Pierre de Richelieu. Was it possible that the man had come to take her for a boat ride and then disappeared? After all that? Was he not lurking about, waiting to collect on a debt now owed? Or had he already received payment? Was that why Cora wore that tiny secret smile?

Will turned and abruptly strode toward the nearest double doors, which led to a porch outside. Once there, he leaned against the balustrade and took in great gulps of air. His imagination was running wild. Even if they had kissed, what did it matter? What right did he have to let it agitate him at all? He was merely a guide, a caring shoulder, nothing more to her—

He smelled the cigarette smoke before he turned. A glance over his shoulder confirmed it. Hugh.

Hugh grinned and tapped the ash off his cigarette over the edge of the balustrade. "What has you in such a state, man?"

Will attempted to move his expression to boredom as Hugh came to stand beside him. "If I see the Hall of Mirrors once more in my lifetime, it will be a hundred times too many." Especially with Cora's face in every one...

"Come now. Don't play me the fool. Might it not be the lovely Cora that has you all up in arms?" Hugh took a deep draw on his cigarette and casually blew the smoke out his nostrils, all the while staring out at the gardens. "Must've grated, to see Lord de Richelieu sweep her away just as you might've coerced her from my blanket to yours."

Will sighed and leaned on the balustrade as he stared out onto the massive gardens reminiscent of Richelieu's. "Go back to the group, Hugh," he gritted out. "I think my uncle was looking for you."

But Hugh stayed where he was. He took another pull on his cigarette and slowly let the smoke out so it billowed around them. Will resisted the urge to cough.

"What do you fear, Will? That you've lost her to that brash Frenchman?"

"You know nothing of what concerns me."

"Don't I? Cora's just the sort of itch I long to scratch. You should've seen her at the lake, coming out of the water under the moonlight, her bathing costume clinging to every sweet inch—"

Will grabbed Hugh by the shirt and rammed him against the doors before he knew himself. Just like the night before.

Hugh only laughed, his breath coming at Will in disgusting waves, sweet with the scent of his French cigarettes. "Ahh, there it is again," he said, staring into Will's eyes with triumph in his own. "Does she know?"

"You know nothing," Will said, glimpsing the others inside, staring with wide eyes at them, on the other side of the glass. He dropped his hands.

"Right. Nothing," Hugh said. "Why not just own up to it? Play your hand? See if she burns for you like you do her?"

Will shot him a look of fury, and Hugh laughed again, holding up his hands in surrender. "I'm only asking."

"You ask too much. And you pry into business that is not your own."

Hugh lifted his brows and pursed his lips. "If she's not your business, I'll keep trying to make her mine. Once her little crush on

Richelieu is over, of course. He's doing the yeoman's work. Prying open her heart. Making her see that she might find love in her new world."

Will shook his head, staring at him in disbelief. Of all the cold, calculating— "You keep away from her, Hugh."

"And if I don't?" Hugh taunted casually, taking another long draw of his cigarette while watching him through squinted eyes.

Will eased toward Hugh and looked down his nose at him. "You don't want to find out what I'll do." He turned then and entered through the doors.

But Hugh's laugh could be heard even beyond the glass.

CHAPTER 32

~Cora~

It was difficult to avoid smiling through supper. Again and again, I caught Pierre and the rest of our traveling party staring at me, clearly wondering what I was thinking. It was then I knew that what had shifted inside me had made a difference in my very appearance.

I'd decided I would go by the name of Cora Diehl Kensington. I would lay claim to both the name of my childhood and the name of my birth, honoring it all. But that mattered little. I'd realized that if Jesus had sat down with the tax collectors and the prostitutes and sinners, making upstanding religious people cringe, then He'd have no difficulty with either Mama or Mr. Kensington.

I'm a sinner...but I've made my peace with my family and my Maker, Mr. Kensington had written. Whether or not that was true, I had yet to ascertain. But I knew that living like a redeemed sinner was what freed a person to live life to the full. Were there regrets? Certainly. I knew Mr. Kensington had them—I'd seen them lurking in the sorrow in his eyes. But if he truly knew

Christ, he was a man who looked forward, not backward. And now I would follow suit.

I would claim what was mine and not fret over the rest. Vivian, Felix, and Lillian could decide whether they wanted me as a part of their lives. I could not make that choice for them. The relief of my new way of thinking allowed me to take my first full breaths in weeks. The Morgans? They were simply flawed human beings that I had to deal with for the remaining weeks of our journey. I'd be polite to them all and accept what came—and what did not. It did not matter. I was Cora Diehl Kensington. Accepted and loved by those important to me. The rest would be like lights on the Eiffel Tower—a gift when seen at night, but not integral to who I was.

Pierre asked if I might walk with him in the gardens after dinner, and I accepted, "as long as Anna might accompany us," I added. I knew better than to put myself in the same situation I'd allowed the night before. And after the boat ride in Versailles…

He hesitated for half a breath. "But of course," he said smoothly. "Anna is a welcome chaperone. Monsieur Will is not." He smiled as he rubbed his bruised cheek as if remembering it all over again.

The rest of our party laughed over that, a bit too loudly. Will gave our host a rueful smile. But his eyes shifted from Pierre to me.

I was certain Pierre had been hoping for more stolen kisses. And I was not at all certain that was wise. But I felt indebted to him—for the incredible generous act of our ride upon the water at Versailles, for not asking for anything from me in return. Upon waking from that dreamlike ride, I'd found my mooring, after weeks of feeling adrift. And I wanted him to know it.

As we walked, he tucked my hand around his arm and stroked it, sending shivers up my arm and neck, down my back. He was handsome and charming, for certain. Was I a fool to try to cool the ardor he genuinely felt for me? But what could I be to him other than a welcome distraction? A curiosity? He didn't even know me.

Behind us, Anna puttered along, turning to pretend to admire the rosebushes whenever we paused. Pierre glanced at her and then gave me a wry grin. He held my hand in both of his. "So, *mon ange*," he said tenderly, searching my eyes. I looked down and to the side. "What is it that you have to tell me?" he asked.

"Tell you?" I dodged, not certain I had the strength to speak the plain truth now that he'd given me the opportunity.

"Our time upon the waters of Versailles has clearly revived you. Never have your beautiful blue eyes sparkled so. But I have had trouble seeing them since this afternoon. You do not meet my gaze." He put his hand beneath my chin and, with the softest of gestures, eased my face up. "Ah, yes," he said, pulling back a little, as if he could read the words within.

I gave him a rueful smile and gently pulled my hand from his, then turned to resume our walk, hands behind my back. He, in turn, tucked one arm across his midriff, holding the elbow of his other, chin in hand, as if already intent on honoring the words I'd yet to speak.

"Pierre, I can't begin to thank you enough. For your kindness," I said, looking at the tiny pebbles on the path. "For your attention and generosity. For not throwing us out the moment you knew who…I was." I resisted the urge to insert "and what." *I am Cora Diehl Kensington*, I repeated to myself. *Important to the people I love. Beloved daughter of God. Nothing else matters.*

"For clothing us for your ball," I stumbled on, "for not sending Will to jail after he punched you last night, and for your grand gesture at Versailles this afternoon."

He laughed under his breath. "But of course," he said. He glanced back at Anna and then touched my elbow, easing me to a stop again. "But why is it that I feel as if you are bidding me *adieu*?"

"Because…" I dragged my eyes up to meet his. "Pierre, what is this? Between us? An idle flirtation? A distraction? I am a woman on a journey, but I intend to go home. To Montana, a place few Parisians will ever see. To return to school to become a teacher. And you…you are a man with roots generations deep in Paris. Your life is far different."

"Surely your life is not so different from mine," he said with some confusion in his eyes. "Granted, the chateau…it is large. Ostentatious. But it has been in the family for centuries. Your own home might be newly built, but does it not compare? At least in some measure?"

I shot him a wry grin, thinking of our tiny house on the ranch. The houses he was probably imagining—even homes as grand as the Kensington home in Butte or the lodge on the lake— were not anywhere near the size or grandeur of his chateau. I shook my head.

He smiled even though his eyes betrayed frustration. "What does it matter? I've courted many women whose families have but apartments in the city." He glanced at the chateau and then back to me, shrugging. "It is not I who built her. I was merely born within her walls. Why does it matter?"

"Because today...today on the boat, as I slept, as I awakened, I remembered who I was, Pierre. And that girl counts it a joy, an *experience*, to be here with you. But she does not belong here."

He considered my words. Slow understanding, and a tinge of defense, lifted his chin. "What if it's something more, *ma chérie?*" His eyes searched mine, hoping. "This thing between us?" His intense look almost had the same power as his kisses to draw me in. I wanted him to kiss me again. God help me, I had the wildest urge to kiss him, just to see, to see if I remembered it right, to see if it had been a one-time thing. But that was exactly why I'd brought Anna along. So I wouldn't get distracted, forget what I needed to say. I looked down at the toes of my shoes peeking from beneath my skirts, and then looked back into his eyes. "There is no doubt that we find ourselves drawn to each other, Pierre. That is not the difficulty, is it? Though our paths have met here in Paris, they are soon to part. And by summer's end, there will be an entire ocean between us."

"Let us address the ocean later. Let us only consider a week at a time. I could come with you to Provence."

"And then what?" I asked, lifting my brows. "We head to Austria next. Venice. Rome. I doubt you have time to follow us about all summer long."

He pursed his lips and then cocked his head. "Perhaps not all summer." He took my hand in his again. "But let us not decide this now, Cora. Let us see what transpires. I will try to see you in Provence. In Vienna and Venezia—I have *business* to tend to in both cities," he added in a rush, shushing my protest. He paused. "You find it so undesirable? Seeing me elsewhere about Europe?"

I laughed under my breath. What could I say? He was merely asking for the opportunity to see me again. "No, Pierre. I'd welcome seeing you anywhere," I allowed.

He grinned at that. And then, ignoring Anna, he pulled me close for a brief kiss.

-William-

As they neared the Eiffel Tower, Will ran his finger under his collar, again wishing he had another half inch to let out. Richelieu had sent two new suits to his quarters that morning. The servant said that Richelieu no longer had any use for them and wondered if Will might be interested in having them tailored to fit. Caught off guard, Will tried them on, curious. But as he admired himself in the mirror, he admitted the truth. Richelieu was a couple inches shorter and narrower in the chest, so clearly these had not been his. He merely had been intent on helping to clothe the "poor" junior guide in some act of charity, regardless of what the servant said.

And even if it was solely a magnanimous gesture on Richelieu's part, Will swore he'd never take charity from him. Walking behind him as he chatted up Cora again, Will was sure he'd meant it as a punch to the gut. Had Richelieu seen what Hugh had seen in his face, his eyes, when he looked at Cora? Was he trying to clarify that Will had no chance against him if they competed for her affections?

He stifled a sigh and looked down the line of neat hedges in the park beneath the Eiffel Tower. He had to get her out of his mind, give up on this crazy dream before it became his undoing. Because after all, he had no more business taking up with Cora Kensington than Pierre de Richelieu did. Neither of them belonged with her. Neither of them.

He'd purchase his own suit before they left for Provence. It would not be nearly the same quality as what Richelieu had offered him; but it would be his, earned the old-fashioned way. It was unfortunate he'd tried the new suits on at all, though, because now his old, too-small collar chafed more than ever.

Studiously attempting to look at anything but Cora and Richelieu laughing and chatting, he followed behind the group as they strolled the park that led to the Eiffel Tower. The two of them intended to go to Richelieu's favorite restaurant after their sunset visit to the Eiffel Tower, and then Richelieu was going on to another event, so Cora wore an exquisite evening gown of cream and pink, with cutout lacework crossing her delicate shoulders, and a feather in her hair. The small train of her dress was held by a tiny strap over her left wrist so it wouldn't drag through the gravel on the path. Truly she had never looked lovelier, and it made Will feel all the more shabby. He had to admit that Richelieu was a fitting companion for her this evening, dressed in a silk jacket, trousers, and hat.

Again and again, Will's eyes strayed to the couple in front of him, then reluctantly to his other charges. Hugh caught his last lingering glance at Cora. He smiled slyly like a fellow conspirator, and Will looked away from him in frustration, embarrassment.

And that was when he saw the man, with hat pulled low, watching the group as they passed. It was not the look of the casual observer, nor the native caught by the intrigue of a foreigner in their lands—Will was well versed in deciphering that expression. It was a cool, calculating kind of stare. As if he were memorizing each one in the group for future reference.

Will stared hard at the man but then saw him gesture across the park, to another neatly trimmed row of hedges in which a second man stood. Will's heart went into double time, and he gripped his walking stick hard. What was this? Why were these men here, and what interest did they have in his clients? Will took several long strides toward Antonio and, with one swift tilt of his chin, drew the older man's attention to the sentinels on either side. But by that time, both were leaving, exiting to the far side of either hedge. Will chalked it up to a fluke, an oddity, but he caught the first man's dark gaze just as he broke away. It was the tiny smile edging his lips that caused Will to shout and run after him.

Will got to the other side of the seven-foot hedge, looking left and right. But the man was gone. Will ran another thirty feet to the next opening between the hedges. Beyond that, there was nothing in a vast lawn of the park. Somehow, somewhere, the man was hiding. But why? A chill ran down Will's back, and he glanced over his shoulder. Antonio was approaching him, dark brow furrowed as he shook his head. No luck for him either.

And now they were both separated from their clients. Will raced toward Antonio, and, belatedly recognizing what Will feared,

Antonio turned and charged ahead of him. They hurried over to their clients. Uncle Stuart met them first, ten feet in front. "Will?" he said in a hushed tone.

Will's eyes scanned the row of hedges on either side, the people inside the park. Nowhere did he see the first man or his companion. Panting, he reached up and ran a hand through his hair. "It's all right. There were simply a couple of men—"

He abruptly stopped speaking as Richelieu approached. "What is it?" the man asked lowly, waiting for Will's answer. His eyes told him he'd not accept anything but the truth.

"Two men. Nicely dressed. On either side of the park's hedgerows. Watching us. Our party, passing. If it had been one, I might've let it pass. But two?" He shook his head. "They were waiting for us. I'm certain."

Richelieu frowned and peered down the bushes again, squinting into the sun. "Perhaps it is not your clients they are watching, but me. If that is the case, I can handle them," he said, opening his jacket and showing Will a small gun, carefully hidden in his vest. "I never leave without it." He gave Will a sly smile.

The man had fearsome enough enemies to prompt him to carry a weapon? Richelieu turned to walk away, confident that all was now in order. Will swore under his breath and met his uncle's eyes, as well as Antonio's.

"Of course the man has enemies," Uncle Stuart said soothingly, trying to dismiss the sense of danger that had fallen upon them. "Men do not reach his stature, his sort of power, and keep it without making others angry en route. He is no different from countless others we've met over the years."

"Except he's set his sights on one of our clients," Will bit back, under his breath. *Cora.* He, his uncle, and Antonio were moving, catching up with the rest, who were now resuming their stroll toward the Tower. Richelieu was regaling them with a story, obviously trying to assuage their concern over Will's actions. "That courtship is already under way," Antonio said with a nod. They all looked forward and saw Richelieu place a hand at the small of Cora's back, pointing something out to her in a nearby tree. A bird?

"It will be over as soon as we depart," Uncle Stuart said.

"Are you sure about that? Is he not friends with those who will house us in Provence?" Will said, keeping his tone low. He still owed Richelieu for not making a big deal out of his attack. He wasn't eager to raise his ire again now. But what if Richelieu had to use that gun under his vest? Would their clients be in the middle of some terrible shoot-out? His hand clenched around his walking stick at the thought of it. There was a reason Uncle Stuart never allowed them to carry weapons. Too many things could go wrong.

"He is a busy man. Deep into his business," Uncle Stuart grunted, clearly not liking the challenge in Will's voice. "He'll forget about Cora after a couple of days. She's a passing interest."

Will shared a look with Antonio behind his uncle's back. A man merely distracted would not go to the same lengths that he'd seen this man go to—the housing, the costumes, the dancing, the boating. Even his willingness to put aside the affront of Will's attack was evidence of the man's infatuation. No, it was by no means trivial, his attention. Will clenched his teeth. If Uncle Stuart insisted on seeing it as such, he was a fool.

Not that he could say anything about it.

Staring upward as a group, they reached the massive feet of the Eiffel Tower. Will thought it might be his favorite aspect of Paris—to stand beneath the elegant structure, each curve and angle as beautiful as it was strong. Uncle Stuart began his lecture. "Built for the World's Fair of 1889, the tower was to be torn down within twenty years. But Parisians adopted it as their own."

As his uncle went on, Will glanced around, studying each person about—other tour groups, begging Gypsies, a couple of businessmen out for an afternoon stroll. Neither of the men he spotted earlier was in sight, which both relieved him and made him anxious. Were they merely waiting for a better opportunity to—to do what? Try to capture or hurt Richelieu? Or one of the Kensington or Morgan heirs? All of them?

He sighed and counted heads, glad they were all in one small, tight group for once. Hugh and Felix were shaking hands and grinning, as if agreeing upon a bet, and glancing up to the top. Then he looked for Richelieu and found him to one side of a small newspaper stand, slipping his wallet out and handing the guard some bills. *So that's how he gains entrance.*

Richelieu approached the old bear and bent to say something in his ear. Looking pleased, Uncle Stuart nodded and gestured for the group to follow their host to the stairwell. "The lifts are still closed, but we've gained access to the stairs," he said with delight. Reluctantly, Will turned to follow. He was the last one in, and with a grunt, the guard closed the iron gate, locking it behind them.

They began the climb, the women exclaiming about the numerous flights of stairs, the men jostling to get ahead—Felix at the front, of course, Hugh right behind him. Andrew stayed with Vivian.

It only took a few turns before Lil, red-faced, paused to catch her breath beside Uncle Stuart, who appeared similarly flushed.

"You go ahead, my boy," Stuart panted. "I'll stay and keep watch with Miss Lillian here."

Will passed them, sure they'd never make it to the top. Climbing wasn't the best idea for Uncle Stuart anyway. His heart wasn't what it used to be. Nell paused next, and her brother Andrew and Vivian waited with her. Will glanced downward, now a couple hundred feet up from the bottom. With the gate locked behind them, he was reasonably sure all would be safe below. He was more concerned with what might transpire up top. His eyes narrowed as he spied Cora and Richelieu two flights above him, on the opposite side. Even from this distance, he could see Cora's color was high and she was flashing Richelieu a shy smile. *Passing interest, my foot*, he thought grimly.

Felix and Hugh were being idiotic, jostling each other, now two turns ahead of Richelieu and Cora. Will doubled his pace, intent on catching up to the young men. If they wrestled at just the wrong juncture, if there was a handrail rivet not quite strong enough—he glanced down to the ground and shuddered at the thought of them going over.

He passed Antonio, who was leaning forward, hands on his knees, panting for breath. The middle-aged man was in good shape, but this was a taxing venture for them all. "Keep an eye on Richelieu and Cora, will you?" Will said. Antonio gave him a red-faced nod before Will added, "I'm going after the boys."

He resisted the urge to call after them, scold them like children. Clients never reacted well to that. But he'd do it if he had to.

In their race, they'd lost all sense of decorum, laughing and practically wrestling right there on the stairs. They'd finally caught the
attention of Andrew and Vivian, who yelled up at them. But their
cries went unnoticed. Hugh grabbed Felix by the back of the collar,
and when he lost his balance and stumbled to the left rail, Hugh
hooted and ran past him on the right, taking the steps two at a time.
Felix ripped off his jacket and left it on the rail, tearing after Hugh.

Will raced on, seething that they would take such foolish risks,
as well as leave behind such an expensive coat. "Felix!" he shouted,
hoping his friend would pause, but Felix remained steadfast in his
goal of catching up to Hugh. Will's breath was coming in ragged
heaves now, his heart thundering in his chest. How could they keep
up such a pace? He kept his head down, watching every stair that
passed, knowing he couldn't afford a fall himself. Finally, he was
gaining on them. Up ahead, Felix had caught Hugh on a small landing where the stairs turned, and they shifted from side to side on the
small platform. Far below, Will heard one of the younger girls scream
when the men leaned far over one rail, but Hugh and Felix could
neither see nor hear anyone but each other, it seemed.

Hugh frowned as Felix grabbed hold of his jacket as he attempted
to resume his climb, and roughly yanked him backward onto the
landing. But when Felix tried to move ahead, Hugh did the same
thing to him. Felix crashed into a beam on the far side of the landing
and then dived for Hugh, bringing the man down on the stairs.

"Stop it!" Will cried. "Stop it, now!" He was but twenty feet
away.

Both men looked over at him in surprise, then, with a grin at
each other, resumed their wrestling match to get ahead.

Will swore under his breath and ran after them. Hugh was again ahead, but Felix grabbed one of his elbows and yanked him backward, sending him to one side of the stairwell rail and running past him, oblivious to what he'd just done. Hugh teetered on the edge, his legs lifting. For a second, Will hoped he'd regain his balance. But then he clearly was not. Will heard the women screaming below as Hugh twisted and narrowly caught the rail with one hand as he went over.

Will was still five feet away.

Hugh swung, grimacing as he fought for a grip. Felix reached him a second before Will. "Hugh!" he cried, grabbing hold of his friend's wrist.

Will leaned over the rail and assessed the situation. "Hugh, give me your other hand!"

"I'm losing it," Hugh cried in desperation. "I can't hold on!"

"Felix has you!" Will said.

Hugh groaned and paused, as if summoning the strength. Will took two steps downward. "Here, I'm right here," Will said, reaching out to the man from a different angle.

Hugh didn't pause another second. Sucking in his breath, he swung toward Will, reaching out. They clasped wrists. Will repositioned himself for better leverage, then nodded at Felix. "Get a better grip on his wrist."

Felix paused, his dark brows gathering over his bright blue eyes, sweat beading on his brow. "It's okay," Will said. "I've got him."

Both Felix and Will grunted with the strain of holding Hugh aloft, now fully dead weight. "Move fast," he grunted at Felix, his breath coming in pants. They wouldn't be able to hold on to Hugh for long. "On three, we're going to yank him up and grab him by the waist. Got it?"

Felix, red-faced, the sweat now running down his forehead, nodded.

"One, two, three," Will said, and with that, both men gave it all they had, yanking Hugh upward with force. Before gravity could reclaim him, they reached out and caught him underneath each armpit.

Quickly, they pulled him backward, collapsing in a heap on the stairwell, Hugh partially atop them. They gasped for breath and held on to Hugh, as if he still might slip from safety.

Cora and Richelieu reached them, panting, faces awash in concern. "Are you all right, monsieur?" Richelieu asked, reaching out to touch Hugh's shoulder.

"Fine, fine," Hugh said.

Felix began laughing first. Then Hugh. But Will seethed with fury. He pushed Hugh off of him and clambered to his feet. "You think it's funny?" he cried. He wanted to kick them. "You almost *died*."

Hugh rose, and his smile partially faded. "Sorry I gave you a fright there, Will," he said, reaching out his hand.

Will stared at it, still too angry to take it.

"Will," Hugh said, now fully sober, "I'm indebted to you. You saved my life."

"Yes, I did," Will said, finally taking his hand. "But if you ever do anything as idiotic as that again"—he looked from Hugh to Felix—"I'll toss you over the rail myself."

CHAPTER 33

~Cora~

I'd never seen him so furious. He'd left us behind at the Eiffel Tower, walking past Antonio's outstretched hand of congratulations, ignoring his sputtering uncle, and rattling the gate at the bottom until the guard came and unlocked it. He strode out and, according to Anna, didn't appear all that evening, apparently electing to take his supper in his room rather than dine with the rest of the group.

We'd moved ahead, making it as far as the first observation deck, a small number of us going all the way to the top. But a cloud had descended since the incident with Hugh, muting conversation. Such was the effect of death—or near-death, I supposed. This seemed to bring the Morgans and Kensingtons to an abrupt halt, but for me, it was a familiar feeling. It was as if the shine had come off of the silver, and all that remained was the basic, utilitarian utensil. I knew how to deal with such surprises; the others did not.

Pierre and I ate our supper at a restaurant, as we had planned, but it was early, and only a few of the tables in the restaurant were occupied, so there was none of the gaiety and subdued chatter I'd become accustomed to in the city. Through the large glass window, I could see Antonio alternately pacing outside the restaurant—keeping a chaperone's eye on me—and then sitting in the Richelieu carriage, waiting to escort me back to the chateau. But my mind was back at the Eiffel Tower…

"What is it, *ma perle*?" Pierre asked, jerking my attention back to him. He looked at me with a tender gaze that felt like a caress.

"It is the boys," I confessed, setting down my fork. I wasn't eating my *coq au vin* anyway. "Hugh and Felix." I shook my head in agitation. "They don't know what they've been given. What they so nearly threw away today."

He studied me with his steady green eyes. "But you do," he said quietly. "Who did you leave to take this tour, Cora?"

My eyes shifted to the front window of the restaurant, watching as people walked by. I imagined them there, my parents. Staring in, their hands on the glass. "My papa," I said, tearing my eyes away. Then I met Pierre's gaze. "The father who raised me, Alan Diehl. Up until last month, I did not even know Wallace Kensington. And Papa, he suffered a stroke… He was terribly weak when I left him."

"And now? You've received word from him?"

I nodded a little. "Before we left the States. He was receiving good medical care, but still I fret over him."

He nodded soberly, unblinking. "Who else?" he asked. This time he reached out and covered my cold hand with his warm one. "Who else are you feeling far from, *ma chérie*?"

I dared to look at him again. Was it that obvious? Did I wear my longing like a mask across my face?

"My mother. She accompanied Papa to Minnesota, where he might enter a proper hospital."

Again, no surprise filled his eyes. Only compassion. "Who else?"

I studied him, confused, and gave a little shake of my head. "No one else."

"Come now," he said, taking a sip of his wine and leaning back. "Tell me. Your father, your mother, it is normal to miss them. But the weight you carry in those beautiful blue eyes..." He shook his head as if he could feel my pain. "Cora, is there not yet more you are mourning?"

I considered his words and glanced back to the front window. I imagined others there, joining Papa and Mama, staring in at me like a window to my soul. "I left more than my parents. When Mr. Kensington...when he came to collect me, we were on the verge of losing our farm..."

I shook my head, feeling embarrassment flood my face. What would Pierre care of such mundane matters? How could he even begin to understand? His world was so different. But his eyes were warm, compassionate. As if he understood me already. As if he wanted to know me better. "It may sound silly to you, Pierre. But I am missing a bit of myself..." I searched his face, wondering if I'd completely lost him in those last statements. "The girl who wore far simpler dresses, who enjoyed a certain comfort in her naïveté..." I paused and studied him, trying again. "Wallace Kensington made a way for me to come here." I waved about the fancy restaurant. "On this tour. But he also made it impossible for me and my folks to ever return home," I said bitterly, "to ever resume our former life."

"And why did he do that?"

Why did he do that? I thought. He could've paid the debt and allowed us to maintain ownership so we'd have a place to come back to once Papa was well again. But he hadn't. The thought niggled at me.

I shrugged a little and wound my cloth napkin into a knot beneath the table. "The farm was failing. My father was ailing. Perhaps he just wanted to force us all *forward*."

Pierre played with the stem of his crystal glass and eyed me carefully. "It sounds as if he was doing you a favor, no?"

"Yes. No!" I shook my head. "I don't know."

"Oh, *mon amie,* I think you do. He was pushing you out of a nest," he said.

"A nest in a dying tree," I muttered, looking to the window again. "But it was all so sudden...and it left me feeling torn between grief and anger...and relief, really."

"Ahh," he said, leaning forward on the table as the waiter took away his empty plate. "And there it is. So your Monsieur Kensington was the storm that forced you to a new nest. And you are not entirely sure it is a nest you want. This is what divides us, yes? I am but a symbol of more—more of what you're not sure you want." He tucked his chin, staring at me, waiting, as if for me to strike him.

"In part," I said with a slight nod. "But, Pierre, Mr. Kensington has promised me only this summer of the tour, and after it, the completion of my education, so that I might teach. I have no inheritance, no funds of my own to speak of. Does that not make me the most pathetic sort of woman you might ever pursue?" I smiled at him. "I attended your ball. That hall was filled with women of refinement, women far beyond my station. Women born to hold your attention."

He shrugged and leaned back in that languid, suave manner of the French, smiling. "Cora, perhaps it is because you are so utterly different from any woman I've ever known—or will likely come to know—that I find you so compelling."

I gave him a little laugh. "I'm a novelty to you, then. Not more. Let's not get confused."

"*Non*," he said, frowning and stretching his hand out, just barely touching mine with the tips of his long, elegant fingers. His eyes were deadly still. "You're far more than mere novelty."

His words left me breathless. Frightened me by their intensity. And quietly, I pulled my fingers from his.

He smiled, compassion in his eyes. "It is all right, *ma chérie*. There is time. Ample time for us to let whatever this is," he said, waving back and forth between us, "unfold."

———◇◇◇———

Pierre put me in a horse-drawn Richelieu carriage beside Antonio and, with a kiss to my knuckles, bid me *adieu*. He was reluctantly off to a political function for the evening. With a quick word from him, the driver pulled away into the swell of Parisian traffic.

"You enjoyed a fine meal, Cora?" Antonio asked.

"I did," I agreed simply. I did not feel like talking, and he seemed to sense my mood and left me to my silence, him looking out one side of the carriage, me the other. The genteel evening crowd was just now emerging, glancing my way, nodding at us as if we were one with them. In my finery, and in Pierre's carriage, I felt like an actress on a perfectly set stage. Pierre's words echoed through my mind.

Could I ever truly be at ease in society? Or would I forever feel like a fraud, a girl playing dress-up?

And what did I care? I was me.

It was Pierre who made me care. My mind went over our conversation, and it warmed me to think that he had so clearly seen the sorrow in my eyes, that he cared enough to draw it out of me.

The driver took the road that followed the Seine, and I stared at the water glimmering with the reflections of streetlamps and buildings. I tried to think through all that had transpired through the afternoon and eve. From those last moments with Pierre back to the near accident at the Eiffel Tower.

My mind was swirling, and I needed some time to let the events settle in my heart. No matter what kind of cad Hugh was, he was a part of us, our group. And none of us wanted to see him dead. But today, we'd come perilously close to watching him fall to his death.

I shivered, thinking of seeing him go over the rail.

"Avez-vous froid, mademoiselle?" The driver held up a wool lap blanket, his eyebrows lifted.

"He wonders if you are cold," Antonio translated.

But I wasn't. It was a beautiful evening, the heat of the afternoon still lingering, radiating up from the cobblestones and bricks as darkness set in. "Non, merci," I said with a grateful smile and a shake of my head. Pierre's servants were terribly attentive. If I stayed much longer, I'd become nothing but a spoiled, fat brat of a girl, I was sure of it. No better than my sisters. But I couldn't deny the flicker of desire it lit within me—the thought of nevermore having to strive for anything. That it all might be simply provided…

And yet that didn't set well either. *You can take the Montana farm girl off the farm, but you can't take the farm out of the girl,* I thought. I considered my long years of chores from sunup to sundown. And then I considered Mr. Kensington and what he did to reach his goals. No, the life of luxury was in neither my blood nor my upbringing. I let a small smile curl the corners of my lips. This was an adventure, a *grand* adventure, to be sure. I was eager to see the coming days and weeks unfold.

But it clearly felt as but a chapter in my life story. Not the entire book.

———◇◇◇———

What might occupy the evening for me? Perhaps a turn around Pierre's beautiful gardens and fountains. I bade Antonio good evening but then vacillated at the front foyer for a good while. The butler frowned at me in confusion before I finally settled on the idea of donning a comfortable, threadbare nightgown stashed at the bottom of my trunk and curling up with a book.

I was on my way up the curving staircase when I met Will, who was coming down.

"Will," I said when he didn't seem to notice me.

"Oh! Cora. Sorry. I was just on my way out."

"I see that," I said wryly. He'd almost walked right over me. "Where are you off to?"

He studied me a moment and then checked his pocket watch. "If I can make it, a Compline service at a church in the city. Figured I needed something to calm me if I am to sleep tonight."

"An excellent idea," I said, hesitating as an idea took hold in my mind. "Might I join you?"

He paused, and I sensed he had really wanted to go alone. But I waited him out, growing surer by the second that attending an evening prayer service might bring me just the measure of peace that I needed.

"If you'd like," he finally said politely.

"Wonderful. I'll change quickly and meet you outside?"

He nodded once, and we passed on the stairs. But his manner was polite, distant. There was none of the heat that I'd felt between us on the ship.

I puzzled over the memory as I pulled the feather from my hair and changed. Had I imagined the whole thing? His eyes bright with interest. The pause when he nearly fell on top of me. Our lips, so near. But ever since, it was as if he had shut that door, never looking back.

Which was all right by me, I thought, pinning a massive hat to my head with one eight-inch pin and then another. The hat matched a light-blue jacket and skirt that would be warm enough for evening temperatures and demure enough for a church service. My thoughts returned to Will. I had enough to contend with, considering Pierre. And my goal was to complete the tour and get back to Normal School, not to get romantically involved. I didn't belong with any of these people. Any of them.

Right? I silently asked myself, staring into the mirror.

But my reflection kept me spellbound for a moment. I looked like one of them.

I thought back to the people in the city, how they'd nodded in my direction, accepting me.

Pierre, unperturbed by my story of loss and lack of resources.

As I stared into my own reflection, I searched for the girl beneath. The farm girl I could not escape—nor wished to. And for the moment, I longed for my old nightgown that smelled of home—of hay and dirt and harsh lye soap with the hint of lemon peel Mama threw in. I thought of pulling the heavy hat from my head and braiding my long hair, feeling the comforting rope of it in my hand.

The grandfather clock in the hallway began to toll, and I awakened from my reverie. I'd committed to Will and had probably made him late by now. It would be most rude to back out.

I hurried down the hall and the stairs again, wondering if Will would be agitated over my tardiness. He didn't seem in the mood to accommodate any inconveniences. The somber butler opened the massive front door for me, nodding as I passed, probably pleased that I wasn't still tarrying in his foyer. Outside waited a small buggy and one horse.

Will gave me a smile when my eyes met his, no doubt reading the surprise I felt. Until tonight, we'd ridden only in motor carriages as a party. He opened the short door and held out his hand to assist me up.

"I wasn't in the mood for a loud motor carriage this evening," he murmured in explanation.

"That's quite all right," I said, settling my long skirts. "Neither am I." Two horse-drawn carriage rides in one evening… I found it soothing. A reminder of my not-so-distant past.

"Good," he said, shutting the door and going around. He climbed in, sitting beside me, and lifted the reins. Without another word, we set off at a quick pace and indeed said little most of the way into Paris. He seemed deep in thought, and I was enjoying the relative quiet, the lack of demands on me, as much as I had my ride aboard Pierre's elaborate boat at Versailles. I closed my eyes and listened to the *clop, clop, clop* of the horse's hooves, the scrape of the wheels as they turned on their well-oiled axles, the sound as we clambered over the ancient cobblestones.

Gradually, the houses became smaller and closer together, the smells now more of city and sewage than of grass and sweet hay. Traffic increased—mostly buggies and wagons, with the occasional motor carriage. Will turned the buggy one way and then the next with confidence until we reached a fine section of the city where beautiful buildings climbed four stories high—most with ironwork in front of tiny corner gardens on the fourth floor.

"One of the better neighborhoods," he said, gesturing around when he noted my interest.

"You have spent a great deal of time in Paris," I stated.

He glanced over at me in surprise, then back to the road. "A good amount, yes. It was here that I came to join my uncle when I was but a boy."

"A boy?" I asked in surprise. "Your parents let you go so early?"

"My parents had little choice," he said gently. "They were dead."

I lost my breath for a moment and gradually had the courage to look up at him, studying his fine profile. "I'm sorry, Will. I had no right to pry."

"That isn't prying," he said, meeting my gaze for a second. "That's merely friendly conversation."

Curious now, I dared, "They died at the same time? Together?"

He nodded and paused a moment. "It was an accident. We were living outside of Minneapolis, and driving home one night, it was raining like I'd never seen. We were halfway across a creek—one we'd crossed without incident on other rainy nights—before my dad knew we were in trouble. It was deeper than before. And in seconds, water was coming into the carriage, then pushing us over. The horse tried to run, which made it worse…"

I held my breath, waiting for him to continue.

"My dad fished me out of the backseat and set me on top of the buggy, but my mom had disappeared in the stream. He told me to stay where I was while he went after her. I never saw him again. I never saw either of them again."

I paused. "How old were you?"

"Eight. Stayed there all night on the side of that buggy, in the rain, with our dead horse, my parents gone. I wanted to jump in, die with them." He shook his head. "I was so scared. So…bereft."

"Eight," I whispered. "I'm so sorry, Will."

He pulled up, and I saw with some surprise that we'd reached the cathedral. He was staring at me—I could feel the warmth of his gaze—and abruptly, I realized that I'd wound my hand around the crook of his arm as he'd been speaking, as if to encourage him, support him. I swiftly pulled it away, but he gently took it again and looked into my eyes, giving me a tender smile. It was the smile of someone who understood the searing pain of loss, the dull ache of grief.

And in that moment, I felt more known and understood than I had in many months. Even more than I had with Pierre over supper. "I am grateful for your friendship, Will."

He lifted his chin, just a bit, and his warm eyes assessed me. "And I am grateful for yours, Cora."

The bells in the tower tolled, a sound that reminded me of the grandfather clock in the chateau, except a thousand times richer. These bells seemed to penetrate my rib cage and ring right inside me. But still we sat there, staring at each other. A shiver ran down my back, the memory of our moment on the boat returning, again and again, with each toll of the bell. I shifted, feeling somewhat awkward. "Shall we go inside?"

He nodded slowly and slipped his hand from mine, going around the buggy to open the door and help me step down. I was careful not to look into his eyes again. Did I not have enough to deal with in allowing Pierre's advances? Getting involved with Will would be far more complicated—especially since we were to be together for weeks upon weeks yet. No, it was best we remain friends and nothing more.

He did not offer me his arm again, electing to walk beside me, hands folded behind his back. We joined a queue of people hustling to make their way inside—mostly older women and a few men, bent over and shuffling past the crooked-nosed priest, who was chagrined at our late entry.

We slipped inside one of the last pews, which were marred by a hundred years or more of use. But the wood held a rich brown patina, burnished by countless skirts brushing by, oiled with the touch of a thousand hands. The sanctuary smelled of beeswax, and I spied massive, dripping candles on iron fixtures, all the way down either side. I glanced up and sucked in my breath, loving the colors in the grand old stained-glass windows.

The cathedral walls were perhaps seventy-five feet high, built in the Gothic style. There were twenty sweeping arches lending their support all the way down to the front. There, a massive altar rose atop a cascading series of steps, and behind it was a gold-inlaid altarpiece, a Renaissance-era painting of the Madonna and Christ child inside. Priests in black robes processed down the aisle, sending a tangy trail of incense heavenward behind them.

The priests began their liturgy, the congregation answering by memory or consulting small prayer books. Will and I only sat there, absorbing the cadence of call-and-response as the soothing balm I knew we both sought. Then came a choir of young boys, all about six to ten years old, dressed in red-and-white robes, marching forward and singing an ancient hymn in Latin a cappella. The priest at the front sang a lead in Latin, and the boys responded, gathering behind him.

Will bent and whispered in my ear. "Do you know Latin?"

I shook my head.

"Would you care for me to translate?"

There was no judgment in his tone, only warmth. "Very much," I whispered back.

He wrapped his arm around the back of the pew, behind me, so he could edge closer. I felt the tinge of blush at my cheeks, wondering what the old women around us would think. But I closed my eyes, preferring to concentrate on the gentle, low timbre of Will's voice, the comforting warmth of his presence beside me. I was so dreadfully weary of worrying over what people thought.

"When I called out, He heard me, the God of righteousness," Will said, pausing to listen to the next phrase. "When I was in trouble, You gave me freedom: now, take pity on me and listen to my prayer."

The priest's voice droned on in Latin, but all I could hear was Will's voice, strong, true, steady. "Sons of men, how long will your hearts be heavy? Why do you seek after vain things? Why do you run after illusions? Know that the Lord has done marvelous things for those He has chosen. When I call upon the Lord, He will hear me."

My thoughts immediately went to my traveling companions, the Kensingtons and Morgans. But then I was filled with guilt. Was it I who was running after illusions? After vain things? Or was I resisting the marvelous gifts that God had given me?

"Be vigorous, but do not sin," Will went on. "Speak in the silence of your heart; in your bed, be at rest. Offer righteousness as a sacrifice, and put your trust in the Lord. Many are saying, Who will give us good things? Let Your face shine on us, Lord, let the light of Your face be a sign. You have given me a greater joy than others receive from abundance of wheat and of wine. In peace shall I sleep, Lord, in peace shall I rest: firm in the hope You have given me."

Was I living the truth of those words? Was I living out greater joy or seeking to find what my siblings had in their worldly abundance?

"Glory be to the Father and to the Son and to the Holy Spirit, as it was in the beginning, is now, and ever shall be, world without end. Amen."

"Lord, have mercy and hear me," the congregation said together.

"A reading from Deuteronomy 6:4–7," said the priest. He went on in Latin again, and Will resumed his translation.

"Listen, Israel: the Lord our God is the one Lord. You shall love the Lord your God with all your heart, with all your soul, with all your strength. Let these words I urge on you today be written on your heart. You shall repeat them to your children and say them over to them whether at rest in your house or walking abroad, at your lying down, or at your rising."

It was one of my mama's favorite verses, oft repeated in our household. Had I been loving the Lord with all my heart, soul, and strength? Or had I been focused on far different things?

"Into Your hands, Lord, I commend my spirit," we repeated after the priest, reading from the hymnal.

"You have redeemed us, Lord, God of faithfulness," said the priest.

"Into Your hands, Lord, I commend my spirit."

"Glory be to the Father and to the Son and to the Holy Ghost."

"Into Your hands, Lord, I commend my spirit."

Will eased away after that, and I felt the draftiness of the old cathedral anew. But my attention was riveted on the priests and choirboys as they moved into a canticle and hymn.

Their voices rose, high and pitch-perfect, like the candles' smoke reaching for the roof. They seemed to echo in the air for seconds after they finished each segment. I closed my eyes and thought about what it meant to fully *commend my spirit* to the Lord. To trust Him in life as well as death. What it might be like to die, to see heaven, as Will's parents had. Would there be singing like this, or even something far grander? I shivered. I hoped so.

The thought of it gave me a sense of peace that entered my chest and spread to my fingertips and toes.

Will had moved on, even after losing both his parents. He was living, fully living, making his way forward. I'd been holding on, holding on to my past and in particular my papa, as if it was my duty to not let go. As if I did not stand guard over him, remain vigilant, he'd slip away for good. As if I'd forget who I really was without him. But God already had us all in His arms. He knew us, whether we were with Him in heaven or here on earth. It didn't matter if my understanding of who I was had changed—God's understanding of me had not. He saw it all, held it all. *He held me.* Through the bad The good. He was holding me even now.

My heart sped up, trying to keep up with my racing mind. Remembering Mama and Papa's words of wisdom, as well as Mr. Kensington's letter about living at peace with God—and what he really meant by that.

It meant not living bent over by the weight of what might have been, what was supposed to have been. Not living with the burden of what had been lost, what had gone wrong, or what we'd done wrong—but rather standing straight, knowing that God still walked before us, beside us, behind us. With us. Through it all. That Christ had made right all that was wrong. Forever and always.

The last notes of the final hymn hung in the air, as if God was saying an *amen* with me. I closed my eyes and thought, *Amen and amen and amen,* seeing, in my mind's eye, Mama and Papa leaving on a train, leaning out the windows and waving. Leaving, content that we were all in the Father's hands. *See you soon,* they mouthed.

And the thought of it made me smile.

CHAPTER 34

~William~

Cora was clearly moved by the service. Being there, gradually, Will's heart settled into a peaceful rhythm as well. He closed his eyes, trying not to think about the pretty young woman at his side, the way she'd slipped her hand around his arm in empathy as he spoke, that she'd asked to come with him, that she'd leaned into him—fitting so sweetly under the crook of his arm—as he translated the Latin.

She was a friend, nothing more. She'd never be anything more.

He'd wanted to come alone. To gain some distance, perspective, on what he'd been feeling all afternoon and evening. He'd searched for some reason to dissuade Cora from joining him but had found none. And now, he admitted, nodding toward the cross at the front, he saw why. God wanted them both there. In their own ways, they were both hurting, trying to find their way home through the grief—new and old—that shackled them. He couldn't help but wonder if God was using Cora to help him over the final hurdles. To see her making her way, rediscovering hope, uncovering true identity, gave him the courage to do the same.

The priest said his last *amen*, the boys' choir echoed their own, and the people silently rose to leave. Will made his way down the pew and waited for Cora to follow.

It was as she passed him that Will looked up and glimpsed one of the men they'd seen in the park. He turned as if he'd seen nothing, then pressed a hand to Cora's back and bent toward her. "Don't be alarmed, Cora. But we have to stay in the middle of this crowd."

Her blue eyes shot up to meet his, and her golden eyebrows knit together.

"Steady. Keep that serene smile. Like you have nothing to worry about."

Obediently, she did as he asked, settling her features back into an expression of calm tranquility. She trusted him, he thought. It sent a jolt of pleasure down his spine and increased his desire to protect her.

If he's even here for us. Maybe he's worshipping, Will thought. *Maybe I've imagined it all.*

But he thought not.

They moved quickly down the stairs outside, toward the horse and buggy. Will helped Cora climb inside, looking about for the man again. It wasn't until he sat down himself and picked up the reins that he spotted him still up by the church, beside a massive column, smoking a cigarette. He grinned down at Will and lifted his chin with a smile. Mocking him, almost.

Will frowned. He *wanted* Will to see him. Why?

His thoughts were a jumble of confusion as they moved out into the evening traffic heading home. As they turned the corner, Will glanced back up at the cathedral, but the man was gone.

"Will, what is it? You're frightening me." Cora reached out to grab hold of the buggy's front wall when they bounced over a hole in the road at a fast clip.

"I saw the same man at the cathedral that I saw earlier in the park." He glanced left and right, examining every face they passed. "He was inside with us. He'd obviously followed us there."

Cora frowned. "Pierre told me that man was probably interested in him. Not us."

"That's what we hoped."

Will abruptly turned left, then quickly right, heading down a narrower, quieter avenue, out of the thick of the crowds, hoping to lose anyone who was following them—and avoid anyone who might by lying in wait. They rode in silence, nodding at the few passersby on the street at this late hour. Unlike the electric lights of the main streets, this avenue had only gas lamps. That was all right by Will. Their dancing flames seemed warm, encouraging to him.

He looked behind them and, seeing no one in pursuit, took another left and then a right. He had to get Cora to the safety of the chateau.

"Why, Will?" she asked. "Why would they be after us?"

He glanced over at her. "Forgive me, Cora, but the heirs of copper kings might make for easy ransom money."

"But why me?" she asked, eyes wide, hand on her chest. "Why not one of the younger girls? They're more apt to wander off…"

"Maybe they see you as an easier target. The others are rather… clannish. Even the younger girls are nearly inseparable from each other. But you…you tend to trail the rest, Cora. Go off…on your own."

"Yes, well, I decided to stop that," she said in irritation. "To stay closer with the rest, whether they want me there or not."

"I've noticed," he said, tossing her a wry grin.

"But it makes no sense," she said, shaking her head. "Why would they allow us to see them before they strike?"

"So when you disappeared, I'd know exactly who had you," he guessed. "That you hadn't met with some unfortunate accident—but that they had you. So when the ransom letter arrived, I'd confirm it as truth."

She thought on that for a moment. "Or could it be that they only wish to confuse us? To make us believe that I'm their intended target, when they're really after another in our group?"

He considered her theory. "Possibly." And the more he thought on it—considering that they did not give chase—the more he feared for his other charges.

"Will, we need to get back," Cora said, voicing his own thoughts.

"Hold on," he said grimly, whipping the reins across the horse's back. "We'll get there as fast as we can."

CHAPTER 35

~Cora~

We pulled up in front of the chateau. Will and I exchanged a worried glance when none of the servants opened the door or came to greet us. The monstrous chateau felt ghostly, grim, and full of shadows without the warmth of people buzzing about. Will carefully wound the reins through a metal ring in a post outside and then grabbed his walking stick from the buggy, reaching for my hand with the other. "Stay beside me until we make certain everything is all right. Understood?"

I nodded, my heart hammering in my throat, glad for the comforting warmth and strength of his hand. There were few lights on inside. It was terribly quiet. Something was dreadfully wrong—we could feel it. What had happened?

We moved up the marble front stairs, and Will pressed on the latch to open the massive door, wincing as it creaked. He peeked around the corner and then abruptly dropped my hand, running to a man on the floor. The somber butler. Blood pooled from behind his head, and I looked away when I glimpsed the gray pallor that I knew could only mean death. While Will frantically felt for a pulse, my eyes searched the empty hallway before us, the abandoned parlor to our left, the stairs to our right. Where were the rest of them?

Will reached out his left hand again for me, and I took it, walking slightly behind him as if he were a human shield. He gripped his walking stick in his right hand, and I drew comfort, remembering how he'd faced the three men in Butte. But how many were here? What sort of force would it take to storm Chateau Richelieu, with all its servants and all its occupants?

He listened at the closed door of another sitting room and then slowly opened it. A maid was tied to a chair, gagged, eyes wide. We rushed over to her, and Will loosened the gag while I worked on the knot at her wrists.

"Who are they?" Will asked in French, his hand on her shaking shoulder. She was weeping from relief at the sight of us. "How many? What are they after?"

"Six men," she said, her voice cracking. She shook her head. "They didn't say who they were after, only to remain here and be quiet if I wanted to live. They killed poor Henri…" She dissolved into weeping.

Will frowned and leaned close to her. "Only six? Are you certain?"

She nodded quickly, wiping away her tears.

"How long ago did they arrive?"

"Ten, fifteen minutes ago. I'm not quite—"

"Where are the Kensingtons and Morgans?"

"Some in their apartments. Mademoiselle Vivian and Monsieur Andrew were in the gardens, the last I saw them."

"Where is the nearest phone?"

She shook her head. "They cut the line. We tried, before they found us."

He took her by the shoulders. "If they wanted to kill you, you'd be dead already. I want you to run for help. Call the constable. Understood?"

Again, she nodded, and the three of us moved toward the door. After scanning the empty hallway, we crept back to the front foyer and past Henri, which sent the maid into another fit of sobbing. When Will was sure there were no intruders outside, he sent the maid running for the nearest neighbor, a half mile distant.

"You should go too, Cora," he said, scanning the vast, empty lawn.

I shook my head. "What if they're out there?" I whispered back. "I prefer to stay." *With you*, I thought.

Will frowned but nodded. We were once again in the foyer. "Take off your shoes," he whispered.

I immediately understood. They were making a clatter on the marble flooring. I bent to unlace and pull them off, along with my monstrous hat, and set them on a chair. He took my hand again, and we scurried down the hall, looking left and right, until we reached the kitchens and found five more bound servants. We quickly untied them. "Grab some of those," Will said to them, nodding at a rack of cast-iron pans. "And if those men come back in here, you beat them senseless."

They stared at him in confusion, and Will stared back in frustration.

"Will, you're speaking English," I hissed.

He took half a breath, comprehension softening his features. Quickly, he repeated his instructions in French.

Wide-eyed, the servants all nodded, and we peered out the window. We could see no one in the gardens. One of the maids said she thought everyone was upstairs by now. Will was asking about routes upstairs, the best I could decipher.

"How do you say it...?" he muttered in agitation, rubbing his temple. "Passage secret?"

The servants exchanged heavy glances, obviously nonplussed at the idea of disclosing such household secrets. But we were in the midst of uncommon circumstances.

The first footman, gripping a fire poker in his right hand, immediately led the way, moving into Pierre's library. One wall, thirty feet high, was dedicated to nothing but priceless books of antiquity, as well as many dime novels. I'd teased him earlier over his passion for the American Westerns, wondering if part of his fascination with me might have been born in those pages. There were narrow walkways on each of the upper levels, as well as rolling ladders.

The servant moved toward the nearest ladder and rolled it two-thirds of the way down of the wall. Then he climbed, gesturing for us to follow. Just as I reached the top, he pulled a golden bookend in the form of a lion outward, and we heard a click.

"To your left, please," he gestured, urging us out of the way. Then he swung it open and entered.

We were in a tiny passageway that smelled heavily of dust and mildew. Gray unpainted wood, so out of place in the Richelieu chateau, stretched twenty feet forward and then turned. We glanced back at the servant.

"This will give you access to the entire west wing, all the apartments and sitting rooms," he said. "It weaves back and forth around each suite, at times above or below windows."

"Will you come with us?" Will asked when we'd entered.

The footman hesitated. Will raised his hand. "It's all right. Return to the others."

The footman nodded. "To enter any of the rooms, flip the latch beside the peephole. To open from the other side, you must find the latch, which is unique in each room. A bookend, a mantelpiece, a vase, in some cases."

We left him then, and a chill ran down my back as he clicked the bookcase shut behind us. We were alone, and unless the constable arrived quickly, it was up to us to save the others. Will didn't hesitate. He moved down the narrow hallway in the near pitch-black, not pausing until we were halfway down. I understood then. He knew we were all housed in the front portion of the chateau; we were making our way to each apartment.

That was when he began checking peephole after peephole, listening. At the third, he peered through twice. We could hear a man's muffled shout and knocking, as if through several walls.

I resisted the urge to beg him for a chance to look, concentrating instead on staying out of his way. Pausing a moment, motionless, he flipped the latch, and we both held our breath at the sound, which to us sounded like thunder cracking. But inside, the sound of a gasp gave me hope. I pressed through, right behind Will, and spied Nell and Lillian, arms around each other, crying in a corner.

"Girls, come!" I hissed, frantically waving them over as we heard something bang against the door. They ran for me, and I rushed them through the doorway as we heard another crashing sound.

"Go, stay hidden," Will said grimly, shutting the door in my face, sealing us away in relative safety before I could say another word.

The girls nestled under my arms, whimpering, whispering desperate questions, but I stood on tiptoe and peered at the empty room. What was Will doing? Could he find his way back in here if he wanted to?

"Will he be all right?" Nell whispered.

"What if they get in? Will had no weapon but his walking stick!" Lillian added.

"Shh, shh, let me think," I said. "The police are on their way. We only need to make it another fifteen or twenty minutes, I'd wager." Silently, I lamented the chateau's distance from her neighbors, from the city. Was I guessing right? Only fifteen or twenty? Or longer?

I considered my choices. Sit here and wait for Will. The police. But the risk was that those who were after us might figure out how two whimpering girls had been exchanged for one grown man. Or we could move on and see if we might save others who were under attack too.

The girls were sobbing now, gulping huge, noisy breaths. I gripped Nell's and Lillian's hands. "Shh, girls. Shh. You must get ahold of yourselves. Now. Our siblings are depending on us. Don't ruin their chances."

The girls sniffed, and I could almost sense them wiping their faces, though I could not see them. "Who was next door to you?" I whispered.

"It's a men's sitting room," Nell said. "The armory. Remember?"

I did. "Right. Follow me." I squeezed past Lillian and took her hand. I assumed she took Nell's, in the dark. As we crept along, we heard men shouting, screaming at each other. A cry about girls escaping…

At the next peephole, I stood on my tiptoes and looked. I could see nothing but an elaborate red-and-gold settee, a fearsome medieval ax above it. I listened, but I couldn't tell what might be coming from inside or what was happening out in the hall beyond. "Come along," I whispered, pulling the girls with me again.

"Do you remember who was in the next room?"

"Andrew," Nell said. "He and Vivian had just returned from their stroll in the gardens."

I peered through the hole and thought I glimpsed Vivian pacing. I pressed my ear against the wall, trying to discern if she was alone or if others were with her. But if the door had been breached, would the intruders be allowing Vivian to pace? Unlikely. Holding my breath, I pulled the lever and watched in awe as the entire fireplace and mantel swung a foot askew.

Vivian gasped. I peeked around the corner. Andrew and Vivian blinked in shock at the sight of me, dusty and covered with cobwebs. I frantically waved them inward, pleased that Andrew had taken a sword from the wall. It was probably a hundred years old, but at least it was a weapon.

"I wondered why Henri said that fireplace didn't function," Andrew said, pressing by me.

"Oh, Cora!" Vivian cried, giving me a swift hug. Someone was trying to get into this room too, ramming and ramming the door. Heart hammering in my chest, I reached up to grab hold of the heavy fireplace door and pull it shut. But it only moved an inch. The men rammed the door again, just steps away. If they came through now, they'd see us all. Know where we were.

"Help me," I whispered, sending a frantic glance up to Andrew.

He leaned over me and took hold of the door's crossbeam and pulled. But it was still stuck.

"Vivian," I whispered frantically. "The latch! It's jammed. Flip it again!"

She was closest, and spying what I referred to at her shoulder, grabbed hold of it and yanked. We heard the click again, and just after it, the crash as the doorjamb gave way and men stumbled into the room. I glimpsed coats, hats, three feet away, the men finding their footing, rising.

"Pull," I grunted to Andrew. And together we rammed the massive fireplace back into place. But there was no way our attackers had missed the movement.

"*Ils s'enfuient! A travers une porte secrète! Trouvez le loquet!*" yelled one, ramming the wall. *They're escaping!* It sounded like he was directly in front of me. *Through a secret door! Find the latch. Find the latch!* he screamed.

"They're after the girls," Andrew said in a whisper to me. "The youngest of both families. We have to get them out of here."

"All right," I said. "The other way. At the far end, you'll reach Pierre's library. The police have been summoned."

Andrew turned and told Vivian and the girls to run, run for the end of this passageway. We could hear the men inside his room, shouting, scrambling, knocking over everything to find the secret latch that would open our doorway again. "How many men are there?" he asked over his shoulder. "Here, take my hand."

Gratefully, I found his hand in the dark and followed behind. "Six. I think they're all down here at the end, trying to get to you."

"Where's Will?"

"I don't know. He stayed behind to stop anyone who tried to chase me and the girls. What about Stuart and Antonio?"

"Stuart retired to bed. I don't know where Antonio was."

A crack sounded behind me, and I glanced back. They'd given up on finding the latch and were attempting to break through the wall. I could see light from Andrew's room coming through. "Hurry, Andrew."

We scurried faster down the narrow passageway, gaining on the girls, when an ax ripped through the wall ahead of us too, barely missing my hand. I recoiled, staring in horror at the massive medieval ax that I recognized from the armory wall. Another one came through, a foot away, driving me farther backward. In the slanted slivers of light, I glimpsed Andrew's face, his frown of concern, the desperation. Perhaps I could distract them, make them think I was one of the younger girls, buy them time to escape, or the police to arrive.

"Go," I whispered to Andrew, hooking my thumb in the opposite direction. If I could get past those behind me, who were trying to break through with lesser tools, perhaps I could find shelter in one of the empty rooms. The first ax disappeared and, a moment later, came crashing through again. I whirled and ran, slowing only when I reached the hole that the men were making in the plaster of the first room.

It was about four and a half feet up and a foot wide. I could see men's hands reaching in to grab hold of the edge of plaster and pry it back. I lifted my skirts and went to my knees, crawling past as quietly as I could. I winced as broken plaster bit into my skin, but continued to move forward. I could hear them talking, urging each other on in rapid French, wishing I could understand all they said.

I was almost clear when I heard a shout. *"Là! Il y en a une là-bas!"* I'd been spotted. I pushed forward, intent on getting past them, when I felt a man's hand grab hold of the back of my jacket and wrench me upward. I squirmed, flailing about. He was losing his grip. But then he got a better hold and bodily lifted me to a standing position. I blinked in surprise, gasping as he rammed me against the wall that separated us. What sort of man had the strength to do that? I shuddered at the thought of him breaking through and knew my only chance was to escape him now.

He rammed me against the wall again, and the rays of light around me began to swirl. He intended to render me unconscious, I concluded dimly. Instinctively, I slumped, as if he'd accomplished his task. His hand snaked in through the hole and wrapped around me, underneath one arm, up and around my opposite shoulder, where he dug his fingers in. I felt as trapped as if I were shackled to the wall with iron. My head spun. I heard the men behind me shouting, more arriving, additional plaster giving way at my lower back. How soon until they were through?

It was then that my head cleared and my vision steadied. To my left, those with the ax were making better progress. From my peripheral vision, I could see a head pop through.

I could feel the hairs of my captor's forearm at my chin and didn't hesitate. I leaned down and bit, as hard as I could, tasting sweat and blood as I heard him scream behind me. He immediately dropped me, and I fell to my knees and scrambled out of reach, then rose and stumbled down the passageway.

I looked back and saw the first man shimmying through the hole made by the ax, in silhouette for a moment, disappearing in the dark, then reappearing in the light of the nearest hole.

"*Je la tiens*," he said to his comrades, obviously telling them that he would fetch me.

I turned back around and ran, headlong, forward.

Will, I thought in desperation. *Where are you?*

CHAPTER 36

~Cora~

Seeing the corner too late in the velvety darkness, I rammed into the end of the passageway, crunching my shoulder and forehead. I almost bounced off the wall, stumbling to keep my feet. I moaned and then took a lurching step toward the nearest peephole, only glancing through it before I yanked on the lever. I slipped through, turned, and rammed it shut just as my pursuer reached it.

He pulled the lever too, of course, and I bodily pushed against the doorway—which in this room was an armoire—to keep him out. But he was stronger, and my stocking feet slid as he pushed it open, inch by inch. I was eyeing the door, wondering if I could get through it and to another room that I could barricade before he caught me.

That was when Will slid into the room as if pursued. Spying me, he ran to my side and helped me ram the door shut again. "Quick, that chair!" he said with a grunt, face red with the effort of holding the armoire in place.

I dragged the massive gilt chair over to him. Will tilted it and rammed it underneath a shelf of the armoire, effectively jamming it. We heard the man shout in frustration and pound the wall.

Will grabbed my hand and led me to the main door. He peeked around the corner, then muttered, "No choice, really." With that he dragged me across the sprawling, high-ceilinged hall into another bedroom. Fifteen feet away to our left, two men were turning. They spotted us.

Will slammed the door shut and turned the key in the lock, then rammed a chair beneath it. He stumbled backward, staring at the glass knob as it turned and the men banged against the door. Then he ran to the window, pulling open the tall shutters and tugging the windowpane open. He glanced down and frowned, obviously considering the height and whether we could jump or climb down. But my attention was on the door. I was trembling with the impact of each charge. "Will…"

He turned around and shook his head at me. "We're too high. There's nowhere to go out there." His eyes scanned the rest of the room. "Think there are any other hidden passages on this side?"

"I don't think so. The footman would have told us."

His eyes stopped moving around the room and settled on me. He reached out and with gentle hands, touched my head. "You're hurt."

I wiggled away. "I'm all right! We have to get out of here."

But his eyes stayed on me, impossibly ignoring the door that was shuddering behind him. "We can't. We'll face them, Cora. I'll hold them off as long as I can. The authorities should be here any minute."

I didn't want to agree with him, and for a moment, I desperately tried to think of another way, but then I gave up, wrapping my arms around him for a quick hug. He hesitated and then wrapped his arms around me, taking one breath, then two. The men at the door had retrieved the axes and were using them on the only thing that stood between us now.

Will turned and stood between them and me.

Had the others made it to safety? I still hadn't seen Hugh and Felix. Where were they?

The ax abruptly stopped swinging. We heard shouts. And then a hole exploded through the door right above the knob, making Will and me both cower and dodge to the side. They'd shot it. But only a five-inch piece of door was gone. The chair beneath the knob still held. We could hear the men outside swearing. Will backed me away, sheltering me in the corner of the room in case they reloaded and shot again. Kicking ensued, and the door cracked, breaking almost in two. I glimpsed the men outside; one huge man had a wounded arm dripping with blood. *The one I bit.* His face contorted in a sneer when he saw me, and he kicked furiously at the door. My heart hammered in my chest. He wouldn't care that I was not one of the intended targets. He would simply want retribution.

But then another shot was fired, and abruptly the attack on our door ceased. We could see nothing but the empty doorway across from us. Shouts filled the hallway, along with the sound of many running feet, boots on wood. *The police,* I gradually understood, speechless with relief. *The police.*

Will turned and, with a triumphant smile, pulled me into his arms again. I wrapped my arms around him, closing my eyes, trying to accept that we were all right, I was safe. Alive I clung to him, burying my face against his chest, treasuring the feel of my head tucked beneath his chin, his strong hands spread across my back, the comforting warmth of him.

And when I opened my eyes, I saw Pierre in the doorway, pistol aloft, staring at us, mouth agape.

"Pierre!" I said, so glad to see him safe too. I pulled away from Will, stumbling toward him, but his expression confused me. It took a moment for me to identify it, and it wasn't until his arms settled around me that I knew what I'd seen—jealousy.

Men in uniform surrounded Pierre and then edged past him, motioning to us to come with them, saying in French that all was well; we were safe. Will passed by without a word. Pierre tightened his grip around my trembling shoulders and seemed to soften as he held me. "Ahh, Cora, I am so sorry. Forgive me for not being here to defend you and your kin."

"It is all right. We never expected—not a one of us could…" I didn't know what I was saying. I stopped trying. Pierre led me downstairs to the library, where the rest of the Kensingtons and Morgans were huddled. Nell and Lil cried out when they saw me, almost knocking me from my feet with their embrace. Their dirty, tear-striped faces looked upon me with pure joy. Vivian rose and walked in a stately fashion toward us, waiting for the girls to release me before enveloping me in her arms. "You saved us, Cora. Thank you," she whispered in my ear, holding me tight.

Andrew was there then too, laying a gentle hand on my shoulder, thanking me with an uncommonly warm look in his green eyes. Hugh and Felix were pumping Will's hand, rapidly telling him that

they'd been blindsided, struck from behind, bound and left unconscious in their rooms. The old bear, Stuart, had suffered a similar fate.
A physician was seeing to him now.

I looked about at them all, such strong people to have survived
such a night as this. And I glimpsed the humanity we shared, as
well as the bond that had been formed between us. Hugh and Felix
held dripping blocks of ice, wrapped in cloth, to their heads. Will
allowed the physician to examine his eyes. The younger girls were
crying again, talking, both at once, to the police constable. Vivian,
trembling as badly as I, stood behind them, until Andrew urged her
to a chair.

It struck me then.

For all their collective glamour, strength, in this hour, I saw
what an illusion it was. Beneath the facade they were as human
as I—fallible, faltering. Struggling to discover themselves, each in
their own way.

Will cupped my elbow. "I think you had better sit down," he
said.

I glanced up at him and took a seat I hadn't seen appear. "Thank
you," I said, more falling into the chair than sitting down. I hadn't
noticed that my knees had turned to rubber.

"Here," Pierre said, beside me. "Drink some tea."

I took the cup from him, but my hands were shaking so hard
that the cup nearly clattered off the saucer. He reached out and took
it from me, bringing it to my lips. "Shh," he soothed. "Shh."

I felt Will edge away. I didn't see him go, but I could sense the
loss of his warmth, of his presence, almost as if a light had been
moved from the room.

Pierre knelt beside me and set the cup on a small table. "Who were they, Cora? What did they want?"

"The girls. Andrew said they wanted the girls. The youngest from each family. For ransom, I suppose." I frowned. My teeth were chattering, but I felt flushed, hot, not cold.

"Not you? They weren't after you?"

"Only as a means of getting to the girls, I suppose. Or when they couldn't get to them…as second best."

I glimpsed Will leave the library with two policemen. Pierre followed my gaze. "How many did they catch?" I asked Pierre, bringing his attention back to me.

"Six men inside, another two outside," he said, laying his warm, dry hand over my own clammy one. "It is lucky the maid slipped away unseen. But now they are all either dead or in custody." He rose and placed a tender kiss on my forehead. "They will not harm you or yours again, Cora. It is over."

"Good," I said, the word feeling hollow in my mouth.

I knew I was affirming a lie. Because if there was one thing I'd come to understand, it was that life was never a guarantee. It was only a daily gift.

CHAPTER 37

~Cora~

The younger girls were weeping over "poor Henri," the murdered butler, and Vivian was trying to comfort them. Our personal maids, finally released from official questioning, now flitted about, doing their best to see to us, their narrowly saved charges. Again and again, I refused tea, another blanket, a glass of brandy.

Stuart was arguing with Andrew over something, and my eyes focused on them. The old bear wanted to send a telegram to Mr. Morgan and Mr. Kensington. "We must dispatch it at once," he blustered.

"They'll only make us return immediately!" Andrew protested. "Why tell them at all? The danger has passed!" I could read the frustration in his eyes. To him, all that remained was further adventure... and the perfect opportunity to ask Vivian to marry him. The old bear sputtered, apparently unable to figure out what to say in the face of such an audacious suggestion. "But, my boy," he said, "I—I'm responsible for your well-being!"

"And we are well," Andrew said, looking about the room. "Shaken, but well. All seven of us. To leave Europe now would be the equivalent of running home to our daddies. And isn't the tour about finding our independence, a greater understanding of our world and ourselves?"

Stuart's mouth opened and closed repeatedly, his old eyes shifting back and forth as he searched for a good argument.

"Oh, don't tell Father," Lillian said, finding her voice and drawing near. "There's so much for us to yet see."

Nell came up beside her and nodded, although she wasn't nearly as fervent. Clearly, the girl was thinking about the safety of her home.

"Drew's right; the ordeal is over," Hugh chimed in from a corner chair, gesturing with his free hand while the other held an ice block to his forehead. "They've caught them all."

Will moved back into the room, and with one glance, I knew something was wrong. Antonio appeared beside him, his jaw wrapped with a white cloth that wound around his head, a lump the size of an egg forming under his right cheekbone.

Will moved to his uncle, bent, and whispered something in his ear.

Stuart's eyebrows lifted, and then he frowned, chin in hand, pondering.

"Here is the trouble," Stuart said at last, glancing about at all of us. "They caught all the intruders who attacked Chateau Richelieu this night. But the men that Will saw earlier in the park, the one Will and Cora saw at the cathedral—they are not a part of those in custody."

I could feel Pierre's glance when Will mentioned the cathedral, but my eyes remained on the bear. What did this mean? That if there was any remaining threat, we couldn't go on?

"I must contact your fathers," he said regretfully. "Only they can decide whether we resume our trek or return home."

Hugh and Felix groaned. Vivian closed her eyes and bent her head as Andrew slipped a hand over her shoulder. The girls looked at each other, huge tears on their lower lids, as if they were about to be wrenched apart. I was torn—half of me relieved at the thought of all of this being over, returning home, reuniting with my mama and papa, returning to school…because after all, I'd held up my end of the bargain.

But the other half longed to continue this journey, to find out more about my half siblings, about myself. About…

Will. The thought came unbidden, and I quickly glanced at him, feeling heat in my cheeks as if he could read my thoughts. But he was staring at his uncle. Guiltily I looked to Pierre. *Why not him? Why did I not think of him?*

The room erupted in arguments.

"You must do what you must, as our guide," I said, surprised by the words that were leaving my mouth. The group hushed, and all eyes turned to me, making the heat of my blush spread from my neck upward. "But might we send telegrams too? Reassure our fathers that we are quite well and feeling confident that if we foiled these intruders' intentions once, we can do so again?"

"Then tell them that we will await word from them in Provence?" Vivian put in.

"And if we get as far as Provence," I rushed on, trying to past the wonder that my sister and I were arguing for the same thing, "if we show them that we're willing to take the next step, might they not see the very independence that they sent us here to discover?"

"You'd be safest here, my friends," Pierre said, gently trying to dissuade me.

"But Pierre," I said, rising and going to him, feeling strength return to my limbs as I made up my mind. I wanted to continue, see this tour through, I realized. We'd take precautions in case the missing men decided to try again. And this time, we would be on the watch for them. It'd be difficult to take us by surprise. "Didn't you tell me you could send us to friends in Provence? Or perhaps your sister? Surely they can provide adequate shelter. And we can hire additional men to protect us, can we not?" I turned to Will.

He hesitated, studying me. Then he gave me one slow, somber nod of assent.

"Then let us go in the morning," I said. "Forget the shadows of this night, and remember what brought us to France in the first place. The art. The people."

"The food!" Nell said.

"And the dances! Oh, the dances," Lil moaned, as if already being torn from the next invitation.

The others laughed.

"My sister *does* live in a castle on the Rhône," Pierre said.

My smile grew. "There. You see? What could be safer than a castle?"

"A castle would be a unique stop along the tour," Will said with a slow grin.

"Then we move on?" Hugh said, rising and looking about. "We're all in agreement."

"Now see here," the old bear grumbled. "That decision is up to me."

"Are we not the clients?" Andrew asked, keeping his tone reasonable, low. "Until you hear from our fathers?"

"And isn't your charter to take us to new territory," Vivian added, "completing our education with an introduction to as many people and new experiences as possible? Is it so wrong to see but one more, while taking reasonable precautions?"

Stuart smiled, slowly, knowing they'd found an argument he might support. "You're certain, then, all of you? Unanimous in this?" His smile faded as he studied each face around the circle.

"Let it be a vote, then," Will said. "All in favor, say aye."

As one, we voted aloud.

"All against, say nay."

The room was silent.

"I see I must ring my sister in Provence," Pierre said with a grin.

"If you'd be so kind," the bear said.

I rose and walked out of the room, then down the hall and out onto the marble porch, taking deep breaths of the night air, wondering if I'd encouraged the group in the right direction, if I shouldn't have grabbed the chance to head home and leave this foreign, challenging world.

I sensed someone behind me but did not turn, wondering if it was Pierre or Will. Trying to decipher in my heart whom I hoped it would be.

He took another step, and as soon as he grasped my hand, I knew his long, lithe fingers. Pierre. He brought my hand up to his mouth and gently kissed the knuckles, waiting until my eyes met his. "You continue to surprise me, Cora." He shook his head. "In good ways. May I call upon you in Provence?"

I smiled. "I'd like that." And I did. I wanted him to come. To know him better. For what reason? I wasn't entirely sure. I only knew I wasn't ready yet to say good-bye. Even if it seemed impossible, anything more between us.

When I thought about it, I didn't want to say one more farewell to anyone I cared about, even a little. Even the Morgans or Kensingtons, as impossible as that seemed.

I was weary of farewells.

I only wanted hellos. Welcomes. Open doors.

So I could walk through them.

... a little more ...

When a delightful concert comes to an end,

the orchestra might offer an encore.

When a fine meal comes to an end,

it's always nice to savor a bit of dessert.

When a great story comes to an end,

we think you may want to linger.

And so, we offer ...

AfterWords—just a little something more after you

have finished a David C Cook novel.

We invite you to stay awhile in the story.

Thanks for reading!

Turn the page for ...

- **A Chat with the Author**
- **Discussion Questions**
- **Historical Notes**

A CHAT WITH
THE AUTHOR

Q. Why the Grand Tour?

A. I've always been intrigued with the concept of the tour—of sending young people out to "finish" their education. I think travel continues to do that for me—to expand my world, challenge my preconceived ideas, solidify truth, and eradicate the lies. There's no replacement for seeing a place yourself, knowing it.

Q. Have you been to all the places the Kensingtons and Morgans will journey to in Europe?

A. I'm focusing on places I've been, for the most part. I took my girls to England and France—a fantastic mother-daughter trip. The only location I haven't explored is Vienna. I'll rely on coffee table picture books, some interviews, and lots of Internet research to cover that stop. My daughter Emma and I just spent a great deal of time in Venice and Rome, where books two and three will largely take place. I yanked her out of middle school for her own little Grand Tour. When her big sis was Emma's age, I took her on a research trip to Italy too. It was awesome…for both of us.

Q. That must be hard, convincing the schools to let you pull her out.

A. The girls have to comply with federal regulations, so they do what they have to. But I'm pretty passionate about the power of travel to educate—whether you can get your kids to the nearest national park, another state, or another country. Happily, her teachers are all supportive, and I can weather any letter the admin kicks out. If I was really brave and had more money, we'd homeschool and travel for a whole year. But this is as brave as I get. And, well, the coffers will only fund a couple of weeks on the road. So we'll take what we can get.

Q. Will you take your son somewhere when he's of age?

A. Nah, my husband is already claiming that one. He wants to go someplace manly with him—Scotland or Africa. We'll see. I might set a book in one of those places too and have to go, at least for part of it. But don't tell him yet.

Q. What's next for you, in writing?

A. Book 2 in this Grand Tour series, and a devotional called *31 Upside-Down Prayers*. Both have to be done soon. Back to the library for me, so I can earn more funds to return to Italy!

DISCUSSION
QUESTIONS

1. In the beginning, Cora knows that something's wrong even before she reaches the farm. On board the ship, the passengers discuss how the families of the *Titanic*'s victims awoke the night the ship sank, aware that something bad had happened (actual, historic accounts verify this). Has anything like that happened to you or someone you know? Discuss.

2. Cora has several blows that rip apart the only identity she's ever known—as a daughter, as a potential teacher, as a poor girl helping to work the land. She's thrust into a whole new world and forced to examine what really makes her who she is. What do you think was the most powerful realization she had about her identity?

3. Have you ever suffered a blow that made you wonder if you knew who you were? Or a transforming experience that changed who you were in some ways, either externally or internally? What was that life event, and how did it impact and change you?

4. What does living at peace with God mean to you?

5. What's the nicest hotel you've ever stayed in? Did the stay leave you satisfied or wanting more?

6. Cora seems to be resisting Pierre's advances, even though he seems like a Prince Charming character. Why do you think that is?

7. If you were in her shoes, would you do the same? Or is there a part of you that wants to be the princess, swept off your feet? Even if you're married now, what drives the Prince Charming fantasy? Discuss.

8. Keeping up appearances, regardless of actual feelings, was important to many of the characters in this novel. Why do we do that in real life?

9. Cora comes to several key realizations about her faith in this novel. The cathedral scene was a pivotal point (pp. 370–374). Have you thought about these things yourself? Did that scene move you spiritually? If so, how?

10. What defines you or makes you who you are today? Did you ever have to let go of something, consciously deciding it did not define you?

11. List the top three places you'd like to see in the world, and, if you wish, why you want to go there.

12. Most of us spend the majority of our lives close to home. What keeps us from a sense of adventure? What keeps us from exploring and expanding our world? Examine both the practical and the mental/emotional barriers.

HISTORICAL
NOTES

The Grand Tour was popular for several centuries but gradually faded in the 1900s. This twentieth-century rendition is entirely an exercise of my imagination, but it follows the general path the old bears led their clients on—from England, to France, to Austria, and down through Italy. At times, they elected to visit Germany, Spain, Greece, and Turkey as well. But that would've extended the series to five or six books, so we kept to the famous highlights—and my personal favorites.

The copper kings of Montana were true forces, wielding great power in the young, growing state. At one point, there were more millionaires per capita in Helena, Montana, than any other place in the world. Mining made merchants powerhouses, and I loosely based Wallace Kensington on those who lived—and dominated—in Butte. But all depictions of Kensington are figments of my own imagination.

The real Duchess of Northumberland—Lady Edith Percy—died in 1913, and the Duke—Henry George Percy—would have been almost seventy years old. My representation of them, as well as of Lord Carlisle and Lord de Richelieu, is completely fictional—no attempt to realistically depict them was made (other than to utilize their titles and their beautiful estates).

The Eiffel Tower has three observation decks, all of which had stairs and lifts; an Austrian tailor did try to parachute off the first deck in 1912 with a homemade chute and, indeed, died. But I have no idea if they closed the decks for a time—I only thought it was plausible.

Richelieu was a name I pulled from a French map. Nobles of his stature and wealth largely lived a good distance from the city center of Paris by 1913—out in the countryside, an hour or two away. But for the purposes of this novel, I portray the countryside and grand chateaus to just a fifteen- or twenty-minute carriage ride away. If you go to visit, know you'll have to travel a good distance farther to see such estates.

Some say Marie Antoinette never tended to her own livestock or milked the cows, as our bear shares with the group. Reportedly, she used her "hamlet" as an alternative "drawing room." My own guide at Versailles shared the milking story, and while it may very well be nothing but myth, I found it charming. Such is the way of history—there are many accounts of similar events, with various perspectives and interpretations. It's rather like how people view fiction, don't you think? Regardless, while I've tried to represent historical facts accurately, I'm no historian. I'm merely a teller of tales…

~ L.T.B.

ACKNOWLEDGMENTS

Rachel Lilley, archivist at the Montana Historical Society, helped me track down information on Montana Normal Schools (aka teacher colleges) in 1913. She was quite thorough, as well as helpful.

Christine Cantera kindly assisted me with all Italian and French translations. You can find her at WhyGoFrance.com. I do.

Dan Rich, Don Pape, Terry Behimer, Ingrid Beck, Traci DePree, and Caitlyn Carlson formed the editorial team behind this series. I'm thankful they caught the vision and helped me bring it together. Amy Konyndyk, Steve Gardner, and James Hall made the vision beautiful, with an incredible cover concept and execution. And I appreciate the sales and marketing team—Marilyn Largent, Jeremy Potter, Ginia Hairston, Karen Stoller, Michael Covington, and the rest of my publishing partners at David C Cook, who constantly strive to bring my books to readers' attention. I appreciate you all.

I've fallen in love with the world of book bloggers, too. Many of them have done so much in getting word out about my teen series, the River of Time (*Waterfall*, *Cascade*, and *Torrent*). For a list of my All-Star Book Blogger Buddies, see my website, www.LisaBergren.com.

STILL WANT TO KNOW MORE?

Find out more about Lisa, read about her journeys, and connect with her by visiting:

Web: LisaBergren.com and TheWorldisCalling.com

Facebook: Lisa Tawn Bergren and River of Time Series

Twitter: @LisaTBergren

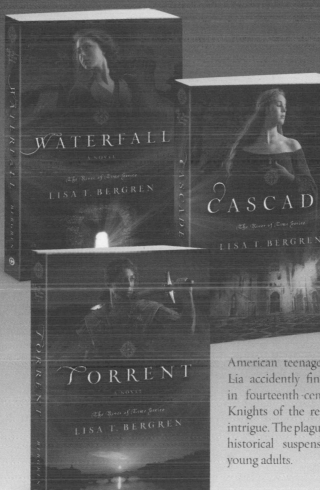

EVERY GIRL WANTS A GUY WHO WILL

FIGHT FOR HER
HONOR

American teenagers Gabi and Lia accidentally find themselves in fourteenth-century Italy. Knights of the realm. Political intrigue. The plague. A romantic historical suspense series for young adults.

800.323.7543   DavidCCook.com   David C Cook

transforming lives together